SOMETHING was moving through the trees and undergrowth with that weighted, dragging step. Only this time it was coming towards us. Susie, my terrier, began to growl.

My skin tingled, and then, as an odd, sweetish smell caught my nostrils, I shivered. Whatever it was was much nearer. I took a firm hold on the leash, ordered my legs to stay put, and said, "Who's there?"

The movement stopped. There was a moment of silence, then a shot rang out and something whizzed an inch from my ear. I jumped, the loop dropped from my hand, Susie barked and plunged straight forward. A moment later she yelped in pain.

"Susie!" I cried and went after the dog. Susie yelped again, and rage swept through me. Then immediately in front of me, I saw outlined a shape, taller than I, and much wider. There was the sound of a heavy breath. And that's all I remembered.

Fawcett Crest Books
by Isabelle Holland:

MONCRIEFF

DARCOURT

DARCOURT

A NOVEL BY

Isabelle Holland

A FAWCETT CREST BOOK

Fawcett Publications, Inc., Greenwich, Connecticut

For Isabel Bosserman

DARCOURT

THIS BOOK CONTAINS THE COMPLETE TEXT OF
THE ORIGINAL HARDCOVER EDITION.

A Fawcett Crest Book reprinted by arrangement with
Weybright and Talley

ISBN 0-449-23224-7

Printed in the United States of America

10 9 8 7 6 5 4 3 2 1

(1)

THE highway slipped by, lined on either side with marshy land covered with greenish gray reeds, and increasingly, the tall oaks that I had heard so much about.

"That part of the South Carolina coast is the same kind of country I grew up with in Louisiana," the editor had said at our final meeting, a little nostalgically, I thought. He sighed. "You can take a boy out of the country—"

"Yes, I know the ending to that one," I said. "But the country boy that allegedly lives in you is buried so deep it would take one of the Darcourt oil drills to get him out."

"True."

Brian Colby, with his fuzzy hair, his scrambled sideburns and turtleneck sweaters, looked like one of those indigenous New Yorkers who almost need passports as they cross the bridges and tunnels onto the mainland. "But the fact remains I was born and brought up within yelling distance of Bayou Lafourche."

"With side trips to New England prep schools and Harvard."

"Yes," he admitted.

"Then it doesn't count."

He grinned. "All right. I'll admit I didn't spend much time there." He sat up in his chair. "Now are you all set? I'd rather you didn't call on this telephone if you need to get in touch." He scribbled on a piece of paper. "Here's my home phone, in case you don't remember. If a woman answers . . ."

"Yes?"

He looked up. Our eyes met and we both laughed. Young at thirty-seven—just ten years older than I—to be a senior editor at one of the news magazines. Brian was divorced and, according to what he said when we had first met a few months before, enjoying his freedom. He had invited me more than once to his apartment. But I had always managed to be too busy to go, because my interest in him, though he didn't know this, was professional, not personal. As a moderately successful free-lance writer, with many contacts, I had had no difficulty in arranging, for my own purposes, to meet him, and make it look accidental. Given his footloose status, it was even less difficult to attract his attention. Especially when I expressed my interest in the Darcourt oil enterprises.

In these days of energy shortages and Middle East unrest, no one had to work to drum up an interest in a domestic oil empire, even one as old and respectable as Darcourt Fuel Industries. Darcourts had been part of the national landscape for a long time, and they had fingers in other pies: land, grain, shipping, tobacco and rice, to name a few. But unlike such dynasties as the Kennedys and the Rockefellers, they had never busied themselves with national politics. Their wealth was legendary. So was their reputation for inaccessibility. In some strange way they had managed for generations to keep themselves aloof from gossip and speculation. No society magazines photographed their homes. Their names never appeared in the gossip columns. Births, marriages and deaths were kept intensely private.

But there had come a rumor, unfounded, even discredited, that no one had been able to trace to any source, reliable or otherwise, that the current administration was going to try to coax the present Darcourt out of his family stronghold to serve as head of a new commission studying the problems of global energy.

When this rumor first surfaced, the uproar was deafening. "It would not be possible," one newspaper pundit had stated categorically, "for a Darcourt to divest himself sufficiently of his commercial holdings to place himself above the suspicion of conflicting interests." And the pundit had gone on to reveal how intricate and interlocking those interests were. "However," the oracle continued, "no citizen should consider himself for whatever reason beyond the call of national service, certainly not one whose family has cornered as much of the national wealth as the Darcourts. Therefore let Tristram Darcourt come before a Senate committee and state his case."

It was at this point that Tristram Darcourt's representative, a family attorney, interviewed over the telephone, had stated in unmistakable terms that Darcourt was not, had never been, nor would be interested in a government post. "How such a stupid idea came to be put about I can't think," he was reported everywhere as having said. "It's nonsense."

Everyone interviewed, up to and including the White House, said the same: it was nonsense. That, of course, just whetted interest.

Representatives of all the major newspapers, news magazines and networks dispatched correspondents to the Darcourt houses in Maine, Lousiana, Montana and, of course, the family headquarters of Darcourt Island off the coast of South Carolina.

All they saw were servants: elderly couples and gardeners and ranch hands who maintained the various homes when they were not in use. On privately owned Darcourt Island they had simply not been allowed to land. The island was not large and it was exceedingly well patrolled by guard dogs. One young network correspondent was well chewed before he made it back to the boat he had hired to bring him over. His acrimony, when describing his attempt, was considerable.

But no one actually saw Tristram Darcourt. Old files were combed. College yearbooks were searched. The only photograph that could be found was an overexposed snapshot taken by Darcourt's prep school roommate, and all it showed was a tall, muscular figure in a track suit. The part that was overexposed was the face. It could have been anyone. Friends, enemies, servants, business associates were sought out. The friends proved almost as elusive as Darcourt himself, and, when cornered, turned out to be remote acquaintances unable to add anything to the meagre public store of knowledge. The enemies turned out to be enemies of the business holdings—none of them had actually met Darcourt. The business associates had known only other business associates.

"You'd think," Brian grumbled, when I approached him with my idea, "that the man is a myth. Doesn't exist."

"Maybe he doesn't," I said.

He looked at me. "Well, it's worth a gamble to find out.

7

Only I'm afraid interest will have died by then. Somebody else is already being talked about for that committee."

That was what I had been afraid of, too. That the interest would die before I could get to the island. "Even if he is," I said carefully, "wouldn't the magazine be interested in a story on Darcourt?"

"Sure. But not as much."

"Not even if it turned out that Darcourt knew about—was instrumental in—the Arab oil boycott of a year or more ago before it happened?"

"What do you know?" Brian asked sharply. "I've never heard that before."

Neither had I. My conscience poked me uncomfortably. "Well, I haven't either. But it might be true."

"What are you up to, Sally?"

"Just what I've told you: getting a post on the island as governess to Alix Darcourt."

"You know, Sally," Brian said suspiciously, "there are two questions I'd like to ask. One, how did you get to know that the Darcourts are looking for a governess for their daughter?—and by the way, what's wrong with school? And two, what makes you think that the Darcourts, who must have spent millions keeping themselves out of sight, wouldn't have you investigated and discover in about five minutes that you're no more of a governess than I am?"

"I've thought of that. You should have known I would. I'm not going as me, Sally Wainwright. I'm going as Thérèse LeBreton, teacher, with credentials to prove it."

"And just who is Thérèse LeBreton?"

"A college friend from New Orleans who's been a tutor for the offspring of wealthy families here and there for several years."

"And where is she now?"

"In France. Being English tutor to some French children. She thinks it's a great idea."

"You trust her?"

"Don't be an idiot. Of course."

Brian fiddled around with the pencils on his desk. Outside, like a theatrical backdrop of gold lights on black velvet, lay New York. We weren't on top of it looking down. We were right in the middle of it, a far more exciting view. I walked to the window and stared out. Above, a single light plane sailed across the arc of the black heaven.

Brian spoke behind me. "How did you find out the Darcourts wanted a tutor for their daughter?"

I turned around. "I didn't. Terry did. I looked Tristram Darcourt up in *Who's Who* and in the newspaper morgue where I was working. I got precious little, but I did find out he had a daughter of fifteen. A lot more digging produced the information that she did *not* go to any of half a dozen of the outstanding boarding schools around the country, and it dawned on me she might be privately taught. It was then I had my brilliant idea about a governess-tutor disguise. So I wrote to Terry and asked her to use her teaching and tutoring grapevine. She's been in some fancy homes herself and knows some of the people. Anyway, she wrote back that as luck would have it the Darcourts were looking for somebody to teach their child. That she had been to some elite boarding school, but had left abruptly. That she's a problem of some kind. So, I applied, sending Terry's credentials."

"If they ever found out what you're about they could make life very difficult for you."

"Why should they, if they haven't found out already?" I said it off-handedly. But my heart was beating rapidly. Even Brian didn't know fully the risks I was running—or why.

"LeBreton," Brian said slowly. "It's a common enough Louisiana name. Have you ever been down there? What if they ask you something about your supposed New Orleans childhood?"

"I've been down there," I said, my stomach muscles beginning to tense. "I did a story down there once while I was visiting Terry."

Brian stared at me for a minute. "What kind of problem is this girl supposed to have? Suppose it's something you can't handle?"

"Like what? If it was something that required a doctor or a shrink or some kind of specialist they wouldn't have been looking for an ordinary governess type."

"You must want to do this story pretty badly." And then he added something I was to remember. "Nobody knows much about the Darcourts except that they're rich and powerful, and obviously want to keep things that way—nobody knowing anything about them. A lot of people have tried to get over that wall. Nobody's done it. But the rich and mighty are not only used to having things their way, they're used to making sure that they do. If they find out you're lying to them, that you're there to do a story on them, they could make you very sorry."

"How?"

"I don't know. But remember, the advantage is with them."

"In this day of investigative reporting? Even the richest have had to mind their manners."

"Only if they want something in return. Like public office. Then they start behaving nicely. But what do the Darcourts want? Nothing except privacy."

"What about this government post?"

"If it's true. There hasn't been the slightest evidence that it's anything but a wild story."

"You know, you don't sound like an eager-beaver news-magazine editor. Where would Watergate have been with an attitude like that? It could be the coup of the year."

"Watergate involved people in public office. But I agree with you, it could be the coup of the year. Which is why I'm talking to you. But you will be using false papers and impersonating somebody you're not. I'm not a lawyer and I'm not sure how our legal department would look on that. All I'm saying is, be careful. There's something about all of this that makes me nervous, coup or no coup."

"Pantywaist," I said.

"Now let's get down to details as to how we're to stay in touch. I don't suppose they have anything as mundane as an ordinary phone number."

"Unlisted. Naturally. But there is such a thing as an office phone on the island. I haven't tried calling it."

"By the way, I'm not entirely clear. Are you actually hired? Or are you just going down for an interview?"

"Strictly speaking, I'm going down for an interview, but the letter I got from"—I rummaged in my bag and pulled out a folded piece of paper—"Mrs. Conyers said that my references were impressive and I might as well come on the premise that I will stay." I opened the letter and scanned it "'. . . if we come to an agreement, and I must say I am impressed with your background and experience, then I'm sure you would prefer to make just one trip.' " I looked up. "*Le voilà.*"

"Sally, are you sure you want to do this? What experience have you had? Can you fake this?"

I looked at Brian, a nice young man of impeccable background despite his modish appearance. "I wouldn't have to fake it, Brian. I've taught and coached and tutored."

"You? When?"

"When I was in St. Catherine's orphanage up in Massachusetts. You didn't know that about me, did you?"

"No. I sure didn't. Is this something else you've made up?"

"Oh, no. I've just been quiet about it. My father died when I was fifteen. My mother had been dead for three years. I ran away, but eventually the state caught up with me, and since I had been brought up in a good Catholic home, I went to St. Catherine's for the next two years."

"I'm waiting to hear you tell me it was another Buchenwald."

"No. It was all right—for communal living. The point is at that orphanage I taught the young kids everything teachable and helped supervise some of the older kids. That was the way I got to that nice Ivy League college I wanted to go to. I worked my tail off for the nuns, and to do them justice, they had the diocese pay me, so I had a head start on expenses, so, what with that and my scholarship I could go to Northampton. But there isn't much in the way of youth I haven't run into."

"Well, maybe you'll be okay. As I said, call me at home. Is there any way onto the island except by boat?"

"Not as far as I can find out."

"Well, good luck. Keep in touch. You're right about its being a great story."

I smiled mischievously. "Glad you admit it. Now tell me that you exaggerated the risks."

"No. I'm not going to tell you that. I'll say instead that I hope I turn out to be wrong."

So did I. Much more devoutly than I had let him know.

He got up and came around the desk. "How about dinner at my place? I sling a mean frying pan."

I got up, too. "Brian, I'd love to. But I have to leave at the crack tomorrow morning. In the meantime, I've got to pack and close the apartment. Can I take a raincheck?"

He leaned back against the desk. "Sure, if you're around to collect it."

Two days later I was driving across the flat marshy shoreland that led by causeway and boat to St. Damien's Island, which led, in turn and by boat only, to Darcourt Island.

"Well, Susie," I said to the Norwich terrier sitting beside me. "We're here." Susie, a small, rough-haired, sand-colored dog, weighed about ten pounds. She had been with me on every story I had ever worked on, occasionally traveling in a rucksack on my back. For all her minute size she had great dignity. Partly because of her age, which was twelve, partly because it struck me that arriving with a dog might not accord with my role as governess, I had planned to leave her this time with the super and his wife, both great fans of Susie's. In fact, I had got as far as Second Avenue before I drove around the block, went back and picked her up. She was waiting at the door, a patient, reproachful look on her face.

"I didn't think you'd get far," the super's wife said.

"Not," I commented to Susie as we drove off, with Susie sitting on the passenger seat beside me, "that you're anybody's idea of what a companion-governess is supposed to turn up with. Well, time marches on. There's nothing I know of in the union rules regarding the etiquette of governesses that says I can't have my own companion with me. *N'est-ce pas?*"

Obligingly, Susie barked.

"Good. I'm glad you agree with me."

Just short of the causeway I pulled to the side of the road under some enormous oaks, their branches trailing that beautiful parasite, hanging moss. The silence around me was complete. My own New England was being lashed by February snows, but down here the air, though fresh, was warm. I sniffed, and there came to my nostrils that faint smell of sweetness and corruption that I remembered from the swampy lands outside New Orleans and down in the bayou country.

I had told Brian that I had gone down there to cover a story while I was staying with Terry. It was true. Using as an excuse my journalism school report on some tinpot local politician lately sent from Louisiana to Washington, I had eagerly accepted Terry's invitation. My real reason was something else: to search out, not my own past, which I knew, or thought I knew, but my mother's.

Mother had told me many things, in her soft, dreamy voice that carried, until her death, the curious intonation of the Cajun French: tales about Mardi Gras; about the ceremonies of All Souls Days, when entire families would troop to the cemeteries to put flowers on the graves of their dead; about red beans and rice and jambalaya and *pompano à papillote* eaten at Antoine's and Galtoire's in New Orleans; about the convent in which she had been educated; about how at home only French was spoken.

But, towards the end of her life, sometimes in the middle

of some tale, she would be given, quite suddenly, to odd silences. And on one or two occasions this was followed by words that made no sense in the context of what we had been discussing. The first time it had happened she'd been telling me something, I think, about my great-grandfather, what a total patriarch he was and how he ordered the affairs of everyone down to the smallest detail in the life of the youngest grandchild. Then her voice trailed off. I waited and then said impatiently, "Well, what happened?"

"I have told you, Sally-Marie, she died."

"Who died?" And because I thought I had misunderstood, "Grandfather?"

Silence. Mother's wide-open dark eyes stared at me. Then she said, "She went away and she died."

I was puzzled and a little frightened. "Who are you talking about?"

Silence.

I tried another tack. "What did she die of?"

"How should I know? She was ill. She went away. I was a child. It was not *comme il faut* to discuss such a thing in front of *une petite*."

"Maman," I said, using the old French term that I knew Mother used in referring to her own mother, "who are we talking about?"

I never got a reply, even though some variation of this odd little dialogue occurred several times.

After another stare Mother usually came back from wherever her mind had been and firmly changed the subject. Once or twice I persisted, only to have my ears boxed. "*Tais-toi*," she said, administering the brisk, old-fashioned chastisement. "*Alors!* Enough!" And went sent off into another volley of French.

There was one thing I learned quite early: that when Mother retreated into French there was no further use in asking questions.

So that was that.

But I was born with a large lump of curiosity and a tenacity about finding out things I wasn't supposed to know. Probably that was why I became a reporter. Unfortunately, as far as Mother was concerned, my inquisitiveness remained unsatisfied because she died when I was twelve, and even before that, in the two years she was ill, I couldn't push my questions: Why did she leave New Orleans? Why did we never visit any relations? Why was there no contact between

13

us and what once must have been her numerous family in southern Louisiana? Why, at odd moments, did that look of fear come over her face? Who was the "she" who went away and died?

I loved my mother. I found her beautiful and romantic, and she aroused in me from as far back as I can remember a strange stir of protectiveness. But I was not close to her. I found her interesting, exotic and glamorous, the more so as she mingled so little with other people, spending her spare time over her exquisite needlework rather than at the kaffee klatches and club affairs that occupied the other women of our small New England town. But for all the everyday things she did not tell me about her childhood and upbringing, I felt the most important things—those that made her the person I remembered—what she felt, what she loved, what she feared—had been left out.

I said this once to my Irish father.

"Oh, leave it, Sally, m'dear. You're chasing moonbeams."

"There's a mystery there," I said, never one to ignore a dramatic turn of phrase.

"There is indeed. And it's why you're bothering me with all these silly questions instead of doing your homework."

"Yes, but—"

"That's all there is to it, Sally. And if you're not passing your tests, it's no picture show you'll be going to, I'm telling you that straight."

And that shut me up as he knew it would. "The picture show," as he put it, was the great delight of my life. In our little town, in those days of the late fifties, there was only one movie house, and to miss Saturday afternoon matinee was the equivalent in other circles of not attending the cotillion.

So, defeated but muttering rebelliously, I went back to my Latin.

"What was that you said?" my father asked in a guileless voice.

I looked up at him over my shoulder. Those smoky hazel eyes that I had inherited were twinkling. His hand, calloused and thickened from years of manual labor, moved towards my head and pulled one of my curls. "I'll thank you to keep a civil tongue in your head, miss."

My father was that anomaly—an Ulster Catholic; and he had the features and the coloring that seem to come only from those coasts that border the Irish channel—the north-west coast of Scotland and the northeast coast of Ireland.

"Yes, but—"

"But me no buts, and leave your mother be," he said, and, with another tweak of my chestnut hair, left.

I stared now into the rearview mirror of the car and pushed a chestnut curl into place. Those springy curls had been a source of pain and embarrassment to me in my college days of the late sixties. The fashion was for the long, straight, flat curtain of hair that my soul craved. Twice had I got as far as a beauty salon to have it straightened, as many of my friends had done. But I never got through the door. Perhaps it was because my father had had the same hair to the day he died. And when I last saw him, after the funeral parlor people had finished with him, lying in his coffin, the only thing about him that looked the way I remembered was his chestnut hair, thick and curly and untouched by gray, for all that he was past fifty.

My eyes were the same smoky hazel, ringed in black lashes, but there my father's bequest ended. The rest of me was like my mother: slight and small-boned, with what one of my roommates described as my triangular cat's face. It was a very French face, and when I had lived in France, until I opened my mouth, I was taken for a native. I was banking now on this, that no one, looking at me, would dispute the fact that my name was Thérèse LeBreton. Sitting there under the huge trees, I opened my bag and took out Terry's last letter.

We had become friends a week after the beginning of our freshman year, drifting together partly because I was drawn by her Louisiana background, and partly because her intense homesickness was assuaged by her learning that my mother came from her part of the world.

"What was her name?" she asked in a voice that was more traditionally Southern and less French than I remembered my mother's as being.

"LeVaux," I said. "She was Giselle LeVaux."

Terry smiled. "She was a real Cajun. There are hundreds of them down in the bayou country."

"That's what she said."

"Ever been down there?"

I shook my head. "No. But one of these days I'm going."

"Come on down and visit me. We'll go look up your relatives together," Terry offered, living up to the generous reputation of Southern hospitality.

And that's what I did, while nominally I was covering the campaign speeches and atrocious guitar playing of Louisiana's favorite son, Congressman Cowboy Calvin.

But the only cousins who seemed to have heard of mother were a few elderly ladies sitting on front porches, fanning themselves with palm leaves and talking in the peculiar patois of Cajun French. Those my own age had apparently never heard of her. Or so, at first, I thought. But after two episodes when I walked in on a covey of cousins chattering excitedly, who stopped the moment I appeared in the doorway, I came to the conclusion that that was what they wanted me to think.

My French then was not as good as it later became, but even if it had been, I'm not sure I would have caught the meaning of those final phrases before they—the LeVaux, LeBoudier and Martin cousins gathered together for a dinner to which Terry and I had been invited—shut up so quickly. Native French, especially Parisians, have a difficult time with the Cajun patois, just as Americans have with broad cockney, or as the English do with some of the more eccentric American regionalisms.

"What were they saying?" I asked Terry, when we were on our way back to the motel.

"Search me. I have cousins who talk like that and I can't understand a word they're saying." Which I knew was likely, since Terry, brought up in New Orleans, did not speak Cajun French.

I glanced down at Terry's letter in which she had proffered some wisdom culled from her experiences as a governess:

"State right at the beginning what your hours off per day will be—and believe me, you'll need them—and then stick to them through thick and thin, even if you don't feel like it. . . .

"Keep reminding yourself that this is not 1850 and you're not Jane Eyre hired for twenty-four hours a day at twenty pounds per annum. If you don't remember this, nobody else will. . . ."

I folded the letter and sat with it in my hand. Off to the left somewhere a bird started up from some bushes with a wild cry. I turned to look, since birds from my part of the country didn't sound like that. But all I saw was a speck rising against the watery gray and gold of the late afternoon sky. According to the arrangements, I was due on Darcourt Island at six thirty. It was now a quarter to five: time for me to move on and over the causeway. Yet still I sat. And I knew that my reluctance to go further was because I was aware that I had reached the point of no return. Once I crossed the causeway, I was committed. And what I would have committed myself to was entering, under false pretenses, the well guarded home of a family that had used its considerable wealth to conceal something—what, I didn't know.

But I did know—or was reasonably sure—that in some way it concerned my mother.

As I said, all during my life my mother had had a curious remoteness, as though, I sometimes thought, in some odd way she were merely visiting my father and me. But then, during her last illness, that seamless wall around her seemed to crack. We couldn't afford around-the-clock nursing care, so Father and I took turns sitting with her at the hospital after the private-duty nurse had left. And it was during those hours that I first heard the name Tristram Darcourt. Mother wasn't unconscious, but her mind rambled. Once she addressed me as "Sister," which puzzled me, because she hadn't had any sisters. I wondered if she were confusing me with one of the nuns at the hospital—a thought that didn't please me at all.

"Sister who?" I asked her, without thinking.

Mother's dark eyes turned towards me.

"Mother?" I said, and took her hand. It felt like a collection of small bones, and aroused in me, as Mother always did, a sort of protective instinct. "It's going to be all right," I said, not really knowing what "it" was, yet aware of the trouble behind her eyes.

"Sis?" she said. And then, "I tried. But he found out anyway. And that's when he—" Then her eyes cleared and changed. "Sally-Marie? What are you doing here?" Her thin hand closed around mine. "What did I say?"

I had been told not to let her get excited. "Nothing, Mother. Nothing at all." I wondered what Father Schmidt would say about my lie. He was very big on no lies at all—not even white ones.

Mother's head lifted from the pillow as her eyes strained towards me. "Are you sure?"

"Quite sure," I said as steadily as I could above the pounding of my heart. Father Schmidt might not have seen it that way, but my lie was an act of love. She had raised my ever active curiosity almost past bearing. The temptation to ask, "What did you say about what?" was so vivid, it almost

17

burned my tongue. But I said as gently as I could, "I don't know what you're talking about. You've been muttering in French, but you know I can't understand that." Which was true, as far as it went.

Mother's head went back on the pillow. Her eyes slid past me to the window and then closed as she drifted off to sleep. Slowly I released my clasp of her hand. For a few minutes I looked at her face with its thin, pale skin and delicate bones. Then I sat back in my chair and stared at the screen the nuns had put around the bed. How much later it was I don't know, but suddenly I looked down and Mother's eyes were open and on me. I leaned forward, in case she wanted something.

"Tristram," she said. I sat absolutely still. Then she sighed and turned her head. "You're afraid, like all the others."

Over the almost audible shout of my conscience I heard myself say, "Tristram who?"

Her eyes turned back towards me. "Why, I told you, Sis. Tristram Darcourt."

It wasn't the name Tristram Darcourt that was bowling over my restraint, it was "Sis." No one ever called a nun that, so it must mean a sister. "Mother—"

But at that moment, I became aware of my father, still in his work clothes, standing in the screen opening. He put his lunch box on the table by the door, along with his tin hat, and came over.

"Now what's this?" he said, bending over the other side of the bed. His words penetrated the fog around Mother as none of mine had. She smiled up at him.

I slipped off my chair and out of the ward. For one thing, only one of us was supposed to be there at a time, and his arrival signaled my going home. For another, I had a lot of homework to do, plus the housework that Mother's illness had made my responsibility. But most of all, I didn't want Father asking me a lot of questions about what Mother had said, and boring in on me as to whether I had taken advantage of her by asking some of my own.

Once I said to him, "Why doesn't Mother ever talk about her family?"

"Why should she? Now have you been bothering her with your silly questions, Sally?"

"I don't see why they're silly. All the kids at school talk about their cousins and relations and so on. Why shouldn't I?"

"Because you don't have any. Me only brother was killed by the Bastards. I've told you that. And me parents are dead." The Bastards, of course, were the Ulster constabulary, made up of Ulster Protestants. My father would have washed my mouth out with soap and a scrub brush if I had used the word in any other context, but he was like proper Southerners with their "damyankee." When referring to his ancient enemy, the word "bastard" was not only permissible. It was mandatory.

"I'm not talking about your side of the family, Father. But Mother's."

"I told you. She doesn't have any. Not close ones, anyway."

"Yes, but——"

"And I'll not have you bothering her with your nonsense. You hear me, Sally?"

My father was an Irish Irishman, and it sometimes seemed to me unfair that he should be so much more authoritarian than the fathers of other girls I went to school with. However, I obeyed. Thinking about it years later, I found it odd that it never once occurred to me to press my questions on Mother herself. I don't know what I thought would happen if I did. But it was as though early in my life, before I could actually remember, a line had been drawn over which I must not step, and daring and inquisitive as I was, I had stayed on my side of it.

That evening when Father got home from the hospital he came back to the kitchen where I was busy making dinner. "What was it your mother was saying?" he asked, with his penchant for coming straight to the point.

"She called me Sis." I looked up from the peas I was shelling. "I thought she was an only child."

There was a second of silence. My father's big features looked strained. Then, "So she is. Don't you know every third girl in the South is called 'Sis?' T'was likely some friend she had you confused with." He put his box and hat down. "I could eat you in a sandwich. What's for dinner?"

"I don't think it was a friend, Father. I think there's something funny——"

And that was as far as I got before Father exploded. I adored him, much more than I did my mother, and I knew perfectly well his rage was more due to his worry over Mother than anything I had said. Nevertheless, as his rough tongue pronounced me wayward, ungrateful, hard-hearted, unworthy of the sweet saint who bore me (Mother!), I could

19

feel the tears brim over my eyes. And I threw down the pea pod I was shelling and went to my bedroom, slamming the door behind me. I had all of my father's temper, and also his pride. And I had no intention of letting him see how he had wounded me. Also, I thought angrily, furiously wiping my cheeks with my dirty fingers, he could get his own dinner.

But after a while the thought of him sitting there, hungry, was too much for me. I knew he hadn't had the first notion of cooking, so with my head in the air and a snippy expression on my face I went back to the kitchen and finished getting dinner.

Silently we sat down at the kitchen table and silently we ate. After about half an hour Father said, "I'm sorry, lass. It's your mother that's worrying me."

I debated whether to forgive him immediately or let him wait a bit. Then inspiration struck. My father was always most malleable when he was repentant. "Can I ask one question?"

He looked at me over the bread he was using as a pusher. "And what would that be?"

"Mother said something about a Tristram Darcourt. Who was he?" It was not the question I wanted most to ask, but at least he wasn't family.

"The only other person to whom the word bastard may be applied in this house. A fancy man, with his money and his great name and his plantation and his lying black heart."

"Yes, but who was he?"

Father looked at me somberly. "The man your mother nearly married. They were engaged. He broke the engagement."

"Why?"

"I told you. Because he was a bastard. And that's all you're getting out of me, with your wheedling, artful ways."

And that was all I ever got out of him. Whether he meant, eventually, to tell me more, I'll never know. Mother never left the hospital. She died the following week. Three years later when I was fifteen, Father was killed suddenly on one of his own construction sites.

Naturally, of course, I had looked up the name, Tristram Darcourt, in every reference work I could lay my hand on, right after mother died, and found precious little that enlightened me about the man himself, let alone his villainy. Various tomes produced the information that the Darcourt family, originally D'Harcourt, had come to the colonies in the days of King Charles II, who had granted them the island on which they now lived. That there had been a Tristram Darcourt in almost every generation, one of whom, in a democratic impulse, removed the apostrophe from the name. That the family also acquired land on the mainland of South Carolina and in Louisiana. That the older brother of the present Tristram Darcourt, Robert Darcourt, had died in a mysterious accident. That Tristram himself, born in 1927, graduated from Annapolis, was married to Nicole Charpentier in 1951. Their daughter, Alix, was born in 1960. All of which I found glamorous and exciting and far removed from my own very humble surroundings, and, of course, it added somehow to my mother's mystery.

But that was the end of all information.

I won't say that my interest flagged in the next fifteen years, but it was overlaid with more pressing matters—my father's death, running away, the orphanage, the endless work with the younger children (which was now going to stand me in such good stead), college, which I managed to complete in three and a half years, two years in Paris, another year roving around Europe and the increasing appearance and prominence of my byline in various papers and magazines.

After that came the rumor about Darcourt's appointment to the G. E. C.—Global Energy Commission. My old interest revived with a vengeance. And the frustration, when I could find little more about him and his family than I had had before, was correspondingly greater. Then, out of the blue, came one of Terry's periodic letters from the family in France where she was honing up her French and improving her connections while she tutored their children in English, and the Great Idea of using her name and credentials to get me into the Darcourt fortress, where all others had failed, sprang fully formed into my mind. . . .

Which had brought me to this stretch of marsh with its moss hung trees and its silence now broken by the evening cry of wild birds.

"So here we are," I said aloud to Susie, who replied this time with the indignant whine that I had learned meant she considered her dinner overdue.

"All right," I said. "You can have a snack to go on with." And I took some dry food out of a plastic bag and held the bits in my hand.

21

Susie's warm pink tongue scoured them up in no time. Then, of course, she had to be allowed out to use the amenities. By the time she was back, giving final grooming licks to her rough coat, it was near sunset, and all the delaying tactics had been exhausted.

St. Damien's Island, I discovered as I drove off the causeway towards the island's center, had a split personality. Far off to the left were walls and gardens of large homes, barely visible to the vulgar eye from the roadway. And beyond them, I knew, would be the ocean, though I couldn't see it. But to the right, on the southern side of the island, the houses, though plainly quite old, were far more modest, and the swampy soil came to the edges of the main road that ran through and around the southern edge of the island. I would have liked to explore this interesting dual personality further, but knew I would have to wait till another day.

The instructions in the last letter had been simple: "Follow the Southern Shore Road to the end, where there is a jetty and a garage. Put your car in the garage—an attendant will let you in—and someone will bring you over to Darcourt."

I knew that I should have taken the Southern Shore Road that was one of the three roads branching from the causeway, the other two being the road to the center, and the Northwestern Shore Road. But I had been unable to resist the temptation of driving to the middle of the island, so now I was faced with either finding a connecting road to the southern highway, or going back to the causeway.

It was while I was thinking of making a turn that I saw a young man on a motorcycle coming towards me. Perhaps he could tell me if there were a short cut. I waited for him to pull alongside and called out the open window, "How do I get to the Southern Shore Road and Darcourt Island from here?"

He put a long leg out to the ground and stopped. Straight blond hair flowed back from a cowlick. From under a prominent forehead, a pair of green eyes looked at me speculatively. A curious silence stretched. I poked my head out and was about to speak again when I was overwhelmed by a sense of hostility coming at me from the youth. Since I had not only never seen him before, but had stopped only on impulse, I found this not only astonishing, but eerie; as though he knew me, who I was and why I was here and hated me for it.

The impression was so strong and unnerving that instead

of my question about the Southern Shore Road, I said, involuntarily, "What's the matter?"

He stirred then, lowering his gaze and fiddling with the handlebar. "Nothing. What do you mean?" Then he looked up again, and he seemed simply a strikingly attractive youth. With his thick, ash blond hair and clear skin he could have been any age between twenty and thirty.

It was Susie, growling, who broke the tension. She's a reserved little dog, not taking much to people. But she growls only with provocation, and I looked at her, surprised. Her tan muzzle, drawn back from her excellent teeth, was pointed straight at the young man. With increasing astonishment I saw the ridge of hair standing up along her backbone.

"Hey, that's a cute dog. What kind is he?" It was a perfectly ordinary inquiry, and lots of people made it, yet I was intensely uncomfortable, as though both the boy and I were playing roles that were lightly put on and had no basis in reality.

"A Norwich terrier." I put the car in gear. I'd find somebody else to give me directions."

"Did you want something, ma'am?"

The trouble was, there was no one else in sight, although there were several houses along the road. Probably they were all inside eating dinner. "I just wondered whether there was a turnoff to the Southern Shore Road ahead, or if I would have to go back."

He looked at me for a minute, then turned, pointing with a long arm. "Go down as far as those houses you can see from here and turn right. There's a road—it's just a track but it's okay. It'll take you to the shore road." He lifted one foot onto a pedal. "You can garage the car there. But I guess you know that." Again the hostility.

"What do you mean?"

"Didn't they tell you? The master doesn't allow cars on Darcourt Island—except his own broken-down jeep and cars belonging to the family and special people like the doctor and the priest." There was no mistaking the anger in his voice, or the sneer at the word "master."

"How did you know I was going there?"

He laughed then, only it was a laugh without pleasure or warmth, and it didn't touch those strange eyes. "There isn't anybody of the island people that doesn't know where you're going." And before I could say a word he came down on the pedal, the motor roared again and he shot away.

I turned my head staring after him. "What on earth—?" I started belatedly. But he was gone. Shrugging, I turned back. A little shiver of unease went through me. "Weird!" I said to Susie, starting the car forward.

Ten minutes later I had made the turn and was reflecting that that unpleasant youth was right when he said the road was just a track. Unpaved, it ran between reedy banks and here, away from the center of the island and the scattering of houses, the rank, marshy smell was much stronger. Also, I thought, as I felt the tires slide and squelch, much swampier. But the birds—I had never seen so many. I am not a bird watcher. I can hardly tell a sparrow from a cardinal. Yet I found myself slowing, peering forward out of the windshield and out of the side window at the flocks of birds that soared up from apparently nowhere, chattering and crying, or out of the copses that dotted the flat landscape. Even if I had been able to identify them, it was now too dark for me to tell one kind from another. And with that thought, I realized just how dark it had become, quite suddenly. I remembered then that somewhere I had read that the further south you go, the shorter the evenings, till in the tropics proper, night seems to fall almost literally, like a curtain rung down.

I stared out of my right window into one of the most awe-inspiring sunsets I had ever seen. The sun, half below the horizon, was blood red, and sent fiery trails out on either side interspersed with gray and gold. Then I looked left, to the east, and saw that there it was night. It was at that moment that the car gave a quiver, as though the ground under it were shifting, and in a strange, retrospective flash I knew that the boy had sent me down this track deliberately, undoubtedly knowing that the marsh would not sustain the weight of the car and that I would be caught by the dark.

What he did not know was how much of my Irish father I had in me. Fear would come later. What I felt now was a burst of rage that was worthy of one of my sire's noisier explosions.

"The black-hearted son of a sweltering seacook," I muttered, employing one of his phrases. "I'll show the—" And with that, almost by reflex, I stepped on the accelerator. Fortunately, it was the right thing to do. Another inch down and the treacherous swamp would have closed its grip on the wheels. As it was, with a protesting squelch, the car burst forward.

"Hold on, Susie," I said, clutching the steering wheel for

dear life. I could see the shore road not too far ahead, and reminded St. Christopher that even though he had been demoted by the pope, this was no time to let me down. A few minutes later, with a final sucking noise, the car left the marsh and hit the tarmac.

"I'll snatch that boy bald-headed for that," I said, this time using one of my mother's expressions.

It was dark now, and I switched on the headlights. A few minutes later the road curved left and I saw ahead a jetty, a dark building, a lighted lamppost, and, shining under the moon, the ocean.

I drove up to the jetty and stopped. It was then I saw a tall figure in work clothes and boots standing to one side of the pier. As I drew up he came level with the window.

"Miss LeBreton?"

I had schooled myself to answer to Terry's name, and had been alert for the first time it was used. But my experience with the young man and swampy track had shaken me. For perhaps five seconds my mind was a complete blank.

The man came closer. "Miss LeBreton?" This time the question mark was more noticeable.

"Oh, yes. I'm sorry." *Stupid*, I thought to myself.

"Anything wrong?" He bent nearer to the window, and in the light from the lamppost I saw the face of a man of about sixty. I also received a blast of his breath. Bourbon, I thought to myself. My father had been rather fond of it. I said, "Only that I almost got stuck in a swamp. I came by that track back there."

"Didn't Mrs. Conyers tell you to take the right-hand road coming off the causeway?"

"Yes, but I forgot and was in the middle of the island before I realized my mistake."

"That track's not meant for cars. How come you used it?"

I hesitated, then thought I might as well tell what happened. After all, I reasoned, there was nothing unusual or reprehensible about asking directions. "I asked a young man how to get to the Southern Shore Road and he told me to go to the end of the houses and turn right down the road there. He said it was a track, but that it was okay."

"What did he look like?" The question came sharply.

"Blond, with a cowlick. On a motorcycle. Why?"

I heard his intake of breath. He straightened and then said, "I'll go and open the garage door and put your suitcases in the boat. What are you going to do with that dog there?"

"Take her with me, of course."

"They don't like other people's dogs on the island."

"That's unfortunate," I said, in my best Ivy League fashion. "She goes with me."

"Them dogs they have on the island will chew her up."

The lamppost by the jetty threw its light on the front of the car where Susie was sitting. I knew her so well that I knew by the way she was sitting that she was tired. She was twelve years old, old for a dog, and had been my father's last birthday present to me. One reason I had run away was that the orphanage had initially said no dogs. Luckily for everyone the nuns relented about this and Susie had spent the night after the cops had caught up with us in the police station with me. A few years ago I had refused a story in England because I would have had to stay there six months and the English would have put her in quarantine. I had only considered leaving her home this time because of her age. And then I couldn't do it.

"They'll have to chew me up first. And if the Darcourts object to her, then they can find another governess."

He shrugged and went to what I now saw was a garage door. Inserting a key in the bottom, he straightened, pushing the door up.

"Okay. You can drive your car in."

When Susie, my typewriter, my suitcases and I were outside I said, "May I have a garage key so I can get the car out when I have to?"

He pulled the door down and locked it. Then he stood up. "You don't need a key. All you have to do is call me."

"But what if I want the car when you're not here?"

"I'm always on duty. Twenty-four hours."

I didn't like this. "I'd rather have a key."

"Then you'd better ask Mrs. Conyers if she wants me to have one made for you. My orders are to give out no keys. Not to anybody."

I have a sharp and quick tongue, and my impulse to come back with something snappy was overwhelming. But, unpleasant as I found this man, he was undoubtedly following orders, and my quarrel, if it was a quarrel, was with the family, or Mrs. Conyers, with whom I had had my entire correspondence.

"Is the family on the island?" I asked, surprising myself by my restraint.

"I guess you'll find that out when you get there, won't you?

The boat's down here." And she picked up the suitcases and led the way along the jetty. Susie doesn't like leashes, for which I do not blame her, and she had been trained to stop at my order and at all curbs. But boats and strange dogs, to say nothing of the dark water and the surly boatman, were something else. I took a leash out of my shoulder bag and bent down, attaching it to her collar. "It won't be for long," I said with a pat. Then I picked up my typewriter with my other hand and followed the boatman to the end of the pier.

The boat was a dinghy with an outboard motor, and we were soon bouncing over the water.

"How far is it to Darcourt Island?" I asked.

"Four miles."

"That's farther than I thought. What happens when there's a storm and the water's choppy?"

"You stay put."

His accent might be flat and Southern, but his manner wouldn't have shamed a stage Yankee. Well, I would engage him in no further conversation.

I stared across the water at the moon. Then I looked back. St. Damien's Island was surprisingly far behind us and in the dark, even with a moon, was a flat shape hugging the surface of the water. After another minute or two I felt the boat rising and falling to a deeper swell or rhythm.

I forgot my resolve to silence. "Are we in a channel or something? The waves feel deeper."

"No. We're out of the channel now and into the ocean. The landing is on the ocean side."

"Why?" I asked before I could stop myself. "I would think they would have put it on the sheltered side."

"Ask them when you get there."

"All right. I will. And I will also ask them why you are so abrupt. Is that their wish or yours?"

I was not surprised when he did not answer that, and we went the rest of the trip in silence, with no sound but the water against the boat.

In a few minutes I saw Darcourt Island suddenly become a shape in front. There were a lot of trees, I thought, far more than on St. Damien's. I was curious about the vegetation, which seemed much more like Louisiana than the little I had seen of the rest of South Carolina, but I was determined not to earn myself another snub. So I deliberately turned my attention to the approaching land, with its huge trees and

27

mossy hangings through which the moonlight was eerily visible.

"Miss LeBreton!"

I jumped, and again my mind went blank. For a few lost seconds, the name had no connection with me at all.

My unpleasant companion gave a cackle of laughter. "Sure is funny how you don't seem to know your own name."

There was a long silence. My tongue seemed paralyzed. Susie whimpered. I knew she was not enjoying the cruise and put my hand on her back. "It's all right," I finally managed to say to her.

Then all at once, trees rushed towards us. There were lights.

"All right," the boatman said, "hang on. We're here." And he reached out and grasped the pier. I saw a shadowy figure standing on the little jetty.

"Miss LeBreton," a cool feminine voice said. "I'm Mrs. Conyers. You're very late. We had almost given you up."

One of the nuns at the orphanage had a voice like that. And I knew from the chill displeasure in it that I had made a bad start.

(2)

AS soon as I and my possessions were all on the dock, I decided to take the bull by the horns. I was tired of being on the defensive.

"How do you do, Mrs. Conyers? Your boatman—I'm sorry, I don't know his name—told me that you don't allow people to bring dogs onto the island here. I'm sorry, but Susie has always been with me. She's old now, and no trouble, and I couldn't leave her. I hope it's all right."

"Petersen, the boatman, was quite right. The Darcourts have their own dogs—mostly guard dogs. Once, when someone brought another dog onto the island without telling us, the dog was killed. I should have mentioned the matter to you."

You certainly should, I thought. And then, in fairness, so should I. I bent and picked Susie up. Our exchange up until this moment had been conventional enough, yet in some way it was a trial of strength and it had become important for me to state where I—and Susie—stood.

"I should have mentioned that I would bring her." I paused, because to say what I was about to say took effort, in view of the importance of me being here. But I had done a piece on the training of guard dogs and knew how they work. "If the rules can't be bent, and the guard dogs instructed to leave Susie alone, then I'll go back with Mr. Petersen here when he returns. Susie is very dear to me. I can't have anything happen to her."

Another pause occurred. Then the cool voice spoke. "Very well. You may bring your dog here. I will tell the doghandler to accept her when they are brought to meet you. This way, please. And leave your suitcases. Judson will bring them. You may go back, Petersen."

We walked to the end of the jetty, and I saw then that a jeep had been parked off to the left behind some trees. The woman spoke.

"Judson, there are some suitcases on the jetty, please bring them."

A man who had been standing on the other side of the jeep came around and walked past us.

Mrs. Conyers walked towards the jeep. "Get in, Miss Le-Breton. This is the only motor vehicle on the island. But it isn't too uncomfortable."

"After you," I said, matching her politeness.

After a second's pause she complied. She was taller than I, and thin. The moonlight was not bright enough for me to see her face or estimate her age. But her voice was that of a middle-aged or older woman. She did not have on a coat, but she was clutching some kind of shawl around her shoulders. I got in and put Susie on my lap.

Judson came back and stashed the cases next to him. Then he got in and started the jeep. We drove for what seemed like a long time. Always around us were the huge trees, moss hanging from their branches, the moonlight pale and remote on the other side of the black silhouettes. There were also small trees, their leaves shining, and flowering shrubs, petals blanched in the strange light. The marshy smell was not as strong as on St. Damien's, but it was there, under a powerful, sweet aroma of something else.

"What is that sweet smell?" I asked.

"Flowering sweet olive."

"It's very strong," I started, and at that point the jeep broke from the trees and I caught my breath.

The young moon was shining directly on the house, and on what looked like a mile of lawn leading up to it. Built in the Louisiana tradition, rather than in the Greek Revival of other parts of the American South, it had no columns, but there was, halfway up the house, a balcony running entirely around, similar to many I had seen on plantation houses along the River Road outside New Orleans. There were wings on either side, jutting from the original square of the house.

Behind and around those were the enormous oaks, mossy lace flowing from their branches.

"It's quite a sight," I said, impressed. "Does the house have a name?"

"Darcourt Place."

"How old is it?"

"It was built shortly after the Civil War, replacing an older house that had caught fire and burned."

"Is there much land behind it? Or just the ocean?"

"No. The island is quite long. There's more behind than in front. But it's almost entirely woods and swamp. There are gardeners that look after it. No member of the household goes into them."

There was that note again, that of stating an order. I could feel my natural resistance to authority rising in me and took a firm hold of myself. I had taken my stand on Susie, and that would have to be enough, at least for the time being. Terry might say what she liked about my stating my wants and hours off, but she would be the first to remind me to remember that the demeanor suitable for a fiesty reporter is a far cry from that which goes with even the most independent governess. I could see, right now, I thought rather grimly, that I would have to watch my step and my tongue.

The jeep bowled along the driveway, incongruously, I thought. Perhaps it was the moonlight. Perhaps it was the eerie silence. But my imagination supplied the coach and four that would have been far more appropriate. As we got nearer, the house, naturally enough, loomed larger. Yet I was surprised at how very large it was, towering above us when the jeep turned in the small circular patch of gravel in front of the main door.

Also like Louisiana houses, the front door was only a few steps above the ground, and neither particularly large nor impressive. What was impressive were the lights that blazed from the front hall and from some of the upstairs windows. I wondered how many people lived in the house. Standing in the doorway was a tall, stout man in the garb of a butler. As the jeep stopped, he came forward.

The voice beside me said, "This is Miss LeBreton, Stevens. Would you please see to her bags."

"How do you do, ma'am? Welcome."

I smiled. After Petersen and Mrs. Conyers his pleasant greeting was all the warmer. "Thank you." It occurred to me as I got out that though his "ma'am" was a Southern form of greeting, his accent was nearer to my own.

"You sound as though you might come from"—I gulped—"New England." Careful, careful, I told myself, frightened at how easily I forgot my assumed role. I had almost said the words "my native" before "New England."

"So do you, miss." He pulled the cases from the front seat. "You must have spent some time up there."

I had prepared myself for this lie, and now would be an excellent time to establish it. "I went to school up there, and was so teased about 'my Southern drawl that I took drama lessons to overcome it." Safe and true. Terry had indeed tried to coach herself out of her magnolia drawl.

"Stevens," Mrs. Conyers said beside me, "Miss LeBreton has brought her little dog."

There was a short pause. I was still holding Susie, reluctant, somehow, to put her down. She was so very small. It seemed silly, however, to be so protective, and I was just bending to place her on the patch of drive in front of the steps when a sudden, furious barking broke out from behind the house. There was obviously more than one dog back there, and the barks were the deep baying that meant large dogs.

Quickly I straightened. "Mrs. Conyers," I started, then to my horror heard the noise suddenly coming towards the house. I turned to the housekeeper, my arms around Susie. "Please instruct those dogs to leave me and Susie alone, as we agreed, Mrs. Conyers," I asked as calmly as I could. But I was frightened. I love animals, but guard dogs are trained killers. And it would be as pointless to be sentimental about them as it would about a Bengal tiger on the hunt.

In the lights from the house I saw her face, set, almost expressionless. "You shouldn't have brought the wee dog," she said, her accent suddenly, and rather touchingly, Scots. But she went to the edge of the porch. "Norton," she called. "Come here at once, and stop those dogs."

But they were nearly up to the house, baying like animals almost on their quarry. And there was nothing I could do. Nowhere I could run. I was sure I stood in no danger. But I was terrified for Susie. That intrepid little dog, though, was much braver than I. Instead of cowering in my arms, she suddenly raised her muzzle and gave a loud, aggressive bark. Then, as though she weighed a hundred and fifty pounds, instead of ten, she growled, and I knew by the sound that her dignity had been affronted.

"Susie, be quiet!"

At that moment a huge black and tan shape streaked into the light and launched itself at me.

"Ranton! Down!" The voice, deep, crisp and incisive, came from around the edge of the house. The big dog, a Doberman, stopped short, less than two feet from me. His lips curled back from fangs that looked three inches long, and a low, guttural noise came from his throat.

"Quiet, all of you!" And the barks and growls that emanated from the animals still hidden all stopped. "Ringwood! True! You, too, Ruby and Bellman!"

And from around the porch came a broad-shouldered man in riding breeches and boots, surrounded by another Doberman, two German Shepherds and a Great Dane. He stopped on the other side of the porch, his face still in shadow.

Susie, furious, was trying her best to bark, but I had a hand around her muzzle, trying hard not to laugh at the absurd picture of ounce-sized Susie challenging those behemoths. But I was indignant, too, at the noisy, bellicose reception and promptly forgot the role I was to play.

"Please reassure your bodyguard that I am not about to walk off with the family silver."

"They are not barking at you, Miss LeBreton. They are barking at your dog, who was not invited. You had no right to bring her here without, at least, the courtesy of asking our permission."

He was right, of course, although there were more tactful ways he could have stated his point. And he had no way of knowing that my decision to bring her here was a last-minute impulse. All of which did nothing for my *amour-propre*. But I swallowed my assaulted pride. "Yes. You're right. I shouldn't have brought Susie without telling you. Only it was . . . Anyway, I'm sorry." And then, although I was beginning to think I knew, "Whom am I talking to?"

"I'm Tristram Darcourt."

Yes, I thought. The calm arrogance with which he pronounced his name bespoke him. Everything about him—his feudal assumption of ownership of everyone as well as everything on the island, an attitude passed along by his minions, Mrs. Conyers and Petersen—ignited my resentment of authority in any and all forms, a useful quality for a reporter, but disastrous for a family retainer, which was, after all, what I had been hired to be. It was, I could see immediately, going to be a bumpy voyage.

"I see. How do you do, Mr. Darcourt. As I said, I should have told you I was going to bring Susie." My voice trailed off. One apology was all I could squeeze out. I took a breath. "I can assure you Susie is old and quite harmless. If I had realized—"

All the endings to that sentence were, under the circumstances, quite unusable. So it was just as well he interrupted.

"If you find yourself unable to accept our ways, Miss LeBreton, you are quite free to go. Judson will take you back to the jetty and ring for Petersen, who will come and get you."

He had very neatly thrown the ball back in my court, which, quite naturally, exasperated me even further. It was then a saying of my father's popped into my mind: *"There's nothing more irritating, Sally, than being all squared off for a good fight, only to have your opponent start being civil. It'd take the heart out of a saint . . ."* And he was there, his eyes crinkled with laughter, his mouth straight and deadpan. I couldn't help it. I started to laugh.

"You're amused, Miss LeBreton?"

"Yes. I'm sorry. I just remembered something . . . my father once said."

"How remarkable," Mrs. Conyers' voice said from behind me on the porch, "since your father died when you were three."

Watch it, Sally. Or you'll be in real trouble. Given my flair for self-revelation, I thought grimly, it might be better if I availed myself of Darcourt's invitation to leave. But if I left, I would remain forever ignorant of whatever it was that shadowed my mother's life. I took a deep breath. "Yes. He did. But my mother was quite determined that though I should never know him myself, I would know as much about him as she could pass on. She was always quoting him. Mr. Darcourt, you are right that I should have mentioned that I wanted to bring Susie, who is now twelve years old and has always been with me. In fact, because of her age, I almost left her behind. But she's never been left, and at the last moment I couldn't do it. However, I will not put her life in danger. If your dogs are going to attack her, I will leave." Let's see what you do with that, I thought.

"She'll be quite safe, but the guard dogs have to be instructed to leave her alone. Bring her over here."

I looked at the immense jaws of the five dogs.

"She . . . she may bark," I said doubtfully.

"Very likely. But that has nothing to do with the matter. Here."

He stepped forward. I saw a prominent, aquiline nose, deep-set eyes and black hair streaked with gray. Beneath were thick, powerful shoulders. "Give her to me."

"I—" I started to say, without moving.

With an impatient sound he lifted Susie out of my arms. "Susie . . ."

"She'll be all right," he said indifferently. Then he glanced down and rubbed her chin.

Now Susie is a flirt. Quite apart from her devotion to me, she likes men. To my female friends she shows polite indifference. But to the male. . . I could see her stump of a tail wagging.

Silently I watched while he took her over. "Ruby, Ranton, Ringwood, Bellman, True, come here."

As all five dogs advanced, a tune or jingle started up in my head; something about Ranton and Ringwood, Bellman and True . . .

Darcourt was saying, "This is Susie. You will guard her." And to my horror, he put her on the ground. Susie gave a bark and sat down. Those long, killer noses came over and sniffed. And sniffed. Susie sniffed back. Then she licked the Great Dane on the nose. I held my breath while a tongue as big as she was licked her back.

"Now call her," Darcourt said.

"Susie," I said and cleared my throat. "Susie! Come here!" She didn't move. Obviously she was enjoying herself.

"Susie," I said more sharply.

"Very well trained," Darcourt said drily.

"I've never believed in military obedience."

"Evidently." He picked her up and brought her back. "Here," he said, putting her in my arms. "Now walk over yourself. They've already been given your letter to sniff, so they would know you when you arrived."

Feeling mildly frustrated over the battle that never took place, I approached the five dogs who went through their ritual sniffing.

"Now they know you," my genial host said. "As long as you stay within the appointed boundaries, they will not only not attack you, they will defend you from would-be attackers. But don't go outside the fence."

I turned. "What fence?"

"The fence that divides the island in two. On this side,

you're free to roam as you wish. But do not go on the other side." He added drily, "Try to restrain that overactive rebelliousness." He paused and said even more drily, "You will have more than enough to do in handling Alix's."

If there was ever a quality that Terry LeBreton had absolutely none of, it was rebelliousness. She was a born complier. I would do well to remember that. I did not for one moment expect for any Darcourt to encounter anyone who had known the real Terry. But you never knew, and it would pay me to be a lot more careful.

"Yes, Mr. Darcourt," I said in my best family-retainer manner.

He walked past me towards the dogs and to the end of the house from which he had come, and I noticed he limped, one shoulder a little higher than the other. At the corner of the house he glanced back. "And don't overtax yourself. Civility, yes. Servility, no."

I opened my mouth to tell him I was delighted to know he recognized the difference, and then closed it again.

He was watching me. "Quite so," he said coldly. "I'm leaving tonight and won't be back for some time. So I'll bid you good-bye for the moment." And he disappeared.

"This way, Miss LeBreton," Mrs. Conyers said, and went up the few steps into the open front door of the house.

I got an impression of a wide, parqueted floor covered by oriental rugs, soft lights reflected in the furniture, and a lovely smell. "What is that delicious scent?" I asked Mrs. Conyers' back.

"Potpourri," she said, without turning around. Her dress was neither long nor sweeping. Yet it gave the effect of being both, though her skirt came to a few inches south of her knees. The stairs, wide and polished with dark red carpet down the center, were to the right. To the left, against the wall, were a cabriole table, a door, another, larger table, another door, and, at the end of the long hall, another door, similar to the front door. Overhead was a delicate and obviously old chandelier.

I was staring up at it when I heard Mrs. Conyers' voice. "This way, Miss LeBreton."

I made for the stairs, still carrying Susie. When I reached the top I put her down and followed the housekeeper down the hall to the left.

The room she showed me into was large and square with windows on two sides. An enormous fourposter bed was against one wall.

"Dinner will be in half an hour," Mrs. Conyers said. "Please don't bother to change tonight."

I glanced down at my rumpled pants suit. "I think maybe I'll put on a dress."

The lips tightened. "As you wish. The bathroom is through the door there. Dinner will be announced by the gong." And with that she started to leave.

"Just a minute," I said as she got to the door.

She turned. "Yes?"

"When do I get to meet Alix?"

"At dinner. That is, if Norton and Mr. Darcourt can find her. You were due here, you know, by six thirty, and she was waiting for you. But she is . . . she is rather impatient. As you know, as I told you in my letter . . . there are problems. If I seemed . . . severe. . . when you arrived, it was because . . . after waiting for half an hour, she had run off."

Spoiled brat, was my mental comment, and then I reproached myself. My prejudice against the rich and well born tended to extend to their children, which was not always fair. Probably it was because my memories of children at the orphanage were of those who had been abandoned, whose parents were dead, or were in jail or in institutions. It occurred to me, at that moment, that in all my calculations and connivance about coming here, I had considered every angle except the child herself. And that for every kind of reason I might be the last person to be able to do anything with her.

"Why does she run away?"

The woman stood at the door, an odd sequence of emotions flitting over her face: doubt, pity, irritation, and—was it fear?

"I told you in the letter, Miss LeBreton. She has problems. There are ʿ . . . difficulties."

"But you didn't say what they were."

"Don't you think it would be better if you found out for yourself? If you met her without prejudice?"

She was quite right, and I nodded. But there was something else that was bothering me. It was becoming plainer by the minute that the Darcourts and their household did not relish personal questions. I was, however (although they did not know that), here to ask them.

As casually as possible I asked, "Is Mrs. Darcourt here? Shall I get to meet her?"

I had been fully prepared for Mrs. Conyers to say, as

indeed she did, "Mrs. Darcourt is not here." Somehow I had known she was not there. And I thought nothing of that. Families of the Darcourt's social milieu seemed to spend more time apart than those of humbler origin and smaller income.

What I was not prepared for was the fear and withdrawal that swept over the housekeeper's face. She said abruptly, "Mrs. Darcourt is not here," and turned back to the door.

"Will she be here in the foreseeable future? I mean, will I get a chance to meet her?"

She faced me, then. "No, Miss LeBreton. Mrs. Darcourt spends most of her time away. I thought you must have known that, since it was I who wrote to you and made arrangements for your coming here. Is there any particular reason you are asking these questions?"

There was something coming from the woman, a powerful emotion that I felt pressing against me, even though that set, locked-up face was unreadable.

"No," I lied. And for a minute we stood there, I, with one hand on the carved bedpost, she with her hand on the doorknob. I took a breath. "I was just interested . . . naturally . . . in view of the . . . work I'll be doing with Alix." To my astonishment and disgust I heard the conciliating note in my voice, as though there were something strange and improper about my interest in the wife of the man who owned this island, and the mother of the child I was to work with. I gave myself a mental shake. "I'm sorry if my question sounded odd, although I'm a little puzzled as to why you should think it so. In my experience, the fact that a . . . member of the household should conduct correspondence and make arrangements for the children is not unknown in families of this kind." It was a bold little speech, but inspired, I thought, touching as it did on experience I had purported to have.

And it worked. Mrs. Conyers' face relaxed. "Of course," she said, sounding more human than I had hitherto heard. "It's just that . . ." She took a deep breath. "Mrs. Darcourt's health has always been frail, and she finds the climate of southern France more salubrious. Mr. Darcourt and Alix join her there when they can."

As I thought, I reflected cynically. It was a neat speech, and translated meant that Mrs. Darcourt was the kind of woman who enjoyed the anemities and pleasures of the Côte d'Azur. She was certainly not alone in that. The Mediterra-

nean coasts of France, Italy and Greece were heavily populated with rich American women whose frail health demanded
more "salubrious" climates than their native shores. For a
minute, and by contrast, before my eyes, there rose up the
picture of my mother, her head bent over her petit point,
her needle threading through the fabric with incredible delicacy, her slender hands rough from the housework that she
did without help. The Charpentiers, Mrs. Darcourt's family,
I had discovered from my pokings in reference books, were
a Cajun family that had fairly recently come into money—
something to do with oil tankers in the Gulf. I wondered
then how many of the Darcourt males had married money
to add to the already considerable Darcourt fortunes. It was
obvious that this was exactly what Alix's father had done,
having jilted my mother for reasons unknown. . . .

I brought my wandering mind back from its conjecture
with a snap.

"Yes. I understand. I—"

At that moment the gong sounded.

Mrs. Conyers made a noise with her tongue. "You'll have
to hurry if you want to put on a dress. We'll await you downstairs." And she went out quickly, snapping the door behind
me.

I didn't have time to explore the room, as I had intended
to. That would have to wait until later.

Hastily I washed my face and hands, aware again of the
tune or jingle that had nagged at me before. I tried humming
it. *Ranton and Ringwood, Bellman and True. . . .*

But it was still elusive. Drying my hands, I slipped into a
light wool dress, the color of smoke. Then I brushed my hair,
which somehow seemed curlier and wilder than I had seen
it for a long time. Perhaps it was the damp climate, I thought
resignedly, pushing it here and there. Above the heathery
dress my eyes seemed more gray than hazel, and the sea air
had whipped some color into my cheeks. But nothing would
add either to my height or my curves, "and there's nothing
I can do about it," I said aloud to Susie, who sat on the
bathmat and watched me fuss.

Then I put down the brush and comb and bent and
scratched her between her ears. "After all, the best things
come in small packages, don't they, love? I'll try and get you
something devastating from the kitchen."

It gave me great pleasure to pick her up and settle her on
the beautiful white linen bedspread before I left. Not only

was she in successful violation of the "no-strange-dogs-on-the-island" rule. She looked, as I left, like the royal, pernickety heroine of the famous fairy story of the princess and the pea.

"Don't take nuthin' from nobody," I counseled her as I left. And she gave a bark of agreement.

Since Tristram Darcourt had told me he was leaving for a journey, I had not expected to see him again, let alone find him standing at the foot of the stairs. "We are waiting for you, Miss LeBreton. Let me show you to the dining room."

I looked down into the strong, arresting face, with its powerful nose and high, bony forehead. Beneath the prominent thrust of the brow, the deep-set eyes were a clear, light gray, and very cold.

"I'm sorry to have kept you waiting," I said sweetly.

"It only matters because we have not yet found Alix, and, after dinner, we must go out again."

I stepped down to the polished floor and saw that though Darcourt was a head taller than I, he was of medium height only, a fact that surprised me.

"This way," he said, and we moved to the back of the hall towards a rectangular mirror in a gilt frame. For a few seconds the two of us were reflected in the glass: he, with his strangely bulky shoulders . . . except that one shoulder, the one nearer me, was higher and thicker than the other. Inadvertently, before I could think, I glanced up and saw the curve where normally his shoulder would be and saw him watching me. Quickly I looked away.

We went through the door beside the mirror into a big, square, lighted room. Down the center was a dining table covered in white linen. At one end was a sideboard. Windows were on either side of a mantel. To the far right, big double doors, now closed, obviously led to another room.

"Your place is here, Miss LeBreton," Darcourt said, limping over to a chair to the right of what was obviously the head of the table. Across from him stood Mrs. Conyers. At the back of the room, near another door, stood Stevens and a small, red-haired woman in a maid's uniform.

Darcourt pushed my chair in as I sat down, and then went to his own chair. Seated, he looked a tall man, as nature had intended him to be, had it not been for whatever accident or illness had distorted his natural growth. As I was thinking that, he looked up, and I could feel myself blushing, because there was something in the ironic expression of his eyes that

40

made me fully aware that he knew what was going on in my mind.

This put me at a disadvantage, which I didn't like, so I said rather briskly, "I thought you said you were leaving tonight and that we wouldn't be seeing you?"

He shook out his napkin. "I intended to. But I couldn't leave until we had located Alix."

"I take it you haven't."

"Not yet." He shifted as Stevens put soup down in front of him. The butler and maid then served Mrs. Conyers and me.

I picked up the intricately chased soup spoon at my place. "Does she do this often?"

"Yes. Often enough so that there's no need for us to get into a state about it."

"Children often run away," I said thinking of myself and the various other orphans in my charge. "But it usually means they're unhappy."

"In Alix's case, it just means she's disobedient."

I could feel my hackles rise, but I said as mildly as I could, "Don't you think that disobedience is a way of expressing unhappiness?"

"Unhappiness, Miss LeBreton, is a relative term. She was unhappy, as you put, because we insisted that she be here to meet you when you were due to arrive. Unfortunately, you were late, so since restlessness is one of her main problems, she took the opportunity, when we weren't watching, to run away."

Mrs. Conyers then spoke for the first time. "Perhaps wilful is the better word."

It was then that the missing element—concern for the girl who was about to become my charge—asserted itself within me (however belatedly) for the first time. This icy, stone-faced man, with his "disobedient," and the chilly Mrs. Conyers, with her "wilful," were grim companions and mentors for any lively child. I, too, would run away, at any and all opportunities, and I wondered again why she was isolated here with a governess instead of being at school. What were the "problems" that Mrs. Conyers had alluded to in her letter and in the short time since my arrival? But remembering her snub when I asked, I decided I'd bite my tongue off before I gave her, or this unpleasant *padrone*, an opportunity to administer another.

"Miss LeBreton—" Darcourt said, and at that moment the

41

baying of the dogs started again. It was one of the most chilling sounds on earth, and despite myself and the fire crackling at my back, I shivered.

"You'll get used to the sound, Miss LeBreton," the master of the house said.

Again I watched my tongue. "Perhaps," I said after a second or two. "But it must be a terrible sound to have at your back if they're pursuing you."

"Fortunately, if you stay on this side of the fence, you won't have to fear that."

The words *And what is on the other side?* were sitting like fever blisters on the end of my tongue. But I kept my teeth together.

Again I was aware of that ironic look. "Among the reasons for the fence, Miss LeBreton, is the presence, beyond the fence, of swamps. A human being could disappear without a trace, with no one the wiser."

The dogs' barking was growing fainter. I could feel my nerves relax.

"Couldn't they be drained?" I asked, as amiably as I could.

"Yes. But it would be difficult and expensive. And it would ruin one of the greater bird sanctuaries of the southern coast."

"Oh. Well—"

But at that point the baying came much nearer again, this time punctuated with just plain barking.

"Alix," Mrs. Conyers said.

Darcourt looked up. The whole room seemed to be poised, for a minute, waiting. Even Stevens, passing around a dish of vegetables, stood, half stooping, his head up. There were footsteps, and a door slammed. Then the double doors were wrenched back and a tall, fair girl stood in the doorway, her long blond hair a tangle, her jeans splattered with mud that extended here and there to the white shirt she was wearing. Afterwards, when it was important to try to remember what my first impression of her was, I tried to re-create the picture she made—the torn, muddy clothes, the tangled hair, the riding crop in her hand. But it was her eyes—her father's silvery light gray eyes—that were the dominant feature. Only in her they were much more brilliant because, different from her father, they were not hidden under her brows, but, large and sparkling, were set flush with the rest of her face.

"I got away from them," she said dramatically. "I got away from Ranton and Ringwood, Bellman and True." She almost flung herself at the foot of the table. "And Ruby, too, of course." And she looked at me, as though she wanted me to pick up a clue. "I named them, you know. I named the dogs."

And then the tune that had been bothering me ever since I had arrived, that I had been trying to hum in the bathroom, suddenly identified itself.

"Of course. It's 'John Peel,' isn't it?"

She smiled then. And I thought she must be one of the most beautiful creatures I had ever seen.

"Yes, I ken John Peel and Ruby, too.
Ranton and Ringwood, Bellman and True,"
she sang.

I groped around for the words that followed, because she was looking at me, her head on one side, and I couldn't bear not to respond as she wanted me to. Then the remaining lines of the old English ballad sprang into my memory:

"From a find to a check, from a check to a view . . ."

Darcourt's deep voice broke in,

"From a view to a death, in the morning."

And I saw the smile disappear from her face, as though it were shuttered. "Daddy—"

"Go to your room at once, Alix. I'll be up later."

Her voice rose. "But, Daddy, I'm hungry—"

"At once." The words cut across the room like a whip. "Do as you're told."

She stood, tall and frail as a flower, her eyes brilliant, then a sob broke from her, and she ran from the room by the door we had used, slamming it behind her.

I stood up. "Mr. Darcourt—"

"Sit down, Miss Le Breton."

"But—"

"I will not be disobeyed. By anyone. Is my meaning quite clear?"

I stood there for a full thirty seconds. He had not risen, but sat there, those hidden eyes on me, one hand on the table. And I noticed, idly, as though I had nothing else to do, that the length and suppleness that had not developed in his body was in his fingers, which were long and well-shaped and strong-looking.

"Do you understand me?" he asked again. And when I did not answer immediately, he said, "Either you obey my orders, too, or you leave tonight. I will not have anyone on this island defying me."

Four hundred years of suppressed Irish rage rose in me then. If it had not been for Alix, I could have, with pleasure, killed Tristram Darcourt. He represented everything I had been brought up to loathe. But I sat down, because in that moment I made a resolve, that though I might leave the island without the information I had come to acquire, I would not leave without rescuing that helpless girl.

To achieve this would require far more acting than I had ever been called on to do, so I might as well begin immediately.

"Yes," I said calmly, not too meekly. "I understand you, Mr. Darcourt. It's just that Alix seemed so . . . upset."

"Hysterical," Mrs. Conyers put in.

He said more evenly, "As Mrs. Conyers says, hysterical. It is not good for her and I will not tolerate it. Stevens, offer Miss LeBreton more chicken."

(3)

I LAY awake that night in the big fourposter, staring at the moon now high in the sky, my mind a chaotic muddle of remorse and reflections, most of which could be summed up in one extremely vivid memory: my mother's voice saying, "Sally, when you get one of your brainstorms, you're like the man who flung himself on his horse and galloped off in all directions at once. . . ."

I had forgotten now which particular exercise in headstrong enthusiasm inspired that comment, but it was entirely, if belatedly, obvious to me now that I had fallen into the old trap: I had once more taken a flying leap, not so much into the dark—I knew what I was here to find out—but without hinting carefully enough as to the means by which I was going to accomplish it. Blithely, I had taken on Terry's persona without seriously thinking what being a governess entailed: that governesses were not known, hired or retained for their perky impudence, or their facility in snappy comebacks.

I sat up in bed and rested my head on my knees. Once, when I had been in a school play that I had also written—something about the American Revolution—I had marched onto the stage after four hours of solitary meditation on my part, word and gesture perfect . . . and stood stunned by the howls of laughter in the audience and my fellow actors. It seemed I had overlooked the little matter of changing into costume. . . . In view of what happened and my floods of tears afterwards, my father tactfully refrained from comment. After we returned home in ignominy, he kindly and silently offered ice cubes for my puffy eyes.

It was a few days later, when I had had time to recover, that he said, "Perhaps that will teach you, Sally, think. . . . THINK, my girl," and he rapped his knuckles on my head.

And since then, except for one embarrassing lapse, I had. The lapse had occurred in Italy, when I was bird-dogging a story on an Italian labor official who had proved singularly inaccessible to the press. By guile, feminine wiles and sheer contrivance, I had wormed my way to his presence, only to discover that he spoke neither English nor French, my only two languages. To find out later that everyone knew this, if I had thought to ask, and that I could have taken an interpreter, was simply salt in the wound.

And now I had done it again.

Damnation, I thought to myself, beating my fist on the mattress. After all, I had not been finally and formally hired. Turning on the bedlamp, I leaned over to the night table and dug the letter out of my handbag and opened it. My eyes found the sentence, "*We can make the final arrangements after you reach here and if we discover them to be mutually agreeable . . .*"

And now, added to other motives for staying—discovering the secret that shadowed my mother's life, and Darcourt's connection (if any) with the foreign oil boycott—was added my determination to do what I could to help Alix Darcourt. That she was nervous and high-strung was patent. That she was receiving exactly the wrong treatment was even more obvious, and my mind went back to my own mother, who, in ways I did not understand, was also a prisoner.

"Susie," I said, leaning over and putting my handbag back on the night table, "we have to do something."

Susie, who had been snoring at the end of the bed, woke up. She gave a "whuff," which was usually her contribution to our conversations. I rubbed her rough head. Her tail wagged. I noted, with a pang, the gray hairs around her muzzle. There was no question about it, Susie was getting old. Which made me glad that, no matter how much trouble it (and my tongue) had got me into, I had brought her.

I leaned over and hugged her. "You're a great girl, Susie."
Her stumpy tail started to wag, and then, to my astonishment, she sat bolt upright facing the door. Her ears twitched forward, and a low growl burred in her throat. Obviously, something—or someone—was there.

Sliding off the bed, I moved, barefooted, over the dark red Persian carpet, my nightgown (really only an elongated shirt) flapping around my calves. Gently, I put my hand on the doorknob. Then swiftly I twisted and opened it.

There was no one there. But someone had been there. A few feet from the door lay an envelope. Looking to either side, I darted out and retrieved it and returned to my door. It was a used envelope, with canceled stamp but no return address, either on the back flap or the upper left corner of the front. Lower down, in the center of the front, in a very English hand, was *Mrs. Tristram Darcourt, Darcourt Place, Darcourt Island, South Carolina.*

I stood there staring at it, wondering why I was experiencing that curious sensation of the hair on one's neck standing up. It was unpleasant. And frightening.

Then I jumped, because far away, in the wing on the other side of the central hall, I heard someone laugh, an odd, eerie sound, then a door slammed. There was a growl behind me and a whine. I turned around. Susie was peering short-sightedly at the floor, preparing to jump. It was a high bed, as so many of those old fourposters were. I sprang back into the room. "Susie, wait." And I managed to get to her just before she slid off and put her down. Trotting straight for the door, she stood in the doorway, her nose testing the atmosphere. Then she gave a short, sharp bark.

"Quiet," I whispered, going back to the door. "We'll be thrown out for sure." But, like Susie, I was uncomfortable. Whoever had left that envelope had probably been the one who laughed, and was only a few yards away behind one of the closed doors in the other wing. All of a sudden I felt rather exposed, standing in my nightgown in the doorway. So grasping hold of Susie's mouth, which was as ready to express itself noisily as my own, I backed into the room and closed the door. Then I looked for a key. There was none in the keyhole. Putting Susie back on the bed, I conducted a search, looking in all the bureau drawers that were now filled with my rather sketchy underwear and stockings. But nowhere, either in the drawers themselves or under the paper that lined them, could I find a

47

key. For a moment I stood in the middle of the floor, reflecting. I had been in a lot of strange rooms in my life, some of them where a young, alien female was considered legitimate game for the local bloods, so I was quite handy with makeshift devices that might not keep out a determined predator, but would certainly warn me of his, her, or its presence.

A few minutes later I had achieved a satisfactory mechanical concoction consisting of a chair under the door knob, a string, and a large, china and highly shatterable ornament poised on the very edge of a highboy. If anyone played around with the doorknob, the chair would move, the string would pull and the china ornament would fall to the wooden floor beneath, because the carpet did not extend to the walls. A quick examination revealed that the vase was Limoges and probably valuable.

Well, I thought, getting into bed, *tant pis*, so much the worse for them. If members of the Darcourt household sneaked around trying to get into people's rooms for which no key had been supplied, then they would have to face the loss of valuable bric-a-brac.

Sitting up in bed, I reached over to the night table where I had put the envelope and examined it again, running my hand inside to make sure it was empty. As I had thought—nothing there. I stared again at the address. Like my father, and for the same chip-on-the-shoulder reason, I was acutely sensitive to the various stigmata, emblems and characteristics of the upper class, and this handwriting was definitely upper class of either English or American vintage. Eying the Greek E's, I decided that if I had to make a guess I would say this belonged to the American Finishing School category. Idly I looked at the postmark, which was stamped Columbia, South Carolina. But it was not the state capital's name that made me sit bolt upright. Somehow I had assumed that this envelope, dug up from Heaven knew where for Heaven knew what reason, must have been sent here when Mrs. Darcourt was in residence. But the postmark, which, unlike most postmarks, was quite clear, was of a week before.

That vague sense of unease that had been growing became—suddenly—a shiver. As though, I thought, as though. . . . But at that I came up against a blank wall in my mind.

After another fifteen minutes of staring at the envelope I put it back on the night table and turned off the light.

Setting my mental alarm for six thirty, I lay back in the dark room. Susie came up to the bed, turned round and round and finally curled into a ball at my side. From the open windows came cool, moist air. I had drawn back the curtains before getting in bed the first time, hating to sleep in a closed room, and now, turning my head, watched the stars and listened to the rustling of the leaves and determinedly refused to think about the envelope. Which reminded me, I thought sleepily, of the story of the girl who was told to go and sit in a corner and not think about a hippopotamus. . . . And at that point I must have gone to sleep.

I awoke to find golden sunlight streaming through the window, and lay for a few minutes, luxuriating in a big bed, the wall covered with delicate blue, green-and-yellow-flowered wallpaper and the tangled vine and ivy hugging the edges of the window. It was an elegant room and bespoke, like the house, a family that for generations had been used to the accouterments of aristocracy, used to being waited upon by a staff of servants. I turned over and wondered how many backs, both black and white, had bent to harvest sugar and rice and probably cotton and tobacco— because the Darcourt lands were many and scattered, to say nothing, more recently, of all that oil—so that Darcourts could live in rooms like this, confident that their meals would be brought, their houses cleaned, their clothes laundered and ironed. Many, I thought. And many heiresses married . . . which brought me to my mother, who was not an heiress.

I sat up in bed cross-legged. "Yes, Mr. Darcourt; no, Mr. Darcourt," I practiced, *sotto voce*. "Whatever you say, Mr. Darcourt; go jump in the lake, Mr. Darcourt you arrogant bastard, sir—" And then jumped myself, because outside the door was the sound of soft footsteps approaching and stopping, and then, as I slung my legs over the side of the bed, going away again.

Dismantling my warning system and pushing the vase to the back of the highboy, I opened the door. There, on a round tray just outside, was a small china pot, a pitcher, covered with a cloth, sugar bowl, cup and saucer and a plate with something on it wrapped in a napkin, all in an exquisite pattern of sprigged blue.

"Well," I said. And bent and picked up the tray. Closing the door, I carried it over to the bed. The coffee was steaming and very black. The milk, I was delighted to see, was hot. I had grown up with café au lait, made with Louisiana coffee, which my father ordered from New Orleans for my mother.

"Ummm," I murmured, as the first delicious sip went down. Then I opened up the napkin on the plate and found a hot buttered biscuit, which I shared with Susie. To have hot coffee brought to the door first thing in the morning was undoubtedly a rich custom, and one I would have no trouble at all adjusting to.

"Watch it, Sally my girl," I said to myself in my father's Irish accents. "Just remember you're a member of the honest proletariat."

It was as I was putting the folded napkin back on the plate that I saw the paper. Evidently it had slid under the plate. Pulling it out, I saw the legend, "Miss LeBreton," written on it in black ink, in an angular aggressive hand very different from Mrs. Conyers' prim, straight up and down script.

I opened it, my heart thudding a little. I was surprised to realize how much I feared the paper would simply say that he—because I had no doubt at all that that writing was the hand of "The Master"—had decided I was not suitable for his daughter's governess, and that he had made arrangements for me to leave immediately.

But all it said was, "Please see me in the library at eight." It was signed, simply, "Darcourt."

I glanced at my watch. It was seven. Susie's control was excellent; nevertheless, she would have to be walked before my appointment.

Hurriedly, I showered and dressed, putting on a green gaberdine dress at the last minute, in place of the khaki pants suit I had planned to wear. Any concession, such as dress, that I could make to the sensibilities of my host and his housekeeper would not only be to the good, they would be good discipline. It was a lot easier to remember my manners dressed inoffensively in a standard tailored dress than in the pants I found so convenient to wear.

"Come along, Susie," I said, and opened the door.

We sent down the stairs, through the hall out onto the flagged terrace below the upstairs balcony and strolled around the house. The air was warm, but crisp and invigorating, with a touch of salt and, occasionally, the faintly sour smell of marsh. But against that was that overwhelmingly sweet aroma—what was it Mrs. Conyers had called it? Flowering sweet olive.

There was a huge magnolia tree back of the house and, behind the east wing, what looked to be stables, at any rate sheds or stalls, built around a court. Then I knew they were stables, because I could hear the metallic sound of shod hooves on stone. At that point a man's voice made itself heard.

"Miss Alix . . . you know your Daddy told you he wanted you to stay in the house this morning. I can't saddle no horse for you."

"It's all right, Duncan. I've saddled him myself. I'll tell Father you fought me every inch of the way. Please open the gate for me."

"Miss Alix, I can't do that. You know your father would—"

"Or I'll jump Brutus over it. I've always wanted to see if he could clear that fence. I guess now's the time for me to find out."

And I heard the scraping of the hooves.

"Don't Miss Alix. You'll break your neck and the horses' legs. I'll open the gate for you."

And there was that silvery laugh I had heard the night before. "And there's no question which would upset Father more, is there, Duncan? My back or Brutus's legs. . . . That's right, push it open."

I saw the wide solid gate being pulled back. Then everything happened suddenly. Those hooves were not walking or trotting, but had sprung immediately into a gallop, and Susie and I, standing just outside, didn't move fast enough.

I saw a huge chestnut horse, above that, a blonde head. I heard Susie bark, and realized that she was right in the path of the big gelding.

"Watch out," I yelled, and hurled myself forward, pushing Susie in front of me, and looked up. It was a frightening sight. The horse had reared, neighing wildly. Suspended above my head were hooves, their steel glinting in the morning sunlight. I closed my eyes and uttered long-forgotten prayers. The hooves came down to one side.

"Sorry! I didn't hurt you, did I?" Alix said, laughing. Then before I could answer, as I got slowly to my feet, I heard her gallop off into the trees.

"Are you all right, miss?" I turned. A black man with grizzled hair stood there. From his stained breeches and the harness in his hand, I could tell he was probably a groom.

"Yes. I'm fine. Susie?" I turned. Untouched by her near fatal accident, Susie was taking care of her personal needs in the flower beds that ran along the house.

I turned back to the groom.

"Does she always take off like that?"

"Yes, ma'am. Almost always. Miss Alix doesn't ever do anything except in a hurry and flat out. That's her way. Just like it was her—"

And at that point he stopped.

"Just like it was who?" I asked, somewhat less than grammatically and trying to sound as casual as possible.

"Nuthin', miss. Do you want me to saddle a horse for you?"

"No, thank you. Not today." I didn't feel it was necessary to tell him that I had never been on a horse in my life.

He touched his rather battered hat and went back inside the stable yard saying quite distinctly as he reached the gatepost, "Her daddy sure isn't going to be pleased. Not one little bit." But he was too far for me to question, which was perhaps what he intended.

I glanced at my watch and discovered that this whole episode had not taken more than five minutes. It gave me an eerie feeling. Those hooves looked wicked above my head. If one of them had come down in the wrong place, it would have sliced my head open and Susie in two. As always with me, reaction came after the fact. My knees suddenly felt quivery. "I'll take you out again later, Susie. Breakfast now."

It was a magic word. Susie promptly lost her interest in the flowers and trotted over to me. Together we went into the house. I picked her up and took her upstairs and settled her on the floor with some dry food. "I'll try and get you something ravishing from the kitchen," I promised her. It was when I straightened up I took in the fact that the bed had been made. More gracious living, I thought, not entirely sure whether I should be pleased that that was a chore done, or socially outraged that some servant now had me to wait on, in addition to everyone else. With a mental note not to get my values mixed up, I was about to turn when something exploded in my head. The envelope that I had put on the night table the night before was nowhere in sight. It seemed incredible that, until this moment, I had forgotten about it. I stared at the night table trying to recall if I had noticed it this morning. It is said that the mind takes in everything, however unconsciously and however unreachable it may become. I closed my eyes, concentrating, taking my memory back to when I woke up. . . . There had been the knock on the door . . . the tray . . . the note. . . . But when I tried to visualize the night table with the white square bearing the upright handwriting propped against the water glass as I had placed it the night before, nothing came. There was no image. The envelope might have been there, or it might have disappeared in the night. I opened my eyes. Disappeared how? I got down on my knees and looked under the heavy flounce around the bottom of the bed. There was nothing there or behind the bed. Nor was the envelope behind the night table, under it, or inside its one drawer. Ten minutes later I had searched the entire room. The envelope was definitely not there. Which meant that either someone had come into the room during the night and taken it, or, which was much more likely, it had been removed while I was down walking Susie. Just to make sure no one had come into the room during the night, I examined every foot of wall. There was no other entrance of any kind, and any sliding or opening panel nonsense that might have existed inside a closet was obviated by the fact that the room's only hanging space was an old-fashioned wardrobe. Which meant that the only way into the room was by the door, and if anyone had tried to come through that, the noisy trap I had set up would have waked me in an instant. So—the obvious conclusion was that while I was down by the stable this morning, someone had come into the room and taken the envelope. Possibly whoever it was who had made the bed. But not definitely. There was a bell beside the mantlepiece, and although I am not given to summoning servants in that way (or, for that matter, summoning servants at all), I walked across the room and started to put my hand out. But short of the actual bell, I paused. Whoever had left that envelope outside my door the night before had done so with a purpose. If I started making inquiries it would be a confirmation of how seriously I had taken the matter. I dropped my hand. Better to treat the matter as a prank and ignore it—certainly for the time being. It riled me to appear to let whoever it was get away with it.

But there were times when the best course of action was—for me, anyway—the hardest: do nothing at all.

"Susie," I said, by way of relieving my feelings, "you have my full permission to bite anyone who comes in this room." And with a pat I put her up on the snowy counterpane. Then I went downstairs. Where was Darcourt's study? I wondered.

"Back of the stairs to the right, miss, then through the library and the blue room to the end of the wing," a voice said, and I turned and saw Stevens watching me.

"Thank you, Stevens."

"That's all right, miss," and his little blue eyes twinkled.

I headed past the tall mirror at the back and opened the door to the right. Comparable in size and space to the dining room across the hall, the big, graceful room was covered, on three walls, with bookshelves from floor to ceiling. Across the fourth wall, to my left, were windows looking out on the magnolia tree at the back and the oak woods behind that. I walked through the room and saw that behind me, dividing the wall, was a white chimney piece and beneath that a fire burning in the hearth. My eyes strayed to the books and around the walls again. It was one of the most beautiful and comfortable rooms I had ever been in in my life, and I stood there, forgetful of my appointment. Then I turned back to the fire and saw, for the first time, that above the mantel, instead of books, was a portrait. How could I have missed anything so compelling? I wondered. For surely it was Alix, an older—but not much older—Alix, laughing, that flowerlike quality apparent in the delicacy of bone, the long, slender neck, the tilt of the flaxen head with the hair cupped around as though dressed for a ball. It was a timeless portrait, with the shimmering white dress foaming off the shoulders, and could, in its implicit elegance, have been painted by a pupil of John Singer Sargent's. Yet I knew that it was as recent as the debut of Alix's mother. Because that, without any question, was who it was.

"Yes," a voice said behind me, "Alix is very like her."

I swung around. A door in the opposite wall that I had barely noticed, so much did its tawny wood match the leather bindings of the books, was open. In the doorway, his crooked shoulders almost filling it, was Tristram Darcourt. He came through and closed the door. "I was planning to see you in my office at the other end of the wing.

But since you were late, I thought I might as well come looking for you, and we can talk in here."

There was some perversity in the train of events, I thought, that had consistently put me in the wrong with Darcourt and his household, thus assuring that out of nervous defensiveness I would forget my part. This time I was determined not to, and made myself pause. Then I said, "Yes. She is like her. I take it that is Mrs. Darcourt."

He limped over to a serviceable modern desk, made of golden fruitwood and, for all its austere lines, perfectly in keeping with the room. Its back to the windows, it stood out a few feet from a book-covered wall. Seating himself behind it, he indicated another chair in front. I went over and sat down.

"Yes," he said, leaning back, his hands in his pockets. "That's Mrs. Darcourt. Now——"

"Will I be meeting her?" I asked quickly, thinking about the envelope, before he could turn the subject, as he was so obviously about to do. And then, as he said nothing, "I mean, it would be helpful in working with Alix, I thought."

"No, you will not be meeting her." He said it heavily. I was reminded of a door, being quietly, but irrevocably shut. "She's . . . away, almost all the time. Now, shall we talk about Alix?"

"Yes. Of course . . . I just thought . . . Yes." My voice trailed off as the full meaning of what he said struck me. *"She's . . . away, almost all the time."*

But the envelope, I thought, which was open, had been postmarked only a week before. I could feel the words form on my tongue. Yet I knew I wouldn't say them. Not now. Not to this man. Though why I felt this so strongly, I couldn't be sure.

Further, I could see it was not going to be easy striking that middle, contained, note between defiance and subservience, both of which, I was beginning to realize, were different sides of the same coin.

The straight brows across from me frowned. "Why did you come here?" he asked abruptly.

The question took me by surprise, unpleasantly so. Did it mean he had gotten wind of the masquerade I was playing, some hint that I was not who I said I was—Thérèse LeBreton of New Orleans, member of a numerous and wide-flung family with roots deep in the Cajun country, the same country, I suddenly and uncomfortably remem-

55

bered, of his wife's kin, the Charpentier clan? But those hidden eyes were watching me, and I had to produce an answer before my hesitation increased any suspicion he already had.

"To be governess and companion to Alix," I replied.

"How did you know she needed one—that I was looking for one for her?"

"One hears these things." I spoke as calmly as I could. "As you know, from my résumè, I have been governess to Melissa Laird and the Fenwick children in Virginia. I've forgotten whether it was from Mrs. Fenwick or from one of the other families of that area that I heard it—there was a lot of coming and going among the people there, particularly during the hunting season—but it was around the time that Ginny Fenwick, the youngest, was going to school, when I knew I would be looking for another position." Just in time I changed the word "job" to "position" which, in my limited experience, seemed more a term a governess would use. And thank God, I thought, for Terry's detailed letters.

"I see."

And there was another pause while I felt my stomach muscles tighten. What would a man as powerful as Tristram Darcourt do to someone he found had penetrated his home and family under false pretenses? And his legendary power, I thought uneasily, was not just of rank and wealth. It was in the man himself, lying just below the polished manners that came from generations of breeding, and were to him as natural as breathing itself. My father, in his ignorance, anger and defiance, always considered that men from such families as the Darcourts would be pallid fops, weaklings, with the guts bred out of them . . . no match for the toughs who walked the high girders with such carelessness, himself the toughest of all. And without giving the matter further thought, I had taken on his prejudices.

But this man in his well-worn riding clothes and boots, sitting in his graceful library filled with books that represented the collection and knowledgeable discrimination of more than two centuries, was just as tough as Patrick James Wainright, and far more controlled.

"Very well," he said finally. "From my brief acquaintance with you I would not say that I would have thought you either suited or happy to fill the role of governess. But you're here now. . . . If I did not have to go away this morning on a business trip, we might discuss your suitability further. But I do. I should have been gone long since, but I wanted to be here when you arrived."

He was telling me two things: the first was that he found me so unsuitable that if he did not have more important matters to take care of—by implication more important than his daughter—he would get rid of me. The second, and more immediately important, item was that it was he who had overseen my hiring, not Mrs. Conyers. It all seemed clear enough, but I decided that the matter should be clarified, especially if he was going away.

"I thought it was Mrs. Conyers who made the arrangements."

"Did you? She wrote at my instructions."

"And when you go, shall I be under her authority, or answerable only to you?"

"In all matters pertaining to the household, she will be in charge. Should there be any question concerning Alix, then I suggest you talk it over with her, and if there is disagreement between the two of you—especially if there is disagreement—then give careful attention to what she says. She's been with the family a long time and her counsel is worth having. But if the disagreement persists, then get . . . have her get in touch with me."

"She will know where you are?"

"At all times."

But I won't, I thought. And then chided my overheated sensibilities and imagination. Hadn't he just said Mrs. Conyers had been with the family a long time? Wouldn't it be natural then that she should be the keeper of the king's schedule? Curious, I thought, that the word king should keep cropping up in my mind.

"Now, about Alix." The long, rather sinewy fingers tapped on the desk blotter. "You thought last night that I was harsh with her, didn't you?"

"Yes. I did. And furthermore—"

His brows went up. "Yes, Miss LeBreton?"

"You humiliated her in front of me. I've always thought that way . . ." I groped for an adequate but not too offensive adjective.

". . . dirty pool?"

The absurd words were on the nose. "Yes. Dirty pool. You put her down in front of someone who had been hired to be a companion to her. How will she feel about me now?"

"That's for you to find out and adjust to, isn't it? I did what, as her father, I thought was in her best interests. If you think I'm in the wrong, I'm willing to listen to you. But not now."

First things first, I thought sardonically. Which means business first.

"As you wish, Mr. Darcourt."

"Yes. As I wish. And that includes some house and ground rules: Alix is not to leave this island while I'm gone. She is not, under any circumstances, to go beyond the fence into the southern part of the island." The cold, level eyes were on me for a moment. "You have shown yourself to be somewhat rebellious, Miss LeBreton. So much so that I must tell you that if I were not compelled to go on this business trip, I would try to find someone more—"

"—docile?" I couldn't help it. The word slipped out.

"Yes. Docile. You are, after all, in my employ. I know a great deal more about my daughter than you do. And I know what is best for her. I will not have anyone encouraging her disobedience." He paused. "If that sounds harsh, please remember what I told you. The southern half of the island is filled with swamps and quicksands. She could ride her horse into any one of those and disappear without a trace." He paused and said in a flat, unemotional, even, colorless voice, "It would be a terrible death—"

Perhaps it was the dimness as the sun slipped behind a cloud that gave his face that gray, strained, harsh look. "I know," he said after a short pause. "I have seen someone die that way."

A shiver went through me. "Are they—the swamps— essential for the wildlife around here?"

"You must know what is happening to the Everglades, Miss LeBreton. Bit by bit, piece by piece, they are being destroyed, the water drained away. I have no intention of that happening to Darcourt Island. And since I own it, I can see that it doesn't."

I was torn. Having done two major stories on the destruction of nature's balance for man's needs, I, too, deplored the slow erosion of the Everglades by bulldozers and housing merchants. On the other hand, I strongly suspected that along with Darcourt's protective impulse towards wildlife was the iron will of the petty ruler whose domain was going to remain subject to his will, and his alone. But I was not here to fight that. There might, however, be practical difficulties attached to all this.

"What happens if she simply takes off, Mr. Darcourt, as she did this morning?" And then nearly bit my tongue. I hadn't meant to disclose that I saw her gallop away against her father's orders. He obviously read my face and gave a rather sardonic smile. "Don't worry. I knew about that."

"I suppose the groom—whatever his name was, Duncan—told you."

"No, Miss LeBreton. He didn't. I saw Alix galloping past my study window."

"Well, suppose she decided to jump the fence? How could I stop her?"

"I would hope that you would be able to—er—induce her not to do such a thing. Surely such persuasion towards moderating her behavior would not be beyond your powers?"

The sarcasm was there, the touch of derision, and for the first time it occurred to me that the Master of Darcourt might be amusing himself by baiting me. There was a silence as I looked back into those silvery gray eyes, in which I felt sure I could detect mockery. Or was it in the mouth, long and surprisingly expressive?

I took a breath. "I don't know whether it would or not, Mr. Darcourt. That rather depends on her experience with discipline in the past, doesn't it? I'm not a . . . an authoritarian person. I've always preferred reasoning to force. I cannot promise that she will obey me. I can only assure you that I will try to . . . to enable her to act in her own best interests. I hope I succeed."

"I hope you do, too. I wasn't suggesting, by the way, that you beat her. Only that you use the authority that your age and your . . . experience . . . should give you. It's not a dirty word, by the way, authority, even though it's unfashionable. I think you will find that authority works very well with Alix. She responds to it."

It was on the tip of my tongue to say, As she did last night? With tears? But in the silent tug of war that was going on between Tristram Darcourt and me as we sat there, I could only lose, and if I lost he would, I was quite sure, get rid of me immediately, convenient or not. I decided to turn the subject a little.

"Mr. Darcourt, does Alix have any friends of her own, young boys or girls she can visit or who visit her?" And as I spoke there popped into my mind the mental image of the blond youth who had sent me down the muddy lane. And there was something else about him that tugged at my mind, though I couldn't, at that moment, get hold of it.

For the first time, I saw Darcourt pause, as though uncertain.

He got up. "That was one of the reasons we brought you here, Miss LeBreton. That you would be a friend to her."

I got up, too. "Both an authority figure and a friend? Don't they cancel each other out?"

"Not necessarily, Miss LeBreton. I hope you don't find them to do so. I must now wish you good morning. Petersen is waiting at the dock for me. I hope when I return, in a month or so, that I will find you have settled very comfortably in your dual role."

He pushed his chair in, gave a slight bow and limped towards the door by which he had come in. Without a backward glance, he passed through and closed it behind him. It was as the lock fastened that I realized I had forgotten to mention a subject I had intended to bring up: a key for my bedroom door. Well, I could talk to Mrs. Conyers about it, although I was also beginning to realize how much Darcourt held all authority, large and small, in his capable, if repressive, hands.

(4)

I WATCHED Darcourt's departure from the iron balcony.
After mounting the staircase, intending to go to my room,
I saw the tall, graceful French windows straight ahead across
the broad landing and, obeying an impulse, went towards
them. Heavy gold curtains hung on either side of the windows,
but here, where there was no other house nearer than the
mainland, the windows themselves were without covering,
although I could see that wooden shutters, or jalousies,
opened out from these frame and glass doors as they did
from all the large number of windows on both floors. The
view through the windows was breathtaking: what looked
like a mile of grass unrolled before the house, green and
moist and smooth as a golf course or, I suddenly remembered
from my travels, as though this were England or Ireland. And
as I peered out I could see why. Sprinklers dotted the huge
green apron, tossing their moisture into the air where the
drops glinted with rainbow colors in the morning sun. And
far to the left and the right, where there were banks of
flower beds forming ribbons of colors as border to the trees
behind, were figures, gardeners, I assumed, moving or bent,
wielding the tools of their trade. My eyes went around the
rim. I could count four figures. Heaven knew how many
there were out of sight.

Without thinking, my hand went to the latch on the door
and pulled it down. The door opened. In front of me extended,

for about four feet, the stone flags forming the floor of the balcony. I stepped out and smelled again the sweet-sour moist air. Only on this side, the front of the house, the sweet dominated. The swamps that Darcourt was so voluble about lay behind the house. And behind the fence that neither Alix nor I could cross. . . .

Use your authority, he had said. And then, in almost the following breath, be her friend. . . . The clever so-and-so, I thought to myself, as I saw, for the first time, the neat trap he had laid: If I became her friend but failed to control her, then I would not have used my authority. If I succeeded in making her obey me (not quite as hard a job as I pretended to myself and to Darcourt. After all, anyone who helped in keeping two hundred and fifteen orphans from burning down the asylum, murdering one another, or mounting a palace revolution, learned something about the uses of power, but Darcourt, of course, didn't and mustn't know that: it didn't come with Terry LeBreton's rèsumè), then I probably would give him cause to think I had failed to become his daughter's friend. Either way, he would have the grounds he needed to fire me. Not, I thought, that he would quibble over the convention of having to have a good reason: his most capricious whim would be reason enough.

"Clever," I thought again cynically, and at that moment heard voices immediately beneath me. I peered over the iron railing and then stepped hastily back.

Wearing a gray business suit, Tristram Darcourt was about to step into the jeep that was parked in front of the door.

"You know where to reach me," he was saying to Mrs. Conyers.

Cautiously, I leaned forward and looked over the railing again. Luckily, part of the wisteria that seemed to be all over the balcony combined with branches of the huge oak that towered over the house to form a moderately effective screen.

"Yes, sir." The voice of the housekeeper sounded anxious. "But what if she—"

I could have killed Judson at that moment for starting up the jeep's engine and drowning out the rest of her sentence. Then the motor quieted. Darcourt's voice floated up, a crisp antidote to Mrs. Conyers' rather wispy tones. "Then you'll just have to see by any means necessary that that doesn't happen. Do you understand?"

"Yes, sir. But what if she decides to see for herself, to visit the house?"

"You simply must not let that happen. You have Norton and Judson. You can always get hold of Monsieur André. If there is no other way, you know how to let the dogs out. Is that absolutely clear?"

Her answer was indistinguishable. He put one leg in the jeep and climbed in, his raincoat over his shoulder, one hand holding a briefcase. Once, when I was poking through various newspapers and news-magazines, I had come across an article entitled "The Ten Most Powerful Men in America." And, in two rows of five, were photographs.

Only the last photograph on the second row was blank, because no one had been able to dig up a picture of Tristram Darcourt. And somehow the empty frame carried far more clout than the other nine pictures. Like the empty chair at a feast, it dominated. And the curious part was, with the mystery removed, it still dominated. Even from this height, foreshortened, distorted, Tristram Darcourt exuded power. It seemed to crackle from his crisp black hair, his massive shoulders, his knifelike profile. . . . Almost, I thought, like an Indian's. And at that moment he glanced up.

Even though I was fairly sure he couldn't see me, I stepped back, and then mentally kicked myself. I could easily have betrayed my otherwise invisible presence by moving, shifting the shadows.

But I could see no recognition in the narrow eyes, silvery even from this distance. Then he made a gesture with his hand and the jeep shot forward.

I stood there watching its passage down the long, curving path, and was about to go in, when I saw a figure, obviously Alix, dart from the trees and throw herself at the jeep. The car stopped. I couldn't even hear her voice, let alone discern what she said, but it was obvious that she was pleading. Every gesture of the frail, slight body was one of solicitation. I saw her father's hand make one of his decisive, sweeping gestures. The jeep moved forward again. I gasped as I saw her seemingly dragged with it, hanging frantically onto the door. Then I saw Tristram Darcourt take his daughter's hand, wrench it from the car, and thrust her back, throwing her to the ground as he did so. The jeep picked up speed and disappeared into the trees.

Behind, her head on the ground, lay Alix, her arms out in front of her, as though still pleading.

63

An anger deep within me stirred. My father was short-tempered, easily irritated and explosive. In the grip of one of his tempers, his tongue could be pulverizing. But he was never, to anyone, cruel. Least of all to me, his daughter. Yet the behavior I had just witnessed was cruel and barbaric past belief. It would have been under any circumstances, to anyone. From a man towards his daughter, it was inconceivable—yet it had happened. I had seen it.

I turned and ran down the stairs again, and encountered Mrs. Conyers as she was coming back through the front door.

"Miss LeBreton," she started.

"Later, Mrs. Conyers. I'm going out to see Alix."

"Leave her be! It is better—"

I swung around. "Better that she lie sobbing on the ground? Did you see what happened, Mrs. Conyers?"

"Yes. I saw. But if you don't notice her hysterical behavior, she will stop that nonsense. Believe me, Miss LeBreton. Her father knows how best to deal with her. You would be wise to follow his example."

"Yet it was her father who told me he wanted me to be her friend. A friend would go to her now."

"No, Miss LeBreton. You are mistaken—"

I decided that the time had come to define my realm of authority. Better now than later. "Mrs. Conyers, Mr. Darcourt told me that Alix was in my care; that I should listen to your advice, but that the ultimate decision was mine [not exactly what Darcourt had said, but it was in the main true]. I am sure you mean well. But even if Alix is hysterical and out of control, she has the right to my sympathy and understanding, and I'm going out to see she knows that. Please step aside."

We stood there for a long moment. With her back to the light, Mrs. Conyers' face was in darkness. But her straight, rigid figure in the dark brown dress expressed her opposition to me and to all I had said. Then the shoulders dropped a little.

"Very well, Miss LeBreton. It is true that Alix is your responsibility. I may, in the future, have occasion to remind you of that." And she stepped past me in the hall and up the stairs. A few minutes later I was standing over Alix, who by this time was sitting up, one hand around the other wrist, her face white. As I approached, she looked up at me. It was the first time I had seen her up close, and I experienced the same curious sense of timelessness that I had when I saw her mother's portrait. There was a very uncontemporary quality about Alix, as though she had stepped out of a time capsule from another century.

"He hurt my wrist," she said.

I went down on one knee. "Let me look at it."

The skin around the slight wrist was a little inflamed. "Let me see your other."

She took her other hand off the ground, shifting her balance, and held her arm out. Yes, I thought, comparing the two, the right one was a little swollen, although by most standards it was still thin.

"Did you fall on it?" I asked unemotionally. I wanted to find out what exactly had happened.

"No! He twisted it when he pulled it off the door handle."

Those huge eyes above the hollowed cheeks were staring up at me. Emotionally, I was all on her side and my indignation matched hers. But instinctively, without thinking, I pitched the tone of my response to one of flat common sense. "You have small wrists. He probably didn't realize how easy it was to bruise them."

"He should. It's happened before!"

I stood up. "The best thing to put on it now is ice. Let's go in and find some."

She got to her feet, as effortlessly as a dancer. "You don't believe me, do you?" The note of hysteria that had been in her voice, and that had evoked my matter-of-fact response, was gone. She might have been saying that it was going to rain.

"Of course I believe you, Alix. Why shouldn't I? If I sounded . . . unsympathetic, it was just reflex, I suppose—"

"Like a slap for hysterics?"

Alix was not stupid. I looked up at her face—she was slightly taller than I—and read a conglomeration of emotions that added up, I decided, to the need for a candid statement on my part.

"Yes. All right. I thought you were a little . . . strung out. Or rather, I didn't think. It's just my . . . governess's reaction to too much tension. I'm not unsympathetic to how you feel."

"You don't seem like any governess I ever had."

"We come in all shapes and sizes. Like adolescents. Like anybody."

For a second or two she didn't speak. Then, "I wasn't

65

lying, you know. It's happened before!" And with that she thrust her loose shirt sleeve all the way up her arm. Above her elbow, the bruises looked green and black against the soft white flesh of the inner arm. She let the sleeve fall down. "Those happened yesterday morning."

And suddenly I saw in my mind those sinewy fingers tapping against the desk blotter. Given their length and power, he wouldn't even have to exert pressure to make marks like that.

"What was happening?" I asked. "I mean, what was he trying to make you do that you didn't want to do, or vice versa—prevent you from doing?"

"Does it matter?" The gray eyes were hostile, and reminded me, momentarily, of her father's. "Are there some things it's okay to beat me up about?" She sounded, now, I reflected fleetingly, much more like the average disgruntled teen-ager.

"No. Of course not. But if hanging on to you like that was the only way he could stop you from doing something way out—like jumping out of a window—then I would find his finger marks more excusable than if he were—as you say—beating you up to exert his authority. But even then," I added after a moment's thought, "I would have to be convinced that he had exhausted all other ways, such as rational persuasion."

"My father doesn't believe in rational persuasion. I once read him that line about 'Come, let us reason together,' and he just laughed. He believes in absolute obedience—to him." She was rubbing her arm as she spoke, and the hostility was still in her face. "I didn't realize you were on his side and that he had hired some kind of a spy. I mean *another* spy. He already has Mrs. Conyers and Judson and Norton, and all I have is—"

She shut her mouth and started walking towards the house. I went after her and caught up. "Is who?" I asked.

"Someone," she said.

We walked together in silence for a moment. This first conversation had not gone as I had planned. Instead of winning her over I had alienated her. "Look," I said, "let's stop and talk for a minute. We. . . . I seem to have got off on the wrong foot. I'm sorry. I want to be your friend, and please believe me, I'm not a spy." *But you are, that's exactly what you are,* some voice in my head said tauntingly. *You're here to find out what you can about the Darcourt secret. . . .* Funny, I thought. I had always thought of it as my mother's

66

secret. But somewhere, somehow, it had become to me the Darcourt secret. And the moment the words formed in my head I knew that my instincts were right, and that there was one. . . . But this had nothing to do with Alix, and as far as she was concerned, I had certainly not hired myself to be a spy.

"You are a spy, aren't you?" she was saying, standing there now, looking at me.

"No, Alix. I am not. Your father . . . your father said he wanted me to be a companion and friend to you."

"That's what he's said to all the governesses that have come and gone. And they've all been spies." She turned back towards the house and started to walk rapidly.

"Alix," I said, hurrying after her. "Listen to me."

But her legs were longer than mine, and with easy grace she was moving out ahead of me.

And then, without thinking, I stopped and said loudly, "Alix. Stop and turn around. I want to talk to you. At once!"

And she did, as I knew she would. That conviction that I would be obeyed had happened before in my life, notably at the orphanage, and had prompted Mother Ignacia, the head of the orphanage, to say once rather drily, after she had witnessed a display of my technique, "You seem, Sally, to have the power of command. I hope you use it wisely."

It was a power, if that was the correct word, that I was a little ashamed of, because it went dead counter to my anti-authoritarian beliefs.

"Look, Alix," I said in a different voice.

"You sounded just like my father." She seemed totally amazed.

"I'm sorry. I'll try not to crack the whip. But if I'm trying to get your attention and you keep walking away from me, what would you suggest that I do?"

She eyed me warily. "I don't know. That's your problem, isn't it?"

I went up to her, intending to take her arm, but something held me back, something, again, that made me think of her father: an odd tension, a standoffishness, a stance, as though, for them both, to be touched would be an intrusion. I stopped a few feet from her. "It becomes my problem when I can't reach you."

She looked down at the ground, and then said, sounding like a sulky thirteen-year-old, "What do you want?"

"To be friends."

She looked up then, with an oddly wise expression, "You can't be friends just like that . . . like it was some kind of . . . contract. It doesn't happen that way."

"No. It doesn't. But. . . . All right, can we have a contract? I won't crack the whip if you won't slam the door. You said that you had quoted to your father, 'let us reason together.' Then maybe we'll get to be friends. Maybe we won't . . . but maybe we will."

She stood with her fair head bent, as though searching the ground for something. Then she suddenly stooped. "I thought I saw one!" Her fingers went into the wet grass.

"What is it?" I asked.

"A four-leaf clover." She straightened. "See?"

I walked a little nearer and looked down into her palm. There were the four green leaves joined into a square clover.

"Congratulations," I said. "Good luck."

"Here." Quickly she moved towards me, her hand held out. "In honor of the contract."

I almost made the mistake of refusing. I wanted her to have the good luck talisman. Being half Irish, I had always been aware of a brilliant green streak of superstition running right through me. But, luckily, I took it. "Thank you," I said. "In honor of the contract."

We turned and walked towards the house.

And for a while we didn't say anything, which was all right, in fact it was restful, as though the silence itself mended the damage of some of the words. Then she said, "What are you going to do with it?"

I looked down and opened my hand. "I think I'll press it."

"In a book?"

"Yes."

"What book?"

"One that belonged to my mother. It's a small, pocket-sized, New Testament in French. She always kept it on her night table."

Alix turned, her interest caught. "Was your mother French?"

I could almost feel my pulse jump. Without planning, by accident, the conversation had fallen very usefully. "Louisiana French. Cajun."

"Oh. So's my mother. Did you know that?"

Careful, I thought. "Yes. I seem to remember that when the . . . opening here came up and I was writing to Mrs. Conyers about it, I looked your family up in *Who's Who* or something, and it said there that your mother had come from New Orleans, and gave her French name. Charpentier, wasn't it?"

"Yes. But originally the family came from the bayou country. My grandfather fell on an oil field or something—you know there's lots of oil down there near places like Raceland and Golden Meadow, the Bayou Lafourche country —and when he got rich he moved his family to New Orleans. But all the cousins and aunts and great-aunts are down in the bayou country."

"Have you ever been there?"

"No. Father won't let me go."

"Oh. Why?"

She shrugged, and I could feel a faint withdrawal from her. "I guess he doesn't get along with Mother's family. After all, his is so English."

"Do you mean old American English, or English, English?"

"Both. The family's been over here a long time, but there are cousins in England that go way back and they've always kept up with each other. And there's a sort of family tradition that the male Darcourts spend part of their schooling in England. Father went to Harrow for a couple of years before going to Annapolis. Did you know that?"

"I didn't know about his being at Harrow. Although I might have guessed. I took his accent to be more New England, but it could be slightly English."

"It's both. We have another place up in Massachusetts, you know."

That accounted, I thought, for a certain, almost European quality to his arrogance. But I was less interested in family history per se than in family oil. "I didn't realize the Darcourt oil holdings were in Louisiana. I guess I always associate oil either with Texas or Oklahoma millionaires, or Arab sheikdoms and I assumed your family had pieces of that."

I had made it sound as casual as I could, but I was holding my breath.

"Oh, I wasn't talking about the Darcourt oil—that's all over the place. Just Grandpère Charpentier's."

"Oh."

And then she said something that really made me jump. "If you aren't a spy, how come you knew what I had been doing? I mean, you must have asked questions, somebody must have told you."

I was completely at sea.

"Alix—I don't know what you're talking about."

I could sense in her, then, the fight, about to happen.

I said quickly, "Please, Alix, remember our contract. Explain. What you are referring to when you said I must have known what you'd been doing?"

I am not a fanciful person, but I could almost see the wings outspread, so much did she remind me of a bird about to take off. But she said, "About jumping . . . trying to jump out of the window. Father would never tell you. Because then he'd have to tell you why, and he'd never do that. So somebody else must have told you. Old Conyers, probably. But I don't think that even she would unless you'd been snooping."

"Let me get this straight. You mean you were trying to jump out of the window yesterday morning?"

Assent was all over her face, though she didn't say anything. Then, abruptly, she nodded.

A little chill flickered up and down my arm. Once or twice I had had to deal with the seriously disturbed. But first I had to do my best to reassure her.

"Alix, please believe me. When I used that—your jumping out the window—it was a shot in the dark, the first contingency I could think of where to grasp someone so tightly as to leave marks would appear justified. No one told me that this had actually happened. You know," I went, "if I were a spy, I'd be an awful fool to tell you that and put you on your guard, wouldn't I?"

It was a minute before her face relaxed. But I saw then that she believed me. "Okay. I guess you're right. But you can see why I thought you were."

"I certainly can—" I was on the verge of telling her that I had seen a man, the previous summer, foiled from jumping off a bridge in London, held by a brawny policeman in a way that would leave bruises similar to her own. But then, what would Terry LeBreton have been doing in London watching would-be suicides when, as far as I could remember, from my memory, she'd been up in Seal Harbor, taking care of the Laird children. Not saying the wrong, revealing thing, I thought, was going to be like treading across a minefield.

We walked for a few seconds in silence. Then, Alix sighed and said, "You know why I was trying to jump out the window?"

"No. Why were you?"

"Because Father said he was going to lock the door, and I can't bear to be locked in a room. It makes me feel caged."

"I don't blame you. I'd feel caged, too. Had you . . . was he punishing you?"

"Oh, no. Just stopping me from going to see Mother, as he always does."

"Going to see your mother?" I was so stunned I halted. "I thought she was in southern France."

"That's what everybody thinks. That's what Father *wants* everybody to think. But she isn't. She's in a house on the other side of the swamp."

"But why—"

I never finished the question, because the silence that until that moment had echoed only with the soft cry of birds about their morning business and conversations was suddenly broken by the noise of frantic barking.

"There are the dogs," Alix said, stopping. "I wonder what set them off."

"Alix, about your mother—"

But she was gone, flying over the turf, the sun on her yellow hair. I was a brisk sprinter at school, and could have overtaken Alix, even with her advantage of leg and start. But I was a great believer in the maxim, begin as you mean to go on, and I was not about to set a pattern of pursuing a fleeing Alix for the rest of my time here. Besides, I was still digesting her astonishing statement about her mother being on the island. As I walked towards the house I dredged up every piece of information about Mrs. Darcourt that had been presented to me in the past fourteen hours—was it only that long since I had arrived? It felt like a week.

Mrs. Conyers' words came back as I pulled them out of my memory, *"Mrs. Darcourt is not here. . . . Mrs. Darcourt spends most of her time away. Mrs. Darcourt's health has always been frail, and she finds the climate of southern France more salubrious. Mr. Darcourt and Alix join her there when they can. . . ."*

And then Darcourt's: *"No, you will not be meeting her. . . . She's . . . away, almost all the time."*

At that moment, like the genie from the bottle, the envelope left outside my door—and later taken from my room—popped into my mind. Put together with what Alix had just said, it could mean—what? Almost anything—from everything to nothing at all. Much as I disliked to give weight to what Mrs. Conyers or Tristram Darcourt said about Alix,

71

there was something about her seesaw swings, her volatility—I preferred that word to hysteria—that produced in me a sense of caution about taking her too literally. Children like Alix—and I had encountered them before—sometimes confused wishful thinking with reality. At that I made a face, catching myself in the kind of psychologists' jargon that often hid as much of the truth as it was supposed to clarify.

On the other hand, I thought, walking towards the house, if one wished to be technical, Darcourt hadn't actually said Mrs. Darcourt was not on the island. Away could mean away from the house. And the same interpretation could be put on Mrs. Conyers' statement. But aside from the fact that I didn't think that was what either of them had meant, it was the kind of deviousness that I had been brought up to call a weasel, and weasels to me were lies, and cowardly lies at that, made by people who kept the letter but not the spirit of the law. "Don't be mealy-mouthed, for the love of God," my favorite moralist, Patrick James Wainwright, had once roared at me. "If you're going to tell a lie, tell a thumping one."

And at that memory, something strange started happening to me. My throat felt thick, and tears stung the backs of my eyelids. I had never cried for my father, never really mourned him, never let him go. Now it was as though, at long last, he was leaving me.

"No!" I said aloud. Why now? What had brought it about?

The tears were in my eyes now, and I wiped them away, aware that the barking, which however rackety had remained more or less constant, was now coming nearer.

I was no longer afraid of those powerful animals, nevertheless it took a little effort to stop in my tracks as they plunged towards me.

"From ghoulies and ghosties and long-legged beasties, and things that go bump in the night," I breathed, automatically crossing my fingers, "Good Lord, deliver us. Hello, whoever you are," and I held out my hand.

The huge Doberman slowed, stopped, sniffed at my proffered hand. Then he liked it, and to my astonishment I found myself patting the formidably handsome head. As the others came up, I patted them, and found myself entirely surrounded by animals. I heard a whimper, and there, at the back, was the enormous Great Dane. Suddenly I wanted to laugh, because I noticed what I hadn't, in my fright, seen before: that he was barely beyond puppyhood, and he re-

72

minded me strongly of Susie when, competing with other and larger dogs for a dish of food—as had happened in our various travels—she had got left out and pushed to the rear. Remembering that he was the one who had exchanged affectionate licks with Susie, I pushed through the Dobermans and Shepherds and rubbed the top of his head. My reward was immediate and quelling. He reared to a full six feet, put lion-sized paws on my shoulders and licked my face.

"Down," I said feebly, my hands against the powerful chest.

"Down, True," a male voice said.

True promptly dropped down. And I found myself staring at one of the handsomest men I had ever seen, around thirty, tall, as fair as Alix, and with her fineness of feature. His mouth curved into a charming smile. "I'm André Charpentier, Alix's cousin. You must be Miss LeBreton."

I had two immediate and diametrically opposed reactions: one was a lift of the heart evoked by the sheer male attractiveness of the man; the other was a spasm of panic. Tristram Darcourt might spring from an old Southern family, but his accent was crisp and incisive, almost English. By contrast, the voice that came from in front of me was pure New Orleans, and anyone from New Orleans would certainly know the complicated network of the LeBreton family down to the last cousin. Here was another obvious contingency I hadn't thought of: that Alix Darcourt would be bound to have Charpentier cousins from Louisiana; that they could be expected to be familiar with other well-known Louisiana families, including the LeBretons, my supposed family; and that they might visit Alix while I was there. Well, I thought resignedly, here we both were: I could not disappear in a puff of smoke. The man smiling in front of me was expecting an answer; in fact, he would begin to think it odd if he didn't get one immediately. As with confronting the dogs, I could do nothing but go forward.

"That's right," I said, watching his face carefully. "I'm Terry LeBreton."

The cobalt blue eyes regarded me sincerely.

"If I had known I was going to meet you, I would have brought greetings from your Tante Julie. I was at her party last week."

Fortunately, I had met Tante Julie when I had visited Terry in New Orleans. I smiled. "How is Pompom?" Pompom was

73

Tante Julie's large, bad-tempered gray Persian. Most of French New Orleans, attracted by the deceptively cuddlesome-looking cat, had been royally scratched.

André Charpentier held out his arm and pushed up the sleeves of his shirt and light tweed jacket. Sure enough, a scratch ran up the inside of the wrist.

"This time I thought I was safe. He looked asleep. I should have known better."

I laughed. "Yes, you should."

Alix came up from behind her cousin. "Have you met my cousin André, Miss LeBreton?" And she turned a radiant look on her handsome kinsman, a look filled with the affection and trust so singularly lacking in her expression when she faced her father.

"I have had that pleasure," I said, smiling. "And it's Terry. I don't want to feel old before my time."

I had my reward then. It might have been the backwash from her feeling for André, but the glance she gave me held the friendliness I had wanted from her, and that she had not shown before.

"All right," she said, with a touch of shyness. "Terry."

André held out his hand. "And may I also, Terry? Except that I think I'll stick with Thérèse. I much prefer the French pronunciation."

I shook his hand. "Of course. If you don't mind the fact that I may not react to Thérèse immediately. It's been so long since anybody used it."

I was just congratulating myself on the neat loophole that would explain any failure on my part to respond to my name, when I saw his blond eyebrows fly up. "Surely not? What about Oncle Pierre and Tante Madeleine?"

And I remembered Terry's starchy, ancient relatives living in great dignity and reduced circumstance outside New Orleans on Bayou St. Jean, and refusing, with astonishing success, to concede in any but the most necessary business circumstances to their English-speaking surroundings.

Boldness, I decided, was my only hope. "Well, if you know Oncle Pierre and Tante Madeleine, then you probably know that they are frequently infuriated when I *don't* answer to my name even though it's easier there, where everyone speaks French, for me to remember it. They accuse me of having given into Anglo-Saxon barbarities."

He threw back his head and laughed then. "Yes, I know. Your Oncle Pierre was giving me a lecture on the subject the last time I saw him. Like me, he's something of a de Gaullist."

Relief restored my bounce and the snappiness of my tongue.

"You mean *Vive la libre Louisianne*?"

His eyes danced.

"Something like that. Repurchase the Louisiana Territory. It was all a mistake. By the way," he continued easily, "what happened to your New Orleans accent? Did you lose it up there among all those New Englanders?"

Once again I trotted out my story of being teased and the drama lessons.

"Tut," he said. "You shouldn't let yourself be homogenized."

To my relief, Alix spoke up, taking his arm. "Cousin André, what are you doing here? We didn't hear you drive up, did we . . . Terry?" And she smiled at me.

"No, we certainly didn't. Nor did we see the jeep." I hadn't thought about it, but I was curious. How did he get to the back of the house? Alix and I had been following the path there from the jetty to the house, and not only had no one passed us, but we heard no sound.

"I arrived before you were up, my dear."

"But why didn't you wake me up? We could have gone riding together."

"I was going to. But while I was busy talking to Tristram, who should I see galloping past the window on Brutus, but you, *ma petite*. And in strict disobedience to your father's ruling, too, he told me." He reached over and flicked her cheek. "Why do you go out of your way to enrage him, Alix?"

For a minute her gaze was on the ground, then she raised her head and said, "You should know the answer to that, Cousin André."

It was an oddly still moment, the patrician young man in his worn tweed jacket and gray trousers, the girl in her riding clothes, their two burnished gold heads turned towards each other, their straight profiles so alike—and both so very different, I found myself thinking, from the harsh-featured man who was her father, with his thrusting aquiline nose and distorted body.

Then the moment was broken. "The trouble with Alix, you will find out, Thérèse, is her wild imagination," André said, looking at his cousin affectionately. "So that sometimes it is hard to tell the difference between what she sees, and what she thinks she sees, *n'est ce pas*, Alix?"

"No," she said, pulling away her arm. "It is *not* true!" Her voice started to rise. "Why do you say things like that, André? Why do you tease me?"

"Because, my dear, you must learn to take a little teasing. Not to take yourself so seriously. Isn't that right, Thérése?"

It *was* right, and I sensed in his appeal to me an attempt to tell his young and adoring cousin something he thought she should be aware of. But I was determined to join no side against her, or even give the appearance of doing so— not even when she was in the wrong.

"Sometimes," I said, as lightly as I could, "what we see *is* the only truth." And won a surprised, grateful glance from Alix.

"Well," he said, and I wondered if I just imagined the withdrawal in those charming blue eyes, "that's an extremely positive answer to an ancient question."

Alix frowned. "What question?"

"A metaphysical one, *cherie*. If a tree falls in an empty forest with no ear to hear the sound, is there a sound?" But I had been wrong about the withdrawal, the blue eyes were now teasing me, and despite my resolution about taking sides, I couldn't withhold a smile in return.

"Oh," Alix said, digesting this. "Philosophy. The Falling Tree. We talked about that."

This time it was André who looked surprised. "You did, Alix? Now with whom have you been discussing such abstruse matters?"

"Father Mark."

"And did Father Mark give you an answer?"

"No. He said that he would ask me again in a year what conclusion, if any, I had come to."

"How wise of him, wasn't it, Thérèse?"

It would have been so easy to make it a close threesome by saying "Yes." Why had I again the feeling that I was treading through a minefield? André was looking at me, and I felt my resistance going down before those compelling eyes. "I—"

"But Father was there," Alix said suddenly, and I felt as though a hypnotic trance had been broken. "And of course he had to say something practical."

But André was fast on his feet. "How debasing! What was his crude interpolation?"

"That if one were under the falling tree, one should postpone philosophical speculation until one got out of the way."

André laughed. "Yes, that is very like Tristram."

Alix took his arm again, glancing at me as she did so. Was she, I wondered, as innocent as she sometimes sounded? Had the breaking of the mood been deliberate?

"What were you and Father talking about this morning? I thought you weren't due back until next month."

"Business, dreary business."

She threw him a sly look.

"*Javelin* business?"

Quite suddenly, the chill was back. Then he reached over and ruffled her hair. "You have been listening at keyholes, *petite. Comme une bonne.*"

Again she pulled her arm away. "You know I don't understand French."

"Like a servant."

"How dare you! Her hand flew back.

"Alix!" I said.

She threw me an enraged glance, and as she did so, her hand was caught by her cousin.

"Or a baby," he said.

She pulled her hand away and stood there for a moment, facing us both.

"Alix," I said, and again this time held out my own hand.

"You're laughing at me, aren't you? Both of you." And she wheeled and ran.

For a few seconds there was silence. Then André spoke.

"You mustn't let her upset you," he said quietly. "She's a lovely child, but both spoiled and neglected, and that's a bad combination. It makes for hysteria."

"Yes," I admitted. "That makes three of you saying that. So it must be true."

"The fact that Mrs. Conyers and her father have both said she was hysterical doesn't make it necessarily untrue," he said, and we both laughed.

"Tell me, Mr. Charpentier—"

"André. Please."

"All right, André." I tried to ignore the lift in my heart. "I am a little puzzled by something. Both Mr. Darcourt and Mrs. Conyers said—or at least implied—that Mrs. Darcourt was away. Mrs. Conyers even said, or at least I thought she said, in France. Yet Alix just told me that she was on the island, in another house on the far side of the swamp. Where is she?"

Despite my warm liking for him, I half expected the put-off that I got from both Tristram Darcourt and his house-keeper, with the added implication that it was none of my business. I was therefore grateful, as well as relieved, when he said candidly and without hesitation or change of voice:

"In France. She has a house there not far from the Italian border. Both Darcourt and Mrs. Conyers are foolishly secretive about it. I suppose it's natural in an abandoned husband, but I find it irritating in a housekeeper, although I suppose she feels she must support her employer."

"When you say, 'natural in an abandoned husband,' do you mean because of his pride? Because she left him?" And then I wondered if my own candor was a little overdone.

But André didn't seem to feel it. Touching my elbow he turned us back towards the house and we walked along as he spoke.

"Yes. The Darcourt pride is as famous as Darcourt Island. People do not leave the Darcourts. It's simply not done." He was looking at me with a humorous lift to his fair eyebrows. And I had no trouble at all believing him.

"Nevertheless, Mrs. Darcourt did, I take it, leave him."

"She did, indeed. When Alix was quite small. And would have done so sooner, but that Alix's arrival, which was unplanned, and unwanted, at least on the part of Nicole, induced her to give the marriage another try. They had been married nine years by then, without children, and the marriage was pretty much on the rocks. But when Alix was born it seemed, for a few years anyway, to revive. Perhaps Nicole thought a child, even a daughter, might soften Darcourt a bit. Humanize him. But he seemed to treat her with no more . . . affection . . . than he did anyone else. Perhaps if she had been a boy . . . the Darcourts are terribly feudalistic"—he smiled suddenly—"I suppose today you could say chauvinistic, about things like that. Especially as there has always been a son—right from the seventeenth century on. Tristram is the first Darcourt not to sire a son, at least a legitimate one, and the family holdings and trust are all tied up and handed down with as much primogeniture and panoply as though they were a dukedom."

"But . . . if Alix's mother, Mrs. Darcourt, is in France—"

He finished the question for me. "Why did Alix tell you she was in the old house on the other side of the island?"

"Yes. Was it wishful thinking? Was she putting me on, having a little fun at my expense?"

"Probably. To both. But with Alix"—he paused, then took a breath—"you always have to be prepared for the fact that she lives in a reality of her own. Not always. But sometimes. That's why I said what I did about the tree falling. Alix may be . . . disturbed . . . but she isn't stupid, and she knows there are times when, with her, objective and subjective reality become one. She knows that and it's good to remind her that other people know it too. Or so old Doctor McIntyre says."

Again I had that slight feeling of chill. "When Mrs. Conyers wrote originally, she said there were problems. I suppose that was what she meant."

"Undoubtedly. Darcourt has always pinned his hopes on her growing out of it. But, although he won't admit it, I think she's grown worse. And her spinning you that tale about her mother being in the old plantation house certainly confirms it. That's the real reason, you know, for his iron rule about her riding over the swamp. He thinks—and Doctor McIntyre agrees with him—that going over there drives her further into . . . well, unreality."

"Why couldn't he have told me so?" I broke out exasperatedly. "Instead of all that talk about the danger of the swamp and what a horrible death it is."

"He's right about that, you know. After all, he did see his older brother die there."

"His older brother?"

"Yes. When he was a young man. And stood there, a few feet from him, unable to reach him."

"Ugh! How horrible!" And then I remembered the newspaper or newsmagazine mention of the older brother's death through a "mysterious accident."

"So that was the 'mysterious accident'?"

"Mysterious? Yes. I suppose so. In the sense that only one person knew what really happened."

"You mean Mr. Darcourt?"

"Yes. Of course. The brothers went out together and only Tristram came back, with, of course, his report of what had happened."

It was an unpleasant story, and, if true, must indeed have been a traumatic experience. If true—

"How old was Mr. Darcourt when that happened?"

"I'm not sure. The whole thing's a little hazy. But I think it was when he was about seventeen. You spoke of 'mysterious accident' as though it were a quote. Had you read about it somewhere?"

"Only in news accounts I looked up—" It was at that moment it occurred to me that a governess would not necessarily go to the nearest newspaper morgue to look up details about the family to which she thinks she is going.

We both spoke at once.

"You see I—" I started.

"Looked up? Do you always do this before taking a job?" André asked at the same moment.

"Yes," I said, deciding, once again, that boldness was the best tactic. "I like to know all I can about the families I am going to be working with."

"I hadn't thought about it before, but what a good idea! And all you could find about Robert Darcourt was that he had had a mysterious accident. Well, true enough, in a way. No one, except Tristram, knows what really happened."

"What does Mr. Darcourt say happened?"

André paused. "He doesn't and I've never discussed it with him. Nor, as far as I know, has anyone else—anyone who's alive, anyway. That's why the whole tragedy was so mysterious. It happened in the Devil's Cup—a nasty area of swamp not far from the old plantation house. The brothers, Robert and Tristram, were riding, and although the swamps are certainly dangerous, the paths around there are well marked and wide and strong enough to accommodate a horse, or even two. The only thing I ever heard, and that was second hand from an old servant, now dead, was that Tristram, who was riding ahead, heard a sound, turned back and found Robert, who had evidently been thrown from his horse, already over his knees and sinking fast. Then, according to the story, as Robert went down, he screamed and screamed."

My flesh crawled. I shivered.

"I'm sorry," André said suddenly. "I shouldn't have told you like that. But I wanted to make you understand why Tristram feels the way he does. Doctor McIntyre says that an exerience like that could leave deep scars."

After a minute I said, "This Doctor McIntyre you mentioned, is he a psychiatrist?"

"No. Just a GP. But Tristram seems to set great store by him. And, of course, when Tristram says jump, he jumps.

Not that he isn't a good doctor. He is, one of the best, and a great guy. He comes over here every month or so to look at Alix and gives her shots."

"Shots? What kind?"

"Multivitamin, mostly. You know, a lot of doctors have come to believe in them for emotional disturbance or imbalance."

By this time we were at the house. Alix and the dogs had disappeared, all except True, who was lying, like a young lion, on the doorstep.

"Hello, True," I said, and was promptly bowled over as True came leaping affectionately towards me.

"No. Down," I said firmly.

True dropped onto his haunches, opened his mouth and yawned. Then, still sitting, he wiggled his entire rear area, and whimpered a little.

"What he wants," André said, "is to sit in your lap."

"Hasn't anyone told him about his size?"

"I don't think so. By the way, I'm about to drive through the swamp to the other house. Would you like to come with me to see it? It's an interesting drive."

"I've been forbidden, in no uncertain terms, to cross that fence."

A smile touched André's eyes and lifted one corner of his mouth. "Tristram?"

"Who else?"

"Well, I think he meant you shouldn't go alone or just with Alix. He wouldn't object to your going with me."

"He sounded awfully unequivocal, though I prefer your interpretation. However, I think I ought to go and find Alix. That, after all, is what I'm here for."

"By this time she's probably resaddled Brutus, and is out on another ride. We can go by the stables and find out."

As André had foretold, Alix had come back, flung her saddle on Brutus again, and gone out for another ride. "Just like an ant in a hot skillet," Duncan added, picking up a piece of harness off the floor, "throws things here and there like they're gonna get back on the wall by themselves."

André's car—a small foreign one—was parked behind the stables. "We might come across Alix," André said, slamming the door after me and getting in his side. "On the other hand, we might not. Parts of the island back here are fairly thickly wooded."

For many reasons I shan't forget that ride: the beauty,

the swamp, the birds, the thick, almost junglelike patches of forest, and, when the birds were quiet, the eerie silence.

We did not talk much as we started off, skirting forest on our right, following a low wooden fence.

"Is that the fence Mr. Darcourt told us not to cross?" I asked.

He guided the jeep expertly around a stump to the right of the path. "No, that's just one of the many holding fences delineating various charted paths and the borders of where the forestation is supposed to be. The big fence is several miles ahead of us."

Overhead towered the high oaks, the long, lacy moss blowing in the wind. Beneath were flowers and shrubs—azaleas, rhododendrons, magnolia trees, cape jasmine, and here and there, indicated by the powerful scent, the flowering sweet olive. The path was hard beneath the wheels, but the soil in the undergrowth on either side looked black and soft. Often, as the path turned and twisted, we passed around and through open gates. Occasionally the branches overhead were so thick the sun was blotted out, and once or twice André switched on lights. It was when the sun was hidden that I became aware of a pervasive damp and a rank smell that made me think of jungle growth—leaves, ferns, creepers, springing from the ground and proliferating overnight.

And then, suddenly we came to a high, woven-steel fence. André had been right: there was no mistaking it.

"There's your fence," he said briefly.

Just a few feet short of it, he turned the jeep again and we drove along it for what felt like several miles. On our left was the forest we had just left, on our right, on the other side of the fence, another forest. Only some thinness on the far side of the black tree trunks seemed to indicate that the forest area there was narrower.

"How thick is the forest around here?" I asked.

"It varies. At some point no more than two miles. But at other points up to six or seven."

"And on the other side of the fence?"

"Here only about a quarter of a mile. Then comes the swamp. Here we are."

Making a final turn, we drove up to a steel gate, with a small house on the other side. Just as we came to a stop, a frantic barking broke out from somewhere behind the house reminding me of the evening before. Then the front door opened and a man came through it. Seeing André, he altered direction and went towards the gate lock. The boots he wore, I noted, were rubber and went several inches up the thigh. On his head was an old cloth hat covered with fishing flies, under which appeared a dark, rather expressionless face. "The water's high," he said laconically. "Watch out for the rims and banks."

"All right, Norton. Thanks. Miss Alix come by here?"

He shook his head. "Once I thought I heard something, and put my hand on the ground and knew she was riding. But I couldn't hear anything and I ain't seen her."

We drove through and the gate clanged shut behind us. "What did he mean, put his hand on the ground?" I asked.

"It's an old Indian trick, although it was known in Europe, too. If you think somebody on horseback is after you, but can't hear anything, you put your ear on the ground; you can hear the *clop clop* of a horse's hooves then, or if you put your hand flat on the ground, you can feel it vibrate."

"So Norton is gatekeeper as well as dog handler."

"Yes. Plus other things: assistant game warden, forester and gardener. There is no one, with the possible exception of Darcourt himself, who knows the whole island the way he does, every last path through the forest, every trail through the swamp, why he even—Damnation!" He braked, and the car stopped abruptly.

"What's the matter?"

"I had a message to give him from Tristram. Do you mind if I go back and give it to him? He might be off on one of his rounds when we get back."

"Of course not. Will we be able to get back in?"

"Oh, sure. I have the key. It's just that when he is here he opens the gate himself. I won't be a minute."

He slid out of the car and I watched him walk quickly back. In a few seconds he had rounded the bend in the path which hid the gates from where we were.

It was odd, I thought, a few minutes after his tall, graceful figure had disappeared, how alone I felt. The birds Darcourt had spoken of must have been in another part of the forest, because I was overcome with the eeriness of the silence. Nothing moved. The air was still. The dogs had fallen silent. I turned suddenly and looked back. Nothing alive and moving was visible. The shadowy path disappeared around a shrub. The big trees almost met overhead. The sun, which was high, passed behind a cloud. The shadows deepened. I opened my mouth, knowing that I was going to call André's name and then, by an enormous act of will, closed it. It was not easy for me to admit that Patrick James Wainwright's daughter was scared. Scared of what? Against my volition, the picture of a young man slid across my mind, his legs disappearing into black slime, the knowledge of his own imminent death coming into his eyes and opening his mouth in a scream, while his brother stood on firm ground and did . . . what?

Then, with equal suddenness, André was back. "Sorry about that." And he got into the jeep.

Less than a quarter of an hour later we were riding through the swamp itself. I don't know what I had expected. Something evil and black and threatening, I suppose.

What it turned out to be was flat land filled with myriad lakes and pools, all reflecting the blue and gray sky, and the clouds and sun. There were shrubs and bushes and a few small trees, and miles and miles of yellow-green reeds. What were overwhelming in their presence were the birds, rising before the jeep, floating gently on the little ponds, twittering in the bushes and reeds, crying, screaming, calling, standing serene, one leg tucked up.

"Ye gods!" I said finally. "It's like the aviary at the zoo multiplied a thousand times."

André looked at me and smiled. "Well, it's a sanctuary. Here they're safe. And they know it."

We drove in silence. After a while I said, "I expected to have the creeps in the swamp. Yet it's less creepy than the forest."

"There's nothing creepy about the swamp, unless you're caught in it at night. Or wander off the paths. The trouble is, you can't be sure which are the safe ways and which are not. Hence Tristram's orders."

"But you seem to know."

"Well, it's part of my job." He smiled at me. "I took forestry at the university, and the whole sanctuary and the wildlife of the rest of the island, plus the vegetation, are under my general supervision. There's another place in Georgia I supervise, and, of course, the Chárpentier place in Louisiana."

"Oh. I see." That answered, anyway, my curiosity as to what André was doing here when Tristram Darcourt had left, and explained Darcourt's answer I had overheard from the balcony, "You can always get hold of Monsieur André

84

. . ." to Mrs. Conyers', "What if she decides to see for herself, to visit the house . . . ?"

There was also something else that André had said in the past few minutes that hovered in my mind, a question. . . . But I couldn't remember what it was. I tried to get my mind back onto what André was now saying.

"And, of course, the state chapters of the Audubon Society visit here regularly. We band some of the birds and keep records in a small shack outside the old house."

"Is Alix interested in all this—the wildlife studies?"

"No, unfortunately. Because of her . . . delusions, she's not allowed back here, and that has biased her against the place and all that goes on in it. Some lonely kids can forget themselves in that kind of study. But Alix, who wants friends and people more than she wants anything else, isn't one of them."

"I asked her father if she had any friends. And he said that was one of the reasons why I had been hired."

"Yes," André skillfully skirted a clump of some poison-green shrub. "I admire Tristram and think he's done an astounding job, given all the problems he has with Alix, but I've often thought he ought to relax his rule not letting her go onto St. Damien's or the mainland sometimes, where she can mingle with kids who've led a less ivory tower life."

It was then I remembered what had sounded a familiar note in my mind: André's original statement about wandering off the paths while in the swamp had made me remember the blond young man on St. Damien's who had left me to go down a swampy path with night coming on. Now Andre's talk about Alix's isolation from other kids had brought it back. "By the way," I started.

But at that moment we went through some low shrubs and into the trees that I had been watching as we approached them.

"The house is just through here," André said, and then, glancing sideways at me, "Sorry. You were about to say something."

But we crossed the narrow belt of trees, and everything went out of my mind. Across fifty yards of tangled long grass and weeds, surrounded by more forest, rose the vine and creeper-covered walls of a derelict mansion, its curtainless windows staring like hollow eyes out of a dead face.

(5)

"GOOD HEAVENS!" I said. "It's much older than the other one, isn't it?"

"Oh, yes. The foundation was built by the Spaniards some time in the 1570s when they put a fort here. That was partially destroyed when the island was taken by the English. Then when the first Darcourt took over, he built this house, more or less in the prevailing Vanbrugh style, to which wings were later added. The family lived here till just before the Civil War. The other house was built just after the inside of this had been burned. One of Tristram's dottier forebears set fire to it."

"Any particular reason, or was he just a natural arsonist?"

"She. And the reason—for whatever that's worth—was that disease had broken out, not only among the family, but in the old slave quarters, and that it was a divine punishment that could only be expiated by burning the place to the ground. The stone shell of the house was left, but most of the inside—especially the upstairs and back—was destroyed."

"Was anybody hurt?"

"Only the old lady herself, and that was because she locked herself in a closet and was dead from suffocation before anyone could reach her."

"Was she diseased?"

He hesitated a little before answering. "I believe so. Which was perhaps why the family seemed to mourn her death less than they might otherwise have done."

"What was the disease?"

Again that odd hesitation. Then he said, "Yellow fever, I think. It was very prevalent in these parts."

By this time we had driven over a faint path—really only a depression in the thick grass to the house.

"But it's astonishing . . . that Alix should think her mother lives here."

André pulled the jeep up in front of the scarred door and looked at me. It was one of those odd moments when I was again overcome with his resemblance to Alix—the wheat-colored hair, the straight nose, the delicately flared nostrils. "That's why I wanted you to see the place. It gives you a much better idea than anything Tristram or Mrs. Conyers or I could say about how far out Alix can be sometimes. It's not a comforting thought, I realize, but I think it's better for you to know."

I sat staring at the house, taking in the mullioned windows on the lower floor, with most of the small panes missing, the soft gray stone, the roof broken here and there, the chimneys that seemed to rise in the midst of the surrounding trees.

"It's big here in front," I said. "Is there a lot of it behind? Does it extend far back?"

André opened the jeep door. "Yes, fairly far—mostly offices and kitchens and stables. The main body of the house was actually smaller."

I opened the door on my side and started to get out.

"Wait!" André said sharply. "This is a sanctuary for more wildlife than meets the eye."

I paused. "Such as?"

"Snakes and scorpions, for two. And they both love the long grass."

I pulled my leg back in. He grinned. "Let me stamp around here for a bit. They're more scared of us than we are of them and they'll go away."

I understood then, as I had not fully before, why everyone seemed to have on boots. André walked around the car, pulling a cane from the back as he did so. With this he swished at the grass in a big circle as he walked, and sure enough, I saw a scorpion dart out of the line of fire from one clump of dryish grass to another.

"Now," André said, coming around to my side, "it should be clear."

My desire to get out was somewhat less than it had been.

However not only was pride involved, but I wanted to get a closer look at the house. André opened the door and held out his hand.

"Okay?" he inquired in a kindly way.

"We LeBretons are intrepid," I said, putting my leg out and hoping for the best.

"That's what I've always heard," André countered, deadpan, and we both laughed.

He slammed the door. "I'll show you inside and then I'll bring you back here and leave you for a few minutes while I go and check the shack."

"What shack?"

He pointed to our right. "Over there to the right, in front of the trees."

"Oh, I see." I peered at the dark frame hut. "That doesn't appear to be an antique."

"Not in the least. It was built under the supervision of the Department of Fish and Wildlife not ten years ago. Most of the sanctuary records are kept there. Here—this is the path to the front door of the house."

The huge, scarred, once beautiful door opened to the touch, swinging creakily on its hinges. Inside was a stone hall with rooms branching to left and right, and it was obvious this house has been built along the lines made famous by the Carolinian architect, Vanbrugh, however inappropriate the style might have been, transplanted from northern Europe to this near-tropic island.

What had once been a polished wooden floor was charred and scratched. Here and there against the walls were the splintered and broken remains of furniture. I jumped as something scurried across the darkened floor in front of us.

"What was that?"

"A rat, most likely, oh, intrepid Thérèse!"

"I was just surprised," I said with all the dignity I could muster.

"So I noticed. You must have jumped a foot."

I decided not to pursue the matter. "Are there any lights?"

"No. Electricity was, of course, not in use, when the place was burned. But I do have this." And he brought a large flashlight out of his jacket pocket and switched it on.

"Here," André said, handing me his cane, "take this. It will make you feel even more intrepid."

Gratefully I took it. There was something about the atmosphere in the house that made me uncomfortable. It's all those snakes and scorpions hiding God knows where, I told myself.

Slowly we walked over the lower floor, passing through the silent rooms filled with the smell of mold and mildew and with spiders' webs hung across the corners of the ceiling.

Yet, I thought, although the ruined house was desolate beyond belief, nothing—not the rank odor, nor the holes and cracks and splinters of woodwork and plaster—could destroy the exquisite symmetry characteristic of one of the great periods of English architecture.

"It must have been a beautiful house," I said once.

"Past tense. *Sic semper*, etcetera. Watch your step. They're loose boards everywhere."

There were still some prints on the walls, dim and yellow behind broken glass. And twice there were portraits, the paint so dark that it was almost impossible to make out what the subjects had been. "Those could be cleaned," I said.

"I've told Tristram that. I even offered to have a friend of mine at the Metropolitan Museum in New York have a go at them. But Tristram is massively indifferent to the arts."

"I'd be surprised if he's massively indifferent to his family history, though, and those look like portraits."

"Yes, you'd think he'd show some interest in them, but he hasn't. And, after all, since they're Darcourts and not Charpentiers, I didn't push it."

He lowered the flashlight off the canvases and circled it around the room. "I think you've seen all there is to see."

I followed André back to the hall. "I still think it's funny Mr. Darcourt isn't interested in his family paintings."

"Tristram's interests are more modern," he said over his shoulder.

"Such as?"

He turned, grinning slightly. "Would you believe oil?"

"Yes. I'd believe it. Easily."

He laughed. Then, as we approached the center staircase, threw the white lights upwards. "I'd take you up those stairs if they were safe. But, as you can see, the last explorer came a cropper." And he circled the light around a big hole in the staircase itself.

"In that case," I said, "I'm quite content to leave the upper floors alone."

It was as we were standing there that I said suddenly, "What was that?"

"What?" André asked.

"That. It sounded like a scream or a shriek."

"Oh, that's the Redtailed Hawk. We have quite a few around here."

"It sounded almost human," I said, as we went through the scarred front door and André pulled it shut behind us.

"I know. The first time I heard it I almost jumped out of my skin. Here, use your cane ahead of you like this." And taking it out of my hand, he swished it around the grass. "I'll take you over to the jeep, and then will be back in a minute."

"Thank you, André. I can get over there by myself. But I'd like to see the shack too. Can I go with you?"

"Of course. It's just dull—mostly full of file cabinets. However, you're welcome. But let me go ahead with the cane." And he took it back.

No unwelcome wildlife marred our single-file progress to the door of the shack which, on close inspection, seemed an unexceptional, if sturdy, frame house painted a dark green and with a shiny modern lock on the door.

"No windows?" I said.

"It's really just a large storage cupboard for records, and there's a small air-conditioning unit that keeps it at the right temperature."

"I thought you said there was no electricity out here."

"For the ancestral mansion, no. But the shack has its own little power unit. Here we are."

Selecting a key from a sizable key ring with a multitude of keys, André opened the door and turned on a light as we went in.

The inside was simple: a big square, the wall filled on three sides with metal file cabinets of various types—those with the conventional drawers, others with shallow, tray-type drawers and yet others that looked as though, once open, they could be display cabinets. Two counters or benches, such as are seen in laboratories, were at one end, with overhead fluorescent lights and burners: backed in a corner was a refrigerator, and on the other side of the room, a plain desk with a telephone on it.

"It looks like a science lab at school," I said, staring around.

"Well, in a sense, that's just what it is." André's hand swept around the file cabinets. "These are full of records of the flora and fauna on the island, including old diaries by some of the Darcourts who kept such things."

He grinned. "Beer. It's hot work out here sometimes. Want some?"

"No, thanks. But I might say yes to a soda."

I had been facing the refrigerator when I spoke, but when there was a silence I turned. André was behind the desk, staring at an open manilla folder in his hand. Yet I could swear, for reasons I could not have given, that until I turned he had been watching me. Then he gave his charming smile.

"Sorry. I just saw something that distracted my attention. What was it you said?"

"Nothing vital. Just that if there were soda in the refrigerator, I might be persuaded to drink it."

"Soda shall be put there instantly. I'm sorry to say, though, that there isn't any now. An oversight."

"You seem sure."

"I am. I'm the one who stocks it."

"And you've never been a soda drinker?"

"I have many vices. But not that. Beer, yes. Wine, always. *Aqua minerale*, if the water is tested as unsafe, but soda—never."

"In the spirit of *vive la libre Louisianne*?"

He laughed. "Of course." Opening the center desk drawer, he put the folder inside, along with one or two papers that had been lying under it. Then he closed the drawer and locked it with another of his keys. "Shall we go?"

As he was closing the door I asked curiously, "How is the place ventilated, since you don't need air conditioning this time of the year?"

He pointed. "Up here, just under the roof, and through vents near the ground."

"I wonder why they didn't put in any windows."

André started down the narrow line of shortened grass that represented the path. "Because it would be a waste of money. Windows are for looking out. Who'd be in there long enough to want to do that?"

"Well, what about those benches and burners and all that paraphernalia for experiments?"

"That's mostly decoration."

"More expensive decoration, I should think, than a few panes of glass."

He turned, grinning. "Are you sure you're all French? Not Scottish?"

Almost immediately I saw it as the innocent, teasing comment it was meant to be. But for the space of two breaths it was a flash of danger, and I was Sally Wainright, being accused of pretending to be my friend Terry LeBreton.

"What's the matter?" André asked sharply, his smile gone. "Nothing." My heart settled after its frantic leap. And then, with an assumption of coolness, "Why do you ask?"

"You looked . . . you looked as though I had accused you of making off with the family silver." Standing still in the path, he was watching me closely.

I had been about to make some flippant return about the shock of having my Frenchness called in question—a comment calculated to appeal to his Louisiana French chauvinism. But I knew, quite suddenly, it was not enough.

"Well, I'm sorry to be such a pantywaist, but to see a scorpion not six inches from one's foot is a jolt to the system."

"Curious. I didn't see it . . . and that's why I went ahead" —there was the smile again—"to spare your . . . er . . . sensibilities."

"You may not have seen it. But it saw you, hence its agitated scramble. Do we have to stand here while its friends and relations come looking for it?"

"Trying your intrepidity?"

"Sorely."

He laughed. "Sorry." He turned back and continued his strides towards the jeep.

The shave, I thought, following him, had been a little too narrow for comfort, however neatly I had extricated myself. And then found myself reflecting, a good thing it wasn't Tristram Darcourt. Having found a flaw in my defense system, he could not have been deflected from tearing it open.

"Why the pensiveness?" André asked, holding open the car door.

I got in. "It's brought on by all this wildlife, particularly the six-legged kind."

He slammed the door and walked around the back. "It's nice to know you're a nature lover."

"Have you any more natural treasures around here I should look out for?"

"Only the black widow spider." And then, as he saw my face, he burst out laughing.

We had covered the long grass of what had once been the front lawn and were into the trees when André said, "I'll drive back by the Devil's Cup so you can see it."

"A treat for me, I see."

"And a warning. I want you to see it so you can stay clear of it."

"I haven't the remotest intention of entering this swamp without adequate guide and protection. However, I agree I should see all the sights—however macabre."

Looking over the wide swampy area, with its lakes, ponds, streams and marshes, and its sea of waving reeds, I was not able to tell much about direction except that on the remote horizon, barely visible in the slight haze that seemed to have settled on the swamp since we had driven through it a bare hour before, I could see a dark shadow that was probably the forested area. But instead of making straight for the trees, André turned the jeep abruptly to the right when we came out of the belt around the old mansion.

"It's east of the main path back," André said, proceeding to follow a zig-zag course through clumps of reed and pockets of marsh.

"How on earth do you know your way? Are there markers I can't see?"

"No. Just familiarity. It's over there." And he pointed.

About five minutes later he said, "Well, there it is." And as he did so, slowed the jeep, bringing it around a circular path that even I could see was at least six feet across.

I stared, following his pointed finger. There, sunk inches below the path which almost completely surrounded it, was what looked like slimy black mud. Here and there were tufts of brilliant green reeds. I was conscious of a feeling of disappointment.

"It doesn't look any worse than any other part of the swamp here."

"No, it doesn't, which is one reason why it's so dangerous. Let me show you something."

Leaning back in the car, André seemed to be scrabbling around the floor of the back. In a few seconds he pulled up his hand in which he was holding a two-by-four piece of wood. "I use this to put in front of the car wheel, but I know where I can get another."

Standing up in the car, he tossed it into the middle of the mud. A bird flew from the nearby bank with a loud cry. The wood disappeared immediately, followed by an unpleasant sucking sound. Then there was silence. The surface of the slime shimmered for a moment, then was still.

André said in an odd, flat voice, "It would take a human

93

being—depending of course on his or her size—a minute or two longer to be pulled down."

I said, "I can see why it's called the Devil's Cup. I can think of a lot better ways to die."

"Almost any way is better than that." He turned the motor on again and drove around the Devil's Cup onto another path.

"Are there any more goodies like that in the swamp?"

"No. There are one or two smaller patches, but they are not as dangerous because it would be easier to throw a log over for anyone caught there to catch on to."

"And are there logs handy?"

"Yes. I've tried to keep logs or branches near or across all the swampy patches."

"But not by this one?"

He turned the jeep back toward the trees. "It would take a tree trunk to go over that, and there's a matter of getting it here."

"How about a wire fence around?"

"We put one. But it started to sink, even though we were sure it was driven into hard ground. And in sinking, it broke the edges of the hard ground and pushed it back. Besides, Thérèse, this whole area is locked off. Who's going to come here?"

"Alix."

"Alix knows the swamp better than anyone. As I told you, her father is more worried about her coming here as an act of unreality than of her getting caught in the Cup. But he prefers the swamp as a reason. He doesn't then have to confront the fact that her periods of . . . alienation . . . are growing more frequent."

"That sounds foolish. And Mr. Darcourt did not strike me as a fool."

"Come now, Thérèse, you sound foolish. The wisest man—or woman—on earth will believe about someone he loves what he most dearly wants to believe. You must have found that out in your meanderings among the young and their parents."

And I knew, of course, the minute he said that, that it was true. How long had my father known, before he admitted it to himself, the fact of my mother's last illness?

"Yes. You're right." And as I spoke I saw again the wild look in Alix's eyes and knew that I couldn't blame her father, however much I might dislike his disagreeable manner.

But at that moment I remembered also the bruises on Alix's arm. "He can be . . . severe with her, for one who, you say, cares for her so much."

"That's his nature. Probably the only way he knows how to express his caring and anxiety. If you had known his wife—but I don't want to gossip, and it no longer concerns the family here."

It took all the control I had to clamp my jaws together and not allow my unruly tongue to ask all the questions that were tumbling off the tip of it. But I managed it, and we drove back more or less in silence, except where André pointed out different birds and talked with considerable knowledge about those native to the region.

"Hungry?" he asked, as we started through the forested area.

Until that moment, I hadn't realized it, but I was starved, and said so.

"Well, we missed breakfast but lunch will be ready shortly after we get back."

"Breakfast? I had breakfast. It was left outside my door."

"Oh, that. That's not breakfast. That's early morning tea, in the best English tradition."

"But it was café au lait—delicious."

"That's Nicole's—Mrs. Darcourt's—doing. It used to be tea, but no New Orleans girl would put up with that when she could have coffee, so she kept the custom but changed the beverage. And the family has maintained it ever since."

But when we got back to the house André refused to come in, saying he could summon Petersen to take him over to the mainland from the pier.

"How?" I asked.

"By phone. There's one there. Just back of the pier."

"But what about your lunch?" I asked, getting out.

"I'll pick up a sandwich in St. Damien's or at the airstrip." He smiled a little. "It's later than I thought. The pleasure of your company distracted me from watching the time."

"A pretty compliment." I wondered how true it was.

"No compliment. A simple statement of fact. See you soon—I hope."

And with another smile and slight wave, he was gone in the direction of the stables.

Odd, I thought, going in through the back door. I could have sworn he intended to have lunch with us, and I was conscious of a feeling of disappointment. And then, I wonder why he changed his mind.

A delicious aroma struck my nostrils as soon as I was a few feet into the back hall, and it seemed to come from doors opening off to the right where the kitchens must be. I paused sniffing. Baking bread, bacon, vanilla and other odors I couldn't place were all component parts of the delectable smell. Mother was a superb cook, giving the whole process the tender loving care that can be present only with true enjoyment. Inevitably, some of her knowledge and competence rubbed off on me, although I did not inherit the love for cooking that generated the higher reaches of her talent. But the kitchen at home was always a pleasant place, so, standing there, I was suddenly assailed with a desire to follow my nose to the Darcourt kitchen.

Wisdom counseled against it. The kitchens of the rich, I had discovered in various journalistic endeavors, were liable to be even more intimidatingly formal than their drawing rooms, where the rich themselves assuaged their guilt by an overlay of democratic bonhomie. Their servants, unburdened with the guilt of wealth, were almost always much greater snobs.

I was still hesitating, when the butler, Stevens, emerged from the dining room door in front of me. As he closed the door, he saw me. "May I help you, miss?"

I smiled. "I was just enjoying that delicious smell from the kitchens."

He smiled back at me. "I was coming out to sound the gong for lunch."

"Then I'd better go and wash my hands. Do you know where Miss Alix is?"

"I expect she'll be in her room or in the old schoolroom at the top of the house in the big attic. She often goes up there."

It made her sound so normal, as though she were any other teen-age girl. Except that the average teen-age girl was not this rich, nor this isolated, nor this—I was tired of the word alienated—this unstable.

"Well," I said, turning towards the stairs, "I'll go look for her as soon as I've washed my hands. Or"—I looked down at the butler as I climbed—"is she like most girls and comes running at the thought of food?"

"No, miss. I'm afraid not. Sometimes she forgets about eating altogether."

That undoubtedly was responsible for the fragility that was so much a part of her beauty. But I thought as I continued up the stairs that even though the majority of adolescents of both sexes seemed to have bottomless appetites, it was not an undeviating rule. There were picky eaters who in every other way seemed to be overwhelmingly average, even though I couldn't, at the moment, recall any to mind except, of course, Alix herself. And then, as I came to the hall landing, I paused, struck by the way I was trying to find excuses for Alix's stranger flights, as though, in fact, like her father, I was trying to persuade myself that there was nothing about her that could be called abnormal.

Not like her father, I said sternly to myself, as the pictures of those terrible bruises presented themselves to my memory, along with the arrogance and insensitivity which I recalled with equal clarity. Furthermore, even if all other aspects of her life were more like those of other girls of her age, her isolation, her lack of friends could alone account for eccentric behavior, the need for attention attributed by her father and Mrs. Conyers to hysteria.

By this time I was outside my own bedroom door. Opening it, I was greeted with a volley of barks from Susie, who plainly had felt neglected.

"All right, all right," I said, and went over to her, and patted her and when she rolled over on her back, rubbed her stomach. "I promised you something devastating from the kitchen, didn't I, Susie?" I said, filled with guilt. I leaned over and hugged her. "After lunch, without fail, we'll have a walk and then a tidbit."

At that moment the gong sounded, reminding me of English households I had been in in various parts of the globe. Hastily washing my hands, I gave Susie another pat, opened up a can of her favorite dog food and put the contents in her dish, and hurried out of the room and down the stairs.

When I got to the dining room and saw Alix seated there, I had a sense of relief, as though looking for her throughout the huge house were an ordeal that had been postponed.

"Was that your dog?" Alix said, as we sat down. In her father's absence she had taken his place at the head of the table.

"Yes. That's Susie." I glanced at Mrs. Conyers who sat

at Alix's left directly across from me. The corners of that lady's mouth were turned down. "I wasn't really supposed to bring her, but I did anyway, and she was introduced to your other dogs by your father. I do hope that they remember her."

Mrs. Conyers, looking sour, said nothing.

Alix helped herself to some sliced ham from a dish Stevens was holding.

"Of course they will. We'll take her for a walk after lunch and introduce her all over again, not that that's necessary."

"I hope not," I said. No one looking at her father could doubt that any dog, however savage, would disobey him. Alix's slight confidence did not inspire me with the same blind faith, but I also knew that the authority frequently had nothing to do with size or age.

As I was helping myself to the ham Mrs. Conyers spoke up, rather pointedly addressing me. "Her father was wishing her to get her lessons."

"But Terry's just arrived," Alix protested. "I planned to take her around this afternoon."

As clearly as though I could see inside the housekeeper's mind, I could sense her disapproval of Alix's use of my first name. "Did Miss LeBreton give you permission to use her Christian name?" she said.

"Yes, I did," I put in quickly. "I'm not used to . . . formality."

Her brows lifted. "Really, Miss LeBreton, I would have thought you would have become used to it, working as you did for the Fenwicks."

But now there was something about her needling that boosted rather than dented my confidence, so I was able to say with perfect civility, "Oh, I've had to live with it, but I prefer less . . . less stilted relationships."

Alix, picking at her food, said nothing. Mrs. Conyers' clear blue eyes met my gaze for a few seconds, then she, too, glanced down at her plate. And I was quite happy to give my full attention to eating. The food—sliced ham with both a sweet and smoky flavor, some kind of rice dish and salad, plus hot bread—was delicious. It used to make Terry—the real Terry—furious that although, in her words, I had a truckdriver's appetite, I remained slight, and, if anything, underweight. To compound the outrage, I was as sturdy as a peasant, had endless energy, and had never been really ill a day in my life. However, I was not a fast eater, and I became aware, after a few minutes, that I was still tucking away the food on my plate, after the other two had stopped and were waiting politely—the housekeeper, with her hands in her lap, Alix, her fingers crumbling the bread around her plate. She had taken little, and had left most of that on her plate. Mrs. Conyers, who had also helped herself rather frugally, had left a small portion.

"I'm sorry to keep you waiting," I said, "but I'm quite hungry."

"That's all right," Alix said, "but if you'll excuse me, I'll just run upstairs for a few minutes before our walk."

"There's dessert yet," Mrs. Conyers said.

Alix stood up. "I don't want any."

"You will sit here until Miss LeBreton finishes and until we've had dessert. You know that Matilda has made ice cream especially for you."

"I won't sit here if I don't feel like it. And Matilda knows that I don't like dessert in the middle of the day—"

"Alix—"

"I won't. I won't!" And with that she threw down her napkin and ran out of the room.

Things, I thought, doggedly finishing what was left on my plate, were not going to be made any easier by Mrs. Conyers.

After a few minutes of silence she said, "I'm surprised you're not running after her, as you did this morning."

I put my knife and fork on my plate.

"This morning I saw her rebuffed in a particularly . . ." I hesitated over the word brutal, which I had been about to use. And then decided not to let this strange, hostile woman stampede me into saying something that could not but anger Darcourt, to whom, almost certainly, she would repeat it. ". . . in an *apparently* insensitive fashion," I said, changing both words and emphasis, "which is why I went to her. But just now she was reacting to your rather rigid order, and I see no reason not to let her get over her bad temper by herself."

I knew Mrs. Conyers would take the word "rigid" as the gauntlet thrown down, as indeed she did. "Alix should not be allowed to run wild, to forget her manners. No good can come out of that. Nor would her father allow it."

I sighed. It was all so predictable, as though the script had been written. I was pondering my next step, when something in that last thought tugged at my conscience. But before

I could sort it out, Alix came back into the room. She walked straight up to me and said,

"I'm awfully sorry, Terry. That was rude. Please forgive me." And then she went back to her place and sat down.

"I should think," Mrs. Conyers started, when I cut directly across her.

"Just a moment, Mrs. Conyers. Alix was addressing me. And I would like to say here and now that Mr. Darcourt left Alix to my care. I had meant to say this to you when she came back down, which by the way"—I turned to Alix—"I really appreciate." And I held out my left hand. Alix blushed and took it, and I squeezed hers before I returned it. Then I said to the housekeeper, "Let's try an experiment. Please leave Alix to me. If there are to be any comments about her behavior, I'll make them. As I said, Mr. Darcourt made me responsible, and I will take that responsibility— all of it. But I will not be responsible for someone else's interference, and so I shall write to him immediately, if we can't arrive at some agreement about this. Come," I said, and this time I held out my hand across to her. "Give me a chance." I felt no real warmth for the sour-faced house-keeper, but I knew that I had spoken more harshly than I actually intended. And I also knew that in her own eyes her dignity was in question, and I had assaulted it. For a second she hesitated, and I thought I had won, if not her approval, at least her consent. But then she stood up, and I knew I had failed to reach her.

"Very well, Miss LeBreton, I will leave Alix entirely to you, and I myself will write to Mr. Darcourt telling him that she is in your care. And if anything . . . if anything goes wrong, the responsibility is yours."

"Yes," I said, noting that the hand with which she was pushing back her chair was quivering, "it is. That's just what I've been saying."

Without looking again at either Alix or me, the house-keeper pulled her shawl around her shoulders and left the dining room.

There was no question but that I was gratified at what amounted to my victory, but I was surprised to discover that I also found something forlorn in the elderly woman's stiff-backed pride.

Obviously Alix didn't. "Good!" she said with satisfaction. "You've routed her. Now we won't have to bother with her."

"We always have to bother with people, Alix, especially if

they're older, and even more especially if they're in our employ and we hold the purse strings."

Alix's haunting gray eyes looked at me. "You didn't sound as though you were worrying about her feelings."

It was a fair thrust, and I knew it would have been better for Alix as well as for Mrs. Conyers if I'd had my say to her in private, without Alix to witness her humiliation.

"No, I didn't, did I? But that doesn't mean I didn't sympathize with the way she must feel being put down in front of you. I should have spoken to her alone, probably. But I wanted to make a point immediately, so I sacrificed her face to do it. But that doesn't give you—or me—the right to think her feelings aren't worth consideration."

Alix stuck her chin out a little, and those gray eyes, that could be so soft and expressive, for a moment reminded me of her father's—hard as granite. "You mean, don't do as I do, do as I tell you?"

I couldn't help smiling. "So! You're not as isolated as all that. You've absorbed some of the clichés of the younger generation. All adults are hypocrites, etcetera."

"Well, it's true, isn't it? You take old Connie over the jumps, but when I say good, you suddenly come over all authority and good manners. If you want dessert, by the way, I'll ring for Stevens. He must have heard the row and been waiting to come in, not wanting to interrupt." And in one of her lightning switches, Alix turned from sulky adolescent to lady of the Southern mansion, complete with ante-bellum overtones, as she airly rang a small silver bell at her right hand.

"You do throw yourself into your roles, don't you, Alix?" I said, as the butler, an anxious look on his kindly face, came in and collected the first-course dishes.

Alix ignored me. I had not abandoned the subject of my (seeming) hypocrisy, but I had to submit to a hiatus in the discussion—as, of course, Alix knew I did—while Stevens was in the room. Little fox, I thought, watching Alix's immersion in her role, her flowerlike head tilted with gracious condescension as Stevens heaped strawberry ice cream on her plate.

"Thank you, Stevens," she said, very much in the grand manner. "And please thank Matilda for making the ice cream."

"Yes, Miss Alix. She'll be glad for that. She was sorry to hear that you had left the dining room."

Several expressions chased themselves across Alix's sensitive face: sulkiness, regret, defiance and—to my surprised pleasure—humor. For a moment her eyes met mine. Then she turned to the elderly butler. "Stevens, Mrs. Conyers . . . Mrs. Conyers had to leave the dining room before she'd finished. Would you take some ice cream to her? I know she likes it."

Stevens smiled. "Yes, Miss Alix. I'll be glad to."

We sat eating our ice cream silently while the butler filled a dish and took it out of the dining room. I glanced at Alix. Her air of benign graciousness was overwhelming.

"Tell me," I said, equally gracious, "which of several sovereigns that come to mind is your majesty's favorite role, Elizabeth I, Victoria or perhaps one of the female Medicis?"

For a moment a look of thunder threatened the fair and royal brow. Then there emerged a rather muffled giggle. "I *was* laying it on a bit thick, wasn't I?"

"Like whipped cream. Have you ever thought of going on the stage?" And knew I had made a cardinal error. Alix's whole face lit up. "Oh, yes, yes, *yes*. That's what I'd rather be than anything. If only Father would—but he won't. He'll keep me locked up here for the rest of my life."

"Not quite," I pointed out with as much damping common sense as I could. "At the worst, two years. At eighteen you become an adult."

"I'll probably be *dead* by then."

It was the kind of expression that any adolescent, temporarily thwarted, would say to dramatize herself. I'd said it myself several times to my father when he was laying down the law. Yet there was something in the way Alix spoke that provoked that chill that I had felt from time to time since I had come to Darcourt Island, as though Alix were not just indulging a typically adolescent taste for dramatic exaggeration, but, for a second, had seen a future that was hurtling towards her.

(6)

ALIX kept her promise and showed me over the house that afternoon, after first courteously inquiring as to whether or not I would like a siesta.

"Everyone takes one, even old Connie," she said as we passed from the dining room into the big square hall. And then added, "Except, of course, Daddy and me."

I smiled. "That's a big except, since you're two thirds of the family."

"Yes. But we're considered funny. Father's too busy and I'm too . . . restless."

I could believe that. "What about your cousin André?" I asked, before I could stop myself. And then wished I hadn't. I had never been one to show overt interest in any young man so obviously attractive. My reasons were rather complicated and obscure, even to myself. But they had something to do with pride, and something to do with growing up in the shadow of an exquisitely beautiful mother, and perhaps most of all to do with the fact that I considered myself a member of the working classes and André Charpentier—like his cousin-in-law, Darcourt—a notable offspring of domestic aristocracy.

"Oh, André's all for the good life," Alix said.

"And that includes a siesta?"

"Of course. Only dull and deadly drones have to work, work, work."

"And yet you say your father doesn't avail himself of that particularly patrician habit."

"No." Alix had been laughing. But at the mention of her father a cloud came over her face. "Come on," she said. "I'll show you the place. Let's start at the top." And in one of her swift mood changes, she bounded upstairs, two at a time.

I resisted the temptation to bound after her and outstrip her and went up at a brisk but more moderate pace.

Pausing only briefly at the landing, to make sure I was following her, Alix then headed up to the third story.

"Whuff," I said, when I got up there. "That's quite a climb."

Alix smiled mischevously. "You aren't finished yet." And she darted down the hall to the left.

At the end of the hall was a narrow staircase going up to a door.

"That's my domain," Alix said, pointing. "Come along."

When we got to the top she took a key out of her jodhpurs' pocket and unlocked the door. The lock, was, I noted, a modern Yale lock, sturdy-looking and new.

Alix's domain turned out to be a long, low attic, with dormer windows both front and back, discarded carpets of all kinds covering the floor, and, around the edges of the room, just under the sloping roofs, pieces of furniture of all periods, including several bookcases, all filled with books.

"What an absolutely marvelous place," I said, turning around.

Alix went over to a low divan just under one of the windows and lay down. "Isn't it," she said luxuriantly, and stretched her arms. "This is where I come when I can't stand the world or anyone in it." She turned over on her side and looked at me. "No one can hear me, because there are about three thicknesses of carpet all over the floor, and I have the only key."

"I see," I said, and strolled over to the bookcases to look at the books.

"What a treasure trove," I said after a while. "There are classics here that have been out of print for more than half a century."

She got up. "Yes. Every now and then Father threatens to have some secondhand people in to sell old books. But I just secretly remove the ones I want to up here and the whole thing blows over."

"Doesn't your father know you've taken them?"

"Oh, he knows." She got up and ambled gracefully over to the door. "He doesn't like me to come up here, where he can't get hold of me. But," she said gaily over her shoulder as she opened the door, "he can't stop me."

Since Darcourt did not strike me as a man who was readily induced to do anything against his will, I put this down to a little muscle-flexing on Alix's part.

"How can you keep him from stopping you?" I asked, following her through the door, and waiting on a lower step while she locked it.

"Because," Alix said, putting the key back in her pocket, "this isn't the only retreat I have. And he'll do anything— even let me have this attic all to myself—rather than let me go to the other."

I had no doubt at all what she was talking about: the old ruined mansion I had seen that morning, where she told me her mother was living. I looked sharply at her, and found her eyes, hard and bright, on me. She started down the stairs towards me, so I turned and went down ahead.

When we got to the bottom she said, in a flat unemotional voice, "André took you to the old house this morning, didn't he?"

I looked back at her. "Yes, Alix, he did."

"And he showed you how empty it was."

I nodded. "Yes."

She laughed. "So now you think I freak out from time to time, don't you?"

As a matter of fact, I did, and everything in her manner since the beginning of lunch showed me, if I needed showing, just how unstable she could be. Yet I was also convinced that she was testing me; that this whole business of showing me over the house, the attic, with its lock and single key, was dragged in front of my eyes for a purpose. Only, of course, I had no idea what the purpose was.

"Come on," she said suddenly. "I'll show you the rest of the place."

So for the next two hours we covered the three floors of the main part of the house, going in and out of most of the twenty-four bedrooms of the two upper floors, and the two drawing rooms, dining rooms and library of the ground floor.

"Where do the servants sleep?" I asked.

"Oh, in the annex at the back, behind the stables. They have a house to themselves."

"Even Mrs. Conyers?"

"No. Hers is the front west bedroom on the third floor—she chose it herself. She could have had any bedroom but Father's or mine on the second floor. But she's very conventional, and feels that a housekeeper should not be on the same floor as the family. Isn't that *mediaeval!*" And she gave a queer, high-pitched laugh.

"Now," she said, before I had time to say anything about Mrs. Conyers and her choice of room, "that's enough for one day. Let's go out riding."

"You know," I said, "Mrs. Conyers was right about one thing. We are going to have to get to those dismal things, lessons. Only I don't think they need to be dismal."

"Why not? I've never known any that weren't."

"You've been at schools, Alix. Didn't you like anything about them?"

"Sure. The riding and theater groups."

"No academic subjects?"

Alix wrinkled her nose. "I liked history and English—the rest is a waste of time."

I tried a shot in the dark.

"Don't you want to go to college?"

"What for? You don't suppose Father's going to let me do anything as . . . as *ordinary* as get a job."

There was a desolate sound to her voice that wrung my heart, and my anger at her father in his stupidity and arrogance increased. One thing struck me as curious: why didn't Alix run away? Since the early sixties a whole society of dropouts had sprung up. Adolescents now had a subculture of their own, to be found easily in any medium to large city —something that hadn't existed in quite the same way since the student vagabonds of the Middle Ages. For one year I had done little else but cover stories of young runaways. And it was probably my knowledge of the futile, if not tragic, end to which most of them came that prevented me from secretly wishing that Alix would take a bolt for freedom. But I would certainly talk to her father at the first possible opportunity. It could only be a matter of time until the idea occurred to Alix herself.

In the meantime I bottled up my strongest impulse: to tell Alix that if she worked hard enough to pass her college entrance exam and could somehow find the money—surely not too impossible a task for a rich girl brought up among rich relatives and friends—she could go to her state college, get a degree and find some kind of a job, all without Daddy's permission. Such a suggestion would, I knew, be considered subversive in the extreme by Tristram Darcourt, who was paying my salary.

I glanced at her as we were standing in the main hall. "Well, we'll postpone the subject of lessons until nine tomorrow."

"Then we can go riding?"

"The trouble is," I said slowly, "I've never ridden. I don't know how."

"Oh!" There was no mistaking the pleasure that that admission gave her. "Well, in that case, it wouldn't be a good idea for you to try. All the horses we have are fairly wild. So I'll see you at dinner." And off she danced through the back hall to the screened back door that I could see from where I stood.

"Alix!" I called.

But the slamming of the screen door was all the response I got.

I glanced at my watch. Four o'clock. Well, Susie would be tapping her paw, waiting for me to take her for a walk.

I went upstairs feeling that for the first time in my life I had taken on something that might prove both more difficult and more complicated than I had realized. Hearing Alix go past on her horse at a brisk canter did nothing to reassure me. As I went along to my bedroom, I had the oddest feeling that around me some plot was playing itself to a planned and foreordained conclusion, and that, without knowing where it came from or where it was going, I was an unwilling part of, an actor in, it.

That thought kept me in the hall, my hand on my bedroom door, until Susie, sensing my presence on the other side of the door, started to bark.

After all her comments about study and dreary drones, I had expected nothing but resistance and foot-dragging from Alix the next morning. But her unpredictability remained consistent. At nine o'clock on the button she led me to the big upstairs bedroom that had become a schoolroom, and we started in on the academic part of our relationship. As an added surprise, she turned out to be further along scholastically than I had expected, and it didn't occur to me until halfway through the morning that that was exactly the state of affairs she intended: reassured by her educational level, I would relax my demands.

"You're a sly one, aren't you?" I said in the middle of

some Latin translation, in which she turned out to be quite adept.

An innocent stare met my eyes. But I was catching on fast. "You know what I mean, Alix Darcourt. All that advance promotion on what an educational disaster you were!"

"Oh that!" she said carelessly. And then grinned.

"Yes, Miss Innocent, that."

And we both laughed. But I tightened my vigilance. It was not too hard to lead me down the garden path, and Alix was obviously skilled at doing just that.

Absently she touched her face just above her jaw line. When she removed her finger I noticed a round reddish spot, almost indented, that I hadn't seen before.

"Did you hurt yourself?" I asked.

"No. It's just some stupid eczema. Doctor McIntyre says it ought to go away eventually. Usually I keep some make-up on it."

"Does it hurt?"

"No. As a matter of fact I can't even feel it."

"Does the doctor give you something for it, or is it just one of the many woes of adolescence that time will take care of?"

"He gives me vitamins." She made a face. "I cover the spots with make-up most of the time. This is a new one. I have one on the other side of my face. But I bet you didn't notice the other one." Her tone had more than a touch of anxiety in it.

"Turn your head. I haven't noticed anything. Let's see if I see it even if I know it's there."

She turned her head, and I was struck again by her resemblance to the portrait of her mother downstairs: the hollowed cheeks, the delicate arch of the cheekbone, the long neck. But as I was reflecting on this, I wondered how I could have missed the same flat, slightly indented mark just under the cheekbone. Perhaps it was the glare of the morning sun streaming through the window, but the cream or salve with which Alix covered the mark looked shiny by comparison with the skin around it.

"Well, now that you've pointed it out, I can see it. But I haven't until now, so I don't think you need to worry about it. After all, practically all teen-agers have spots. It goes with the condition."

"Yes. I know. But not like these. The nurse at the last school was going to take me to see some kind of specialist, but then I had to leave, so nothing came of it. Anyway, Doctor McIntyre says they should go away after a bit, when I've taken enough of the vitamins."

"Why did you have to leave the school?" I asked, curious.

"I don't know. I didn't like it much." She avoided my eyes. "Let's get on with the lousy Latin."

My reporter's instinct was awake and alert. I had not tried to reach either of the two schools that, according to the rumor and gossip Terry had written to me, Alix had attended.

"What school was that?" I asked, as casually as I could.

"Randolph—" Alix started, then looked at me with sudden suspicion. "Why do you want to know? I wasn't there that long."

"Because I have friends and schoolmates teaching in various schools, and I thought you might have come across one of them." The lie fell, in the words of Prince Hamlet, trippingly from my tongue. It seemed such a reasonable explanation, that I was unprepared for Alix's next question, delivered in a hard, angry voice.

"So you could write to them, snooping as to why I left, I suppose."

"No," I said, with the calm that her hysteria always provoked. "Why should I do that? Anyway, what was so mysterious about your leaving?" The question dangled between us. It was now quite obvious to me that there had been something strange about her departure.

Finally Alix said sulkily, "Well, Daddy said it was because they were a bunch of interfering idiots who didn't know how to run a halfway decent school. . . ." Her voice ran down.

"But you don't agree?"

Alix looked so unhappy that I decided, against all my reporter's principles, not to press my questions. "All right, Alix. Let's move on to some history."

She closed her Latin book willingly enough, and opened her history text, but sat there staring at it in an oddly rigid way.

"Alix?" I said gently, and was startled at the words bursting out of her as though a cork had been removed.

"It was all that loathsome nurse's fault. They ran all the students through her office once a month, just to make sure nobody was coming down with anything or was pregnant or on dope, and when she saw a place like this on my face"— her finger went again to the mark below her cheekbone— "she wanted to know what it was and how long I'd had it, and said it was pretty funny-looking and wanted to haul me off to some doctor in Washington. Only Father had told me that since I already had close medical care down here, he didn't want some school quack making himself rich at our expense, so I wasn't to go to any doctor without telling him. So I wrote and told him. And about a week later, he suddenly appeared and took me home. Only just before that." Her voice trailed off again.

"What?" I asked.

"People were so *funny*."

"What do you mean funny?"

"Well they—the kids and teachers at school—didn't say anything. Only I had the feeling they were talking about me, you know—in groups. And I think it was the nurse's fault. Anyway, when I went into the front hall with my bags I heard these angry voices from the headmistress's study where Father was, and then the nurse came out with her face bright red, the way it went when she got angry, and she gave me this furious look before she went barreling up the stairs."

"Well, her professional dignity was probably bruised. After all, it was her job to see you were all kept in the pink, and when she made a suggestion, your father—" I hesitated, realizing I was about to come out with one of my less tactful sayings.

"Practically accused her of malpractice. Yes, that's what I think, too. And I told Daddy so. And when I described that funny atmosphere among the girls just before I left, he said he was well acquainted with it, having come across it often when he had refused to be bilked out of some easy money. He said he called it the 'you're-so-rich-you-wouldn't-miss-it' attitude. And that probably the girls were saying, with all that money, you'd think they'd be able to afford a doctor's bill."

And the truth was, I thought, I couldn't blame them. It was, I reflected, like a Rockefeller or a Getty dickering over the cost of a taxi ride.

Alix, well launched into her grievance, tumbled on. "And then there was another row when I got home, because I hadn't got my vitamin pills. I'd forgotten to tell father that the nurse had confiscated them. She said all medicines had to be administered in her office, and when I told her they were just vitamins, she said those too. Some girl had been caught taking too much Vitamin D or something, and all her bones melted, or were about to."

I couldn't help smiling. "It presents a pretty terrible picture. Was this supposed to happen all at once? Like that woman in *Lost Horizon* who went from looking nineteen to about ninety in five seconds?"

Alix giggled. "I don't know. I haven't seen the movie."

"I suppose not. It used to be around on the Late Show. Quite a scene. All smooth youth one minute, all wrinkles the next. How often does your personal private doctor come to see you? I must say, it sounds like the court or the White House physician—not a terribly demanding job. Sort of like that of the nurse at your school."

"Well, she'd been a missionary nurse in the Pacific islands or Africa or some such place, and had gotten some ghastly tropical disease and was doing this as a kind of rest cure, because she and the headmistress had gone to the same school or come from the same town. But she wasn't exactly overflowing with Christian charity."

"I'm not sure that taking care of a bunch of over-privileged teen-agers wouldn't demand an unusual amount of Christian charity, particularly if she was recuperating from a severe illness. Now that I think of it, I'd find her job a lot harder than paying an occasional visit to the island here and passing out vitamin pills."

"Doctor McIntyre does more than that. He's in the hospital over in St. Damien's and treats everybody there. He's coming sometime in the next couple of weeks or so, so you'll get to meet him."

That'll be a thrill, I thought cynically. But, since Alix obviously liked him, I bit back any acid comment, even though I thought being court doctor to the Darcourts, when there were thousands in heavily populated areas who needed medical attention, was not my idea of how most usefully to practice medicine. But then, I reminded myself, where the Darcourts and other such families were concerned, tolerance was not my leading characteristic.

"Well, back to the books," I said. "And if I were you, I wouldn't rub that. It could get infected."

Alix made a face at me, but put her hand down and started turning the pages of her history text.

The rest of that week passed without any noteworthy incidents, a state of affairs I took for granted, and therefore paid no particular attention to. It was only later, when I looked back, trying to find the moment when I first became aware of an unknown and frightening element manipulating all of us, that I attempted to pinpoint my first consciousness of something wrong. Something other, that is, than the envelope left in front of my door and its subsequent removal, which I had by this time decided was just a freakish prank. And more wrong than the general outlandishness of the whole Darcourt setup, which struck me as not only thoroughly feudal, but injurious to any modern teen-ager, let alone one as delicately balanced as Alix. But, since I had made up my mind to stay for professional and personal reasons, as well as my growing affection for Alix, I had come to accept as the norm—at least for this island remnant of another age—both Tristram Darcourt's abrasive authoritarianism and Alix's periodic flights from reality. (And as a firm believer in psychological cause and effect, I laid the full responsibility for Alix's instability on her father's insensitive, iron-fisted tyranny.)

But, having swallowed the bizarreness of the situation as a whole, I found the days of that first week or so followed on one another with unremarkable, if pleasant, monotony. Occasionally, and especially if the sun was out, Alix tried to balk at having to stay inside. But once she accepted the fact that I was not about to be wheedled, persuaded or connived out of doing the morning studies, no matter how glorious the weather, she took the discipline with relatively little fuss.

All of which put me unpleasantly in mind of what her father had said: "*I think you will find that authority works very well with Alix. She responds to it.*" I found it profoundly irritating that he should be proved right. Further, I discovered, if her interest was caught, she showed herself to be brighter, with a quicker, more analytical brain, than I would have thought. Despite her scorn for mathematics, she displayed a remarkable facility in both algebra and geometry, in which I managed to stay one jump ahead only by selective cramming the night before.

"Where did you get all this mathematical talent?" I asked her at the end of one morning session.

She sighed. "From Daddy, of course. Where else? You know he graduated from Annapolis with one of the highest marks ever given in math? But I'd much rather be good in something else."

"Such as?"

She stretched languorously, and with much sensuous writhing. "Sex appeal," she said in a breathless voice.

It was a beautiful performance. "Or theater?" I inquired, deadpan. "And anyway, who'd you practice it on, on the island here?"

She gave me her sly look from under her eyelashes. "Oh, I have a boyfriend."

"On Darcourt?" I asked incredulously.

She shrugged. "Why not? Or even off."

I looked at her lowered eyelids, more of her father's words on my mind, as though written on a placard in large print: *"Alix is not to leave the island while I am gone. She is not, under any circumstances, to go beyond the fence into the southern part of the island."*

I said, carefully casual, "But do you go off the island frequently?"

"Wouldn't you like to know, Terry? And wouldn't old Connie and my father like to know?" she grinned.

"The answer to all three is yes. And since I am here as governess-companion, I think I'll have to know. If I didn't, your father would be quite justified in thinking I wasn't doing my job."

She gave one of her elaborate shrugs. "There's nothing to stop you from finding out—if you can." And she giggled. "I'll give you a hint. He's blond."

Suddenly I remembered the boy on the motorbike who sent me down the mired road. "Straight blond hair going back from a cowlick?" I asked quickly, watching her face.

But she was looking down at her boots, which she was piling together. Then she stood up. "School's out," she said, with her mischievous look. "I'm going to ride. Pity you don't, isn't it?" And with a wave, she was off.

It was more than a pity, I thought, then and increasingly as the days passed. Because when Alix was not at her studies in the morning, or at meals, she was either in her attic or out on her horse—in both cases out of my, or anyone else's, reach. Then, as the first week melted into the second and the second into the third, I started noticing Alix's restlessness, which seemed to hit her earlier and earlier in our study period. Being restless myself, I was sympathetic to it. Sitting still for three hours for a sixteen-year-old, without even the tension-relieving activity of changing classrooms or talking to other youngsters her age, must, I knew, tax her considerably, and I had made allowance, even periodically getting up halfway through the morning and leading her downstairs, out the house and around it, at a brisk jog, before going back upstairs and settling down again. But the fidgeting, the getting up and walking around the room, the dropping of pencils, which had always started around a quarter to twelve, with the end close in sight, started occurring at eleven thirty, then it got pushed back to eleven and a quarter to.

"What's the matter, Alix?" I asked one morning as she went around the room, moodily flicking at the curtains, picking up a book here and there on the shelves and putting them down again. "I thought you liked the Tudors. You said it was your favorite period."

"They're okay. It's just that they're . . . they're not about anything important."

"If you mean history isn't, you're wrong. Somebody once said that history is nothing but gossip down the ages, and everybody likes gossip."

"I don't. I'd rather be out on Brutus. And what's the use anyway? Father's not going to let me go to college."

"As I told you. In two years, with a little money and/or luck, you can probably do as you wish. But you're not going to any college anywhere unless you can at least get a high school diploma."

"I don't care about a high school diploma," she said pettishly. "I'd just as soon be a waitress."

"I worked as a waitress for two summers. It can be wearing—both on the feet and on the pride."

She hunched a shoulder. "I don't care. I don't care. What time is it?"

"Where's your watch?" I asked, knowing she usually had one on.

"I left it somewhere."

"How could you leave it somewhere?"

"All right. I forgot to put it on. Is the time of day a national secret? Would you be letting dear Daddy down if you told me?"

I had been highly critical of Mrs. Conyers when she had used the word "hysterical" of Alix. Yet I found that it was in the front of my mind. There was a note now in her voice that, much as I would have liked to deny it, was undoubtedly hysterical.

I hesitated. There were two ways I could deal with this: I could use my authority, and I was fairly sure—this time at least—she would obey. Or I could let her go, voluntarily. It was a risk, because it would give her a precedent. Yet my instinct told me to do that. I shut the book in front of me and looked at my watch. "It's just after eleven. Why don't we call school out for this morning?"

I expected her to take off like a rocket. But she stood, as though frozen with surprise, for a few minutes.

"You're free," I said. "Go! Scram!"

Then that smile that could still dazzle me blazed in her face. "Terry, you're a darling!" Coming over, she threw her arms around my neck and was gone.

More moderate in her expression, but just as rapturous was Susie, whom I took for an unscheduled walk cum jog-trot in the woods and out to the little pier, on which we sat for a while. Even on a dry, clear day St. Damien's was a bare smudge on the northern horizon. The dour Petersen and his boat were nowhere in sight, the only sign of life being a neat motor schooner, headed southwards, its graceful white hull cutting through the water with considerable speed. I eyed the various rods and appendages soaring up from its upper deck.

"Off to the fishing grounds, Susie," I said, running my hand up and down her back. "I wonder what they'll catch." Susie, who loved having her back scratched, gave a whine of pure joy.

I watched the boat disappear around the outer curve of the island and then sat for a while longer. Susie was not as spry as she used to be, and I liked to rest her from time to time. How long it was after the boat had gone, I don't know. But it came over me, sitting there on the pier, how lonely the island was, and how cut off. Supposing I wanted to get off . . . had to get off . . . how would I do it?

The moment that question struck me, it seemed astounding that I had not thought of it before. Because the answer was so obvious: I wouldn't. And as that realization hit, I shivered.

"Come on, Susie," I said, scrambling to my feet. "Time for lunch."

It was as we were walking back through the fringe of forest, so thick in parts that the sun was almost obliterated, that Susie stopped, barked, growled and then whined. Even in the half-light, I could see her fur stand up.

"What is it, Susie?" I whispered.

Her growl grew louder.

It was then I heard, as she was momentarily silent, a rustling. I stared at the bushes, shrubs and undergrowth covering the ground and clogging the base of the trees. The rustling—

a dry, almost dragging sound—stopped. Then, as though in answer to some unseen signal, started again. It was at that moment that I remembered André's allusions to the less romantic forms of island wildlife—poisonous spiders, snakes and scorpions.

Bending quickly, I picked Susie up, to her great fury. She barked in angry protest. "Quiet!" I said, and put my hand around her muzzle. Then I stood still and listened.

There was no rustling or dragging now. The silence was total. Everything was still. Even Susie, who had been frantically wriggling in my arms, had stopped and lay quiet against me. The only motion was her heart, which I could feel, through her skin and mine, beating quickly and steadily against me.

And as I stood there, I wondered, with one part of my mind, whether I was going mad. Because a feeling that I was being watched became, slowly, a conviction. And as I stared into the shifting dusk ahead of me, I also became sure that I could see—though dimly—the person who was watching me. If it was a person. There was a shape, or an arrangement of shadows, or something standing behind a low bush next to a tree. Then a breeze moved the branches of the trees, the curtains of moss quivered above and around me, and I wondered if I were suffering hallucinations. Surely, that tall, bulky shape was—And then everything happened at once. A twig snapped.

I cried out, "Who is it?"

Susie, galvanized into action, wiggled free, jumped to the ground, barking, and took off straight ahead, and there was a sound of more breaking twigs and crashing undergrowth.

"Susie!" I yelled. "Come back!" I ran off the path into the bushes towards her, frightened of whatever was there, but even more frightened for Susie. I could hear something—or someone—moving ahead of me.

"Susie!" I called out again, pushing through bushes and shrubbery and across small, relatively open spaces, always with that heavy noise receding in front of me. A while—I'm not sure how long—later, I tripped and fell on my face.

I don't really know whether I was knocked out or just dazed. But when I sat up my head swam, and when I put my hand up to it, I found a growing lump over one eye. I was feeling this in a gingerly fashion when there was the sound of paws on dirt and leaves and Susie appeared, her ears back, her tail wagging. And in her mouth, born like a prize and a gift, a dead mouse. After laying this, with pride and tenderness, at my feet, she wagged her tail some more and barked.

"Yes, Susie, you're a good dog. But I don't think that solves our problem."

Slowly I got up and was relieved to find myself mostly intact, though one ankle was swollen and sore. I am often careless and scatterbrained, but I am not accident prone, and I was curious to find, if I could, what I had tripped over. Technically, I suppose, it could have been anything: a stone half trodden on and then kicked out of sight, a root, some other piece of natural debris in this untamed wilderness. Yet, though I couldn't exactly recall my sensation at the moment of tripping, none of those seemed right. I wish I had a flashlight, I thought, peering around on the ground. A shaft of sun would appear now and then, but not for long. And it was too dim to make any kind of intelligent search. I finally decided that the only thing to do was abandon the search and get back to the path leading to the carriage drive.

If my ankle had been badly sprained, I wouldn't have been able to walk on it, so the fact that I could walk at all, however slowly, argued for no more than a twist. Usually it was I who moderated my pace for Susie. This time it was she, marching proudly ahead, still bearing her dead mouse, who would pause and look back at me as though to say, Hurry up, slowpoke.

"I'm coming," I said a bit crossly. "And if you hadn't taken off after that mouse, I wouldn't be in this fix."

But I couldn't believe it was only the mouse she was after. No mouse—or even rat—could make that heavy, dragging sound. There was something else, and I was quite sure Susie was chasing it when she got diverted by a target more her size and taste. This though did absolutely nothing for my peace of mind as I limped as quickly as I could out of the densely wooded area toward the path.

"And furthermore," I said. But at that point, I rounded a bush and there was the road again. I hadn't, before my little adventure, paid much attention to it, but I could see now, by the stumps lining the road on either side, that the woods and undergrowth had been cleared to make a path, and that by comparison with the near darkness that began a few yards to right and left of the path, it wound ahead like a tunnel of light.

I stepped onto the road and winced as my sore foot came

117

down on the harder surface. Then I glanced at my watch. Twelve thirty-five. Well, I thought resignedly, I hope they either send out the jeep to look for us, or keep something hot for us from lunch, because with my dot-and-carry-one mode of progress, it would take more than half an hour to cover the distance to the house.

I didn't enjoy the walk, and it was not just because my ankle was painful. I still could not shake off the feeling that eyes—human eyes—were watching me. I could not explain it, so as an antidote, I mentally ran through some of the more stinging comments on the subject of superstitious hocus pocus made by that great rationalist, James Patrick Wainright. The trouble was, I recalled at the same time another comment of his, tacked onto the end of one of his antisuperstition diatribes: "Still, Sally, there's no getting around a sort of animal intuition. It's saved many a man's life. If, with no evidence at all, you can't help but think something's wrong, then pay attention! There probably is!"

"Thanks a lot," I muttered out loud, and at that moment heard a most welcome sound: the jeep.

It was coming from behind me, so I called Susie, who came trotting back, still with her mouse, and picked her up. Then I waited, more willing to welcome the sour Petersen or truculent Norton than I would have believed.

But I had never seen the two men in the jeep. More astonishing still, the young man who was driving wore the round collar of a priest. Next to him was a man of around fifty, with a square, powerful face under a bald head, and blue eyes behind steel-rimmed glasses. On his knees was a black bag. I knew without being told that this must be Dr. McIntyre.

The priest, an angular man, who, on close inspection, did not seem quite as young as I had thought, pulled the car up.

"You must be Miss LeBreton." The dark eyes glanced at Susie in my arms. "May we give you and your friend a lift?"

Susie, her mouth full of mouse, made a token bark in her throat. I smiled. "We accept with pleasure. I was hoping somebody would come by." I limped up to the jeep. The doctor opened the door and got down on the ground. "I'll get in the back," he said.

"No. I can manage easily." And I got up and into the back before he could argue.

"What did you do to your foot?" he asked.

"Turned my ankle."

"Bad luck." He didn't sound overwhelmingly concerned. "But you should stick to the paths."

"I would have done, only—"

The doctor turned his head. "Only what?"

"Susie and I heard something, and she took off into the bushes. So I went after her."

"And it turned out to be a mouse."

"No mouse ever made that much noise."

I was aware of two pairs of eyes on me. The doctor's and, reflected in the rearview mirror, the priest's.

"Well," the doctor said, turning back, "there's a lot of wildlife around here."

"So I've been told."

We drove a few more minutes in silence. Then I asked, "How did you know who I was? Process of elimination?"

The priest smiled. "More or less. Besides, news travels fast around a small community like St. Damien's."

"But this island seems so cut off."

He looked at me in the rearview mirror. "In some ways it is. Very cut off. But there are such things as telephones and boats. By the way, I'm Father Mark. This is Doctor McIntyre."

"Yes. I guessed," I said, smiling a little. "I've heard a lot about you, Doctor McIntyre, from Alix."

He half turned his head. "How is she? Taking her vitamin pills?"

My previous image of the doctor as a somewhat fuzzy-minded, well-intentioned vitamin freak, happy to earn his money being a medical step-and-fetchit to Tristram Darcourt, was proving very remote from the reality sitting in front of me.

"I suppose so, Doctor. I mean, I don't watch her."

He grunted and turned back front again.

"You really must believe in the potency of those vitamins," I said.

This time he shifted so that he could face me. "I do. Why, are you one of the skeptics where vitamins are concerned?"

"No. I guess not. I don't know really. I've never taken any, and I've always been perfectly healthy. But I went to school with people who took handfuls three times a day."

"And you thought they were hypochondriacs or freaks?"

Since that was more or less exactly what I thought, I hesitated. "Well," I said, trying to remember to be tactful, "I sometimes wondered."

"Haven't you read about the megavitamin treatment for various forms of mental illness being tried in some of the mental hospitals around the country?"

"Yes. But I think I've also read that the results are not in."

At that, somewhat surprisingly, he smiled. "You're very young to be such a conservative. You don't believe in trying anything until it's been proven and documented?"

I grinned. "Touché. No. I'm not that much of a conservative. But I suppose I was thinking about all the fuss the vitamins caused Alix's school. After all, weren't they more or less the reason why Mr. Darcourt took Alix out?" I had an impression of his eyes boring into me. But it was at that moment that the jeep emerged from the woods onto the drive and the sun was like a floodlight. I blinked and closed my eyes. By the time I had opened them again and let them become accustomed to the light, the doctor had half turned back. Then he said over his shoulder:

"It's just that Tristram doesn't like his orders interfered with. And he was right. You can't have been around Alix without noticing that she is inclined to get overexcited easily. Neither he nor I wanted some unknown doctor, without all the facts, not only not encouraging her to continue with the vitamins, but maybe prescribing something like a tranquilizer. Which would be very bad for her."

"Yes," I said. But I had my own views, and I was not going to lose this opportunity of venting them where there was the remotest possibility of getting some support.

"I can't help but feel, Doctor McIntyre," I said firmly, and was gratified to see that again he turned so that he faced me, "that a lot of Alix's instability comes from psychological causes." I paused, wishing I had the courage to specify what I was talking about. But there was no point in making gratuitous critical comments about my employer that would, unquestionably, get back to him. At least not yet. Rather abruptly, the doctor finished for me.

"Such as no mother and a seemingly harsh, frequently absent father."

I was surprised. "Exactly."

Those very blue eyes behind the thick glasses were on me again. "I entirely agree with you, and so I have told Tristram. But even such a"—he smiled a little grimly—"conservative as you must know that psychological causes have physiological results, to which powerful doses of vitamins can—and do—act as a counterirritant."

"Yes. That's true," I said, wondering why I still felt dissatisfied.

We pulled up at the front of the house. The doctor got out and went straight into the house through the front door, which was unlocked. I jumped down from the jeep with Susie under my arm. "Thank you," I said to the priest.

He reached out and scratched Susie on the head. "Well, Nimrod, I see you've been on a successful hunt."

Susie, still clutching the mouse, wiggled her backside against my arm.

He rubbed her between her ears. "What a nice dog! She seems to have dignity and serenity."

I warmed towards him, because those were Susie's essential qualities. "She has. You're a perceptive man." And then, in my enthusiasm, put my foot where it so often finds itself: in my mouth. "Especially for a priest."

The dark eyes looked at me over Susie's head. "A dumb lot, eh?"

"I'm sorry, Father. All the priests that have come my way were either very old and crotchety or young and relevant."

He smiled. And the smile reminded me of someone. "What a terrible choice," he said lightly. But his eyes had become intent and watchful, and suddenly I understood why: My flippant comment was perfectly appropriate for a girl brought up among the Irish priests of a small town in Massachusetts. But the French priests of New Orleans and the bayou country, home of the many LeBretons, were—as I had found out even in my brief visit—of a different type: running less to movie stereotypes and current trendiness.

Swiftly and briefly I wondered if I could redeem my slip, and decided to leave bad enough alone. "Aren't you coming in, Father?"

He put the car in gear. "No. I think I'll visit some of my other parishioners first. Tell Alix I'll be around this afternoon, will you?"

"Of course," I said, and wondered, what parishioners? At this point the priest and I were watching one another like two dogs circling before a fight.

"Do you have many on the island?" I asked. And then, as he didn't answer, "Many parishioners, I mean."

"Some," he said, unsmiling. His hand sketched a wave, and the car moved off.

I put Susie down. "I'm afraid you can't take that mouse

into the house." I bent down. "Now give it to me," I said, feeling like a betrayer.

That obedient, devoted little dog put it at my feet and wagged her tail. I picked it up and straightened.

"What do you have there?" Alix's voice came from behind me.

I turned, and saw her coming around the house. "A present from Susie. I don't want to hurt her feelings, but I'm not sure what to do with it."

Alix came up. "Maybe there's something you could use to distract her while we buried it."

"I could go and get some dog biscuits I have upstairs if you will hold the mouse."

"If you'll tell me where they are, I'll get them."

"All right. They're in a plastic bag sitting on top of the bureau. Thanks a lot. If we can put a few of those down, one of us can bury the mouse."

Alix ran off and in a few minutes was back. "Here," she said, and going around to where Susie could just see her out of the corner of her eye, put a few of the biscuits down. Susie, who was undoubtedly hungry, trotted over. I quickly went to a nearby azalea bush, out of Susie's sight, and buried the mouse, covering it with a lot of dirt, and pulling some twigs over it.

Susie had finished her snack and was sitting contentedly while Alix, down on her knees, was stroking her.

"By the way," I said, "I have a message for you. Father Mark said to tell you he'd see you later this afternoon. He and Doctor McIntyre picked me up in the jeep in the woods at the north end right after—" Incredible as it seemed, I had, until that moment, temporarily forgotten what had happened in the woods and my feeling of being watched.

Alix looked up and then stood up. "After what?"

"Well," I said, choosing my words carefully, "Susie and I took a walk and then came back through the woods. I thought I heard a sound. Like somebody moving around. Susie took off after whoever it was. That's when she caught the mouse. Anyway, I went after her and tripped and when I looked up, there was Susie with the mouse in her mouth. But I still had the feeling that someone was there."

It sounded terribly lame and prosaic as I said it, yet I could feel the old horror and chill. Alix's eyes were watching me. Rather like the doctor's, I found myself thinking. Rather like the priest's. It suddenly occurred to me that the people on this island were a watchful lot.

"I suppose," I said, "it could have been Judson, or Norton."

Alix turned and started to move towards the house. "I suppose."

I joined her, and Susie trotted behind us. "Father Mark spoke of visiting his other parishioners. Does he have many on the island?"

"Oh, I guess so. Among the servants. Norton, too."

The gong was sounding as we went in. I went upstairs, settled Susie with a few more pieces of dry food, washed my hands and came down. The doctor joined us at lunch and sat at Alix's right, between her and me, and across from Mrs. Conyers.

"Isn't Father Mark going to have lunch?" I asked as Stevens passed around a big bowl of jambalaya, a delicious New Orleans dish.

"No," the doctor replied. "He brought his own sandwich, and is busy attending the souls in his charge on the island."

"Yes. So Alix said."

"Didn't you believe me?" Alix asked.

"Oh, sure. I just didn't realize there were that many people on the island I hadn't seen. You mentioned Norton, Alix. Is there a Mrs. Norton?"

Alix looked up and giggled. "Norton's a misogynist. Doesn't approve of women at all."

"There are also Rosa and May," Mrs. Conyers said quickly. "May is the maid and Rosa, the cook," she explained to me.

As soon as lunch was over Alix disappeared with the doctor. I loitered downstairs in the library, reading a copy of *The New York Times* and a news-magazine that had just been delivered. About an hour later I started upstairs and was halfway up when I heard Susie's bark, followed by a high whine I had heard only once or twice.

I flew up the rest of the stairs as fast as my sore ankle let me, along the corridor and flung open my door.

I had seen scorpions in zoos and in their native state. But never this size, although I had read they could grow to eight or nine inches.

Susie, brave if not very bright little Susie, had the monster cornered. Its tail was waving dangerously. In a second it would spring and sting her, and if (as I remembered reading somewhere) the sting of a scorpion could be fatal to a child, it would certainly be so to a small dog.

For a second I stood, frozen. Then I ran and snatched Susie and backed off. The scorpion, with no avenue of retreat, ran toward us. Carrying the wiggling, protesting Susie, I ran out the door. The doctor was coming down the hall.

"Doctor," I all but yelled.

"Yes. What's the matter?" He did not look pleased.

"There's a scorpion in there—a huge one. One more second and it would have killed Susie."

"Nonsense," he said. Pushing past me, he went in.

For a moment I was afraid the scorpion would have disappeared, then I saw it move across the rag carpet.

"Yes. It is large," the doctor said calmly. "What I need is a broom. I think there's a broom closet down the hall. Please get me one."

I had seen the closet in my tour of the house and in half a minute I was back with the broom.

My prejudices against the doctor vanished as he dealt with the scorpion and finally shook its corpse out the window.

I stood there, watching him and thinking about Susie.

"It would have killed her," I said.

"Probably." He gave the broom a final shake and turned back.

"Doctor McIntyre," I said. "I know there's a lot of wildlife on the island. I've been told so again and again. I could see where they could run in and out of a ground level bungalow. But how could they get up here?"

The doctor, who had been eying a box of tissues on the dressing table, reached out towards them. "May I?"

"Of course."

He started to clean off the end of the broom. "In answer to your question, they come up walls and pipes."

"How nice," I said. "That does a lot for my sense of security."

He was looking rather grim, but after glancing at me, said in a kind voice, "Don't worry. It's very rare and is unlikely to happen again. I'll put this down the hall."

At the door he hesitated. "As I said, don't worry. I can almost guarantee it won't happen again."

"Almost, but not one hundred percent?"

"Nothing is certain, Miss LeBreton. The whole island might be washed away by a tidal wave."

"Somehow that doesn't frighten me. Scorpions scaling walls and pipes to my bedroom does. Especially with Susie here."

"I told you. The chances of its happening are small. Of it's happening a second time even smaller. Good day, Miss Le-Breton," and he closed the door with a snap.

I decided to make sure that there was no more of the island's treasured wildlife anywhere around my bedroom. After looking carefully over the bedroom and bathroom, and scanning the entire bedroom floor, I was about to put Susie (still in my arms) down, when I saw the ruffled skirt to the fourposter.

"Stay there," I said to Susie and put her on top of the bed. Then I got out my flashlight and lifted the ruffle.

The shoe box was lying about three feet inside. Reaching out, I pulled it towards me, then sprang back with a cry. Inside was the remains of a second scorpion. I am not an entomologist, but I guessed that the first scorpion had attacked and killed and partly eaten the second. Feeling queasy, and holding the box at arm's length, I went to the window, and flipped out the cannibalized scorpion. What to do with the box? It was an unlovely sight, and I decided to wrap it in paper before I did anything else.

As I turned my hand, the box fell out of its top, which had been fitted onto the bottom. It was then I noticed the holes that had been punched low down the side of the box and in the top.

I stood there, the box in my hands, for a long time, thinking. Since the sting of a scorpion almost never kills an adult, I didn't think anyone was trying to do away with me. And if Susie were the target, it would only be indirectly. But simply finding the creature in the room might very well speed my departure if, for example, anyone of three things happened: I was frightened out of my wits into leaving, I was stung and made ill, or Susie was stung and killed.

Ergo, someone very much wanted me out of the way.

(7)

AFTER thinking it over, I decided not to mention the matter of the shoe box. To broadcast that I knew someone was trying to get rid of me would, I felt, perhaps superstitiously, lend strength to that person's resolve. If everyone knew about a first try, then everyone would be expecting a second, and whoever was playing this little game would feel almost compelled to another attempt. The doctor might, or might not, mention the matter of the scorpion. But since, according to him, scorpions could get into my room by themselves, the story wouldn't by itself be anything but an example of non-native squeamishness, amusing but not significant. To everyone, that is, but the person who placed the scorpions in the shoe box and put them under my bed. He, or she, might well feel frustrated that, merely annoyed and repelled by such vigorous and proliferating wildlife, I hadn't taken the hint the way it was intended, and would give up trying to chase me away.

Or would try again?

It was that step in the logical sequence of my thinking that I liked the least, along with the fact that the more I went over in my mind the various people who could be interested in my departure, the more I was faced with the unpleasant fact that I did not trust anyone—not even Alix. No matter how much I might empathize with her loneliness, her virtual imprisonment by her father, her isolation from the real world, there was no question but that the mood swings, caused unquestionably (I felt) by her circumstances, showed her to be capricious and unpredictable.

There was an example of this towards the end of the study period, the morning after I found the scorpion, when, with Susie's safety in mind, I told Alix about finding the scorpion (without mentioning the shoe box), and made a point of stating the danger of a poisonous insect to a small dog.

"Oh, how silly," Alix said. "Susie's got more sense than to attack a scorpion."

"She certainly hasn't. She had the wretched thing cornered when I got up to the room."

"I think you're making a mountain out of a molehill. You're just not used to our——"

"If you say wildlife, I'll throw this book at you. I'm tired of hearing about it. I was very sympathetic when your father told me about half the island being a sanctuary, but if it's a sanctuary for large, lethal beasties with nasty habits, then I'm not sure housing units aren't preferable."

Alix's lips curled a little. "Scorpions have their mode of living. Who are you to upset nature's balance?"

"Because it is normal for a lion to eat freshly killed flesh doesn't mean I want to keep one in my garden or send Susie to play with it."

Alix shrugged. "Why are you telling me all this? Do you think I put it there?"

I looked her in the eye.

"Did you?"

"No, I didn't. And I don't appreciate your asking me that."

"Since you seem to look upon the whole thing as good clean fun, I don't know why you feel insulted by my asking you."

Her brows climbed up in a way I was becoming familiar with. "Aren't you forgetting your position here, Terry? You're my governess-companion. Not my guardian or guide."

It was I who closed the book in front of me then. "Alix," I said very calmly, "don't ever use that tone, or words like that, again, when you're talking to me. I'm not your servant or your serf—or your father's—and if you had fifty times all the money in the national treasury, and were descended from all the families in the *Almanach de Gotha*, I still wouldn't be. Wake up, Alix, equality's just around the corner!" I stood up. "I'm going for a walk. You're free to ride or do anything else that you want to do."

And I left, taking Susie for a walk and this time sticking to the paths.

The matter was not brought up at lunch, since Mrs. Conyers was there and her presence was always something of an inhibiting factor. But Alix apologized the next morning from motives that I sensed to be a combination of good manners, genuine contrition and a sense that she had gone too far. I accepted her apology without rancor—after all, her upbringing was not her fault but, I felt strongly, that of her father and possibly of her absent mother. My sentiments about the latter, like Alix's motives, were mixed: sympathy for her inability to live with the feudal lord who was her husband, however compelling his physical presence, and condemnation for abandoning her daughter to his rigid and constricting authority.

After Alix's apology, things seemed to go back to where they were at the beginning—at least for a few days. Alix's interest in the Tudors revived, her facility with mathematics and Latin returned. Lessons, which had started being a drag, became interesting again. And my mind, freed of more urgent matters, nibbled again at the puzzles I had come down here initially to unravel: why Darcourt had jilted my mother, and why he was so secretive about himself, his business pursuits and dealings. Of the two puzzles, the first, the one involving my mother, looked both harder and easier to solve: easier because the subject was simple and personal; harder because the answer would be most likely to turn up through family or servants' gossip, and the servants at Darcourt (including of course, Mrs. Conyers) were either tight-lipped or remote.

As far as Darcourt's business dealings were concerned, they were easier of approach in the sense that they were vulnerable to the usual reference books and reports from government regulatory agencies. But not only did I have a poor head for business, I didn't know what to look for. Even, if, by some miracle, I found myself alone with the company's books, I wouldn't recognize fiddling or finagling, let alone outright embezzlement, unless it were framed in red arrows. And Brian's answer when I had posed that question was not reassuring or constructive.

"That's hard to say until you stumble over it."

"Not very helpful."

"Well, it was your idea, going there. Given my druthers, I'd prefer sending an experienced business spy who'd know how to smell out fraud or misrepresentation or skullduggery with burnoosed foreigners and where to find it. But, as I said, I have a shrewd idea that you've another plot up your sleeve. Am I right?"

"Yes."

"Wanna tell me what it is?"

"No. Not until I find what—other than business chicanery—I'm going after, and I have a pretty good chance of knowing where to start with that."

"Okay. I'll hold off, if you promise me an exclusive story when you've found it."

"Of course." I grinned at him. "It would go with the cover story."

"Nothing unambitious about you, is there, Sally?"

I looked at him eyeball to eyeball. "Nothing at all."

"All right. Keep me posted."

But I had been wrong about the accessibility of what I wanted. Going on my small experiences of the rich, I had expected a larger, more gossipy staff, far more amenable to bribery. But considering the size of the house, there were remarkably few servants, and they were kept well out of sight.

Further, I had not been able to phone Brian at least to let him know I was alive and still looking. There were, of course, plenty of telephones, but I was not about to use one of those in the house which I was quite sure would be bugged or monitored. But I had now been on the island more than a month without being in some kind of touch, and when I thought about it, I realized I had assumed that long before that I would have had occasion to visit St. Damien's. Obviously I had underestimated not only how remote Darcourt Island was, but how seldom anyone—that is anyone in the household—left it. And I thought again of that moment, sitting on the pier, when I realized how powerless I was to leave.

It was not a comfortable thought, and I considered simply stating that I was taking the day off, and commandeering the jeep and Petersen and his boat. It was not impossible, nor had I any real reason to think I would be refused. But it would, to put it mildly, draw attention to me, and I didn't want that. Another solution would be to take Alix over for a day's outing, except that her father had expressly forbidden it. The whole place and the circumstances surrounding it were far more claustrophobic and restricted than I had envisioned.

I was turning over possibilities in my head when things took a turn for the worse. Alix's restlessness, which I had decided must simply have been an initial and temporary manifestation of her getting used to me, abruptly came back, from one day to the next. One morning she was interested and cooperative and full of discussions of the subjects at hand. The next morning she was restless, inattentive, prickly and by turns languid and keyed up.

"What's the matter with you?" I asked.

"Nothing," she said defensively.

"Then let's get on with our work."

She shrugged, and seemed to apply herself for about five minutes, then she dropped her pencil, picked it up and wandered over to the window.

"Looking for someone?"

"No." She came back, yanked out her chair and sat down.

"When's your father due to return?"

"You know as much as I do."

Well, I thought, if that's the mood you're in, I'm not going to play ball to your bat. "Okay, let's go on to the next chapter."

I had tried being sympathetic. I had tried to find out what was wrong so I could, perhaps, be of help. But all my experience in the orphanage plus my own deepest instinct, plus my knowledge, by this time, of Alix, indicated that she would respond now only to authority and discipline. It was regretable that this further bore out what her arbitrary parent had said, but there it was. I decided to ignore the performance to which I was being treated, and ploughed on as though she were no different from the way she had been the previous half-dozen mornings. It was hard work, but I was not about to let her see that I found it so. Nor did I let her close her books till noon, at which point she slammed out of the schoolroom with the statement that she was going riding and would be late for lunch.

I informed Stevens of this, who accepted it philosophically, and took Susie for a walk.

When we finally sat down—just the two of us; Mrs. Conyers sent a message that she was not feeling well—I asked Alix, "Have a nice ride?"

"Yes. Thanks."

"Where did you go?"

"Oh. Around."

It was plain she was not going to be any more informative.

Also, catching a sidelong glance from her, I had the distinct impression that she was enjoying her evasive action. So I changed the subject.

That afternoon after the official siesta time she did not appear in the schoolroom, where it had become the custom for us to meet for a walk or picnic or even just to talk. Nor was she in her room. I debated going up to her attic and finally climbed the stairs. The door was locked. Annoyed at the solicitating position in which I found myself, I knocked sharply. No answer. I finally went to the stables. Yes, Duncan said. She'd gone out right after lunch. Nor did she return till just before dinner.

In one sense, she had a right to do what she wanted with the time she was not supposed to be in the schoolroom. But I knew her father had hired me to do more than just train her for her college entrance exams. He had stated that he wanted me to be her companion and, if possible, become her friend. I could certainly not do that if she was avoiding me. And it was obvious she was doing just that.

Patience, Sally, I counseled myself, knowing that impatience was one of my besetting sins. She had gone through one of these moods before and come out of it; she could do so again. And pushing against all my impulses to help her come around was an ineradicable feeling that this was the way she had manipulated others. And I was not going to join their band.

So the strange tug of war went on: the fidgeting, moving around and doodling:

"Those vitamin pills certainly don't seem to be bringing you serenity," I said drily one morning.

"They're not supposed to. They're for my skin." And in an automatic gesture, she put her hand up to her face. I forbore to mention that I had noticed yet another round, slightly indented spot which, carefully covered by make-up, nevertheless showed through by the end of a restless morning.

"Is that what's bothering you?" I asked gently. I had all the sympathy in the world for a girl struggling with what she felt to be a major physical problem. The fat or thin or spotty or gangling girls at the orphanage, lost in adolescent self-hatred, had always wrung my heart. Other than being undersized, I had had no soul-searching adolescent disabilities, but being the daughter of a beautiful mother had given me some understanding of the problem.

She snatched her hand down. "No, of course not. It's just my age."

"Is that what the doctor says?"

"Yes. He says they'll go away in time."

My opinion of the doctor's modernity was not very high. "Does he actually *do* anything about them?"

She shrugged. "He scrapes them and takes a slide back to put under a microscope."

I decided not to say what I thought, which was that it sounded like the kind of thing some horse-and-buggy medico would do to look like he was up to date. To push the whole thing off as a matter of age was easy and obvious.

Furthermore it was unquestionably true. Yet there was something about Alix when she answered that struck me as forlorn. No, I amended, my perceptions alert, not forlorn. That was not the right word. . . . The right word was. . . And when the right word came, it both astonished and dismayed me. Because what sprang to my mind was "frightened."

"Why—" I started.

"Bye, see you at lunch," Alix said, and darted out, before I had time to finish my question. I glanced at my watch. Ten to twelve. Well, it was almost quitting time.

Finally, a few days later, before she had made what I had come to think of as her "getaway," I said, "How about a walk?"

"A walk! Who wants to walk?"

"I do."

She grinned at me, and there was a touch in her grin of the insolence I had glimpsed from time to time. "How about a ride?" I could feel my anger rising, but I said evenly enough, "You know I can't ride, Alix."

"That's too bad," she said, and I had the distinct impression that I was receiving a double message: the words conveyed conventional regret. But the tone in which they were delivered made it equally plain that she was laughing at me—and intended me to know it.

Careful, I said to myself. You're being baited. While I was gathering my wits, Alix went on more or less in the same tone,

"Maybe Connie would like to walk. Why don't you ask her?"

"Because, strange as it may seem—and at the moment I'm astonished at myself for my taste—I'd rather walk with you."

She got the point, as I intended she should, and said rather sharply, "Well, Father didn't buy me Brutus just so he could sit in the stables. If I don't exercise him, he'd be impossible to handle next time I try to go out."

"What about the other horses? Don't they get impossible to handle?"

"Oh, Duncan exercises them. So do I. That's why I go out so often."

"Your father told me he doesn't want you to go riding beyond the fence into the swamp."

Her blonde brows rose. "Who says I do? There's plenty of land on this side of the fence."

"I'm not saying you do. But I am asking you, Alix. Do you go over or through the fence into the swamp beyond?"

She looked at me, an urchin grin on her face. "Of course not," she said.

Again, the double message. Her words said one thing: she was not going beyond the fence. Her tone told me she was lying and thoroughly enjoying my discomfort. I looked back at her steadily. Then, for a second, I saw something quiver across her face that I could hardly believe: a malevolent hatred.

"Alix!" I said, startled and . . . afraid.

She jumped up. "There's nothing to prevent your finding out, you know. All you have to do is get on a horse and follow me."

She ran to the door but turned back before going through. "If you can." There was a contemptuous look on her face, and an eerie laughter came out of her mouth, quite unlike the occasionally irritating but entirely normal adolescent giggle that would overtake her during lessons. Then she disappeared through the door.

For the first time since her father and cousin André had left, Alix did not return for lunch that day. The luncheon gong normally rang at one o'clock. At ten after one, Stevens came to where I was sitting, trying to read, in the drawing room, and said, "Miss Alix hasn't returned yet, has she, Miss LeBreton?"

"No, Stevens. Not to my knowledge."

He hesitated, then said, "I've waited to ring for lunch, miss. What do you think I should do? I know Mr. Darcourt does not like her to miss meals."

I thought for a minute, and then smiled at the kindly, worried butler. "Wait half an hour, then sound the gong, Stevens. I know Mr. Darcourt doesn't want her to miss meals.

But I don't think it would be according to his wishes that we let ourselves be . . . diverted from the usual schedule more than that, do you?"

"No, miss. I don't suppose so." He withdrew and thirty minutes later I heard the sonorous brass tone ring out.

I had, at the last moment, substituted the word "diverted" for the one that was in my mind: manipulated. Because I could not rid myself of the feeling that that was exactly what Alix had been doing. When I was a child my father called it "trying it on," and his response was always immediate: he spanked me, which I protested vigorously at the time, but never looked back on with the slightest resentment. The rules were clear, and if I got caught breaking them, punishment would follow. My mother, on the other hand, would raise her large dark eyes to me and ask how I could do whatever it was I had done, knowing that it would hurt my parents. And the mixture of guilt and anger that that provoked followed me for years, and, as much as her reserve and withdrawal, inhibited me from giving her the same unfettered unfearing love that I gave my father.

But, I reflected, sitting down in the dining room, Alix's rides, both before lunch and after her siesta, had been growing longer, as though she were testing the limits of my authority.

"Isn't Mrs. Conyers joining me?" I asked Stevens, as he offered me a big platter of red beans and rice from which to help myself.

"No, miss. Mrs. Conyers said she was not feeling well and would have just some broth and rice in her room."

"I hope she isn't seriously ill."

"I hope not, miss." He took the platter back to the sideboard, covered it with a silver top, and brought a salad bowl.

This was the second time the housekeeper had missed lunch, but Alix had been present on the other occasion, and answered my query with, "Oh, Connie has tummy trouble sometimes. All she needs to do is lie down for a while. She doesn't like people to make a fuss about it."

I had accepted it then, but now I wondered. On the other hand, I didn't feel I could put Stevens on the spot by asking him questions.

After lunch, however, I went up to the third floor and knocked on her door. For a few seconds I thought she hadn't heard, or was asleep, and was debating whether to knock again or not, when I heard her voice. "Yes? Who is it?"

"It's Terry, Mrs, Conyers."

Another pause. And then, "Come in."

It was like stepping into twilight, after coming from the sun-washed hall into a room where the jalousies had been pulled almost shut. For a minute or two I stood there, until my eyes became accustomed to the dusk. Then I saw I was in a room almost as big and high as the one on the second floor beneath it. It was a corner room, as mine was, and through the half-open slats of the blinds, a cross breeze cooled the air. Yet, though the room was furnished much as the other rooms were, there was something comfortless about it.

"Yes, Miss LeBreton?" Mrs. Conyers asked.

She was sitting up in a brass bed, a skimpy-looking pillow behind her back. I could not see her face, but I could make out, on the night table beside her, a tray with a cup and small bowl, evidently the soup and rice that Stevens had mentioned.

"I just came to see how you were, Mrs. Conyers. Alix . . . Alix said the other day that sometimes you had stomach trouble. I'm sorry. Is there anything I can do?" Hearing the conciliating note in my voice, I knew that I was trying to apologize to her for humiliating her in front of Alix. And I despised myself for not having either the guts or the humility to apologize outright.

"No, Miss LeBreton. There's nothing you can do."

I wondered then if I had embarked on a tendency to imagine double meanings. Because, just as I heard both denial and challenge in Alix's assertion that she'd not gone past the swamp fence, I was now equally sure that the house-keeper was answering more than a simple, civil inquiry as to her temporary indisposition.

A heavy silence lay between us. Then I said, "Alix didn't come back to lunch."

"She'll be long gone through the swamp," Mrs. Conyers said, as though stating an obvious truth we had both accepted.

I said, "Her father said that under no circumstances was she to go to the south part of the island. When I asked him how I could stop her, he seemed to think that somehow my authority would be enough. But, of course, it isn't."

I wanted for her to pick up the opening I had given her to say some form of "I told you so." And I wouldn't have blamed her if she had. But all she said was, "No, nothing can stop her."

"I asked her if she rode through the fence, or jumped it at any point. And she denied it. But. . ." My voice trailed off. It seemed so absurd to say that Alix denied and confirmed it with the same words at the same moment.

Mrs. Conyers picked up my sentence. "And she said she didn't, but all the time you knew she was lying, and knew she wanted you to know it."

I almost jumped. "Yes. That's exactly right. Has she done it to you?"

The older woman shifted against her pillow. Perhaps the dim light fell on her face, or my eyes were becoming accustomed to the dusk, but it seemed to me her face was drawn and grayish. "Often," she said, in the same flat tone. And then, "I tried to warn you."

"Yes. I know you did. I'm sorry . . . I'm sorry I spoke to you the way I did in front of Alix when I first came. It was wrong, even though my motive was to try and win her confidence, so that she would feel I was on her side."

"It's all right. I was angry at first, but I understood. You're not the first to try." She moved again, and this time I was sure about the strain and pallor of her face.

"Mrs. Conyers. Are you ill? May I get a doctor for you?"

"No, I have . . . I have a little digestive trouble from time to time. I'll be all right in a day or so."

"Alix said the doctor, Doctor McIntyre—"

I got no further. "I have no wish to see the doctor. None at all. Please do not mention anything about my . . . my indisposition to him."

"But—"

Suddenly she sat up in bed. "I do not wish to see the doctor. Is that clearly understood?"

"Certainly. I wouldn't mention it if you did not wish me to."

I hesitated for a moment, and then decided that there was nothing I could say or do, and started to leave. But as I got to the door, the question that had been working its way to the front of my mind for days sprang to my tongue.

I turned, my hand on the knob. "Mrs. Conyers, why does Alix ride into the swamp? Is it just defiance? Because her father forbade it? Isn't there enough land and paths on this side of the fence for her to have a reasonably good ride?"

The housekeeper sank back on the pillow, and her face half turned away from me. "Oh, yes. There's more than enough room. There are miles of paths through the forest.

And it's not even just to defy her father, although I used to think that." She stopped.

"Then what is it?" I tried not to sound too impatient.

"It's because," she started to say, her mind apparently far away. Then she sat up again, her eyes on the window, as though she could see out of the half-open slats. And even across the room I could feel the tension that went through her. Sharply her head turned in my direction. "I'm sure I have no idea. She's always been a hysterical, rebellious girl. Now, if you don't mind, Miss LeBreton, I would like to get some sleep."

"But—"

"At once, if you please."

Ordinarily the snap in her voice would have made my hackles rise. But my curiosity was far stronger than my resentment, and, again, I had a feeling that I was being given a double message, only, unlike the two previous occasions, not because the speaker was aware of doing so.

"As you wish," I said agreeably, and left. Then I hurried down the hall to the next bedroom which faced in the same direction as Mrs. Conyers'. Like the housekeeper's, this was furnished with a brass bedstead, a bureau, a chair, a night table and an old fashioned wardrobe, but, unlike the room next door, had a more cheerful quality. I didn't, however, wait to analyze why I felt this. As rapidly as I could I went to the front window and peered out. A view of the lawn, the carriage sweep and drive lay in front of me. But there was no human being in sight. And yet I was as certain as I could be, without having seen for myself what caused the change in the housekeeper, that she had seen something through the window that had frightened her into breaking off our conversation.

Walking over, I sat on the bed and half lay against the head, the brass cutting into my back. The beds were old-fashioned and high, and it was possible to see part of the drive and lawn and the trees to the north end of the island, but not the carriage sweep in front of the house. But what if the blinds were closed?

Getting off the bed again, I went over to the window and opened it. The blinds were flat against the wall of the house and it took a little tugging and a lot of squeaking of rusty hinges to pull them half shut, and more tugging to give them a half slant. As soon as I did, the room plunged into semi-dusk. Then I got back on the bed. And my curiosity rose to fever point. Because while I could see, in the inch or so of space between two folding louvers of the blind, a strip of drive ending in what really amounted to a green smudge of trees, I realized I would have to have the eyes of a hunting falcon to recognize someone at that distance—or I would have to know him or her very well indeed.

What had frightened her? Or rather, who?

After pushing the blinds open again, I closed the window and left that floor. Once on the second story, I hesitated. Susie had become used to having me to herself for an hour or so after lunch, since that was the time Alix invariably either rested or rode. But before I went to my room, I turned down the opposite hall and went and knocked on the door I knew to be Alix's.

There was no answer. I knocked again. When I heard nothing, I turned the knob. The door was locked.

"Well, Miss LeBreton, where is your charge?"

I swung around, not believing what I heard. There, an unpleasant and sardonic smile on his face, stood Tristram Darcourt.

For a minute I stared at him stupidly. Then I said, "You're back!"

"Obviously. Where is Alix?"

There was, in his voice, that note that so irked me, as though, I thought, he expected me to cower in front of him. Naturally, it had the opposite effect. I stiffened and decided he might as well know the truth now as later.

"She's gone out riding, Mr. Darcourt, and whether she has gone through or over the fence into the southern part of the island, I don't know. I have asked her, and told her your instructions, but—" I stopped, thinking there was no point in invoking more of his wrath against her than was unavoidable.

"But you still don't know whether she has."

There seemed no way around the bald truth. "No."

"As a companion, you leave something to be desired, Miss LeBreton. Why, in the name of everything, didn't you go riding with her?"

"Because I don't ride. There are millions of people, Mr. Darcourt, who do not have horses and private stables available to them for the purposes of the aristocratic pursuit of riding. I am one of them."

I hadn't meant to be quite so vehement—or perhaps impu-

138

dent would have been a better word—but it had come out that way, and I was not sorry.

To my astonishment, he laughed.

"You do have a chip on your shoulder, don't you? All right. But why didn't you tell me that when I first talked to you about her riding? It would have saved both of us a lot of trouble."

"I don't know. Maybe I didn't think of it. Or want to admit it." And then I was surprised that I said that.

He smiled and said in a different voice, "Well, you should learn. It's not that mysterious or difficult."

"Learn to ride? I thought that was the kind of thing you learned at six, or not at all."

"Afraid, Miss LeBreton?"

I was about to reply in the best push-button fashion. Of course not, when I decided to tell the truth. "Yes. A little. They all look so large."

"Yes, but they're not too bright. Remember that and you won't be nervous."

"I thought people who rode adored horses. How can you say they're not too bright?"

"Because it's true. Besides, do you like people only according to their IQ?"

"No. I've known some extremely bright people who were impossible."

"Yes. So've I."

Without my thinking about it, I had been walking with him down the hall and now came to the second-floor landing. "I'm sorry about Alix," I said. "She's been strange." And then marveled at myself again. One hour before I would have sworn I would never have made such an admission to her father, since I looked on him as the harsh and repressive enemy.

Darcourt had started down the curved stairway, but turned, looking at me, his eyes on a level with mine, since he was standing two shallow steps lower. "What do you mean, strange?"

In the shadows of the hall before, his face had been partly hidden. Now in the strong light from the hall windows, it looked as I had remembered it, austere and hard. And yet, perhaps, hard was not the right word. Then he frowned, and I realized I had been staring. I said quickly, "I mean that Alix changes so rapidly. When you first left—" And suddenly, as I said that, I remembered the scene I had witnessed,

139

Darcourt thrusting her from the jeep, and the bruises I had seen later on her arm. How could I have thought anything about this man could be kind?

"What are you thinking about, Miss LeBreton?"

His question caught me off balance. "Why . . . why do you ask?"

"Because you are, or would be, a very poor poker player. You were about to tell me something about my daughter, and then your expression changed. If you had suddenly discovered I was the emperor Nero, your face could not have shown more recoil."

"*For the love of God, Sally,*" my father had once said. "*Never play poker. You'd lose your shirt.*"

Remembering, I laughed. "Yes, that's what my father said."

"The father who died when you were three, Miss Le-Breton? Or was that something your mother quoted to you afterwards, to keep his memory green, so to speak, as you mentioned once before. Since you could hardly have been playing poker when you were three, he must have had second sight."

We stood there, silent, in some backed-up moment of time. Vaguely I wondered if his more human approach of the past few minutes had been deliberate, so that I would lose my caution and trip myself, as I just did.

"Well?" he said. And then, after another silence, added, "Before you start concocting one of your elaborate lies, let me tell you that the reason—one of the reasons—I have come back is because I have been in New Orleans and southern Louisiana—among other places. And I have been visiting the LeBreton's. They were all very fond of and chatty about their cousin Thérèse, now teaching some French children in the Auvergne. I even managed to see a photograph of her. You're both dark and French-looking, but there the resemblance stops. However, one of the photographs the proud relatives showed me was a college group picture. And my diligence and tact were rewarded, because there you were, among the other damsels. It was, I believe, Miss Julie Le-Breton who remembered your name. So, Miss Wainright, shall we go down and discuss why you are here under a false name, or would you rather talk about it to the police, who are waiting for you in St. Damien's?"

(8)

AS I followed Darcourt down the stairs, I reflected I knew exactly how a bird felt while being mesmerized by a snake. I could no more have not followed him than the bird could fly away.

But, when we were about two-thirds down, I heard Susie bark, and then came that strange high whine that had sounded when she was facing the scorpion. The captive spell holding me snapped.

"Susie!" I cried, and turning, went racing back up the stairs, forgetting my still sore ankle. I heard Darcourt's voice, angry, behind me, but I ignored it. Pushing open my door I went in. And the scene replayed itself—only this time with a difference. It was not a scorpion, but a small red and black snake, around which Susie was performing a sort of war dance. I knew nothing about snakes, any more than I did about scorpions, nor did I know whether this particular snake was poisonous. But any creature, if frightened, would attack, and my approach might just be the *coup de grâce*. I stopped, wondering how I could distract it.

"Stay where you are," Darcourt's voice sounded right behind me. "Don't move." And a hand came down on my shoulder. The next thing I knew something whizzed past me, striking the snake on the head and crashing to the floor. The snake lay still. Pushing me out of the way, Darcourt went over, reached out for Susie and handed her to me, and then, picking up the snake, just behind its head, took it to the window and threw it out.

My tongue at last seemed able to move. "Was it poisonous?"

"Yes. It was a coral snake."

"And do snakes come up the walls and the pipes?"

He frowned and said slowly, "I suppose they can get up, though not by climbing walls. But I've never known it to happen here."

My fright had now given way to anger. "Well, someone seems eager for me to have a wildlife sanctuary right here in my bedroom. I don't like either snakes or scorpions. And I like them even less when they're put here while Susie's alone."

Darcourt, who had come back across the room, picked up the bookend he had thrown and returned it to the shelves beside the door. Then he stopped in front of me. "I take it you found a scorpion up here."

"Yes. I did. All six inches of it. And there would have been two, if one hadn't grown bored and killed and partly eaten the other. I found the remains of the second corpse in the shoe box that they were obviously conveyed in. Somebody either has a great sense of humor or is trying to get rid of me."

Darcourt's mouth settled in the grim line I had come to know well. "The latter could be achieved in more direct ways than that."

I should have been frightened. As a matter of fact, I was. But he aroused my basic pugnacity. "Are you threatening me, Mr. Darcourt?"

"No. I am telling you. I came back to discharge you and get you off the island within an hour."

"Good! You will have my full cooperation. In fact, I don't think it will take me fifteen minutes to pack."

Putting Susie down, I went to the wardrobe and yanked out my suitcase.

"Just a minute, Miss Wainright. There are one or two questions."

I turned around. "Yes. I have one or two myself."

"We'll discuss them downstairs. But first, you spoke of a box, a shoe box. Do you still have it?"

As a matter of fact I had. After wrapping it up and putting it in the wastebasket, something had made me take it out again, wrap it in yet another two or three layers of newspaper (the thought of the smeared inside made my stomach queasy) and shove it on the top shelf of the linen closet in the bathroom.

"Yes," I said, and went into the bathroom to get it.

After looking around, and then running my hand over the shelf I came back out. "It's gone. Its—"

I went over to the bed, lifted the ruffle and looked underneath, pushed by an eerie conviction. Yes, it was there, resting in its top as it had been before. Pulling it out, I got up and handed it to Darcourt. "As I said, someone has a raging sense of humor. Same box. Same place. The only change was a snake not a scorpion."

He looked inside the box. There could be no mistake. The smears were still there.

He stood there, staring at the box, for a few minutes. Then he looked up at me and said, "Do you have any idea who could be doing this, or why?"

"No, Mr. Darcourt. I do not. And it says a great deal for the atmosphere around here, and the people themselves, that I can easily suspect anyone—except, perhaps, for Stevens. Somehow I don't see him either being spiteful enough, or hostile enough to do something like this."

"Hostile, yes. But why spiteful?"

"Wouldn't you call it spiteful to kill a dog—an innocent and quite inoffensive small dog, however much you, personally, may dislike her, to get at the owner?"

"It seems a minor point to get involved with now, Miss Wainwright, but why do you say I personally dislike your dog? If I did, all I would have to do was to hesitate a few seconds. The coral snake would have dispatched her for me."

Since I had said that only because I was angry, I didn't have a very good answer. Particularly, I thought with a guilty pang, since he had saved her life. "True," I said. "I'm sorry. I shouldn't have said that."

Susie, whose timing was sometimes uncanny, stopped sniffing at the suitcase, trotted over to Darcourt, wagged her tail, and sat down in front of his feet. I couldn't help it. I laughed.

With his eyes back on the box, he bent and rubbed Susie between her ears.

"Not only do I apologize," I said, deciding I had to swallow the whole humiliating bite (it was maddening to be indebted to him), "I thank you for saving Susie's life. She . . . I'm very fond of her."

He straightened. "You don't say," he commented ironic-

143

ally. "This is undoubtedly evidence of softening of the brain on my part, because history is full of villains who were fond of their dogs, but I find your affection for Susie the most powerful argument against believing the worst of you. However, you owe me some explanations, and I intend to get them. Now. So let's go down to the library where we can talk. I'll take this box."

And with no more ado, he left the room. There was nothing I could do but follow, leaving the door open so Susie could go with me. "If you don't mind," I said, as I trailed after him down the stairs, "I'm going to bring Susie with me. I don't wish to risk coming back and finding her inside a boa constrictor."

He didn't reply, and I felt better, having (at least for the moment) the last word. In silence we went down to the ground floor and back to the big book-lined room where I had first talked to him.

"Please shut the door behind you," he said, limping over to the desk. He waited behind it while I closed the heavy paneled door after Susie. "And sit down." He indicated the chair in front of the desk and sat down himself.

"Now," he said. "I know your name. But I want to know who you are and why you're here under someone else's name and what you came to find out. And try not to lie to me."

I could feel the blood rush into my cheeks when he said that. It was true my father had counseled me to tell a thumping lie if I found I had to tell one at all. But he did not like lies, and neither did I. "They're cowardly things, lies are, Sally. And are usually told either to get out of something or to please somebody—and they're both no good."

"No," Darcourt remarked calmly, watching my face. "You don't like that, do you?"

"No. I don't."

"Yet you've asked for it. Because when you take someone else's name and assume a false identity, the whole thing is a lie. And that's what you've done. Why?"

I leaned forward in my chair. "Why did you jilt my mother?"

I flung the bald words at him, and then waited with pleasure to see his astonishment. I was therefore stunned and disappointed when he showed none at all.

"I didn't. She jilted me."

I sprang up. "That's a lie."

"No, it is not. I don't lie. Unlike you. I don't know what

144

she told you or why. But it was she who wrote to me breaking our engagement, and, after learning your real identity, and that of your parents, I had the forethought to get out her letters." Taking a key from his pocket he unlocked the middle drawer of his desk and took out a thin package of letters. I stared as though hypnotized at the familiar handwriting. "Recognize it?" he asked, extracting the top letter from under the rubber band and handing it to me.

I had never been away from home so Mother had never written to me. But I had seen that writing on countless grocery lists, and I did have, locked away in a trunk now in storage, letters she had written to my father and which he had saved. For all that she was brought up in the United States, it was a very un-American hand she had been taught by the French nuns who ran the little school she attended.

Taking the letter out of the envelope I unfolded the single page and read:

"My dear Tristram:

I know now that you know about my sister, and I have been told that you wish to be released from our engagement, but feel it dishonorable to break it yourself. So, I will release you. In return I ask only that you do not write or telephone or get in touch with me in any way. I am going away immediately, and I do not wish ever to hear from you again."

It was signed, Giselle La Vaux.

Odd, I thought. I should feel more, reading this letter written when my mother was eighteen to the man she loved and was, for his sake, renouncing. But I felt nothing except a burning curiosity and a vague indignation, as though, in some way, I had been misled.

"I didn't know Mother had a sister," I said. "And my father said she didn't when she referred to someone named 'Sis' when she was ill. But," I eyed him, "according to this she was simply releasing you from an engagement you didn't want, anyway."

"That was her explanation. It was not true. That letter, sent, as you can see, by surface mail, reached me when I was halfway across the world in the Philippines with the navy. By the time I got home, six months later, she was married to your father. I tried to see her, but for my pains I received this letter from your father." And he threw another letter from the drawer over to me.

Then I could feel the tears in my eyes. Unlike my mother's beautiful, convent-trained script, my father's was an aggressive scrawl, slanting every which way, and with the tall letters sometimes meeting in the middle of a word. But it was so characteristically his that I almost felt I could hear his voice. And despite my dislike of and prejudice against Tristram Darcourt, I could see why anyone would consider such a letter final. It was my father at his most Irish and most explosive.

"*Dear Darcourt:*

If you ever bother my wife again, or try to see her, I will have you arrested for molestation. And it will give me a great deal of pleasure to beat you up. Haven't you done enough harm to her already?

Yours, etc.,
Patrick James Wainwright"

It was so like my father, particularly the offer to beat up Darcourt, and the "Yours, etc.," which he had brought with him from northern Ireland, that it was almost as though he were standing beside me and I could hear his voice with the rough Scotch-Irish burr that came from around the Mourne Mountains. It was not till I became aware of Darcourt standing beside me, holding out his handkerchief, that I felt the tears wetting my cheeks.

"Who are you crying for?" Darcourt said, handing me the big square of linen, which I took without thinking. "Your father or your mother?"

"My father. The letter is so like him. Well, Mother's is, too, I suppose. Certainly her handwriting. But—"

"It is your father you mourn?"

I nodded. Then blew my nose. "And something so strange has happened to me. He died when I was fifteen, but until I came here he never *felt* dead. Only now he does."

"Perhaps you never let him go until now."

"I suppose not. Only I don't see why it should strike me here."

"No. Neither do I. Especially as you were supposed to be busy thinking about and looking after my daughter." Darcourt had limped back behind his desk and was sitting down.

"I did look after your daughter, as well as I could—which is when she would let me. But, in view of the brutality you used towards her when she tried to stop your leaving—I saw it from the upstairs balcony—and the bruises on her arms which you gave her, I can see why she doesn't easily trust people."

Darcourt was staring at me. "Then you should also have

146

seen that if I had not pushed her away she would have been dragged along by the jeep."

"I don't suppose you could have waited until she was able to accept your leaving?"

"No. I could not. I was late as it was."

"Business first at all times."

"Since you don't know what business I was engaged in, nor why it was urgent, I consider that remark impudent and presumptuous. And I would like to remind you that it is not I who have lied to you, nor come to your home with a false identity. You have injured me, not I you."

"I find it difficult to believe that anyone could injure someone as rich and powerful as you are, Mr. Darcourt."

"That comment shows your impoverishment, not my wealth." He stared at me for a moment in silence. Then he said, "For someone as imbued with radical and egalitarian notions as you, Miss Wainwright, you give an amazing importance to money. Does that mean that you wouldn't resent someone entering your home under false pretenses, even if your home were a one-room apartment? Do people of modest means have less sense of privacy, less dislike of being deceived?"

I hadn't thought of the matter that way, and it caught me (for the moment) without an answer.

"Conversely," he continued implacably "is money so all conquering that it can safeguard the owner against loss or grief?"

Without thinking I quoted, "If you prick us, do we not bleed? If you tickle us, do we not laugh?"

His mouth twisted in a half smile. "Precisely."

I pulled myself together. "Yes. That's all very well. However . . . someone once said that money could not buy happiness, but it could make one very comfortable while one was being unhappy."

"And that gives you the right to invade my home?"

He had, I noted irritably, the knack of being on the right side of an argument. And the fact that I'd told him only half my reason for being here did not make my path easier. Nevertheless, I was willing for him to chastise me for being in his house under a false name if it would keep him away from the other reason for my presence.

"I can understand your annoyance," I said, hoping to steer him away from the danger area.

Darcourt was staring at me, his eyes narrowed. "So, you

came here to find out why, as you put it, I abandoned your mother?"

"Yes. She was never happy. Not really. She was always withdrawn. And my father told me that you had thrown her over to marry somebody rich."

"Your father, who was as pigheaded an Irishman as ever crossed the Atlantic, believed what he wanted to believe, which is what your mother told him."

"Why should she lie?"

"I'm not saying she did. But someone did, somewhere. She says in her letter that I had discovered her sister's secret. I hadn't. I didn't even know she had a sister. But, unless she made the whole thing up and invented a sister for herself, someone told her something."

"But why?" I said, baffled. "And why should she hide a sister?"

"Why indeed! Perhaps there was some skeleton in the closet."

"If so, you can't make me believe, Mr. Darcourt, if you were as upset at the broken engagement as you imply, that you didn't make an effort to find out."

"Oh, I made an effort all right. I went down and questioned every LeVaux in the bayou country. And they talked— My God! How those Cajuns talked, and half the time in a patois I could barely understand, which, I became convinced, they deliberately assumed when I was around. I did, finally, extract the information that there had been a sister. But she had been, as the saying goes, put away. And the entire family, to the ultimate cousin, considered it a disgrace, never to be mentioned."

"You mean to tell me that because Mother had a sister who was mentally ill she considered this so shameful that she would not only break an engagement, assuming that you would want out the moment you heard of it, but that she wouldn't even mention it to her husband and daughter?"

"Have you ever visited your relations in southeastern Louisiana, Miss Wainwright?"

"Yes. I went there with Terry while we were at college."

"And did you find them forthcoming about your mother's sister?"

I thought back. "Obviously not. Since I didn't know she existed."

"Well, did you find them forthcoming about anything intimately to do with the family?"

I thought for a while. "No. But I just put that down to my being such a Yankee."

His eyes were on me, watchfully. "Well, in close-knit somewhat provincial communities a quarter of a century ago, mental illness was viewed as consumption was among the Victorians. If somebody had it, nobody mentioned it."

"All right," I said after a minute. "I can see that. But I find it hard to swallow that she didn't tell my father."

"Perhaps she did. But he didn't pass it on to you."

"That's nonsense. Mother died when I was twelve, and I lived with my father for three years after that. He would have told me."

"Would he? Feeling as he did about your mother?"

It was true, I thought. My father, who was much older than Mother, looked upon her as some kind of cross between a saint and a rare exotic treasure, too easily broken to be handled except with extreme and loving care. And that feeling did not stop with her death. I adored him. And I knew he adored me. But there were times when I felt impatient at his continuing worship of a woman who had died. It was almost as though he had built a shrine for her in the house and made me chief vestal virgin. I had once, feeling somewhat overlooked and underappreciated, said just that to him, and it was the only time he was so deeply angry that he didn't speak to me for nearly a week. And I never made that kind of mistake again.

"Would he?" Darcourt asked again.

"Perhaps not. I don't know. I'm not so sure."

"But it doesn't solve the mystery, does it? We are still left with whoever it was who told her that I had been informed of her sister, your aunt, in the mental home, and there is the further obvious fact that she was also told that because of it I didn't want to marry her."

"Would you have wanted to back off? If you had known?"

"Who knows? I doubt it. I was young and much in love. But thinking I would care is just what a conservative Louisiana family would believe, because of the possible effect on any children."

"And—for the same reason—you wouldn't have cared?" I countered quickly. It was just the kind of thing a Darcourt would care about, I was convinced. And I wasn't going to let him off the hook.

"I told you. I don't know what I would have thought or decided to do—then."

"You mean when you were young and in love? In contrast to now, when you put business first, as with Alix?"

"You don't let up, do you? You know, you have your own fascination. I have not only told you, I have produced evidence to the fact, that I didn't jilt your mother. She jilted me. I tell you that I pushed Alix away from the car to keep her from being hurt. I'll further tell you now that most of those bruises you saw on her arm I gave her when I was trying to keep her from jumping off the balcony outside her room, and before you get in a state about that, she's tried it before when she wanted to have her way. And, since both Mrs. Conyers and Stevens were in the room when this happened, they'll affirm this. But you still won't believe it. You are the living, breathing embodiment of the saying, 'Don't bother me with the facts. I've already made up my mind.' The main thing I am curious about is why? Is it political? Or is it, as I suspect, just that you are your father's daughter? The more I think about it, the more I think that's it. Despite the fact that you have your mother's face."

The trouble was, everything he said was true. The moment he said it, I realized I had worked from my violent prejudice against him to the facts, instead of the other way around. Was it indeed because my father had said he was a capital "B" bastard?—a title otherwise reserved for the Irish constabulary.

He was watching me as I struggled with this thought. Then he said, "It was that, you know, your resemblance to your mother, that sent me searching down in Louisiana. That was one of the reasons I didn't send you packing immediately, because it was fairly obvious that you were just about as unsuitable a companion as I could have found for Alix. But I was nagged by the question of why your face should have come circling back into my life. Especially," he finished drily, "since every time you opened your mouth you sounded like your obstreperous father."

"I—" I started. Then stopped, caught by what he said. "You mean, you met my father?"

"Of course. You don't suppose I'd let a letter like that just stand, do you?"

"And did he beat you up?"

For the first time in a few minutes he smiled. "It was a draw."

"He never told me," I said slowly.

"I have a feeling there are quite a few things he never told you."

"What do you mean by that?"

He got up. "Since you are hardly candid with me—oh, yes, don't bother to deny it; there's something still you haven't told me—I don't see why I should explain myself further to you. By the way, I've changed my mind. I'm not going to discharge you. I'm going to teach you how to ride. I think it will serve my purposes better if I keep you under my eye and enable you to do what I hired you for—stay with Alix. Go and put on some suitable clothes. If you don't have any, I'm sure Mrs. Conyers can tell you where to find some."

The arrogance of it took my breath away. "Just like that, you're going to teach me to ride? Not, may I? No nonsense about would you like to learn?"

He leaned forward over the desk. "Shall we get something straight? You will go along with what I ask or the St. Damien police will meet the boat when it takes you there. And I'm sure I don't have to point out to you that they will do exactly what I ask them to do, including holding you indefinitely for questioning as to why you entered my house under false pretenses, and for heaven knows what planned felony."

I stared at him, my mind racing. If I could just get word to Brian Colby, he could raise so much unpleasant publicity for Darcourt that his tame police would be glad to let me go. I wished now, ardently, that I had managed to get word to him before. Even so, if enough time elapsed with no message, he would make it his business to find out what had happened to me. But in the meantime I could be rotting in jail. And, while doing, for the moment, what the autocrat in front of me had ordered might put my teeth on edge, it would at least give me time to reach Brian, and to see what I could do to help Alix.

"All right," I said. "I'll go put on some jeans."

"That's better. I'll wait for you here."

The horse Darcourt chose for me looked like a house, for all that it was not quite as big as his own huge black.

"Don't you have something smaller?" I asked, trying to sound casual.

"Yes. But Rusty's the best-natured and has the smoothest ride. Now take the reins and get up on the mounting block."

"I should tell you," I said a minute or so later, sitting precariously in the saddle, "that I have no head for heights."

"Then start to develop it."

Twenty minutes later we were walking our horses down one of the bridle paths that lay behind the house. Much to my amazement, I found I was enjoying myself. Even more surprising was my lack of fear. Sometime within the first five minutes it had vanished.

I had just decided that it was all a piece of cake when Darcourt, who had been watching me in silence, said, "Now we're going to trot. Listen to me while I explain how you rise and fall to the jogging of the horse. It's simply a knack. Once you get it, you won't find it hard."

For the first few minutes after we started trotting I thought my spine would disassemble and my teeth fall out. Then, as Darcourt said, "With every *other* jog, rise. Hold with your thighs and knees," I began to see what he meant.

After a while he commented, "I can't see how you missed learning to ride. You like animals. You have good coordination. You catch on fast. And your father's an Irishman."

As a matter of fact, now that I was actually sitting on a horse and enjoying myself hugely, neither could I. Nevertheless, I repeated something I'd heard my father say many a time. "Horses are for gentry. We're not gentry."

"Ah, yes. I recognize the touch. What was he training you for? The IRA?"

"As a matter of fact—"

Darcourt's head turned. "Yes."

I hesitated. "Well, I suppose now that he's dead it can't matter. But he was a member of the IRA. That's why he left—one jump ahead of the police."

"Naturally."

"Naturally what? That he was a member of the IRA or that he was being pursued by the police?"

"Both."

To my surprise I laughed. "Yes. 'Name y'r givernment and I'm agin' it.' That was my father."

I thought I saw half a smile on Darcourt's profile. But all he said was, "Hold on. We're going to canter. Press your heels into the horse's side—gently."

At first I thought I was going to come off. But then it was like flying, only better than flying. A great sense of exhilaration filled me as we cantered along the azalea-lined path with the swaying moss above us. Time seemed to stop.

After a while I heard Darcourt's voice.

"All right. Pull in the rein. Firmly, but not too hard."

The horse slowed to a trot, and then a walk.

"That was marvelous," I said, forgetting my animosity. "You're right. I wish I had learned long ago."

He smiled at me. "With such a handsome admission, let me say that I have never seen anyone with more aptitude. You'll be very good. Now we'll go back, or you won't be able to sit down for a week."

It was about fifteen minutes later, after we had broken again into a trot, that it happened. The silence of the forest was shattered by the sound of a shot, and something whizzed past my head, between Darcourt and me. With a loud neigh, Rusty rose, and it was though a giant force was pitching me backwards.

"Grip with your knees," Darcourt yelled.

I suppose I must have obeyed, because I remember being surprised that I didn't come off. Barely, it felt, pausing to touch the ground, Rusty came down and took off. And I knew now that there was a world of difference between an easy canter and a flat-out gallop, which is what Rusty was doing.

I had no idea of what to do, nor any hope of staying on. I pulled on the reins with all my strength, but it was like trying to stop a bulldozer with a piece of string. My father's phrase about so and so getting the bit between his teeth now had graphic meaning. Instead of being back behind Rusty's teeth, where the slightest touch would be felt on the soft corners of his mouth, the metal bit was now gripped between his powerful teeth and my tugging had no effect whatsoever. I was not enjoying myself at all, yet the panic that I had expected did not come. I knew what the dangers were. Anyone who had read as much as I—let alone using common sense—could foresee those: roots and holes that a heedless, galloping horse would not see; overhead branches or other, harder obstructions that a horse could pass under but would knock out the rider or even slice off the top of his head. I could hear Darcourt's horse thundering behind me. But Rusty, following his own bent, had abandoned the wider path early on, and was now hurtling down a much narrower one, with undergrowth on either side, so that the bigger horse behind me could not overtake him.

Time had ceased to have any meaning at all, so I don't know how much longer it was till I saw, far ahead, a glint of silver. My mind had barely taken in that it was the fence when I saw something far more worrying coming nearer by the second—a low thick branch as wide as the trunk of most trees. "God save me," I thought, and gave a frantic, futile pull on the rein. The branch was so low that even lying flat on the horse would not help me. I would have to get off. It was when I started to pull my feet from the stirrups that I found my right foot was caught, and the fear—rather than jus the thought—that I would be killed became real. I tugged at my right foot, but something—the shoelace—had tangled with the stirrup. As I pulled at it frantically, I became aware that where the bushes and trees had receded a few feet to the right the path had widened, and Darcourt's horse, Sebastian, was drawing up beside me.

"Get your leg out."

"I can't. It's stuck."

We were within yards of the branch. Something heavy thumped behind my back. Arms came around and took the reins, and a mighty battle ensued between the powerful horse and the almost equally powerful man, with me in between. I wouldn't have believed it possible, but Darcourt wrestled Rusty to a canter and finally to a stop only a yard or two from the branch. The horse's head hung down. I became aware of his sweat and foam-soaked hide and heaving flanks. And there was something else, very strange: far in the distance, the sound of horse's hooves, galloping. After a moment they faded away.

Darcourt had transferred the reins to his right hand. His left arm was still around me. The forest was still around us. I felt weak, purged, curiously at peace, aware of the hardness of the muscles of his arm and chest and waist.

Then Darcourt said in an odd voice, "Can you get your left foot out of the stirrup?"

"Yes," I said, and did so. And felt his own foot go in.

Using the stirrup, he dismounted. Then, still holding the reins, he went around Rusty's head to the other side and disentangled my sneaker's lace from the stirrup's join. "Now get off. Just bring your left leg over and slide down."

There was no mounting block so it was a slight drop. It was not until my feet were on the ground that the reaction set in. I started to shake.

"Are you all right?" he asked.

I tried to forget about my knees and unclenched my teeth. "Yes."

"Liar," he said. But not in the least in the way he'd said it before. Curious, I thought, glancing briefly at him. The crooked shoulder hadn't shown when he was in the saddle.

Not that it was obvious. Nor, of course, did the fact that one leg was shorter. I looked up at his face to find it looking down at me.

"You're shaking," he said.

"Yes." My teeth were inclined to chatter, making it difficult to talk. "I'll be all right," I managed to say.

"You're a brave girl. You did very well."

It must have been the aftermath. It could not, I told myself sternly, have been the tone in his voice: kind, warm—so different from what I'd heard before. Whatever the cause, those traitorous tears started down my face.

"I'm all right," I said sternly as I could, almost willing them back up in my eyes.

For some reason I found it necessary to say it again. Only this time the words were muffled against his chest. Those strong arms were back around me. Then one of them removed itself. A hand came under my chin and forced my face up. To my shock, I found myself standing on tiptoe to meet his kiss. My arms went around his neck. It was like drifting downstream between green banks through the gates of heaven.

Then I remembered who he was and who I was and sprang back.

"How dare you?" I said, hating the fact that it came out a squeak. "You took advantage of me when I . . . I . . ."

He slid the reins through his hands. "I took advantage of one of the rare times you weren't spitting insults. Your mother forgot to give me a good-bye kiss. Now I consider I've collected it. Get back on your horse."

I didn't have to drum up the rage I now felt. "That was a cheap thing for you to do."

"Yes, wasn't it? But, in view of my character, entirely in keeping, don't you think? I told you to get back on."

"Thank you. I've had enough of your aristocratic pursuits for one afternoon. The amusements of the upper classes are a little too rich for my blood."

"Would you rather I'd lift you on?"

"No. But you may have noticed there's no mounting block."

He pointed. "What's the matter with that stump? Lead Rusty over there, turn him around and get on."

"What if he starts to run away again?"

"I suggest you don't let him. Or you'll be killed. The branches get lower and lower on this path."

Well aware that Rusty was even more worn out than I, I gathered the reins with as much dignity as I could muster and led him over to a stump and got on. When I collected myself on top, I saw that Darcourt was up on his big black again.

"After you," he said.

We walked in single file for a while. I finally said, "That was a shot, wasn't it?"

"Yes."

"Was it for you, or me?"

"I have no idea. Do you?"

"No, but if you count it for me, that makes the third try. After the scorpion and the snake."

"You would seem to be unpopular, Miss Wainwright."

"Considering it is your house and your land, you don't seem unduly upset at the idea of one of your guests, or perhaps I should say, employees, having her life threatened."

"I'm not. Mostly because I don't think your life is in the least danger. If any of those attempts on your life, as you've put it, had been serious, at least one of them would have succeeded. I don't want to arouse your protective rhetoric over Susie, but the scorpion and the snake were both put in your room when you weren't there. Quite apart from the fact that even if the scorpion had stung you, you would have survived, anyone who wanted to attack you would have arranged to have the wildlife loosed at night, when you were in the room."

"What about that shot?"

"It was a good two feet from both of us. Most people around here are born with a gun in their hands. If they'd wanted to hit either of us, they would have."

There was no question but that his calm—if not downright insensitivity—was having its effect, but I resisted acknowledging it. "I'm so glad you can take the thought of my death or injury so philosophically."

"I've told you I think the chances of that are small, if they exist at all. But even granted they might, my attiude shows more charity than the pleasure I am certain you would feel if all this were directed at me."

He had a point, but I decided not to give him the satisfaction of hearing me admit it. Instead, I considered it was high time and more for me to give myself a refresher course in everything my father had ever said on the subject of the rich, the elite and aristocratic, all three of which perfectly described Darcourt.

But as I ran some of the well-remembered phrases through my mind, I found, to my dismay, that though the words were there, the sound of his voice had grown dim. And his fiery statements, instead of being Ultimate Truth, became the provocative exaggerations of a fiesty, lovable man who enjoyed nothing more than a good fight.

But where did that leave me? I wondered, feeling a little lost, as though the compass I had always depended on had broken.

"What's the matter?" Darcourt asked abruptly, and, as we trotted out of the narrow path onto the wider one, drew up beside me.

"Nothing."

Reaching out, he took my arm. "Look at me."

A little reluctantly, I did. "You look," he said, with devastating perception, "as though someone had just proved to you that black was white and down was up."

I couldn't help it. I laughed. "That's a fair description." After a minute I said, "I was just thinking about some of the things my father used to say. He disapproved of everything you are and represent."

"Well, given where he came from and the history of his country, I don't blame him. And when you add to that—"

"That Mother was in love with you, and . . . But why did he think you jilted her instead of the other way around?"

"Because he believed it to be true. I told you, there's someone else moving around in this."

"What makes you so sure?"

"Well, what other explanation would you suggest for her certainty that I wished to break the engagement?"

"The fact that you did, and she knew it, though you never actually said so."

Darcourt reached out and stopped my horse and pulled up his own. "Now let's get this straight. Why should I all of a sudden want to get out of an engagement that I had been eager to get into?"

"I've always thought . . ." And then my voice trailed off. There was no way I could say that tactfully.

He looked grim. "Yes. Go on. Don't spare my feelings."

"All right. I've always thought it was because Mother had neither family nor money. The woman you married had both."

"The woman I married was fifteen years old when I knew your mother. And while Nicole's family certainly had money —her father cleaned up during World War Two in shipbuilding and off shore oil—she was no more aristocratic than your mother. In fact . . . but of course you know that."

"Know what?"

"That Nicole Charpentier and Giselle LeVaux were cousins. Nicole, of course, was brought up in New Orleans, in the Garden District, although born down in that section of Cajun territory where your mother came from. Giselle— your mother—was visiting there when I first met her."

I stared at Darcourt unbelievingly. "Your wife and my mother cousins?"

"Surprise, surprise," he said sardonically. "Yet it shouldn't be. All those Cajun families are related somewhere." And then, "W'd better get back." He touched his horse with his heels, I followed suit and we moved off.

He glanced at me. "Other than the rapacity and general obnoxiousness you feel are my natural attributes, was there any other reason you thought I had for wishing to break the engagement?"

I hesitated. "No."

"You don't sound very certain."

"What are you fishing for?"

"As I said before, there is more in your coming here than you have told me. I'm not sure how much more."

Unbelievably, I opened my mouth to tell him that Brian Colby and my research on his business dealings were the only other thing, but, fortunately, stopped before I put my foot in that far.

"Yes?" he said.

I shrugged.

We rode in silence for a while. My mind went back to the shot. "Who do you suppose shot at us?" I asked. "Or do you care?"

"Strange as it may seem I do. I would prefer to think it was not Alix."

I turned my head. "Alix?"

"I thought you suspected everyone. Is she to be spared?"

"Well . . . I can see her putting the scorpion and the snake into my room. But shooting—"

"If she *is* responsible, have you any ideas why?"

I looked at the big man riding beside me. "Wouldn't you

be more liable to know that, Mr. Darcourt? After all, she is your daughter."

"She is indeed. And yes, I do know her."

"Do you think she's the one who is trying to get rid of me?"

"I think if she had a good enough motive, yes. What I am not sure about is the motive—what she hopes to gain by driving you away."

"Perhaps, Mr. Darcourt, freedom."

"Ah, yes. Freedom." He turned his head. "That's the commodity you prize above all else, isn't it?"

I met his gaze, eyeball to eyeball. "A lot of people do. More every year."

"And you feel that freedom is worth any price?"

"Don't you? Or should I ask? After all, have you ever known anything else, Mr. Darcourt, given your wealth and power?"

I stopped short at the expression on his face, which was intimidating—almost frightening. But when he spoke his voice was level, even flat. "You might be surprised, Miss Wainwright, how little . . . freedom . . . wealth and power can buy. You know—" His eyes, half hidden under the heavy brow, were looking at me with an odd intensity. "You don't consider yourself to have either wealth or power, yet you can leave this island, and this house, and Alix, and me, in an hour if you wish. And never give us another thought."

"Could I, Mr. Darcourt? They've been times when I've wondered about that. When I've felt cut off, powerless."

"Did you put it to the test? Call Petersen? Or Norton? Or Judson? And ask them to take you to the pier and ferry you over?"

I had to shake my head. "No, but what makes *you* so powerless? After all, this isn't a monarchy. You don't hold the property in fief. You can sell the land, the house, the holdings. Liquidate them all. Buy a yacht. Go around the world. What's to stop you?"

His laugh rang out then, savage and mocking, and seemed to go on and on. After a moment he stopped and took a breath. "Ah, Miss Wainwright, what an innocent you are. And what a little materialist! So the only chains are ones of privation? I can tell you they can be the least." And he laughed again. "Get down now, and go in and take a bath, or you'll eat from the chimney piece for the next several days."

My cheeks were burning with anger, because I knew he

was mocking me and I bitterly resented it. But, looking up and seeing the stable gate in front of us, with Duncan standing there, I slid off, and without a backward look, marched into the house.

The first person I saw was Alix. "Where have you been?" I asked without thinking, and then, seeing the mulish expression on her face, added, "We've . . . I've . . . been worried about you."

"I know Daddy's here," she said sullenly.

"Yes, he is. But where were *you*? I looked all over for you. Alix, if you're going to take the day off, stay out for lunch, please tell me. When your father arrived and wanted to know where you were, I couldn't tell him, which makes me look pretty poor."

"If you *must* know, I was in the kitchen, baking cookies and cakes. I love to cook," she added defiantly, "and Louise says I can always come back and she'll teach me."

"But why didn't you tell me?"

She shrugged. Then said, "If you don't believe me, you can ask the cook. Or Stevens," she added, turning as the butler came into the hall. "Tell Miss LeBreton, Stevens, that I was in the kitchen with Louise learning how to make *pralines*."

"If you say—" I started. But Stevens was already affirming her statement. "It's true, miss, she was. And made a regular mess all over the place." He looked more grieved than angry. "Until Mrs. Conyers came down and made her clean it up."

"Mrs. Conyers? But she was sick upstairs. I went up to see her."

"I'm better now, thank you, Miss LeBreton," the housekeeper said, coming into the hall from the dining room. "And thought I would get up for dinner."

"Well, if you feel all right. Though now that Mr. Darcourt's here—" I started, and then paused, remembering that might have been Darcourt coming through the trees at the end of the drive, which was all that was visible from where she sat in bed.

But somewhere I was wrong. Because she turned to Alix.

"Mr. Darcourt? Here? Alix, why didn't you tell me?"

She couldn't be lying, I thought. Her reaction was too fast. Equally fast, I said, "So it wasn't Mr. Darcourt you saw through the blind?"

"No—I didn't know he was coming. I thought it was—"

She had been speaking, obviously, without thinking, her eyes on Alix. But she suddenly looked at me and remembered. The color drained from her face, leaving it gray. Her eyes held an expression I couldn't read. Then her whole face changed. Her cheeks flushed. Her expression resumed its usual frosty distance. "It was Judson, I saw. In the jeep. And now if you'll excuse me." And she went quickly through the swinging door into the kitchen quarters.

If it was not Tristram Darcourt she saw, I wondered, then who was it? I couldn't conceive of her having that horrified reaction to glimpsing any of the servants. Then, as I mounted the stairs to take the hot bath Darcourt had counseled and my muscles were already crying out for, I found myself thinking about the heavy dragging sound that I had heard that day in the forest.

All of a sudden I shivered.

(9)

I HAD been fully prepared for Darcourt's announcement—
probably at dinner—that he had discovered my masquerade
as Terry, which would, of course, lose me what little credit
I had acquired with Alix, and even further alienate Mrs.
Conyers. But when we gathered at the dining table, Darcourt made no reference to it, and managed to address me
without using my name. I decided to question him about
this as soon as were alone, on general principles and because
I found his restraint suspect. The opportunity occurred
sooner than I expected, around ten o'clock that evening. Mrs.
Conyers had long gone to bed. Alix, who had been playing
chess with her father, gave a huge yawn and said she was
going up. I closed my book and prepared to go with her.

Darcourt was putting the chessboard away, but turned
towards me. "I wonder if you'd wait a minute or two. There's
something I want to talk to you about."

"Of course," I said. Alix glared at us both, then left the
room. I watched him put the board on a shelf on one of the
book shelves. While he placed the chessmen in position, I
glanced around the big library where we had been sitting.
The weather was mild, and the windows were open, yet there
was a small fire burning in the grate, its flames flickering over
the leather backs of the books. Above the mantel, Alix's
mother's face reflected the shifting light. It was astonishing,
I thought, how much Alix resembled her although, if the

portrait were to be believed, Nicole Charpentier had even greater beauty, if not as much intelligence. There were times, I had discovered, that Alix could look astonishingly like her father in one of his more disputatious moments.

Out of the corner of my eye I saw Darcourt go over and shut the door. Then he limped back to the fireplace where I was standing and threw an extra log on the fire.

"I decided, Miss Sally Wainwright," he said straightening, "not to . . . er . . . unveil your charade to Alix and the others, at least not at present. As you may have noticed."

I eyed him suspiciously. "Yes, I noticed. I also wondered why."

"I was sure you'd be full of suspicion, if you had not already made up your mind that my motives were sinister."

Since that was just what I had done, I didn't reply. I simply scowled a little.

"Why are you frowning?"

"I suppose because I expected you to sweet-talk me in some way, and I was resisting it. Although sweet-talk isn't exactly the word I had in mind."

"Isn't it? I think it serves very well. And your suspicions are entirely accurate. If I can't get my way in one fashion, I'll try another."

I heard that mocking note again, and I could feel the anger begin to uncoil inside me. "I'm sure you would."

He stared at me for a moment or two, and I returned his gaze. Then he put his hand into his pocket and brought out a white envelope. "I have a letter here from Father Mark. Among other bits of information, he tells me that he and Doctor McIntyre encountered you in the forest and that you seem to have had an adventure there. Tell me about it."

"I don't know why he should have considered it worth writing about, since neither he nor the doctor seemed to think anything of it at the time."

"Apparently you heard something large moving around and went after it."

I was surprised that he was asking me these questions, and baffled as to what lay behind it. The whole thing was so unexpected. But—and this lept to the mind—it was, or seemed to be, more important than either Dr. McIntyre or Father Mark appeared to think at the time, or allowed me to realize they thought. Curiouser and curiouser, I reflected, quoting the immortal Alice of *Alice in Wonderland*.

"Well," Darcourt said, "aren't you going to tell me about

it? Apparently you acquired that bruise that is still showing on your temple and a twisted ankle."

"Yes, I did. Susie took off into the underbrush and I went after her. Then I fell, I'm not sure why. But I heard something moving ahead of me. Something heavy, that dragged a little. When I sat up after falling I was dizzy, and was still trying to figure out what was making that noise when Susie trotted back, holding a mouse that she had found and killed. She was terribly proud of herself. But when I got into the jeep and told the doctor and the priest about the noise, one of them, the doctor, I think, said it was the mouse. I said no mouse on earth made that much noise."

"But you didn't see anything?"

Again, I was aware of that watchfulness—the same look I had seen in both the doctor and Father Mark. My skin tingled a little.

"What was there to see?"

His brows went up, very much the way Alix's did when she was trying on her lady-of-the-manor role. Only with her it was amusing and sometimes endearing. With her father it was the real thing. "I was not there, Miss Wainright. You are—"

It was then the noise came—a sound on the other side of the door rather like something, or someone, falling, followed by scurrying.

For a man of such height and powerful build, Darcourt moved quietly and quickly to the door. Grasping the doorknob, he flung it open. Alix was halfway up the stairs.

"Alix! Come down at once."

She paused, but didn't return. Instead she started up again.

"If you don't come down, I will come up and carry you down. And you know I will."

Alix stopped again. Then she shrugged, turned and came down the stairs, her head high, a defiant expression on her face. Her father held the door for her and then closed it again when she came in.

"All right, now," he said. "Why were you listening at that door?"

His tone was not mild, but it was not as harsh as I would have expected it to be, in view of what he had caught Alix doing. Or perhaps that reflected my own aversion to keyhole listening.

Alix didn't reply.

"Answer me, Alix."

She shrugged again. "Because I wanted to hear what you said."

"Don't be disingenuous, my dear. And don't underrate my intelligence. Why was it so important for you to hear what I was going to say to"—his eyes flickered towards me and away again—"your governess?"

"You mean Miss Wainright. Miss Sally Wainright." She swung around to me. "Do I have it correct, Miss Wainright?" The insolence was back in her tone.

"Don't be impertinent," her father said before I had a chance to reply.

"Impertinent!" Alix turned back to her father, her voice rising. "If I did something like that, you couldn't find enough words to describe what you thought of it. Dishonest would be just the first."

I took a breath. "She's right, Mr. Darcourt. It *was* dishonest, and she is entitled to an explanation."

"Perhaps," he said. "But she is not entitled to listen at doors, and I want to find out why she did." He looked back at her. "This is something you've never done before. But you must have had an idea of what was going to be said, or why should you listen? Who has said what to you?"

Alix stared back at her father, sullenly, saying nothing.

"Either you answer me or I'll punish you."

Listening, I was torn. Part of me resented the authoritarian approach on Alix's behalf. But against that was a wealth of experience with the orphans: a rule, if it is just a rule, has to be obeyed, or you will have some very confused young people. There was also the fact that I didn't feel I had the right to interpose myself between father and daughter under these circumstances, plus my own eagerness to know why, indeed, she felt it worthwhile to listen at the door.

Alix stuck her chin in the air in a characteristic pose, but said nothing.

"Alix, I am your father, and little though you may want to believe this, I don't like either punishing you or playing the heavy parent. But I do have to have an answer to the question I just asked. And if you continue to defy me, then I will give orders to Duncan that the stables are to be locked, and you are not to be allowed inside. You will not ride."

Knowing how Alix loved to ride, I knew it was a telling punishment, but I was not prepared for the cry that broke from her.

"No, no, no, no . . ." The single vowel sound rose like a wail.

"Be quiet!" her father thundered, and for once I did not have the inclination to protest. Alix's plunge into hysteria had all the signs of a childish tantrum.

I saw Darcourt make an involuntary move towards her, then stop. Her sobs quieted.

"Now," Darcourt said, not unkindly, "what is this all about? Who've you been talking to?"

"Father Mark," she said sullenly. "He was here again just the other day and said he was pretty sure she wasn't . . . Miss LeBreton."

"Yes," her father said, glancing at me. "That was something else he mentioned in his letter."

I remembered my brief conversation with him, including my revealing statement, "*All the priests that have come my way were either very old and crotchety or young and relevant,*" and the intent look it produced on the face of the young priest. Yet, by itself, it hardly seemed enough.

"Was it something I said?" I asked.

Alix looked at me, started to say something, then shrugged. "Don't just shrug, Alix," Darcourt said irritably. "A civil question deserves a civil answer."

"I suppose, Ter—Miss *Wainwright*." The emphasis carried sarcasm.

"Sally," I corrected, without much confidence that she would use it or that I would regain her good opinion.

Alix looked at me, her eyes steady and angry. "I only call my friends, people I *trust*, by their first names."

There was a silence. "Well, Miss Wainwright," Darcourt said. "Any comment on that?"

I shook my head. "No. I can't criticize Alix if she doesn't trust me. But I think I will explain . . . explain just why I took Terry's name." I stumbled because at that crucial moment I caught Darcourt's sardonic expression.

But when he spoke, his voice was perfectly pleasant.

"Yes, Miss Wainwright. Do."

I turned to Alix. "It was because of my mother. She, too, came from Louisiana. Her name was Giselle LeVaux, and she and your father were engaged. I'd always been brought up to believe that your father . . . broke the engagement. But he showed me the letter from my mother, breaking the engagement herself. She was, by the way, your father tells me, a cousin of your mother's and was staying with your mother's

166

family in New Orleans when she met your father."

I made the account as brief and simple as possible, and, temporarily suppressing any doubts I had about Darcourt's claim as to who was actually responsible in severing the relationship, incorporated his statements with mine.

"So you came to see if it was true?" Alix asked.

"Yes." I was uncomfortably conscious of all that I wasn't saying. Again I felt Darcourt's gaze upon me. Deliberately I avoided his eye and addressed Alix. "But you haven't told me if it was something I said that aroused Father Mark's suspicions."

"Well, only that it didn't sound at all like the Terry Le-Breton that he had known back in New Orleans when they were children living in the Garden District. He said he couldn't be sure because it was so long ago, or about whether you looked the way he remembered. So he wrote to some cousins and was told Terry was in France. Of course, Terry could have come back over here in a hurry. But he thought it sounded funny."

"I can see why," I said drily, understanding, retrospectively, the intent looks the young priest had directed at me. "But I think it's odd that he didn't mention that day in the jeep that we had known one another."

"Well, he said he meant to," Alix explained. "But that it didn't feel right. That's one of the reasons he wrote to his cousins and then to Father."

"I wonder why he didn't confront me with it."

"Because," Darcourt put in, "he undoubtedly knew I would prefer to deal with the matter in my own way."

I glanced at him. "Undoubtedly." And then, "I suppose it should have occurred to me that he, too, came from Louisiana."

"It might," Darcourt said agreeably. "But it's even closer than that. Father Mark's full name is Mark Charpentier LeVaux. He is the son of a cousin of your mother's and is, of course, related to the Charpentiers, too."

I stood there, experiencing the oddest sensation: as though, when all the pieces of my mother's story were fully revealed, they would make a circle, like a chain, or a rope. And that rope was around my own neck.

"Isn't it . . . strange," I asked, "that he should be here as priest to the island? I mean, a queer coincidence?"

"It's not a coincidence at all," Darcourt said calmly. "He
167

went to a great deal of trouble to get permission from his order to work here."

"Because he is related to Mrs. Darcourt's family?"

"Why do you find that so strange?" Alix asked. "In the South families are very important."

I turned towards her father. "Is that the reason? Family solidarity?"

"That reason and others."

That suffocating feeling was back. "What others?"

The light gray eyes bored into me. "Why don't you ask him?" For a moment our eyes held. Then he turned to his daughter. "Alix, I don't want to scold you more than . . . than is reasonable. But listening at doors is both dishonest and cowardly. No—it's no use having an hysterical tantrum." With Darcourt, I saw the danger signal flying red and then white in her cheeks, and the wild look in her eye. "It's something I want you to think about. It would be better to come in here and claim your right to listen."

"And what would you have done, Father? Let me stay? Or blasted my head off?"

Her father looked at her in silence for a moment. "I suppose I deserved that. I'm beginning to realize that I've made too many demands on you with insufficient explanation. You can thank Miss Wainright—Sally—for that piece of insight. I'll try to do better. But let's make it a dual effort."

Alix stared at him. I wondered if it were wishful thinking on my part, but for a moment I thought she was going to meet him halfway. Then, without moving, she gave the effect of withdrawing. Her eyes flickered in my direction. "Well, you seem to have won him over, anyway. Congratulations!" And she turned on her heel and made for the door.

"Alix. Come back here!"

But this time she paid no attention, just walking through the door and out into the hall.

Darcourt glanced at me.

"Please excuse me. I'm going to have to get something straightened out with her." And he followed her out the door, pulling it to him after her. In a second I heard their voices murmuring, although I didn't hear what they said. Then I heard them going up the stairs.

I found suddenly that I felt both drained and restless. For a few minutes I paced the length of the library, looking at the books on both sides. With one part of my mind I registered the fact that there was, in this room, the beginnings of a fine reference library, particularly in some areas: history, both English and American, early Spanish history on the southeast coast of North America. My fingers flicked over the leatherbound backs: the ancient Greek and Roman classics —I pulled one or two out—in the original, and not only read but underlined. I moved to the other side of the room, and in a total change, saw a great many medical texts—mostly, it seemed, on tropical diseases—and by the looks of the backs and insides, well read. Some Darcourt, I decided, must have had missionary yearnings or perhaps some young son or daughter had indeed gone to remote tropical areas to carry the Gospel, and remained to learn all they could about some of the more virulent and feared diseases endemic there.

What a strange thing for rich sophisticates to do, I pondered, and then reproached myself. There I go again, I thought, waving my prejudices. But what an odd family! Odder still was the fact that some of the medical books were relatively modern. Did Darcourt have a sister or brother or cousin, unmentioned in *Who's Who* and other references, out somewhere being a medical missionary? I pulled out a book. If I understood the polysyllabic title, it meant a study of diseases of the skin. Skin, I thought idly, and flipped open the cover. There, in black ink, in a strong, slanted hand, was the name Tristram Darcourt. Curious.

I put the book back and, still restless, walked behind the desk to the window. The moon rode big and high and could be seen between the branches and leaves of the trees. I stared up at it for a while, through the thick, shiny leaves of the magnolia. Then, with a crick in my neck, lowered my head.

The central drawer of the rather startlingly modern desk from which Darcourt had taken the packet of letters was closed. Probably locked. Certainly Darcourt had unlocked it when taking out letters. But the bottom drawer, a deep, double drawer, the kind made for files suspended from rods running parallel to the sides, was unlocked and was half open. It had probably, on its steel bearings, rolled open, I thought, having seen many drawers of that kind before. They were usually locked automatically when the middle drawer was locked, or the drawer above them. But often the locking device didn't catch. And if that happened, the bottom drawer often slid open of its own weight.

Without thinking I went to close it. There were only a few files in the hanging folders, I noticed, each marked by a white label in a plastic case sticking above the file. There were the categories you'd expect: Bills, Claims, Darcourt—Estate Reports. . . . My eyes backtracked to the name "Darcourt." This was an unusually long label, because underneath, in upper and lower case, was "Nicole Charpentier Darcourt—Medical History."

Medical history. Why should a woman disporting herself on the French Riviera have a medical history? Suddenly I felt as though the hair on the back of my neck stirred—usually a sign that my unconscious had caught the trail of something before my conscious mind was aware there was something to catch.

I stared at the file for a few minutes, almost willing my hand to stay at my side. After all, Alix was upstairs being reprimanded by her father for listening at a keyhole. Would reading someone else's personal file be that different or excusable? It was astonishingly hard to force my eye back to an idle examination of the other labels, because something was beginning to move and stir at the edges of my conscious mind: words, bits of information starting to make a pattern. . . . But the moment I paused to take a direct look, whatever it was vanished. And I was left with a queer feeling and a void.

I dragged my eye away from Nicole Darcourt's file and went on: Estate reports, Grants, Grants? My finger started to itch again. What grants? Onward, I told myself. Houses . . . There were several folders for House: House—Employees, House—Expenses, House—Old House. . . . Then Island, that was a thick folder, Javelin, Kennel. . . . *Javelin*, I thought. I'd heard that word before. But when? And where? I was staring at it when I heard Darcourt's step on the stairs and moved rapidly back to the fireplace. I was gazing pensively into it when Darcourt came back into the room.

"Well," he said. "We seem to have arrived at a truce—however temporary. At least the matter of your identity is resolved, which should be a relief to you, given all your difficulties in maintaining your part."

"Well, that should prove to you that I'm not a born liar."

"You can put your fists down. I didn't need proof."

He came over to the fireplace and stood on the other side near the desk. Idly, with his foot, he shut the bottom drawer. As I had suspected, it had failed to catch the lock running down from the drawer above and started to roll open again. So he opened the upper one a little, shut the bottom one, which closed with a click, and closed the top one.

Then he said abruptly, "I tried to explain to Alix how you felt about your mother, having believed for so long that I had abandoned her."

"That was kind of you." I was dismayed to feel my heart give a little flutter.

His eyes glanced at me briefly from under his brow. "Come now, Miss Wainright, you mustn't let yourself fall into such easy acceptance. Your father wouldn't like it at all. We both know my motives are devious, if not diabolical."

"Yes," I said briskly, smothering a desire to giggle, "I do. Did you happen to ask your gently bred daughter if she had taken a pot shot at us?"

I expected him to smile back, but he didn't. "In a manner of speaking. I asked her if she knew if anyone had been out with a gun. Since this is a wildlife sanctuary, shooting anything is strictly forbidden. She denied it, but I think she does know."

For a moment the obvious question hung heavy between us. Then Darcourt said, "In answer to the question you're trying not to ask, I don't know whether she fired the shot or not. No more than you is she a liar, but she was evasive and looked guilty."

"It could mean she simply knew who was doing the shooting."

"Yes."

"Well, surely that's better, I mean, there's a difference between her knowing who fired the shot, and her doing it."

He didn't answer for a moment. Then, "I suppose it would seem that way."

"But you think one is as bad as the other? Why?"

Darcourt took the fireguard and placed it around the fire. "I will tell you that, when you tell me the real reason you're here. I'm going to bed. Good night." And with a curt nod of his head, he walked out of the room.

I waited until his footsteps passed out of hearing on the floor above, glanced at the desk drawer, then went out myself, and upstairs.

Susie was sitting three feet from the door, waiting.

"Was I long, love?" I asked, going over and patting her. She barked in a way that I knew meant she wanted to go out. "I suppose you can't wait," I said, looking down at her.

She barked again. I stroked her, and found in myself a

strange reluctance to go downstairs and outside the house. I stood up, listening. To anyone town- and city-bred as I had been, the total silence of the country could be unnerving. Then Susie barked again. Well, I thought, knowing I had no choice made it easier. I opened the bedroom door. "Come along," I said. Susie darted through and trotted towards the stairs. I was about to follow when I went back and got her leash. Then I ran down the stairs as quickly as I could to catch her.

"All right, all right," I said finally, snapping the leash into her collar. "It hasn't been *that* long."

In the hall, I paused. The design of the house was the classic "shot gun" variety. That is, if you fired a shot through the front door it would pass straight out the back door, each door being at either end of the central hall. Susie and I were standing about midway between the two doors, so it was a tossup. Afterwards, I wondered how much my life might have been different if I had decided, for no special reason, to let Susie do her thing outside the front door.

I had discovered, when visiting my and Terry's relatives, down in the bayou country, that no one locked the front door at night, something that took a little getting used to for anyone brought up near Boston and resident in New York. I was, therefore, however illogically, relieved to find out that Darcourt's front door was locked, and I assumed also the back door, although, it struck me as I went through the front door and out onto the grass, while Susie squatted and then sniffed around the bushes, that I had never tested the back door at night to see if it were, indeed, locked.

Susie was taking her time, and tugging at the leash. "Come along, Susie, hurry up," I said. But Susie, who did not like a mode of existence which demanded that she be kept upstairs while I was elsewhere, was not going to be rushed. And it was obvious to me, knowing her, that she had several bushes to investigate and several stops before she was through.

My hand through the loop of the leash, I stared up at the moon, now higher and smaller. Once, at school, I had taken a beginner's course in astronomy, and I tried now to make out the constellations that hung bright and enormous in the southern sky.

It was Susie's whine that brought my head down. It was a little the way she sounded when confronted with the scorpion and the coral snake. But now she sounded more afraid, and to my surprise had backed against my legs. I could feel her shaking.

"Susie," I found myself whispering, and then stopped. Because now I heard what her sharp ears had caught a few seconds earlier. The open sweep of lawn was on one side of us, but there were bushes and trees on either side of the house, as thick, almost, as the woods at the back, and from where we were standing, only a few feet away. Something was moving through the trees and undergrowth with that weighted, dragging step. Only this time it was not moving away—it was coming towards us.

My skin tingled, and then, as an odd, sweetish smell caught my nostrils, I shivered. Whatever it was was much nearer. I took a firm hold on the leash, ordered my legs to stay put and said, "Who's there?"

The movement stopped. There was a moment of silence, then a shot rang out and something whizzed an inch from my ear. I jumped, the loop dropped from my hand, Susie barked and plunged straight forward. A moment later she yelped in pain.

"Susie!" I cried and went after her, pushing between an azalea bush and a big cape jasmine tree. Susie yelped again, and rage swept through me. Then immediately in front of me, I saw outlined a shape, taller than I, and much wider. There was the sound of a heavy breath. And that's all I remembered.

When I came to I was lying on the sofa in the library.

"Susie," I said, and felt my hand being licked. I patted her and sat up.

"Oh," I moaned. I put my hands on either side of my head, which was not only hurt but was swimming. Feeling a little sick, I lay down again.

Susie jumped up and curled herself up on my stomach. Since I was feeling queasy, I wasn't too sure how well this would work out, but I was glad to have her there and to discover that whatever had happened to her was neither lethal nor damaging. I was just making up my mind to try sitting up again when the door opened and I could tell by the firm strides that it was my employer.

Coming over, he looked down on me. "So you've come to," he said, without, I noted, sounding either relieved or overjoyed.

Rather gingerly this time, I sat up again, moving Susie as

gently as I could down onto the sofa cushion beside me.

"He hit me," I said.

"Yes," Darcourt agreed. He had gone over to the fireplace, and was running the poker through the dying embers. He was wearing, I noticed, not the suit he had had on at dinner but work trousers, an open-neck shirt and worn jacket.

"Well, you don't seem unduly upset or disturbed by it. I could have been killed. And whoever it was hurt Susie."

"Not seriously. And may I ask what you were doing wandering about by yourself outside at this time of night?"

"What do you mean, what was I doing? Susie had to go out, so I took her. Isn't this protected private property?"

He put the poker down and stood facing me, his hands in his pockets, anger on his face. "Yes, this is private property. But since you yourself came here with purposes other than your declared ones, I don't see why you should be so surprised that someone else obviously has, too."

"But I don't go around hitting people on the head and hurting small animals."

"How do I know what you intended to do, or still intend to do? In one sense you're far more dangerous, because you're inside the house. You're able to do more damage with greater ease than administering a tap on the head."

"*Tap*! Have you gone mad or something? I was the one who was attacked, I and my dog, and you're standing there as though I had attacked you. Who was it out there who tried to shoot me and then struck me on the head? Whoever it was was also in the woods the other day. There was that same dragging step I heard."

"Nonsense. You've been watching too many movies or too much television or something. Your imagination is clearly unreliable. Now go to bed."

I put my feet down on the floor and stood up. After pausing for a minute or two, to make sure that I could stay perpendicular, I said, with emphasis, "Somebody took a pot shot at me and hit me on the head. And I want to know who it was!"

"There is no need, Miss Wainright, to raise your voice in that uncomely fashion. Do you want the whole household to hear?"

"I don't care if they do."

"Well, I do care. I have enough trouble with Alix's overactive imagination as it is. As for who it was, this may be private property, but there isn't a wall around it. Anyone

174

who wants to can land anywhere he likes. And if the . . . marauder . . . is here to shoot the abundant wildlife—which has happened more than once—then of course he'd knock you down rather than have you able to identify him."

"You never said there was poaching around here."

"I didn't think I had to. Any wildlife preserve is badgered by hot shots who take a double pleasure, not only in killing, but in doing it against the law. Now go to bed." He nodded towards the desk, where I saw a tumbler with a cloudy white liquid in it. "Take that with you and drink it before you turn off your light."

I was furious at his punitive attitude, and frustrated that I felt much too shaken (at the moment) to do battle. "Thank you, no. Who knows what's in it?"

"Don't be a fool," he said. "It's only a little aspirin with a mild sedative. If you don't take it, you'll wake up with a cracking headache."

"Better to wake up with a headache than not at all, or to find Susie missing."

"Thank you very much."

"Don't mention it." I collected Susie's leash and made for the door.

It was not until I was in bed a few minutes later that it occurred to me that it was undoubtedly Darcourt who had brought me in and that I should have thanked him at least for that. Not that he deserved thanks for anything. I lay in the dark, feeling drowsiness creep on me, and found myself wondering how long I had been unconscious. Yanking my eyes open, I looked at the illuminated dial of my traveling clock. The clock said nearly eleven thirty. I lay back and did some figuring. Alix said her unofficial good night at ten. Then, perhaps ten minutes later, she was caught listening at the door. After perhaps another ten or fifteen minutes—no less—her father went up with her. How long was he up there? Fifteen, twenty minutes? Perhaps. At the most. Then he had come down and I had gone up no more than ten minutes after that. Ten minutes later Susie and I were outside, and loitered for another ten. . . . That would take us past eleven, but not much. So . . . give ten minutes for our conversation downstairs . . . that left fifteen minutes or so unaccounted for. I was still wondering what had happened during those fifteen minutes that I had been knocked out when I went to sleep.

Darcourt was right about one thing, I did have a cracking headache when I awoke at six thirty the next morning. When I went to collect my early coffee, I found an envelope on the tray in Darcourt's slanted handwriting. Tearing it open, I pulled out a single sheet of paper.

Please be at the stable at eight, dressed for riding. A hot shower will make you feel better. I enclose two headache tablets. If you want to be a stubborn fool, you may, but these will help your headache.

It was signed, T.D.

Whether my resistance to pain was less, or I was more worn down, I don't know. But I crawled back on the bed, poured out some steaming hot coffee and milk, and swallowed the pills with my first sip. Then I sat there, with the tray on my lap, watching the early morning light streak across the sky, with Susie curled up beside me, and thought. And thought. At the end of concentrated thinking I had come to some interesting conclusions.

Half an hour later I had had a hot shower and was in my jeans and prepared for action. What I was about to do entailed the risk of being caught by Darcourt, or Mrs. Conyers or even Alix, but there was no way around it. There were extensions of the telephone in each room, but I decided my best course of action was the boldest. I would go down to the library and use the phone there. It would be the room where I would be most liable to be caught, but, on the other hand, I figured the telephone on Darcourt's desk would be the least likely to be monitored. I didn't understand too well how telephones worked, but for all I knew, Darcourt might have, in his bedroom, the kind of instrument adorned with push buttons, that would not only light up if anyone picked up an extension anywhere, but would indicate in what room the phone was being used. And if the call came from the telephone in my room, Darcourt, if he were keeping a watch—and I was quite sure he would be—would know instantly. If, on the other hand, he saw the call coming from the library—a room used by everyone—anyone might be using the telephone for the most pedestrian household purpose. Or so I argued.

There was also something else I wanted to do in the library, but I needed to borrow some courage to do it. And I knew just who would lend it to me. Leaving Susie, I went downstairs and into the big book room prepared, if Darcourt were there, to pretend to be looking for a book. But the room was empty. Closing the door I went over to the phone and dialed. Brian picked up the telephone.

"Hello," he said, sounding as if I had waked him up.

"Hello, darling," I gushed, going into my act for any possible listening ear. "Did I wake you?"

"Who—"

I ploughed straight through him, "It was so *marvelous* of you to insist I call. It's been such a long time."

There was a pause. Then in a voice that sounded much more alert, he almost mooed. "Where've you been, baby? Why haven't you been in touch with me?"

Good boy, I thought, and he had the sense not to use any damaging names. If he had called me Terry, and Darcourt were listening, he would know beyond doubt that this was no social call.

"I've been busier than you would believe. Haven't been able to get away a minute." I took a breath, knowing that with what I was about to say I would be crossing a line. There would be no doubt about my incriminating intentions. "Darling, I wonder if you'd do something for me—" Was that a click I heard, as though someone had picked up a receiver?

"Yes?" Brian said.

"Did you hear a click, Brian? I wonder if I'm on someone's line."

"No click." Brian replied abruptly, sounding much more like the newsman he was than the lover I was pretending him to be.

I took a breath and blew my cover.

"Could you look up two things for me, Brian? One is called 'Javelin.' Something to do with oil—either domestic or foreign, I'm not sure which."

"Consider it done." The enthusiasm of an investigating reporter on a promising scent would have been plain to a backward child. No actor, Brian. But it couldn't be helped. In for a penny, in for a pound had always been the motto of the immoderate Patrick James Wainright.

"Also—"

"Yes."

The trouble was, I wasn't sure what I wanted to ask for, because I wasn't even sure what I was looking for. "Could you look up everything you have or can scrape up on Nicole

Charpentier Darcourt? That is, the present Mrs. Darcourt? Particularly anything medical."

"What are you on to?"

"I'm not sure. But I do know that locked away in the desk I'm talking from are two files. One says 'Javelin,' and from something the daughter dropped when I first came, I think it's something to do with oil. And the other says, 'Darcourt—Nicole Charpentier Darcourt—Medical History.'"

"Well, don't just stand there, baby. Get the file and read it."

"People can be jailed for that, and—I have been carefully informed—the police down here are most eager to do any Darcourt bidding."

There was a silence. "It's up to you. But I'll tell you what I'll do. I'll call in a couple of days to see where and how you are, and if I can't talk to you, or anything sounds fishy, I'll send forces of my own—or rather my employer's—to get you out with a blast of publicity."

I was silent, struck, suddenly and quite against my will and intention, with a pang of conscience. I tried to summon up an image of Darcourt's tyrannical manner and arrogant face to boost my resolve, but all that did was to make me feel worse.

"Are you okay?" Brian asked suddenly.

"Fine," I said, and then jumped nearly a foot as the door opened and Darcourt came in. My heart started to pound. "Oh, here's Mr. Darcourt now. We're going riding, as I told you."

Darcourt, seeing I was on the phone, paused, then went to the other end of the room and picked up a magazine from the table.

"I must go now, darling," I said, quaking, and, because I was afraid, laying on the lover-like camouflage extra thick.

"Okay, love," Brian said, throwing himself into his role, "I'll keep in touch. Don't do anything foolish. Smack, smack," and he made two loud kissing noises over the phone.

Despite the fact that Darcourt himself was at the other end of the room and couldn't possibly hear, and that no one seemed to have picked up an extension—at least I'd heard no click since the one I asked Brian about—I could feel myself blush. I looked up and found his eyes, not on the magazine, but on me. When I saw his grim expression, my heart gave an ominous thunk. It was all very uncomfortable, but I decided not to be cowed. "The same to you," I said heartily into the receiver.

I hung up and Darcourt put down the magazine and came towards me.

"Excuse me," I said, trying hard not to sound either nervous or apologetic, "but I wanted to call . . . a friend."

"You don't need my permission to use the telephone."

I glanced at him, wondering, first, if he'd listened in anywhere, and if not that, if he'd heard what I said through the door as he came in. If he had, I had certainly given him more than enough justification for having me arrested. If he needed justification, which, being the kind of man he was, who acted first and considered people's feelings afterwards—if ever—he unquestionably didn't.

He was certainly looking grim. I braced myself, but all he said was, "Are you ready?"

I nodded.

When we got to the stable Rusty and Sebastian, saddled, were in the courtyard, and Duncan had tethered Rusty near the mounting block. I was about to go over when Darcourt stopped me. "Just a minute."

He stepped inside a room to the side of the stalls and emerged with a pair of boots which he brought over to me. "Put these on," he said abruptly.

"I prefer sneakers." I didn't, of course, and knew that they were too pliable and slick for safety—to say nothing of having laces that could get tangled. But I was grappling with an unfamiliar feeling that I could not identify, but which had the effect of making me determined to be as independent as possible.

"I don't care what you prefer. You're on my property and this is my horse. If your shoe should get caught again, or Rusty take off, even if your lace didn't get tangled, your whole foot could slide through the stirrup. You could get killed. Put on the boots; they're about the right size."

Knowing that he was right did not help my stubbornness, but I was on shaky ground, and besides, I have a strong sense of survival. So I sat down on the mounting block, took off my sneakers and pulled on the boots, which turned out to be an exact fit, and, though old, had been neatly polished.

"Now," Darcourt said, picking up the sneakers, "push your jean bottoms into the tops of your boots. It's easier on the horse as well as on your legs, and the less loose material you have flapping around the better." And without stopping to see if I obeyed him, he took my sneakers back to the small tack room.

I winced as we started off through the stable gates. Even two hot baths had not entirely removed the soreness from my muscles, but after a short while I found that while using the same set was agony at first, they limbered up with use and became less sore.

"All right. Let's trot," Darcourt said.

So for the next hour we trotted, cantered, trotted again, walked, cantered and trotted. Darcourt, whose face did not relax its sternness, politely pointed out birds, bushes, flowers and other items of interest. Yet it was a very different ride from the previous one. Even though Darcourt was at all times abrupt and dictatorial, nevertheless I found myself thinking of his manner and tone of the day before as warm. Today, by contrast, there was a total absence of that quality for which I could find no other word.

So, I concluded unhappily, he'd overheard the phone conversation with Brian. In that case, I wondered, even more unhappily, why he hadn't referred to it in any way, at least as a prelude to arresting me. The answer was obvious, if depressing: he was showing a little muscle while playing cat and mouse. Once I grasped that, however, I perked up. If he could play games, so could I. If he were going to be the courtly laird, pointing out features of note (no, I decided, courtly wasn't right, either—there was nothing courtly about Darcourt, whether warm or grim), then I could, with equal enthusiasm, mimic the eager and grateful tourist.

"What is that bush over there?" I asked disingenuously, waving vaguely to the left.

It was exhausting. The trouble was, it was hard to keep remembering that if he had heard my telephone conversation he had every right to be angry, and to snatch back, unsaid, the words, "Why are you angry with me?" that kept threatening to fall out.

It wasn't as though I cared, I thought, digging my heels into Rusty's side with more vigor than I had intended. And then, as the big horse took off, damn, damn, damn, *damn* . . .

Rusty did not have the bit between his teeth, but it was still hard to stop him, and we had traveled quite a way down one of the narrow paths before I managed to draw him to a halt.

"Go up there to that fork," Darcourt said from behind me. Too shaken to argue, I picked up the reins and barely touched the chestnut flanks with my boot. Rusty walked sedately forward.

"All right," Darcourt said, when I reached the meeting of the two paths. "You can stop now."

He's going to bring his horse up and give me a royal dressing down, I thought miserably. I was right.

My father may have been more explosive when dealing with my transgressions, but there was no question about it, Darcourt had a far more fluent vocabulary.

After a paragraph of well-chosen words, he finished up, "And if you like being run away with and probably jumped over a fence that will injure the horse and kill you, then you're going the right way about it. If, however—"

I had no conscious plan of doing what at the moment I proceeded to do. But the only alternative—bursting into tears—was unacceptable.

As Darcourt had brought Sebastian up, I had turned Rusty around so the horses were standing head to tail while Darcourt treated me to a rundown of what he thought of me.

I picked up the reins. "It's a great pity, Mr. Darcourt," I said, trying to keep my voice steady, "that you don't have a regiment to do this in front of and I don't have chevrons you can pull off." And with those sentiments off my chest, I once again dug my heels into Rusty's side and took off.

Fortunately for me, Rusty had run off most of his excess energy. But we enjoyed quite a brisk canter back home. At any moment, if he had wanted to, Darcourt could have caught up with me, but he seemed uncharacteristically content simply to follow me back.

By the time I had ridden into the courtyard, dismounted, and retrieved my sneakers from the tack room, it was nearly nine. "Take the boots up to your room," Darcourt, who had ridden in behind me, ordered.

I bristled. "There's no need—"

"Will you for once do as I ask without arguing about it? My motives are your safety and the horse's comfort, as I told you."

"My safety is my own affair," I threw back at him, with a passing reflection that in that case it was in poor hands.

"As long as you're on my land, riding my horse, at my orders, your safety is my responsibility. If you should injure yourself and decide to sue me, your defense attorney would be the first to point that out."

That was an aspect that had not remotely occurred to me. For some reason, I found it infuriating, and was betrayed into a *bêtise* that even I blushed to remember. "I suppose," I said, ostentatiously carrying my sneakers through the stable gate, "that that is the kind of contingency you have to be prepared for—if you're very rich."

"Of course," Darcourt agreed smoothly. "When one is dealing with the middle and lower classes, one can't be too careful."

I stalked towards the house and managed to reach the back door before I broke into a giggle.

Fifteen minutes later, after a quick hot shower and a change of clothes, I went down to the dining room for scrambled eggs and bacon and more coffee. Alix, who was sitting there nibbling at a croissant, looked up at me and then down at her plate.

"Good morning, Alix," I said.

"Good morning."

Her tone was indifferent, aloof, and I knew I would be in for a hard time. Nor could I blame her very much. My masquerading under a false name was the worst possible thing I could do if I were trying to win the confidence of someone who found trust difficult. Not for the first time since I had come, I reflected that to be a successful investigative reporter, one had to be able to shrug off the fallout on other—and often innocent—people. The reflection depressed me, not only because it made me question my own suitability for my own chosen profession, but because I had become fond of Alix. I helped myself to eggs and bacon, both kept in warming dishes on the sideboard.

I was turning over various approaches to Alix in my head, when she surprised me by asking, "So how do you like riding?"

"Very much. I'm sorry I didn't learn sooner." I looked up at her and smiled. "I understand much better your impatience to get on a horse."

Alix, who was crumbling some bread beside her plate, looked at me thoughtfully. "Have you been through the fence yet, out into the swamp?"

"No," I said wondering which way the conversation was going to jump. "So far I've been only where I've been taken—or mostly so. Rusty once ran away with me."

"You shouldn't let him get the bit between his teeth."

"How do you stop him?"

"You just have to react faster than he does. If something

182

frightens him, that's what he's going to do if he gets the chance. You have to get the bit well back before he gets that chance."

"It sounds to me like the kind of thing you learn by experience. When you begin to think like a horse."

Alix smothered what was obviously an appreciative giggle, and I grinned back, feeling more encouraged about the progress of our relationship.

At that moment the dining room door opened and André Charpentier walked in.

"Greetings to one and all," he said. "I trust there's some breakfast left."

"André!"

I had been smiling at André, but Alix's voice made me look at her. Ye gods, I thought. The sulky, pouting child had gone. In her place was a radiant young woman, the light, silvery gray eyes shining. "How wonderful! I didn't know you'd be back soon!"

"Oh—some business with the wildlife service cropped up." His smile to her across the table had a tender quality. "*Va bien, petite?*"

"*Très bien!*"

She was about to say something else when Darcourt came in, still, I noticed, in his riding clothes.

"Hello, André. What brings you?"

Less than totally enthusiastic, I thought, surprised.

"The state wildlife department wrote. Wants me to check something about last year's banding."

"The red-tailed hawk?"

"No, we don't seem to have any of those anymore. Some of your poachers must have gotten to them. I haven't seen or heard any this year."

Why did that statement bother me, I wondered, buttering some croissant?

Darcourt sat down at the head of the table with his plate of eggs and bacon. "The poachers seem to be worse, not better, this year. One of them got right up to the house last night and knocked . . . our guest . . . on the head."

André turned. "Thérèse?" he inquired. He came to the table carrying his plate and sat down beside Alix across from me. "Good heavens, Thérèse. That's terrible."

"Only she isn't Thérèse," Alix said. "She's Sally."

André looked bewildered. "Thérèse? Sally? I don't understand."

"Neither does anyone else," Alix said sulkily.

"*Tais-toi*, little one. There must be a good reason."

I smiled at him. "Thanks for the vote of confidence. I came here in the best investigative reporter tradition to dig up some information about my mother, who was engaged to Mr. Darcourt long before either one was married."

"But how exciting," André said. "Just like on television."

"No. I'm afraid not." I threw a quick glance at Darcourt's unyielding profile. "I don't think I have either the *sang-froid* or the ruthlessness to be a really good reporter of that kind."

"Some people," Alix commented, not looking up, "would consider it dishonest to come to somebody's house under a false name."

"And they would be right, Alix," I said. "I haven't pretended to excuse it."

André had been frowning. "But Tristram was engaged to a New Orleans girl, or at least a Louisiana one. Giselle someone."

"Giselle LeVaux," I said.

"But the LeVauxs are remote cousins of the Charpentiers."

"So I've just learned from Mr. Darcourt."

André looked at Darcourt, who had been doggedly eating his breakfast. "But how delightful. I'd far rather have you a LeVaux than a LeBreton. You are then a cousin, and you know what we in the South feel free to do with cousins."

"Not that close," I countered quickly. André was charming and good-looking, but I suddenly discovered that I had no desire to be kissed by him.

"But of course that close." He was motivated, I was quite sure, by the purest mischief.

"I think that's a stupid custom," Alix said rather violently.

"So do I," I agreed. Something was ticking over in the back of my head.

"But no, I am all for the ancient traditions, aren't you, Tristram?"

Darcourt swallowed some coffee. "I have no views on the matter whatsoever," he said. Then, "No, that's not entirely true. I'm inclined to agree with Alix."

"But how unromantic, Tristram!" I looked at the young Louisianan. There was an odd, challenging note in his voice. "And how untrue!"

If it was a challenge, Darcourt chose not to see it as such.

"Do you think so?" he asked prosaically, pouring himself some more coffee.

It was like an electric current between them, I thought, sparking and flickering, as though a live wire had been touched with metal.

"I don't know what you're talking about," Alix said, and I saw the radiant young woman had again become the pouting child.

Her father smiled at her, "Neither do I. Would you like me to declare a day's holiday for you so we can go for a ride?"

For a second she looked pleased, then she glanced at her cousin. "Thank you, Daddy. But André said we'd go for a ride the first thing when he got back. And now he's back. Could I still have the holiday and go with him?"

"All right." Darcourt got up. Then he glanced at me. "I trust that has your approval, Miss Wainright."

"Wainright," André repeated. "What a lovely English name!"

"Irish," I corrected.

"It's English," Darcourt commented, picking up the mail that had been beside his plate. "Your father was probably descended from one of the soldiers who went to Ireland in the army of William of Orange or Cromwell."

I looked straight across at him. "If you'd said that in front of my father, he would have killed you."

That odd, crooked smile of Darcourt's flickered across his face. I'd glimpsed it once or twice before and discovered that it had a disturbing effect on my insides. "It would have taken a brave man to have said that to your father, Sally."

Alix pounced on that. "You knew Sally's father, Daddy?"

"Briefly."

"Why? I mean, how come?" She looked at me and then back again at her father.

Her father looked at her for a moment over the letter in his hand. "When I got back to the States after my stint in the navy and found that Sally's mother had married Sally's father, I tried to get in touch with her. By way of reply I heard from her father, who told me to lay off or he would beat me up."

"He did?" Alix said, plainly awed. And then added naïvely, "He must have been very brave. Perhaps he hadn't met you."

Darcourt made a face. "Ouch! My reputation is made very clear to me. The terrible-tempered Mr. Bangs."

Nobody said anything. Darcourt's eyes glanced from his daughter to me. Incredibly, I found myself feeling sorry for the austere, rather isolated man. "Well," he said, "I'm going over to St. Damien's to do some business. Anybody want to come with me?"

André said nothing. Alix gave him a glowing look. "André and I are going riding."

"Why don't you take Miss Wainright with you?" her father asked.

There was a short silence. Then, "How delightful. Do come," André said.

Any hesitation I might have had vanished when I saw Alix's face. That she was furious at André and even more furious at her father was plain from the looks she was darting at each. Idly I wondered if the fragile brake of good manners would hold her tongue, or whether the spoiled child would win the contest that was visibly going on with her.

The spoiled child won. "Three's a crowd," she said.

"Alix!" Her father's voice was cold. "That is rude and I will not tolerate rudeness. Go to your room!"

"Well, it's true!" she stormed. "Why should Sally, who's a liar and a sneak—"

"Go to your room at once!" her father thundered. "How dare you speak to a guest in that fashion!"

But it was André who delivered the *coup de grâce*. "That was not well said, little one. Bad manners are for *la canaille*, not for a Darcourt—or even a Charpentier. You must not disgrace us, *petite!*"

Alix gave a gasp and burst into tears.

"Well, speaking as a card-carrying member of *la canaille*," I said, "I have never found their talent for insult equal to that of their so-called betters. But I think I will accept your invitation, Mr. Darcourt, to go to St. Damien's. I have a little business of my own and I'd enjoy the day off. When do we leave?"

"As soon as you're ready. I await your pleasure."

I wanted to say something to Alix. Despite the fact that she called me a liar and a sneak (descriptions I didn't relish —yet, by coming under a false name and pretenses, hadn't I been both?), I felt sorry for her. She had, in this little incident, been caught between the upper and lower jaws of the crocodile. And there was an uneasiness about the whole thing that was making itself felt in the back of my mind.

But I left the room without speaking to her partly because she had indeed shown poor manners—and however much I might sympathize, it would do her no good for me to condone them—but also because there was really nothing I could say that wouldn't make bad worse.

But we were destined to get a later start than Darcourt had planned. More to cheer myself up than anything, I had put Susie and me into matching outfits: a bright green summer dress for me and an even brighter green collar and leash for Susie, and was on my way with her downstairs, when I heard below me the unmistakable sound of the back door being thrust open.

"Tristram," a man's voice said, and I recognized it almost immediately as the doctor's.

I was about to continue my descent, when I heard the library door, hidden by the stairs, open. Then came Darcourt's voice.

"Hello, Gilbert, what brings you back so soon? No trouble, I hope."

"I'm afraid so, Tristram."

I came farther down the stairs as the doctor walked towards the library door. For some reason, I wasn't paying much attention to what he said, probably because I was disturbed at what had happened in the dining room, at what I was increasingly feeling had been a trap set for Alix to fall into. But Tristram's voice, sharp with concern, snapped my attention down to the two men.

"What do you mean? Nicole or Alix?"

I paused, one foot halfway down to the next step.

"Both," the doctor said. "Alix's problem is less urgent—but she's not responding to the drug she's been taking as well as I want her to. I want to talk to you about a new one they're using at Carville that's just out of the experimental stage. But that's not the urgent matter. It's Nicole. I think she's finally lost touch with reality. She's got out—"

I love Susie dearly, but at that moment I could have killed her. Because she barked.

The doctor's head jerked up. He went white. Darcourt rounded the back of the stairs, and saw me standing there.

For a moment none of the three of us said anything. Then Darcourt spoke, his voice harsh. "The doctor and I are going out for a while. I'm afraid we're going to be delayed. Please wait for me in the library, Miss Wainright." And he and the doctor disappeared through the back door.

(10)

IT WAS ironic, I thought, walking slowly around the library, reading and rereading the various titles of the books that mounted on shelves to the ceiling.

Darcourt had made it so deliciously easy for me to find out, at least, whether his desk drawers were locked. From the back windows of the book room I had watched him and the doctor drive off in the jeep, Darcourt at the wheel. A few minutes after that André and Alix trotted their horses through the stable gates, by the expression on their faces, totally engrossed with one another. Except for the servants, I was alone.

Nicole had got out, the doctor had said.

Which meant, given all the implications of his white face and disturbed manner, that she was here, not on some spot of the remote French coast.

So Alix had been right all along.

But why?

And what was the disease Alix had, which the doctor was treating with drugs to which she did not respond?

And then I saw the answer that all along had been staring me in the face: mental illness. Mental illness which, today, was treated by drugs. Mental illness which caused a woman living in virtual imprisonment on the island to wander, out of touch with reality, into areas not permitted to her, such as the forest, where Susie and I had heard her; in front of the house, where Susie heard her again, and she knocked me on the head. . . . And then there was Alix, with her freaks and starts, so like her mother . . . not only in appearance and genetic flaw, but in her isolation.

Everything my father had ever said about the rich and mighty poured through my mind. He was right, I thought. Not prejudiced, right. An ordinary family with ordinary views of its status would send its emotionally disturbed members to hospitals or sanitariums, where trained psychiatrists could help them and other patients could communicate with them in a general fellowship of shared mental and emotional suffering.

But not Tristram Darcourt. No Darcourt could be known to suffer such a shameful and shaming disease. Hadn't he talked to me about conservative Cajun French families and their frightened, mediaeval attitude towards insanity? No wonder he knew it so well! Just so was his own.

No wonder Alix—but I was too outraged simply to stand thinking. Going quickly over to the desk, I pulled at one drawer after another. Well, I thought, Brian was right. It was my duty to find out what was in those files. A blast of publicity would let in a lot of fresh air. But how to open the desk? My mind went to movies I had seen, detective novels I had read. Those skilled and practical gentlemen were able to jimmy locks with no more than a paper cutter—like the ones on the blotter!

I was reaching for the cutter when the door opened and snatched my hand back as Mrs. Conyers came in. For a few seconds we stood facing one another. Perhaps it was my overwhelming sense of guilt, but I felt that she was looking at me accusingly, aware of what I had been about to do.

But all she said was, "Good morning, Miss—er—Wainright."

So the household tom-toms had been at work. "Good morning, Mrs. Conyers." I toyed with the rather attractive idea of saying nothing at all about my pretending to be someone else. Who was it who said, *Never complain, never explain, never apologize*? A stoic, no doubt. But I felt the housekeeper deserved some acknowledgment from me. "I'm sorry about the deception."

"It wasn't," she said, "a very nice thing to do, coming into someone's house and violating his hospitality."

"I'm not Mr. Darcourt's guest. I'm his employee."

She looked at me, her eyes direct and sad. "There's no

difference, Miss Wainright. You have eaten his bread and salt, and you have lied to him. That is a breach of trust."

And as she spoke the old-fashioned words, it seemed to me she was right: that she had invoked some ancient, immutable law; a law that applied equally, whether acknowledged or not; one that had been breathed into our bones by ancestors both more primitive and wiser than we had become, with our shifty moral bookkeeping and our clever ways of using words to cover the truth.

"You are probably right," I said finally. "But if that law were fully and publicly observed, in the spirit as well as the letter, it would put most journalists out of business."

"And are you a journalist, Miss Wainright? I've been wondering."

And there it was, lying out in the open. *That which I greatly fear has come upon me.* My father had a great fondness for the Book of Job, and used to read it to me at bedtime. . . . Was it that I *wanted* to be discovered? The self-fulfilling prophesy? To admit that I was here to nose out a story would insure my instant dismissal. Mrs. Conyers would be doing less than what I was sure she would consider her duty if she did not tell Darcourt at the first opportunity. I opened my mouth to deny it. What I said was, "Yes. I am." And stopped, astounded and horrified at myself.

"I thought you were," she said, drawing her shawl around her shoulders. But her voice, which was tired and flat, held no accusation. Beneath the knitted wool her thin shoulders shivered. It was only April, but in New York this would be considered June weather. The housekeeper turned then slightly, and the light fell on her face. The strained, white look of the previous day was there.

"Mrs. Conyers, are you all right?"

"No, Miss Wainright. I'm not. The doctor says I have to go into St. Damien's hospital for X-rays. But I know—I have known for a while—what he will find."

"I'm sorry," I said. "Perhaps treatment—"

"No."

It was final. She walked over to the magazine tables. "I'll be going into St. Damien's with you and Mr. Darcourt, and the doctor."

"I see. Is there anything I can do?"

"Yes. There is something I must tell you. I can't condemn what you've done, because I, too—"

At that moment the door opened and André walked in.

Behind him trailed Alix, looking like a thundercloud.

"Connie, my sweet. What's all this I hear about your being under the weather? Alix tells me you're to go into the island today to the hospital."

I glanced at the housekeeper, and then stared at her, astonished. Her face, which had been whitish before, was gray. Her mouth seemed to have sunk in. She looked suddenly old and frightened to death.

"Because," André went on, going over to her, "if you're going to have to do anything as unpleasant as that, of course I'll take you in. I wouldn't let anyone else do it."

Something was going on but none of it made sense.

André looked up at me. "You know, Connie here was maid and companion to my cousin Nicole, and is very dear to me."

"Master André," she said. And her hand, trembling, went out. He took it, and my heart warmed to him. In the death sentence under which I knew she was suffering, she certainly would not receive such warmth or tenderness from the iron-hearted Darcourt or his spoiled, self-centered daughter.

"I really think—" Alix began.

André whirled on her, "Must you be so selfish and self-centered, *petite*?" he asked in a voice like the lash of a whip.

She just looked at him, then turned on her heel and walked out.

"I'll wait outside," I started to say, when Darcourt came in.

Mrs. Conyers looked at me and then at him. "Mr. Darcourt—"

Here it comes, I thought.

But he brushed both of us aside. "If you're both ready, we'll leave." He glanced briefly at André. "I thought you'd taken Alix out for a ride."

"I had. But when I heard about Connie's having to go to the hospital for X-rays, I came back to take her." He paused. "I'm sure, if she knew, Nicole would want me to do that."

"Very touching," Darcourt said, and I could have struck him, knowing that he knew something—Mrs. Darcourt's presence in the old house—that André didn't know, though perhaps he suspected. "But there's no need. Miss Wainright, Mrs. Conyers, go and get in the jeep."

"I really think—" André said.

But Mrs. Conyers put her hand on his arm. "No, Master André, this is best, I'll go with Miss Wainright."

André hesitated, glanced at Darcourt, then covered her hand with his own. "All right. I'll submit gracefully—if not willingly. But remember"—he shot a challenging look at the saturnine Darcourt—"any time you want any help of any kind, Connie, all you have to do is shout."

"Yes, Master André, I know." She sounded weary, defeated.

I looked at Darcourt's cynical countenance and said, a little belligerently, "If Mrs. Conyers would feel more comfortable going with André in his car, I don't see why she can't."

"Perhaps not, Miss Wainright. But the fact remains she will go with us. Now, if you please, let's not waste any more time."

It was a comment calculated to bring out the worst in me. I opened my mouth, but closed it when Mrs. Conyers put her hand on my arm. "Please, Miss Wainright. Let us go."

"All right," I said, with a hard look at Darcourt. "I'll go out to the car with you."

It was a silent drive. Mrs. Conyers and I sat in the back, with Susie on my lap. When we reached the pier I saw the doctor's car parked nearby and a much larger boat awaiting us than the putt-putt I had come over in.

"You and Mrs. Conyers go down to the cabin," Darcourt said, not bothering to ask what we'd like to do.

"Yassah, boss," I muttered, my hand under the housekeeper's elbow as I shepherded her towards the gang plank. As I put Susie under my arm and stepped down after the housekeeper, I looked up. Darcourt was watching me intently, his black brows brought together over his aggressive nose. His mouth was set in a grim line. "We have a lot to discuss, Miss Wainright," he said with cold anger in his voice.

"We do indeed," I threw back at him and went down to join Mrs. Conyers.

There were a lot of things I wanted to ask the housekeeper. But she was sitting back against the cushions on one of the bunks with her eyes closed. Obviously now was not the moment. So I sat on the bunk across the tiny cabin, with Susie next to me, and thought.

Circumstances had prevented Mrs. Conyers from telling Darcourt that I was a journalist. He already knew I was after something other than information about my mother. I hadn't actually told him I was a freelance news reporter, but, given his considerable resources, he had probably long since found out. His abrasive hostility since he had discovered me

192

on the phone this morning—and undoubtedly overheard my conversation with Brian—could only be attributed to that.

After a while I felt the boat slowing and wished I could go up on deck to watch the approach. I glanced over at Mrs. Conyers. Her eyes were still closed, but somehow I doubted that she was sleeping. There was nothing at the moment I could do for her, and I wasn't even sure she was aware of my presence. I put my feet on the floor and said softly, "Mrs. Conyers?"

She opened her eyes. "Yes?" It was astonishing, I thought, taking in the vague, withdrawn look, how much she had changed in the past few weeks.

"I think we're about to dock. I thought, if you didn't need me, I'd go up to the deck and watch."

That was undoubtedly all too true. I didn't think there was anything anyone, except a doctor, could do now. And yet . . . and yet . . . why did she look so frightened? Did the oldest fear of all, fear of death, account for the look of terror I had seen on her face?

I put Susie under my arm and went up the steep, narrow steps and out onto the deck. St. Damien's, looking very flat and ordinary, by comparison with the almost tropic lushness of Darcourt Island, was coming nearer. The doctor was sitting up by the bow. Darcourt was leaning against the railing.

"Why are the islands so different?" I asked, before I remembered I wasn't speaking to him.

He turned when I spoke. "What do you mean, different?"

By this time I had recalled my resentment. "Never mind," I said, remembering.

"Don't ask a question unless you mean to wait for an answer."

"Don't do this, do do that." The words tumbled out. "Don't you ever get tired of giving orders like some mediaeval sultan? Sir?"

Silence. The doctor looked back; Petersen, who was steering the boat, glanced at me. Was it astonishment on his face? Or satisfaction?

"Yes, Miss Wainright," Darcourt said in a level voice, "in answer to your second question, I get very tired of giving orders, which would be quite unnecessary if people would behave with intelligence and courtesy. Unfortunately, they seldom do. As to your first question. I still don't know what you mean by different, but if you're speaking about the vegetation, then it's because St. Damien's has been tamed to meet the needs of human living. Darcourt hasn't. It's been kept, in so far as possible, the way it was originally. Thanks, Petersen." He took the rope Petersen, who had jumped onto the dock, had thrown to him, and lashed it around a capstan.

His answer enlightened me but did nothing for the sweetness of my temper. I didn't like rebukes under any circumstances, but especially not those that were merited. Feeling unexpectedly unhappy, I put Susie down and tied her leash to the railing. Then I went down the companionway to help Mrs. Conyers up.

Darcourt took her hand as she reached the top, and handed her up to Petersen. Then he turned to me. "Miss Wainright?"

I nodded towards the doctor. "After you." There was something I wanted to say, and knew I had to say it immediately if I was going to get it out.

The doctor stepped up on the dock and walked with Mrs. Conyers the few yards to the roadway. I turned to Darcourt.

"I'm sorry I was rude," I said.

Those strange, brilliant gray eyes watched me for a moment. Then he turned and called to the doctor. "Will you drive Mrs. Conyers to the hospital with you? I'll come later."

The doctor nodded, and he and Mrs. Conyers walked to a car parked along the big apron in front of the garage. Petersen went into the garage and, from the sound, started revving up a car inside.

Darcourt turned back to me. "You're very annoyed with me. Why?"

"If we start talking about that, then I'll undoubtedly be rude again."

"Undoubtedly. But with you that's inevitable. So please answer my question."

"All right. I think it's outrageous that you have locked your wife up in the old house—yes, I've put that much together—because, like the Cajuns you talked about, her mental illness is some kind of disgrace. And because, for the same reason, you've isolated Alix. People used to lock their disturbed relatives up in attics and stick food to them through a hole in the door. But that's not done now."

"And you think that's what I'm doing with my wife and daughter?"

"Their prisons are rich and splendid, but, in effect, aren't you?"

He was silent for a moment, his eyes on me, his fingers

idly playing with Susie's leash, still tied to the rail. "Yes," he said finally. "I am."

"And all because of family pride? Darcourts don't go to sanitariums or hospitals like ordinary people?"

He laughed. "I'm afraid all your suspicions are right. That is the reason." And before I had time to think of a reply, he had leaped up onto the dock and bent down, holding out his hand. "I'm afraid we have to be getting along," he said agreeably.

I untied Susie, handed her up to Darcourt, and then took his proferred hand up myself. Petersen had backed another car out of the garage. "Come along," Darcourt said. "I'll give you a lift to wherever you want to go."

But I had other plans. "Thank you. I have my own car in the garage. Just tell me when you want to take the boat back, or if Petersen is available at all times to take someone over."

"He's available at all times. If you want to take the bigger boat back, then be here at five this afternoon. Otherwise, Petersen can take you over later in the dinghy."

"All right. Thanks." I nodded and went off towards the garage.

With Susie in the front seat beside me, I drove off behind Darcourt.

I had three purposes in mind: One was to find a public telephone well beyond the hearing of anyone. The second was a visit to the local library to look up some Darcourt Island history, and the third was to inquire if there was anything for me at General Delivery. Before I left New York, Brian and I had arranged that should he wish to send me something that he did not want to direct via the Darcourt residence, he would address it in care of General Delivery, St. Damien's Island. Since he had not made any reference to it, however guarded, when we talked on the telephone, I was sure he had not availed himself of our arrangement. Still, I would check, and I might as well go there first.

Since I had no notion where any of the places I wanted were located, I just kept on going along the Shore Road, knowing that sooner or later it would converge with the road coming off the causeway, and that that would lead me into the center of the little town. At some point I passed the mud track in which I had been so nearly stuck, and waved my arms towards it. By an obvious sequence of thought, I was reminded of the blond young man and that, in turn, made me think of Alix's (alleged) boyfriend.

Had she invented him? She was quite capable of it, either to show off or to make mischief or simply to give herself a boost. If it were the latter, she had all my sympathy. While other girls her age were holding hands in the movies or indulging in other, less innocent, pastimes, she was stuck in her family home, which, in addition to its other repressive aspects, was an island.

But, much as I sympathized with her trying to palm a fantasy off as reality, there was no denying the importance of attempting to find out if it were objectively true or not. Who could I ask? Certainly not Darcourt or Mrs. Conyers. Then who? . . . The answer, of course, was plain and obvious and lying in front of me. André. Her handsome cousin, who was not only closely related, but had the additional advantage of being the subject of an intense crush on Alix's part, would be the person who would know. I would ask him about this as soon as I returned. If Alix were getting off the island at night, or the blond young man (if it were he) was managing to get on, then, much as I disliked thinking about the harsh steps he would unquestionably take, her father would have to know.

By the time I had arrived at this thought, we had also, in another sense of the word, arrived, this time at the confluence of the three roads leading from the causeway.

Turning right, I drove towards the town, and in a few minutes was coasting down the main drag. It was a beautiful street, wide, with huge oaks soaring up on either side. Their interlocking branches, from which the characteristic hanging moss trailed and moved in the breeze, met and crisscrossed, so that the houses and shops and people were in dappled sunlight, protected from the fierce intensity of the southern sun.

I drove slowly along, feeling as though I had moved back into a different, younger world. What were now shops had obviously once been houses, their windows square and neatly partitioned, a frame here and there a little crooked with age, but beautifully kept, the paint spanking new. I slowed the car even more. A grocery, a shoe repair store, a shoe shop, a drugstore, a bookshop, a dress shop, and a hamburger and coffee shop were all on one side, a few of brick with white trim, most of white frame. On the other side was a restaurant, another dress shop, a needlework shop, a dry goods store, a men's store, a liquor store, another grocery, a butcher. What had once been hitching posts still lined the pavements under trees, and the pavements themselves were crooked where the tree roots had started to grow up through the surface of the road. There were also, I noted, those recent bastions of urban self-service—parking meters. After traveling a few more yards I found an empty space and parked the car. Getting out, I locked the car and stood, considering. The post office did not appear to be here. Well, I thought, there were some drugstore items I had to renew, so I might as well start there instead.

An hour later, I had also visited the grocery, where I had replenished my supply of canned and dry food for Susie, bought a sweater that was not on my agenda (or in my budget) but which sent me a siren call through a shop window, bought some paperbacks and some stockings and decided it was time for lunch.

Between the restaurant and the hamburger joint, I chose the hamburger place. Marching in, I ordered a cheeseburger with everything on it, French fries and a coffee, and while I waited, asked for a paper cup of water for Susie. I had been in places where this was either refused or given grudgingly, and I marked the place accordingly. I was therefore happy to give this particular beanery my triple star. Not only did Susie get her cup of water, she got a small piece of hamburger, put on a napkin by the chef, who had overheard my request. I smiled at him. Encouraged, he came and stared over the counter at Susie, who was happily cleaning up the hamburger and turning her attention to the water.

"Smallest dog I ever saw," he said. "But pretty." And went back to his griddle.

"Sit where you like," the waitress said, putting my order on the counter in front of me.

I turned, remembering tables by the window facing the street. It would be nice to watch the passing parade as I ate.

With Susie's leash looped over my wrist, and carrying my plate and the coffee, I walked along the tables hoping to come on an empty one. But this was the regular lunch hour, and they appeared well filled. I passed a couple, two girls, two young men, another couple, a single male with his back to me, another couple, then was jolted to a halt, by the pull of the leash loop around my right wrist.

"Hey," I said, and turned.

Her paws up against his leg, her mouth busy with more hamburger, Susie had found a friend.

"Susie!" I said, looking down at her.

"Won't you *both* join me?" a familiar voice asked. I looked up. Darcourt, upsetting Susie, had stood up.

My heart gave a funny leap. Against all my will and intention, my mouth smiled. And the odd, half smile of Darcourt's that raised such havoc with my interior flickered over his face in response.

"Please?" he said.

I put down my plate and coffee and secured Susie's leash under the chair leg. "Between you and the chef, her food regimen is being shot to pieces."

"A little sin now and again gives you something interesting to confess," he said. "As a good, brought-up Catholic you should know that."

"Umm." I wondered what Mother FitzAlan of the convent school and Father McCarry would have made of that theology. "I don't know about good. Certainly brought-up. I'll try it on Father Mark sometime and see how he reacts."

"He would take you very seriously and give you a lecture on the innocence of all animals with periodic dialectical excursions into the theories of Father Tielhard de Chardin."

I made a face. "He sounds a drag. Father Mark, I mean, not Teilhard de Chardin."

"He's worthy but humorless."

There were all the ingredients there for a promising discussion, but my mind was preoccupied with my surprise at seeing Darcourt sitting in the hamburger joint. I glanced up over the big shoulders to the thin, dark sardonic face, and, once again, I had the eerie feeling that he knew exactly what I was thinking. He grinned at me suddenly and I burst out, "I can't get over your being here."

"Because I'm so rich and mighty?"

"Yes."

He fed a small piece of hamburger to Susie, who was looking up at him devotedly. "What a dreary view of life you have, Miss Wainright. The whole world, like your Susie, here, waiting eagerly for hamburger from the tables of the rich."

"Well," I said more sharply than I intended, "isn't that the way it is?"

"I would hate to think so, entirely. Because that would mean that the . . . er . . . affections and favor of all those who have little hamburger, or no hamburger at all, are for sale." Those light eyes were penetrating. "Do you think that's the case? Is that the way you operate?"

I was so angry I felt dizzy.

He laughed softly and crumpled his napkin. "If I offered to take you to lunch, I'm afraid you'd throw what's left of it at me." He picked up his check and rose. "Good morning, Miss Wainright. It's been, as always, a pleasure."

Depositing a tip, he walked off. Seething, I watched his back as he limped towards the door. But it was a slow progress, because several people spoke to him, including, finally, the waitress who had given me my order and Susie her water. This time he stopped her and they spoke for a few minutes. She was a young, attractive woman, with blonde hair and a figure that would have made millions for her if she had chosen to exploit it. But perhaps she had, I found myself thinking, watching her profile turned up towards Darcourt's face. After all, with a crazy wife. . . .

Stop it, stop it, stop it, I told myself, shocked at the disorderly feeling that seemed to be racing through me.

"Here," I told Susie, "since you're so fond of hamburger you can have the rest."

But such was the perversity of human and canine nature, that Susie sniffed, then sat back and looked at it. Then she went under my chair and lay down. For some reason, I felt spurned, and had to remind myself that she had had more to eat this morning than she usually had in a day, and that Susie, unlike many humans, knew when enough was enough. I stared down at my plate, and was leaning down to pick it up when the waitress came along.

"Gee, you weren't very hungry, were you?" She bent and picked it up for me. "Will that be all, or would you like some dessert?"

"No, thanks," I said rather brusquely. For some reason I couldn't put my finger on, she irritated me.

"How do you like Darcourt Island?" she asked, as she wrote.

Not only, I thought, had she probably been seduced by all that wealth and power and attractiveness, well anyway, wealth and power . . . into being his mistress. She had also undoubtedly been recruited as a spy.

"Why do you ask?" I countered.

"Just curious." She tore off the slip. "You see—" She looked at the slip, then put it back on her pad and altered one of the figures, giving herself time to think up an answer, I deduced. So I said quickly, "I suppose Mr. Darcourt asked you to ask me that."

She put down her pad and stared at me. "What a funny thing to say," she commented.

Silently I agreed. It was. Not to say insulting. And I could feel my cheeks get red and wondered what on earth had made me say it. I had opened my mouth to apologize, when I realized suddenly what it was that had motivated my question. And I closed my mouth, my humiliation complete.

"I was asking you how you liked Darcourt," the woman said, putting the check down on the table, "because my sister works there as housemaid, and she told me about your being there."

"I'm sorry," I said, getting up. "I realize I was offensive, and didn't mean to be." Liar, I thought to myself. Of course I meant to be. "Come along, Susie." I lifted the chair releasing her leash.

The woman started cleaning off the table. "Mr. Darcourt was asking me about my husband, who works for him, and who's in the hospital." She straightened, her hands full of cup and glass and plate. "The best of medical care. All expenses paid, by Mr. Darcourt. And he didn't have to do it. Jim wasn't hurt while on the job."

Feudal patronage, my rebellious mind commented. "That was nice of him," I said out loud. "But wouldn't his union take care of it?"

"His union wouldn't take care of an injury got when Jim came out of the local roadhouse with a skinful and then drove eighty miles an hour."

Darcourt the enabler, I thought. Also, this will put the wretched man in Darcourt's power.

"Of course"—the woman went on balancing her burden with one hand while she mopped off the table with another— "he made Jim promise to go to AA—you know, Alcoholics Anonymous—when he gets out of the hospital."

I could have thought up an evil motive for that, too, if it hadn't been exactly what Patrick James Wainright did to some of his construction men who had booze problems. "Ye go to AA or you're out. And that's flat. I'll not have any drunks out on the high girders, killin' himself and, worse, puttin' others in danger. Take it or leave it." Some jeered and left. Others did as they were told, and then stayed with AA of their own accord.

I sighed, frustrated. The woman gave me an odd look. "He's a good man, is Mr. Darcourt. I know, I used to work up at the house before I married. He has had a lot of unhappiness—but I shouldn't say more." And she hurried off.

Frustrated with myself over what I knew to be my own unattractive motives, I left the hamburger place and headed for the car.

It was then, as I was approaching the car, that I saw the motorcyclist with the cowlick. In fact, I could hardly miss him. Astride his motorbike, my erstwhile guide was right behind my car, talking to a friend standing beside him. In order for me to back out of my parking space, either he would have to move or I would have to run over him. Any doubt I might have had as to whether he was behind my car on purpose or by accident vanished as I saw him watching me approach. On his not unhandsome features was an expression compounded of equal parts of insolence and defiance. Without altering my pace or my direction, I walked towards him. I was just level with him when he sneered at me, on a strong whiff of bourbon.

"Been stuck in any good roads lately?"

I made a stab at playing it cool. "No. Not lately."

"Had a nice lunch with the master?"

This time the calculated slap was unmistakable.

Perhaps if I hadn't been saying something of the same sort to myself, if I didn't already owe this obnoxious, overage brat a grudge, if his friend hadn't sniggered, I mightn't have succumbed to my weakness for the flip, snappy comeback. But I did.

"Better than with the servant," I said lightly, violating all my social principles, but meaning nothing in particular except to be offensive. My words had a startling effect. The man's face flooded crimson. The word he flung after me was not polite, and it effectively removed any remorse I might be feeling. Getting in the car, I started it, looked back, sounded the horn and went into reverse. At the last moment he got out of the way—fast, and I was a little ashamed of the satisfaction I had out of seeing him move. One thing was sure, though I would have to ask someone how to get to the post office, I was not about to ask my previous guide.

Still, as I backed out and turned, I couldn't help puzzling over his hostility. The only solution that made any sense was the obvious one: that if he were indeed Alix's boyfriend, he would naturally be hostile to a governess specifically hired to make Alix toe the line, which undoubtedly meant not allowing her off Darcourt Island, and not allowing him on.

True, nothing had been said to me about keeping him—

or any other young man—off. But he wouldn't know that. And, from his point of view, if his coming and going were freely allowed, wouldn't I have been told?

By this time I had arrived at the end of the street. The buildings were thinning out and, a few yards ahead, there was another road running at right angles to the one I was on. Just short of the corner I stopped and asked directions of a pleasant-looking woman. Both the post office and the town library were to the left, she told me. What about a phone booth? I inquired. There were public telephones in the post office and also stationed in front of both buildings. I thanked my informant and turned left.

I drove for a few yards along another oak-shaded street, this time, though, without buildings, and I was wondering if my pleasant guide was one of those people who meant right when she pointed left, when the road suddenly widened into a small plaza. Off to the right was a tall piece of sculpture that looked like it might be a war memorial. To the left was a neat concrete building with junior versions of the New York Public Library lions in front. Next to that was another concrete building that, going by the lettering outside, seemed to comprise all federal, state and local offices, plus the post office. And—just as described—dotted up and down were several phone booths.

I went first to the post office and ascertained that Brian had not, indeed, sent me anything. I was coming down the steps with Susie when I saw the motorcyclist again. This time he was alone, but he was still in his characteristic pose, astride his machine with one foot on the road, his eyes on the front entrance to the post office building. When he saw me he stared at me unsmilingly for a few seconds, then raised his eyes above my head and gazed into space.

I found myself wishing strongly he would go somewhere else. For a moment I pondered confronting him and demanding to know the reason for his belligerence. But, remembering the liquor on his breath, I didn't think it would do anything but give him the satisfaction of being rude again. So I decided to let it go.

Susie and I went up the library steps. I was a little doubtful as to how welcome she'd be in a public library. I could, of course, lock her in the car. But she didn't much like that, and even though this was not New York City, I didn't feel like exposing her to someone's sudden rapacious impulse.

I went through the big glass double doors of the main

entrance, pushed open the door to the right marked "Reading Room" and went over to the Information Desk where a young girl was sitting.

"I'd like to look up any historical material you have on Darcourt and St. Damien's islands. Do you have some?"

She smiled. "Oh, yes. There are several books over in the second stack, there to your left. But," she glanced down at Susie, "I'll have to tell you—dogs aren't allowed in here."

"I can't leave her outside," I said. "She's quite old. Someone . . . I just can't."

The girl looked at me. I looked at the girl. Then she looked down at Susie, who had the intelligence and diplomacy to make a slight motion with her tail.

"Go and sit over there, at the end of the table in the corner. Nobody'll see her. I'll bring you the books."

"Thank you very much," I said. And did as I was told.

The "corner" was near a big front window. I settled Susie and stared out. There was the youth still sitting astride his motorbike and staring in a fixed manner at the library.

When the girl came back with the books I asked her, "Who's that?"

She followed the direction of my nod and looked out. Then she made a noise that sounded like "Tcha!"

"That's Boyd Lambert," she said. "Why?"

"Because he seems to be following me. And because owing to him I almost got stuck in the mud on my way to Darcourt Island."

I said it casually and with a smile. But the effect of my words was electrifying. The girl, who had been open and friendly, stepped back. Her face seemed to close up.

"What's the matter?" I said.

"Nothing's the matter. Why should anything be the matter? But please leave as soon as you've checked those. Like I said, dogs are not allowed in the library." And she turned on her heel and left.

I started after her, totally perplexed. It had all happened so fast. And her sudden reversion to the matter of Susie's presence in the library was ridiculous and transparently an excuse.

It was also eerie and more than a little disturbing. But there was something about the way the young woman looked pointedly at the big clock on the wall and then at me that made me realize I didn't have too long before I—or rather Susie, which amounted to the same thing, because I wouldn't leave her outside where I couldn't see her—got our eviction notice.

I started going through the island histories with a divided mind, but after a while forgot the librarian.

One would think, I reflected fifteen minutes later, that a small dot of a place like this, going back to before the English settlements, would have island chronicles lovingly put together by local historians down to the last detail. Yet there was a strangely elusive quality about the accounts. One startling fact emerged: both islands were, and always had been, owned by the Darcourts. Perhaps, I thought, this accounted for the lack of local gossip. If one lived on what amounted to a private fief, pride of township might be stunted at birth.

Darcourt Island had once been the fortified residence of the Spanish governor, and there had been, as André had stated, also a hospital on Darcourt Island, well behind the fort, used for the victims—seemingly numerous—of local fever. Damien Island was a port for Spanish ships, and a harbor from which they could launch raids against stray English merchantmen. After it had finally been taken by the English, King Charles, in gratitude to Gervase Tristram D'Harcourt for various military services, removed the islands from a previous grant to someone else and bestowed them on his new favorite, General D'Harcourt. And the D'Harcourts, through what appeared to be a clever combination of wealth, patriotic service, ruthlessness and politics, had managed to retain the islands, even during the Civil War and, even more remarkable, during the Reconstruction after the war was over.

I couldn't help getting the feeling, reading between the lines, that no one showed any outstanding eagerness to take the islands away from the Darcourts and make them state or federal territory. And it wasn't because male Darcourts hadn't fought in the Confederate Army, because they had.

I closed one book and opened another. Nothing much new there, except that the Darcourts at some point had moved the fever hospital onto Damien Island—certainly well before the Civil War. A little later emerged the interesting fact that both islands had been called Darcourt, the smaller island, where the family lived, being designated by the name Darcourt Place. The name Damien—just Damien, and not St. Damien's—appeared in references to the island some years later. But no date was given for the change of name. In fact, the change was not mentioned at all. Then sometime between 1945 and 1960 Damien Island became St. Damien's. Only since it was referred to even more frequently as "the larger island" than by either of the other names, it was impossible to pin down the date of the second change any closer than that.

And that was about it.

As far as I could make out, most residents lived either by farming, or by buying and selling to and from one another, and from the tourist trade.

I closed the last book feeling frustrated. There really was very little to go on. My reporter's instinct oddly aroused, I wondered if there were some skeleton or scandal that had been carefully left out, or if Darcourt had used his *droit du seigneur* to keep out all but the most vapid and uninteresting facts.

The thought of Darcourt did nothing for my serenity or peace of mind. Partly to shake off his ghosts, I put the books in a neat pile and looked around.

Was it my imagination? Was I indeed growing paranoid, or did I catch several covert glances, all of which, on catching my eye, seemed to hasten back to their books or papers?

At that moment, the young woman looked up, looked at the clock, looked down in the corner where Susie lay peacefully asleep and then at me.

"All right," I muttered to myself. "I get your point."

Leaving the books stacked, I picked up Susie. I was headed for the door when something made me change directions and go over to the librarian's desk. I had no very clear purpose in mind. For some reason I wanted to see her close up again and test out her reaction.

"Yes?" she said. "What is it?"

Her hostility, or discomfort, or something, was unmistakable. "I—" I started to say.

"I told you we don't allow dogs in here," she broke in in a whisper. "Several people have asked me already why the rule doesn't apply to you—people who have dogs themselves, and who don't like leaving them any more than you do. Please take her out."

I glanced around. There were those covert stares again. Well, it could be indignation over having different rules for different people. I stared at the library's main entrance, of which I had a clear view through the glass door of the Reading Room.

"Just a minute," I said.

I took Susie outside, and to her sorrow and indignation, ran the leash through the metal door handle and then snapped it onto her collar. "I won't be a minute," I said, patting her.

I went back inside, turned around to see her sitting there with forlorn dignity, then went through the glass doors to the Reading Room, and backed towards the librarian's desk. Still with my eyes on the front door, I went on going till I was past the librarian and could see her face.

I still had no very clear idea of what I was going to say. But suddenly the words were there. "Why did you change so suddenly? One minute you were friendly and the next hostile."

My frontal attack surprised her. Her face flushed. "I don't know what you mean."

"Oh, yes you do." I didn't bother to keep my voice down.

"Be quiet," she whispered fiercely.

"Only if you tell me what I want to know."

There was now no question about the heads that were up. Everyone in the big Reading Room was listening.

Far towards the back a door opened. A gray-haired man stuck his head out, frowning. Behind him there was a glimpse of a handsome office.

The girl whispered, "That's the head librarian. If we make any more noise, I'll be in trouble."

I dropped my voice accommodatingly and whispered. "Then what was it that made you change?"

If I hadn't been so determined to get an answer to my question, I would have felt sorry for her. She looked torn and confused. Then she said something I couldn't catch.

"What?" I whispered, and moved to the side of the desk where I could hear her better.

"Nobody wants to be unkind," she said miserably. "But it could ruin the tourist trade we're trying to build."

It made no sense. I went closer, wondering if I had misheard. "What could?"

She looked up. "They already have hospitals for that. They don't need to put another on the island here."

I could feel my pulse speeding up with a familiar excitement. Somehow I had stumbled on a story. Nevertheless, I hesitated. If I said, What are you talking about? I was sure she'd withdraw from such a direct approach. So I sifted through various sentences that could be taken as though I knew what she meant. "Are the people very much against it?" I finally asked.

"Well, wouldn't you be? If it were your town? And we're even afraid of holding meetings, in case Mr. Darcourt were to hear. In the modern world it sounds inhumane, I *know*, but—"

I had been staring absently at the bookstacks behind her desk. At that moment, I heard Susie's yelp. I also realized that it was several minutes since I had moved and lost sight of her.

Going swiftly around the desk I once again saw the outside glass double doors.

Susie was no longer there. I ran.

When I got outside there was no sign of Susie.

For a minute I felt so sick that it was all I could do to keep my lunch down. Dreadful scenes went through my head: Susie in some thieving, uncaring stranger's grasp . . . someone who—but I yanked my mind away from that. And as I did a great rage, like a hot fire, swept through me.

Turning, I ran back through the double doors, through the doors to the Reading Room and marched up to the desk. Reminding myself that I needed her help, I said as evenly as I could, "Boyd Lambert has taken Susie. I'm sure of it. I fastened her leash to the front door and was watching her as I talked to you. And I know he was out there when I went out. But she's not there and neither is he. Whatever's happened to upset you and the others, it's not her fault. Where would he take her?"

She stared at me, a look of consternation on her face. "He wouldn't do that."

"Wouldn't he?" I asked, not bothering to keep my voice down.

She stared back at me. I could see she felt distressed. But after a minute or two she shrugged, "I'm sorry, there's nothing I can do."

I leaned forward. "Isn't there? Well, let me tell you something I don't think you know. I'm not a governness. I'm a newspaper reporter." (That blew that cover, I reflected in passing, but it didn't matter.) "I'm doing a story for—" And I mentioned a well-known and popular news magazine. "You spoke of the feeling over the hospital. Now, I can do that story two ways. I can do it from your point of view, and I can write it in such a way that even a man as powerful as Darcourt wouldn't care to push the matter further. The kind of magazine I work for would love to have something they could use to push the Darcourts of this world around.

"On the other hand, I can write the whole thing in a way that will make the islanders look like inhuman monsters in opposing a hospital for the ill and needy. By the time I'm through you couldn't *pay* people to come here. And if I don't get Susie back, that's the way I'll write it."

These were all shots in the dark. And what connection they had with Alix's boyfriend I didn't know. Furthermore, they amounted to bald-faced blackmail. But Susie was Susie.

The librarian really looked white now. Then she got up. "Just a minute," she said. Passing around the desk, she went across the Reading Room to the office I had seen. Going in, she closed the door.

I hadn't made up my mind what to do if she stayed in there. But she was out in a very short time. She returned to her desk and got her bag out of a bottom drawer. "Come on," she said.

I followed her outside and down the steps. When we got to the bottom she turned. "I think I know where he'd take your dog. But I'm going alone."

I started to object, but she said, "If he saw you coming, he'd hide her or even . . . maybe . . . try to get rid of her. I'll meet you at the Darcourt pier—or anyway, I'll see to it you'll find Susie there—in an hour."

I stared back at her in the waning afternoon.

"If I don't find my Susie—and find her alive and well— then I will go to the nearest telephone and phone my story."

"Yes. I know, I think the others . . . he . . . will return your dog to you for that reason. He wasn't supposed to do anything. But then he's so erratic."

"Why can't I wait here?"

"Because both buildings close soon. It's nearly five. And it's better for you—and for Susie—if I . . . or someone . . . if you find her on the Darcourt jetty." She paused, and then made her meaning more unmistakable. "Mr. Petersen will probably be there. You'll be safer. Here, in this area, town feeling runs high."

I shrugged. "All right. In an hour."

She nodded. Then crossed the little plaza to a small car parked on the other side. I watched her get in, start the car and drive away.

Without her there my fears and imaginings rushed back. As much to keep those at bay as anything, I went to one of the phone booths set like sentinals around the little square.

I dialed Brian's direct line at the magazine.

"Where are you?" he said.

I told him. "Did you look up those things for me?"

"Of course. The one place where the word 'Javelin' hit pay dirt was the Pentagon. Our Pentagon guy dropped it casually in a certain office, then found himself in Army Intelligence being questioned within an inch of his life. He kept talking about freedom of the press, and they kept talking about national security. He couldn't get much. But what he did get was dynamite, involving some kind of big oil deal between Sultan Darcourt and his Arab friends, and an Arab takeover of one of our off-shore islands. But that's when everybody clammed up. Good work, baby!"

Normally I would cherish those words of professional praise. But I was too far gone in misery to feel anything. "Thanks," I said, not caring.

I couldn't come out with the other agony that was tearing me in strips. How could I say, *Having felt nothing more exciting than affection for all the decent men I've known, I now discover that I've fallen in love with the monster of all time, who according to what you've just told me, has a cozy plan going to add to his already indecent wealth and incidentally sell out his country's interests?*

I couldn't tell Brian that. So I told him about Susie, which also was a terrible pain. "All because these selfish people seem to be afraid that a new hospital for the mentally ill is going to mess up their trade."

There was a silence at the other end.

"Brian?" I said.

"That was the other thing I was going to tell you," he said. "I poked around a little on that medical trail you gave me, and dug up the damndest rumor I've ever heard. It can't be true—not today. But, of course, realistically, I guess it can be."

"You mean about Mrs. Darcourt being nuts? What's so unusual about that? Lots of rich people are—as well as the poor and in-between."

"Yes. No. I mean . . . you got the right idea, but the wrong illness."

"Then what's the matter with her?"

He told me.

(11)

AN HOUR, the librarian had said. And it wouldn't be in my interest to wait here.

I glanced at the library behind me. Given Brian's astonishing information, the temptation to go back into the library's Reading Room and embark on an altogether different research project was overwhelming. But if the girl brought Susie to the pier in less than an hour, and didn't find me there. . . . There was simply no question. I had to get to the jetty and stay there, whether it meant fifteen minutes—or four hours.

I don't remember the drive there at all. Thoughts chaotic and topsy-turvy seemed to chase one another through my head.

One fairly solid conclusion came floating to the surface: Given what I now knew—if it were indeed true—the hostility and resulting act of the blond boy, Boyd Lambert, stemmed, not from amorous frustration over being forbidden to see Alix, but, along with other St. Damien's people, island indignation over Darcourt's plans to build a special hospital there. That the indignation stemmed from an ancient ignorance I was pretty sure. But, under the circumstances, and in view of what Brian had told me, understandable.

What I could not understand was Darcourt's role, which argued either a high level of insensitivity to the way the townspeople felt, or incredible stupidity—or both. It was some kind of gloomy testament to something that while I could not accept the thesis of his stupidity—Darcourt was manifestly not stupid—I did not experience the same difficulty over his insensitivity. At least, in my head I didn't.

I turned away again from this unhappy subject back to Boyd Lambert. And that took me in another direction. If he were not Alix's boyfriend, then was one of my other guesses true—that she was merely trying it on to be interesting and mysterious?

It would be quite like her. Yet I didn't think so. At this point, my cogitations were interrupted by my arrival at the jetty.

Drawing up beside the apron in front of the pier, I got out and looked around. The garage doors were all closed, undoubtedly locked. Two boats bounced up and down at the end of the pier: the big dinghy with the outboard motor—the putt-putt, I had first come over in—and an ordinary rowboat. Of the cruiser in which I had crossed with Darcourt, the doctor and Mrs. Conyers, there was no sign. Nor of Petersen.

Mr. Petersen will be there, the girl had said. Petersen is at all times available, Darcourt had stated. Yet Petersen was nowhere in sight.

"Well, Su—" I started and then stopped, my words echoing. I stood there a moment. I am not an anthropomorphist. Susie was all dog. Words were not her medium of communication. But the strength of her personality was none the less for all that, and her absence was a sore void. "She will come back," I said aloud, whistling to myself in the dark.

And then I remembered Delilah, a white mouse I had had as a child. One evening when I got home from school Delilah had gone.

Several hours later my father, who had lent me his big white handkerchief to cry into, said, "Ye'll not be forgetting St. Anthony, will you? He finds things that are lost. And then there's always St. Jude, patron saint of lost causes. Isn't that so," he turned to my mother, "Giselle, me darlin'?"

My mother bent her black head over her needlework. "Yes, I believe so," she said in an unenthusiastic voice. Staring at her out of my puffy red eyes, it occurred to me dimly that Mother had never shown much interest in the pets—domestic and wild—that had shared my room with me. And she was even less taken with Delilah than with the rabbits and guinea pigs I had brought home. Mice to her were mice, regardless of color, and were the housewife's foe.

"So," my father said, getting a clean handkerchief out of the kitchen drawer and giving it to me, "you might, when you say your prayers tonight, mention the matter of Delilah's return to both St. Anthony and St. Jude." And I had. Fervently. And although overjoyed, was not totally astonished to wake up the next morning to the sound of skittering feet. My eyes sprang open. There, at work on her little treadwheel, was Delilah.

From then on, and through many lapses, I had retained a fondness for the two saints, even though I sometimes wondered how much my father had lent assistance to the miracle by inducing my mother to return the wretched Delilah. It was not too hard to figure out that Mother had kidnapped her, but found herself reluctant both to set her loose and have her running around the house, or to dispatch her. (Mother would not be up to the act of execution.) I never asked, so I never really knew.

Standing, staring out over the water, I sent up prayers to both saints on behalf of Susie, and then, for good measure, to St. Francis, patron saint of animals, and to the Lord of all Creation Himself, Defender of absolutely everybody.

When that was done I found my mind going back to my parents. How very different they were. . . . And then, like a wall opening, another scene entered my mind. A very different one: a quarrel filled with bitterness and accusation. How old was I? Five? Six? Even, perhaps, seven. Curious. The memory must have been there all along, but only now, for the first time, did it come flooding back.

We were living then in two rooms, the walls as thin as paper. They were in the bedroom, and I was in what was meant to be an oversized closet or dressing room. It had no windows, so, to make sure I was never shut inside, a block was put between the lintel and the door. The voices—my father's bellowing, my mother's soft with her special brand of anger—as clear as though my parents were standing by my bed. In fact, of course, they were only a few feet away.

"Ye should tell the child," my father roared, getting more Irish, as he always did when excited. "Not now, maybe. But later. It's not fair for her to know nothing of what happened to your sister."

Then my mother's voice, but too soft for me to make out the words. In reply, my father's again. "I'm telling you, that's daft. Nobody thinks that now. . . ."

Then Mother: one or two words I didn't hear. Then, "Tristram did."

Silence—as baffling as the fight and much more frightening. Then, following a sound that could have been Mother quietly crying, my father's voice, soft and tender.

Now, nearly twenty years later, I felt the terrible discomfort of my younger self lying there on my cot, pulling the covers over my head. Somehow their tenderness was so much harder to listen to than their rare fights.

I stood there, my hands jammed in my sweater pocket, grateful for the extra cover as the evening breeze came off the water.

Had Mother's reference in her delirium to "Sis" shaken loose that memory from the forgotten past, only to surface now? Or was it what Brian had told me? I shivered, and decided to go back to the garage and try the doors to see if I could find Petersen.

There were three doors in all and, I noticed for the first time, an outside staircase on the far side, obviously leading up to an apartment above the garage itself. Over a bell was a white card saying, simply, "Petersen."

I rang the bell and could hear it faintly, echoing above. After a minute I rang it again. Still no reply.

I had no hope really of being able to pull up any one of the garage doors, or even what I would do if I could. Still, out of reflex action, I tugged on the first, then on the second, without budging either, and then, without even thinking, on the third. Consequently, when it went rolling up I almost fell over backwards. The light in the garage was on and I stood staring. In the space where my car had been lay Petersen.

Running over, I knelt down. He lay on his back, his eyes staring, one side of his head a bloody mess. I had hardly known Petersen; also I'm not particularly squeamish. But it was an ugly and shocking sight and I closed my eyes and fought back nausea. Then I opened them again. There was no question but that he was dead. Overcoming reluctance, I put my hand on his. Although not yet cold, it was not warm.

Standing, I looked around. It was then I saw there had been some kind of a struggle. A rickety table was overturned, and what had obviously been on top—tools of one kind or another—scattered over the floor. A can of white paint had fallen, making a pale lake on the oily concrete. I stared at the shambles and then saw one of the tools, an oversized monkey wrench, lying apart from the others, as though thrown. Even from where I stood I could see it was sticky with congealed blood. At that the nausea threatened to return. Somehow the wrench, with its dreadful stains, seemed to bring violence into the room in a way that even the body itself didn't.

Feeling the need of air, I went to the door and took a couple of breaths. Then I checked my watch. Six thirty. The big boat, now missing, was to have taken Darcourt across at five. Depending on how long Petersen had been dead, he had had time to take Darcourt (and the doctor? And Mrs. Conyers?) back and return. But in that case, where was the big boat? Of course, Darcourt could have taken it back himself and docked it there. I had doubts about Darcourt's character and motives that threatened sorely my peace of mind (let alone my peace of heart). But I had no doubts whatsoever about his ability to handle far more challenging and complicated devices than a speed boat.

More to the point: Who had killed Petersen? And why?

The girl had said that town feeling ran high over the matter of a new hospital. But what did the dour boatman have to do with that?

Unless Petersen had been killed as a warning to Darcourt, as, perhaps, Susie had been taken as a warning to me simply because I was connected—however remotely—with the Darcourt interest.

Susie. . . . But I had tried to tie her safety to their self-interest, and I said another prayer now that I had convinced them. It was at that moment that I saw, far off, headlights approaching.

I started to walk out to stand in front of the apron. Then I hesitated. Should I pull the garage door shut? If this were the handiwork of a furious town, what would they do to me if I had discovered the body? But, somehow, I couldn't pull the door down and pretend he wasn't there, so, quaking, I walked slowly to the edge of the road, my mind and hope and will concentrating on having Susie restored to me.

I don't know what I expected. Certainly not to have the car stop about twenty yards away. I started to walk towards it.

"Stay where you are," a man's voice said. And to my horror the barrel of a rifle came through the side window, pointed at me.

"You can't see us from there," the voice went on, "and that's the way we like it."

It was true. I was facing almost due west, and the orange setting sun was straight in my eyes, which were even further blinded by the headlights.

"Do we have your word that you ain't gonna write us up in a way that'll hurt the town?"

"Yes, I promise."

" 'Course," the voice said, as though presenting another viewpoint, "promises at the point of a gun don't mean much, do they?"

"I keep my word," I assured him as steadily as I could. "I always have. And," I said, "you also have my word that if I don't get my dog back, I'll write that story so as no one will be caught dead here."

It was an unfortunate way of putting it, I thought, staring at the round black hole at the end of the gun barrel. My mind went to Petersen's body. For the first time I wondered if I, myself, were in danger.

"And if," I said, my eyes still on the gun, "anything happens to me, the man at the magazine in New York for whom I'm working will come down here with reporters and photographers and TV cameras and *really* do a job on the island."

It was a risk, threatening them like this, and I knew it. They could just as easily decide to bump me off, push my body into one of the marshes, and hope for the best. I held my breath, standing in the road, the car a black blob against the flaming orange ball about ready to sink into the mainland.

Then I heard and saw one of the car doors open. Since I was braced for a human form to outline itself against the brilliant background, it took me a moment to realize that a very small dot was running along the road towards me.

"Susie!" I cried.

The next moment my arms were full of Norwich Terrier and my face was being ecstatically licked.

"Thank you!" I called out. "Thank you very much!"

"Just remember what you promised. We can get her back any time. Don't matter where you are. We'll have somebody there."

The car engine revved up, and then quietened again. "What did you say that dawg is?" drawled another voice.

"Norwich Terrier."

"Never heard of no breed like that. Nice dawg, though." And the car revved up again and started to turn.

Suddenly something hit me. My mind went back over an old track: *They could just as easily decide to bump me off, push my body into one of the marshes and hope for the best. . . . Push my body into one of the marshes.* Why didn't Petersen's murderer push his body into one of the marshes? There was no time to work out all the whys and wherefores, at least as far as the occupants of the car were concerned. But I was quite certain that if they had killed Petersen and wanted to hide the fact, they would have ample means of doing so.

"Hey!" I called out. "Stop!"

The car, now broadside on, stopped. "What you up to, lady? Trying to see who we are? That won't do you or your dog no good." It was not the man who was interested in Susie's breed.

"I'm not trying anything. But I think you ought to know. Petersen is lying dead in the garage."

Silence. Then, "Say that again."

I repeated it.

I heard the sound of their voices then, dimly, and tried to figure out how many of them there were. Three, I thought, but I couldn't be sure.

"Lady, you'd better be telling us the truth and not be up to some dodge to get us out of the car so you can identify us."

No, I certainly did not want to be able to identify them, and have Susie taken again or have us both shot. "I'll walk to the end of the jetty," I said. "And sit with my back to you."

Susie was still in my arms. Putting her down, I picked up the leash, which had been restored with her, and walked out to the end of the pier, then sat down and dangled my legs. Susie sat beside me.

I heard footsteps coming off the tarmac onto the concrete. This time I was surer that there were three people. They went into the garage, their voices murmuring as they walked. But from where I sat their voices from inside the garage didn't reach me. I stayed put for what felt like a long time, and despite the astonishing beauty of the view, in no great comfort. I kept thinking about that gun, and the inviting target my back must present. Nevertheless, knowing that my safety lay in keeping my eyes forward, I kept them trained on the thin smudge dead ahead that was Darcourt Island. To my left advanced the blackness of night. To my right the last of the fiery arc was slipping below the horizon. After a while I put Susie on my lap. No need to leave her back exposed if her late captors were feeling restless and nervous.

Suddenly one of the men spoke from behind me, his voice much nearer than I liked. It was obviously the third man, because I had not heard this voice before. At least, I amended mentally, not tonight. But I had heard it before somewhere.

I realized then that he had asked a question to which I had paid no attention.

"What?" I asked.

"I said, do you know who did this?" Unlike the other two, he did not sound friendly, or even neutral. He sounded hostile.

"No. I certainly don't. He was like that when I got here."

"Was the garage door open?" he asked suspiciously.

"No. I was told that he was available at all times to ferry people over, so I rang his bell, and then tried all the garage doors. The last one was open. And I found Petersen. Then you came."

He said nothing but, after a few seconds, walked back. I could hear them consulting. Then the man who just spoke to me said, "Where's Darcourt?"

I kept my head rigidly forward, but my mind scurried around trying to place something familiar in it.

"I don't know," I said. "But he said he would be going back to Darcourt Island at five."

More consultation. After a few moments I realized it was less consultation than disagreement, which obviously started to get heated, because they forgot to keep their voices down.

"I tell you, we shouldn't let her go back. She'll tell Darcourt and he'll think we did it and will be out gunning for us. He thought a lot of Petersen." It was the voice of the third man, the man I'd heard somewhere before.

"Yeah? He can't prove anything. But if we get her mad at us she sure can gum up our works. You know what these Northern newspapers are like. It's too big a risk."

"So's letting her roam loose. I'm for—"

"Can't you keep your voice down? You're the one who—"

And with that they abruptly lowered their voices and moved away. That piece of overheard information did nothing for my happiness. If the man whose voice I knew had had his way I would not only be free, I might very well be dead. I clutched Susie and prayed that the others would win out.

217

Evidently they did, because the first man called back, "All right, we'll tell the cops."

Their steps retreated from the concrete back to the asphalt. Then one pair stopped. One of the voices—that one that drawled—said, "If Petersen was supposed to take you back, how're you gonna get back now?"

"That's going to be a problem," I said.

"It sure is." He sounded amused. "Well, sorry we can't help. Lotsa luck."

"Thanks a bunch," I murmured.

The car engine went on again, revved, and then, after a few seconds and what sounded like a turn, drove off with a roar.

"*The ploughman homeward plods his weary way,*" I quoted dolefully, more to keep my spirits up than anything else. "*And leaves the world to darkness and to me.*"

Well, at least that particular covey of ploughmen not only left me. They left me Susie. I gave her a hug. Her tail moved. Her tongue found my chin.

"Now how are we going to get across?" I said half aloud. Because after what I had just learned, there was no question about my going. If I stuck around here the ones who were for leaving me alone might easily be out voted and/or over persuaded. My mind was drifting off towards the problem of transportation when I suddenly knew where I had heard the third man's voice: it was the day that André was driving me through the swamp. And then I knew who it was—Norton, keeper of the gate and the dogs.

My head was in a whirl. One of Darcourt's household employees defected to the islanders against him?

Well, I thought. And what about it?

Hadn't I gone against him also? Wouldn't anybody who wanted his or her freedom?

And then I remembered Brian's weird information. What if it were true? The islanders thought it was. And if Norton had joined them, they could, if things got heated up, overrun the whole place. As keeper of the gates and kennels, he probably had a complete set of keys, could turn the dogs against Darcourt and the rest of the household, and knew every nook and cranny of both the forest and the swamp. And if Darcourt himself resisted—which, given his nature, was inevitable—they might have a little more hesitation about killing a Darcourt than they did over dispatching his servant. But with all those marshes handy. . . . And Darcourt, who had undoubtedly left Petersen alive and well and ready to make the return trip back to St. Damien's, would not know that his servant had been killed.

"We have to get back, Susie," I said. "The only question is how."

The sun had gone, but there was still some twilight left over in the western sky. However, I would have to move fast if I wanted to see what I was doing.

I went to the side of the jetty and stared at the two boats: one a dinghy with oars, the other a slightly larger dinghy with outboard motor. Fumbling in my bag, I got out a pencil flashlight, mostly useful for peering at tenants' names in dark doorways. But it sent a thin beam towards the outboard motor. As I thought, the engine was turned on with an ignition key which, of course, was missing.

I turned and looked at the rowboat. I have rowed a fair amount in my life, mostly in Maine lakes—some of them quite large—where my father used to go fishing. Despite my small size, I was strong. But this was not a lake. It was the ocean, where there were drifts and currents and tides. And there was Susie who wouldn't have a prayer of getting to shore if the boat overturned too far out.

It was at that point that an obvious idea hit me. I stood up. "Come along, Susie. Let's run. The police will be here any minute and we have to get the key and be out of reach before them." Picking her up, I ran back along the jetty and over towards the garage. I really did not relish approaching the late Petersen, but I had no choice. I found a switch and turned on a light. Then, keeping my eyes away from that dreadful head as much as possible, I rummaged in his pockets and found his key ring. There were quite a few keys on it, and I had no way of telling which was the one I wanted, so I put them all in my bag. Standing, I looked around and saw a shelf running almost the length of the garage. On it— and, now, the floor—were every kind of tool, device, appliance and piece of equipment that I could imagine a man in Petersen's job would need, and many whose purpose altogether eluded me. My eyes came to rest on two large flashlights, one to hold, and one that either stood in its square frame or that could be hung. There was also some kind of tote bag which I appropriated.

I was putting the flashlights in the bag when I heard, faintly, the sound of a car. Dropping what looked like a kitchen knife also in the bag, I went quickly to the light switch, turned it off and, holding both the tote bag and Susie, retreated back down the jetty as rapidly as possible.

Putting Susie down in the dinghy, I got in and crawled to the back, keys in hand. By taking the keys I had done what was known as tampering with the evidence. People had been jailed for that, I reminded myself. The car was coming nearer. I had tried three keys and there were six more to go. The big flashlights were no good to me here. All they would do would be to advertise my location for miles around. But I trained the thin pencil light on the keyhole and pressed on. The car was only, as far as I could tell, about two hundred yards away when the seventh key went home and turned. The engine caught. I blessed fate that I had once or twice before handled outboard motors (on those same Maine lakes) and opened the throttle a little. The boat darted away from the jetty and out into the bay. I kept the boat headed straight out and heard far behind the slamming of doors and shouts of voices.

"Come back," yelled a man's voice, carrying far over the water. "Come back, Miss Wainright. We have to talk to you."

But I kept on going, devoutly hoping that their eagerness would not take the form of gunshots.

It was, I reflected, entirely likely that the island police would have a boat of their own—a more powerful boat than the one I had stolen. And it was equally probable that it was accessible by walkie-talkie and radio. Well, there was nothing I could do about that. I was going as fast as I could. There were other things I had to worry about: For one, where was Darcourt Island? In what direction, given the fact that I was not sure where I was now? I had only made the crossing in this direction once before. As far as I could remember it was directly opposite St. Damien's, but I had gone at a slight angle when I had shot away from the jetty, and although the night was clear, the moon was thin and high, and the stars, though brilliant and like low-slung lamps, did not reveal either the land ahead or behind.

After what felt like a long time I switched on the hand flashlight and swept it in an arc in front of me. Nothing but blackened water. As far as I knew, I could have gone in a large semicircle and be headed straight out to sea. This led by obvious sequence to the next problem: How much gas did this engine carry? Was it full when I started? How far would it take me? I looked at Susie, sitting up on the seat in front of me, facing the prow, like a minute figurehead.

At that moment we hit a choppy wave and she was nearly unseated.

"Susie," I said, closing down the throttle, "come here."

She picked her way back over to me and I had started to loop her leash over the seat when it occurred to me that if something sank the boat, she'd go down with it. Instead, I looped it around my wrist and pulled the tarpaulin in the bottom of the boat over so she could sit on it. Then I opened the throttle again, sweeping the water ahead of me with my flashlight.

It seemed to me we went on and on for hours. Once, Susie whined. I reached down with my free hand to stroke her and she licked it. I wondered if somewhere, somehow, she knew we were heading into worse danger. Or perhaps she had picked up my fear.

I had no way of knowing how long we had been on the water because I had forgotten to look at my watch when we started. Nor had I paid any attention to how long the first trip over had taken. It could have been twenty minutes or less. It could have been forty or more.

So I had no basis of comparison for what seemed now like an endless trip out to the open sea, but reminded myself—with diminishing success—that my own sense of the passage of time could be profoundly affected by the dark, and my growing fear.

I started to think about what might happen if we were really heading out: how far from shore we'd be when we ran out of gas. Against my volition, every story about people stuck, without means of navigation (or food or water), in an open boat drifted into my mind. I pushed them away and took a firmer grip on the flashlight. Maybe my hand had grown numb. Or fear had sent its destructive poison into my muscles. Whatever caused it, I watched, fascinated, as the light seemed to leap from my hand and into the water with a "plop."

I stared after it, my other hand automatically slowing the throttle. As the engine died to a murmur, the huge silence, like a living force, engulfed me. The only sound was the faint wash of the water against the boat. I sat there for a few moments, terrified to reach out for the other flashlight in case I found it dead, terrified that the motor would stop and the key fall out or the gas finish.

"This is nonsense," I said loudly. Reaching into the tote bag, I pulled out the square flashlight, with a hand not as steady as I would have liked, and pushed the button. Light blazed out over the water. It was only then I realized I must have been holding my breath, because relief made me let it out like a spent balloon.

"Well, Susie," I started to say, and then jumped. While I had groped for the switch, I had held the light twisted far to the right, much further around than I had been directing the other light, and it was now shining on shoreline. Shifting, I turned it even further. There was absolutely no doubt about it. Against the slightly lighter sky above it, the line of trees showed thick and black. How far I was away from them I could not tell. As I remembered from my days on the Maine lakes, the water did funny things to one's estimate of distance. Besides all of which it was night. I could see nothing below the trees—no rocks, no pier, no light; just black. I was fairly sure now that when I shot out from the pier I had gone too far to the left—too far east. A small navigational error at the beginning—a yard even—could, if followed long enough in a straight line, take me miles out of my way. And obviously had. And what I had done was to miss the narrow northern end of Darcourt Island and was now some distance along its longer eastern shore. But how far along? Was the northern end near? Or was I in the big midsection, the sanctuary, the swamp?

I sat there, appalled, for a few minutes and then figured I was wasting gas, with no idea at all of how much I had left. The first and obvious thing to do was to go straight to the shore. After that I could figure out whether to try to make for the northern or southern point.

But going straight for the shore turned out to be not that easy. The moment I tried to turn the boat I found myself pressing against a powerful current. And the boat, which had been sailing smoothly, was being slapped and pushed in an alarming way. The best I could do was to achieve a compromise: we did not go straight in; we headed in a long slant towards the southern end.

Abruptly, as we were about halfway there, the land curved away to my right and I saw we were approaching the southern end. And then I saw an amazing sight, the trees thinned out, so that they were no longer a heavy smudge drawn with a thick brush, but tall silhouettes, their arms visible against the sky, the hanging moss a lacy curtain beneath. Showing through between the trees was the outline first of a house, seen from the side, and I recognized the old plantation that

André had shown me. But it was what spread out behind that astonished me.

Squared-off walls, with round towers at the end, reared starkly against the starlit sky. What was it I had read earlier that day in St. Damien's library (only it seemed a thousand hours ago)? Once the island had been the official residence of the Spanish governor. Probably, almost certainly, any "residence" of a Spanish governor—given the time and place—would of necessity be fortified.

I had assumed that the fort had long since vanished—crumbled or been pulled down. But I had not actually read that. Nor had anyone told me. Odd. But then, I reminded myself, all I was seeing was a wall. It could be, and probably was, a shell. Still, there was something about it that made me shiver.

At that moment I realized that the time had come to make a decision. I could land on the shore that was rapidly approaching. Or, once I reached the shore, I could turn the boat around and head up the east coast of the island towards the northern end, where Darcourt Place and Darcourt himself were. And at the thought of the name, my heart gave its disgraceful, now familiar, thump before I remembered that it was not Darcourt I could trust. If I were going to wish for someone, I thought, turning the bow towards a collection of rocks that could be used for a landing—if I decided to land—I should wish for André. André, who took trouble with Alix and cared for wildlife, and probably fought for it against the oil-hungry Darcourt and his Arab friends.

Somewhere, at the back of my mind, I was aware of something that bothered me about all that, something other than the pain and disgust I felt over Darcourt's sordid business dealings. . . . There was something there that didn't fit, that had registered with me before. . . . But I couldn't work it to the surface.

I sat in the boat, idling the motor and staring at the house and fort. Alix had said her mother lived there. I was now quite sure she was right. If so, she was indeed to be pitied. Nevertheless, I did not relish meeting her. Whatever her physical condition, her mental state was, I was (with good reason) quite sure, neither healthy nor reassuring. And I could not get out of my head those heavy, dragging steps. I did not want to land here. Nevertheless, to head back up the island and run out of gas in the middle of the swamp was not, either, a consummation devoutly to be wished. On the other hand, I might make it as far as the northern end. It was a risk. But I decided to take it.

Turning the boat, I headed it north again, realizing, as I tried to keep it parallel a few yards from the shore, that I was going to be fighting that current again.

"Damn!" I said aloud, and then nearly jumped out of my skin. A shot rang out, and a bird flew up from the trees with a wild shriek.

Hunters were not allowed in the sanctuary, Darcourt had said. But this was south of the big swamp. Time to get out of here, I decided, not daring however to open throttle for fear of its noise attracting attention.

That the shot most likely had nothing to do with me, I was fairly sure, once my fright had died down. It was some distance away in the swamp area, and no bullet went past me. I had certainly not been hit, and if Susie. . .

In a panic, I put my head down, promptly got it licked, and conducted a cursory examination. No, she was fine. Well, onwards, I thought. At that moment the engine coughed.

"Oh, no!" I muttered and opened the throttle a little. It coughed again and sputtered out. The silence was overwhelming, broken only by the sound of a plane flying quite low, a plane I was suddenly aware I had heard off and on for the past hour or so. I looked up. A thin beam of light came from the plane, as though a searchlight had been strapped to a wing. I held my breath, not sure, when I remembered the mood of the islanders, whether I wanted them to find me or not. But the matter became academic when I saw the plane was heading out. It was then I discovered that in the few moments that had passed the tide had tugged the unresisting boat outwards. Hastily, I turned the key first off, then, after a brief pause, on again. It caught.

My options had been removed. I had to use the remaining gas to get the boat as close to land as I could. I turned it and headed back to the rocks. We almost made it before the engine coughed and died.

With an enormous effort I flung my arm out and managed to catch hold of a corner of the last rock, and then clung with hand and knees and feet to keep the boat from sliding back out to sea from beneath me. When I managed to secure my balance and get a better grip on the rock, I tucked Susie firmly under the other arm and eyed the rocks. Once I let go of the rock I would have to get up fast, or I would find myself wading back to the shore. Standing up swiftly, if unsteadily, I sprang. To my gratification, and somewhat surprise, I landed on a rock and not in the water. One up for us, I thought. I put Susie down and made a stab at the stern of the boat. It would be no use to me *sans* gas, but my New England soul rebelled against letting it go out to sea and be lost. It was a worthy impulse, but I didn't make it. The boat, looking rather forlorn, was already several feet out and drifting southeastwards.

Well, I thought resignedly, that's that. I stared up at the ghostly trees straight ahead. A few yards to the left they thinned out, and even here I could see stars and a pale, thin moon drifting behind the upper branches. As I remembered, the swamp began almost half a mile north of the house. I didn't know whether or not trees grew in swamps. But I decided not to take any chances. I would hug the shore until I got to the clearing around the house. And then—?

And then, if I walked out in the clearing, even on a moonless night, I would be visible to anyone who was watching; to the woman hidden there by her husband in who knew what state of mind or body. Should I, after all, have taken my chances in an open boat that could drift for days in the trackless ocean, without water, in the broiling sun? A dinghy could be lost for days and weeks, invisible to any ship unless on top of it. No, of the two horrors, I preferred the one I could meet on my two feet, even if I were caught between the ocean and the swamp, even if there were no safe place I could hide.

And then I remembered the shack—that blessedly modern hut with lights and airconditioning and a door that locked.

A door that locked, and that would, almost beyond question, be locked now. But, with nowhere else to go, it was worth a try, however remote the hope that I could take shelter there. At least it was somewhere to head for.

With memories of the active wildlife, I decided to keep Susie under my arm, and started walking south along the edge of the shore.

It was both beautiful and eerie. The wind played through the trees and the moss with a constant sighing sound. There were other noises, twitterings, stirrings, whether bird, reptile or mammal I was not enough of a naturalist to know. I had worn rubber-soled loafers for my trip to St. Damien's, not knowing how much I would have to walk, and the ground under me was soft. So I heard no sound. After a while the trees grew more sparse, and I found myself, almost abruptly, under the towering shadows of the house and the fort. I paused, wondering how I could have missed seeing the fort before, but, after a while, I understood. The house was both higher and wider than the ancient Spanish structure whose massive impact was revealed only from the side. Seen from the same side view, the house was a flimsier and thinner structure, but viewed from the front it would conceal the powerful but rather squat walls behind. Also, the trees, though sparser, were carefully left or arranged or grown as a frame for the ante-bellum mansion.

Rather gingerly, I walked in from the shore and towards the front of the house. Fortunately, the dress I had on, a two-piece affair, was a Kelly green which showed up as dark, and my hair was dark. Susie, however, was sand colored, so I kept well in the shadows of the trees. I still couldn't see the shack, but I knew that it was hidden in the bushes and shrubbery beyond the opposite wing of the house.

At that moment I stepped on a twig, and appreciated immediately the reality of a phrase I had often read: it echoed like a shot. And I wondered if that was what I, unused to the sounds of gunshots, had heard before. There was the flurry of wings and a dry scamper of feet. I almost held my breath, and, for good measure, put my hand around Susie's muzzle.

But, after the flurries had died down, there was no other sound. Releasing Susie's muzzle, I went forward. The big square flashlight had gone the way of the rowboat. I still had my pencil light though, and pondered shining it, well protected by my fingers, onto the path. It seemed, on the whole, a good idea. It was not as dark as it had been under the trees. On the other hand, it was a long way from being moonlit. I tried to see where I was stepping, without much success—as witness the snapped twig. There was also the matter of snakes and scorpions, not to mention small stones and roots. I was fairly confident that the snakes and scorpions would be as happy to get out of my way as I out of theirs. But I didn't think that anything would be improved by my turning an ankle. To get at the light, however, meant I had to shift Susie to reach my over-the-shoulder bag.

It was while I was engaged in doing this that I thought I heard the sound I had been dreading—the slow, heavy, dragging step. I stopped, waiting, holding my breath. No, I decided, it was my ever- and over-active imagination. There was—

This time there was no mistaking it. Still far behind me, but unmistakably. Step, drag, pause. Step, drag, pause. It was all I could do to keep from taking to my heels. For how far, I wondered sardonically? Six feet, maybe, before I tripped and fell or crashed into something.

Nevertheless, I was not going to let whoever, whatever, it was, overtake me without putting my all into getting away. Shifting Susie back to a comfortable and more portable position, I walked as quickly as I could, as far out of the shadows as I dared. Fortunately, the trees, though not thick, were above and around me, lending me some shelter and forming a line just in front. Knowing there was no point in stopping to listen, I just kept moving.

A few seconds later and I had passed through that front line of trees. Then I stopped. Ahead of me was the wide clearing in front of the house. To my left loomed the house itself, larger in the dark than I had remembered. The new moon, far up, lent almost no light, but the stars were like globes let down from the heavens. To my eyes, now used to the dark, the starlit clearing seemed an open, lighted stage. There had, I thought, been that sound that could have been—probably was—a shot. There were those feet behind me. The eyes of whoever was there were also used to the dark, and I, crossing the open space, would make a perfect target.

But the alternative—to skirt the edge of the trees—was not attractive either. It meant going far out of the direct path to the shack, because the trees formed a wide and deep circle facing the house. To keep within it, at my limited pace, would take a long time, and my pursuer, knowing, very likely, that I did *not* have a gun, might openly cross the clearing and head me off. It was undoubtedly that, the fear of being cut off and confronted, that fed my sense of urgency. The shack, I reminded myself, would be locked. The chances that it would not be were just about zero. Yet something in me prodded me to cross that clearing as quickly as possible. Susie, tucked under my arm, whined. I clamped my hand around her muzzle, held my breath and waited. And once more heard the step, drag, pause, step, drag, pause that I thought—hoped—I had managed to lose.

At that moment, when I could feel panic begin to uncoil within me and was trying to will it away, a light blazed out from the shrubbery on the far side. I had been in the dark so long that it took me a minute or two to see that it came from an open door. From, in fact, the open door of the shack itself.

A huge relief washed over me. By some miracle for which I could only be grateful, André was there, where and when I most needed him. Forgetful of the target I made I ran across the clearing, oblivious of stones, roots, holes and wildlife, and arrived at the door, panting.

"André," I said, "I was never so glad to see anyone in my life."

He had been making notes in a file, but he looked up and smiled.

"Good. It's mutual."

I stepped in, feeling curiously lightheaded with the release from fear and tension. Just suddenly the strain of the past hour or two, now that it was over, attacked not only my head, but my knees. Putting Susie down, I sank onto a chair.

André was watching me. I gave him a faint smile. "It's been quite an evening."

"I'm sure it has." He looked down at the notes he was making.

Something was beginning to bother me, but my head was still a little dizzy, and I couldn't seem to fasten on what it was. Idly I glanced at my watch. Eight twenty. I had missed dinner, which could account for the hollow feeling in my middle. On the other hand, I was astonished that it was as early as it was. It felt more like midnight.

"It's because it's dark, I suppose," I said aloud. And then, as I realized I had been staring at the refrigerator, "André—I'll take some of that beer, if you have it."

He got up. "Better yet. I have soda for you this time, unless you'd rather have the beer."

"No. I'd prefer the soda. How come you put in soda?"

"I've been expecting you."

He said it in such a kind, warm way, that it seemed churlish to feel that it didn't make much sense, and it would be rude to say so. I drank my soda and watched him go back to his note-making. Vaguely I remembered something he'd said before.

"Are you recording your banding results of the red-tailed hawk?"

He looked up briefly and gave me his charming smile. "That's right. The Wildlife Department likes regular reports."

Perhaps it was the fresh, cold soda, or the sugar it contained restoring my energy, or just sitting down. But quite suddenly my head cleared and I knew what was bothering me: André's total lack of surprise at seeing me here at this hour. It was as though he had known all along that I would come.

I put the soda bottle down on the table. "André—how could you be expecting me when I didn't know I was going to be here myself? I was trying to cross the channel to the pier at the north end of the island. But it was dark and I was in such a hurry to get away I went too far to the left and didn't discover my mistake until I was halfway down the island's east coast."

"I know. I was at the pier waiting for you and saw your light when you flashed it. I knew then that the tide had caught you. After that it was simply a matter of time till it brought you down here somewhere. Of course, you might have continued sailing down the coast but I was counting on your common sense to make you check your whereabouts and head for the shore. I've known these currents and tides for years, so it wasn't too wild a gamble."

"Why were you waiting for me—" I started, when I suddenly remembered the other thing that didn't fit, that annoyance in my unconscious that kept sending up distress signals, and I blurted out, "But you said to Darcourt that there weren't any red-tailed hawks, that the poachers had gotten them all."

He had been watching me. "Did I? How careless of me."

My heart was thumping. Something was wrong. Very wrong. "And yet that day in the old house when I heard a shriek or scream or something, you said it was a red-tailed hawk."

"You know," he said, his charming smile still lifting his mouth, "you shouldn't go around displaying your facility for total recall. It could be dangerous. I was simply trying to distract your attention from Nicole whose . . . er . . . illness can sometimes take rather noisy forms."

As I stared, his eyes slid up and past me. "Oh, there you are, Nicole. Come in. Didn't I promise you I would deliver Miss Wainright? Well—I always keep my promises. Here she is."

The hand that had been hidden by the desk came up with a gun, which he pointed at me. "Now, Sally, you can have the answer to all the questions you've been asking about Mrs. Tristram Darcourt."

I stared at the gun, and then turned.

(12)

MY FIRST thought was, so Brian's crazy rumor was right.
And, with a sense of terrible pity, I stared at what had once
been the beautiful girl in the cotillion dress.

The "leonine look" the ancient books called the facial dis-
figurement characteristic of the illness when far advanced:
the flattened nose, ridged brows, lesions and coarsened areas
of skin. The modern name was Hansen's Disease, its use
encouraged by sufferers and doctors alike, to help remove
some of the crushing stigma that still existed and was frequently more painful to bear than the disease itself.

The ancient name was leprosy.

"No, Nicole," André said. "Don't come any nearer. We
must get her—alive—to the house, and as quietly as possible."

I stood up and moved back to where I could see both
André and Nicole Darcourt. André's gaze shifted to me.

"And you stay where you are, Sally. This gun is on both
of you."

André rose to his feet and backed to the wall. "Now,
Nicole, I'm going to tie her up and we'll get her out of here.
Then you can have your fun." He started forward.

How on earth could I have thought this man had an
ounce of warmth or kindness or even human decency? His
finely featured face was as handsome as ever, but now that
I saw him clearly, I wondered how I could have found those
bonnie blue eyes anything but cold and pitiless.

"What do you intend to do?" I asked him quickly, because I wanted to know, but also because I wanted to divert him, delay him. For what? Some inner voice sneered. Who knew I was here?

"You'll see," he said, a look of pleasure on his face that was like ice water down my back. "Won't she, Nicole?"

The sound that came from her was like a hiss, although I knew she was just drawing in a breath. But I was stopped short by the look in her eyes. André's were chilled with merci-lessness. Not so much inhuman as unhuman. But Nicole's were filled with the most dreadful of all human emotions: hatred.

I saw now that she carried a cane—which probably had a lot to do with the dragging sound I heard. Suddenly, she took a step towards me and raised the cane. If she had suc-ceeded in bringing it down on me, that would have been the end. But André sprang forward between us and caught her hand.

"No, Nicole. Do you want to spoil everything? Darcourt must be here when she dies, so that he will be accused of it. We planned it that way. Don't you remember? Only it was going to happen at the house. Now, because of Boyd's stupidity, we've had to alter the plan a little to get Darcourt here. But it's all the same. You will have the double pleasure of killing her and seeing him punished for it."

For the first time she spoke. Out of that grossly fat body, carrying its fearful death, came a soft, cultivated Southern voice, rather like Alix's. "What does it matter? We'll say he did it. Both of us."

"But, Nicole, what good would that do if, at the hour she died, he had evidence of being elsewhere, evidence backed up by somebody else? We talked it all out, Nicole. Remember? Think."

His voice was soothing, almost rhythmic, to the point of being hypnotic. I could not see her face, which was behind his shoulder, but I could hear her loud breaths slow down. This gave me a clue as to her other problem. He talked as though to a child, or a retarded adult, but it could equally be to someone who was badly disturbed. If I could just, some-how, knock André out, or at least make him drop his gun, I might. . .

But that was as far as that thought went before he leapt back facing us both. "Don't get any ideas, Sally. I've come too far and planned too much to have you spoil anything."

He backed to his desk and around it. "Now for the next step." Reaching down with one hand he opened a drawer and brought out a bottle and a cloth. "It'll be quite painless," he said, picking them both up in his free hand.

I made a wild but probable guess. "Ether," I said.

He smiled that nauseating smile. "How clever of you! Cleverness, I'm afraid, will be the end of you, Sally. Quite literally!"

I had, perhaps, three seconds. I turned my head and called over Nicole's shoulder, "Tristram!"

It worked. They both swung to the door. I bent down and snapped off Susie's leash. I didn't want it catching on anything and choking her. As it was, I was probably sending her to her death. But better death out there among natural hazards and wildlife than at the hands of these two mad people. And there was always the possibility that she might make it back to Darcourt Place, or someone might find her.

"Run, run, run, Susie," I whispered, as in all our games, and slapped her behind. She took off, a light streak, through the door.

"André! Nicole!" I then cried and started to run around the desk. I didn't have a chance and I knew it. But I prayed it would occupy their attention while Susie got free. And it worked.

"Where the hell do you think you're going—" André yelled, and came after me. But his voice was drowned out by the noise that came from Nicole Darcourt's throat as she came at me, her cane up.

"Stop it, Nicole," André barked out. The cane wavered. He held me with one hand and clamped the ether-soaked cloth against my nose and mouth with the other. My last two thoughts, as I sank into unconsciousness, were that Susie had got away, and that the file on the desk right under my eyes was stamped red with the word "Javelin."

When I came to and opened my eyes I was lying on a bed, staring at the tattered remains of a four-poster canopy. I also felt extremely sick, and lay there without moving, hoping that by being still I would not aggravate the nausea that was threatening to engulf me.

After a while I must have gone to sleep, because when I awoke for the second time I felt much better. Gingerly, I sat up. I was in an immense room that looked, in some respects, like rooms I had visited in European mediaeval castles. The walls were naked gray stone, hung here and there with fading tapestries. The light in the room—such as it was—came from candles, four altogether: two on what looked like a bureau, one on the night table beside the bed, and another on the stone mantel above the fireplace. The room smelled overwhelmingly of damp and mildew and general decay and, I decided, after sniffing once or twice, dirt and rodent.

It was not a thought that I found at all appealing. But I didn't have a chance to develop it because dizziness hit me again and I sat very still for a while fighting it.

After it had gone away I slid to the edge of the bed, noticing as I did so that the sheet or counterpane under me—it was impossible in its rotten condition to decide which—was disintegrating as my legs moved across it. It also radiated a musty odor. Ugh! I thought, and decided to lose no time in getting off.

The bed towered above the floor, and I was about to slide down the side when I heard a slight sound. The floor was so far down that it was in shadow. Leaning over, I took the candle from the night table and held it up. Then, in reflex action, I drew up my feet.

Whoever had brought the scorpions to my room at Darcourt Place knew where to get them. Looking down, and only in the area of the floor lit by my candle, I counted four. They were all now still, but something at the periphery of my vision moved. I swung the candle further to the left. Another scorpion? No, a spider, about the size of a demitasse saucer, with hairy legs.

Backing from the edge, and still carrying the candle, I squirmed my way to the end of the bed that projected into the center of the room. Then, steadying myself (I didn't want to set fire to those highly flammable hangings), I held up the candle again. Since the threadbare ruin of a Persian rug lay across the floor it was hard to be sure. But counting those that became visible on the carpet simply because they moved, along with those on the stone floor, there were at least six. Strange things go through one's mind at such moments. Through mine went the foolish, calamitous boast of King Solomon's son:

"My father chastised you with whips, but I will chastise you with scorpions."

Sister Teresa, a convert, had brought to our parochial school the rich fruit of a Protestant, biblically oriented upbringing. Looking down at the six-legged horrors, I could hear her voice repeating the words of young King Rehoboam's disastrous taunt.

Remembering then the half-eaten corpse in the shoe box, I wondered if they dined upon one another. At that unattractive thought my nausea threatened to return, and I decided to examine the less animate fixtures in the room.

It must, I finally decided, have been the master bedroom in the days of the Spanish governor. Twenty feet from the end of the bed was the fireplace in which a tall man could have either stood up or lain down. To one side was a heavily carved table with curving, massive legs. Against the walls were a chest, a wardrobe, a smaller table and a prie-dieu, all in the same heavily ornamented wood. And over everything was generations of dust.

Abruptly, the door opened.

"Ah, there you are," André said, much as though he thought I might have wandered off for a spot of rest after an afternoon's tennis.

"Yes," I said. "Exactly where you put me. Where else?"

He strolled in, holding, I noticed, a powerful flashlight in one hand. As he moved I heard his shoe scrunch on something. Feeling sick again, I turned my head away.

"Tut, tut," he said. "Don't you like our native wildlife down here? Here!"

As I turned, something dropped on the bed and scuttled towards me. I heard my own shriek, along with his laugh and the ripping of the bedclothes, as I squirmed and crawled as fast as I could away from it.

"What a coward you are!" André said, and brought his curved hand around what I finally recognized as a giant member of the species known in New Orleans as cockroaches, and in New York as waterbugs.

"Here, children, dinner!" And he dropped the roach in front of a scorpion who pursued the fleeing creature and then caught it.

This horrible room with its voracious insects had had exactly the effect on my nervous system that André had planned. I was ready to scream, be sick, promise anything, to get out.

But when André then turned his powerful flashlight on the scorpion relishing his meal, he took one step too far.

I didn't like being afraid. I liked even less André's psychologically clever manipulations. I had read somewhere that a snake pit, or a room full of scorpions lay buried in the chaos of everyone's unconscious, perhaps, even, in some way part of the collective unconscious. What, then, could be more effective than surrounding a person with the reality—a sure prescription (given the vulnerable person) for madness, a bourne from which few travelers returned undamaged.

But the net effect on me was not quite what he had calculated. Whether he was treating me to my own horror movie for a purpose or the pure pleasure of the thing, I didn't know. But anger came to my rescue, burning before it both fear and horror.

"Just what is all this in aid of, André?" I said, furious at myself for reacting when he dropped the roach. "What do you want?"

He switched off the flashlight, and for a minute his handsome face looked extremely ugly. Then he strolled farther into the room.

"Shoo, shoo, children," he said to the creatures scuttling out of his path. "What I want, dear Miss Wainright, dear cousin, is a letter from you to Tristram Darcourt, asking him to come here and . . . er . . . rescue you. You can be as fervent in your pleas as you like, my dear. In fact, the more so the better."

"And what will that get you?"

"His presence, dear cousin. His presence."

"Why?"

"I don't really think that concerns you, you know."

"It does if I have to write the letter."

He stared at me, his blue eyes wide and dark in the dim light. Then he shrugged. "What does it matter if you know? After all, you won't be able to tell anyone."

Despite my reminder to myself that everything he did and said had a calculated effect, I shivered.

He smiled. "The gallant Tristram Darcourt having, despite all his efforts and best judgment, fallen for you, will come. And I will be waiting."

I stared defiantly back, trying not to show the spurt of pleasure (even in the midst of scorpions) his statement gave me. But then my pleasure went. I had forgotten in my silly eagerness what a liar and manipulator André was. If Darcourt came, it would be out of the purest self-interest. As he himself had pointed out, he was responsible for what went on on his property. I scowled more than ever so that André couldn't read my face.

"What makes you think he wouldn't arrive with the state police at his back?"

"Because you will write that unless he comes alone, along a certain path that I can watch, you will be"—he smiled—"dispatched."

"He won't believe you."

"Oh, yes. We won't be here. We will be at"—he smiled even more broadly—"your place of execution. He will see that all I have to do is push you a little. And you will die a very unpleasant death."

I didn't have to ask, but I did anyway. "And where is that?"

"But, my dear," he mocked me gently. "Where else? The Devil's Cup. Why else do you think I showed it to you?"

Once more, I fought against jumping to his clever manipulation by showing the horror I felt.

"You mean you planned this right from the beginning?"

"Let us say the possibility occurred to me."

"But why?"

"For the money, dear girl. For the money and the power and the glory." For a moment then, his voice lost its slight, drawling affectation. "And because I hate Darcourt's guts." Then the debonair mask slipped back. "And the only way I'll get what he has is for him to leave it to me."

I looked at him curiously. "Why do you hate him?"

"Because he has what should be mine. My unspeakable grandfather left Tristram, his son-in-law, all his shipping and shipyard holdings, instead of his own son, my father. I, a Charpentier, should have them. They're all centered in Louisiana—and that is our home. Not some American outsider."

I had heard old Cajuns speak of Americans that way, as though they were another nation, and from what I had read and researched, until a generation or so ago, most French New Orleanians felt similarly of the world beyond the Vieux Carré. But it was odd to find it in this young man.

"So now you know," André said viciously, "why it will give me so much pleasure to take it all back."

Tristram's sardonic face slid across my mind. And I was shocked by my desire to see it—touch it. But as the thudding of my heart slowed, something more rational, less emotional struck me.

"You mean Darcourt made you his heir?" Cool, intelligent, cynical Darcourt, with his quick perceptions. "I don't believe it."

"Oh, no. Darcourt has as little use for me as I for him. His heir is Alix. He's the first Darcourt not to produce a son, by the way." There again was the vicious pleasure.

"He's not dead yet," I found myself saying coolly. "Nor disabled, nor old. He could have a dozen sons between now and quitting time."

"Legitimate? With Nicole, his lovely and gracious wife as the mother? I don't somehow think so, my dear. Oh, no. Alix will inherit and I will marry Alix."

Of course. It had been there all along. The shining, radiant look, the kind of look a girl gives only to the man she's in love with. After all, she did say he was blond. But my attention was so fixed on the young man with the cowlick, that I ignored the blond male who was far more attractive and far more accessible. How could I have been so *stupid*? The answer to that was obvious, too, and sprang into my mind from the past.

"*Get an idea in your head, Sally, and the good Lord Himself couldn't make you see anything else,*" my father had said.

"*And just where do I get that from, Father?*"

"*From me, Miss Impertinence. But that doesn't mean I want you to ram your head against a wall for lack of seeing it.*"

He sounded so uncharacteristically gloomy that I said, "*Has that happened to you?*"

He looked at me in silence for a moment, the smoky hazel eyes, usually sparkling either with fun or the joy of battle, somber and inward-looking. "*Ay, Sally. It happened to me. I had an idea in my head.*" He paused. "*Something I wanted more than life itself.*"

I remembered feeling an odd, unexpected sense of fear. "Did you crash your head? Not get what you wanted?"

"*Oh, yes, Sally. I got it. But—I hadn't figured on the price.*"
"*Was it—a lot?*"

"*Yes. But that wasn't it, Sally. It was seeing that somebody else had to pay it. And me having to watch. . . .*

It was the only time I ever thought I saw him cry. Even later, when Mother died, if he wept, he wept alone. But at that moment he got up and changed the subject so hastily that I couldn't be sure if those were indeed tears I'd seen. . . .

I looked up now at André. "So it's been you, all along. I
237

thought it was that blond boy with the cowlick—Boyd Lambert."

He threw back his head then and laughed.

"Our local trouble-maker? What a joke! Not that he doesn't have his own ax to grind. He'd like to see Tristram knocked off his eminence as much as I would. It's not easy being a Darcourt bastard."

My stupid heart gave a lurch. "Darcourt's son?"

André grinned. "Who else?"

I was astonished at the pain. Well, I asked myself cynically, what did I expect Darcourt to be, a monk?

André, watching my face, grinned even more broadly.

"Who is his mother?" I asked, fighting back a humiliating wave of jealousy. Somehow Nicole Charpentier Darcourt—even the beautiful girl in the portrait—had not aroused my jealousy. But a mistress—that was something else.

"Was. She had been a maid at Darcourt Place and drank herself to death when Boyd was about ten. Darcourt's always paid for his upkeep, of course. But he was brought up by grandparents. Naturally, he thinks he should, as a son, however illegitimate, inherit the Darcourt throne, and is bitter about his illegitimacy. That's why that little comment of yours this afternoon was a body blow and galvanized him into stealing your dog. You should watch that tongue of yours, my dear Sally! Something about a master and a servant, wasn't it? You see, he's quite sensitive about his mother's having been a maid. and since he, too, has her fondness for the bottle, he's liable, under pressure, and especially with a grievance, to hoist a few and act impulsively."

"If I'd known that—about his mother—I'd never have made that crack. I shouldn't have anyway, it's not my style. But he got to me." I looked at André. "Somebody told you all about that pretty fast."

"Naturally, I make it a point to remain informed, and pay rather well for it. The two of you weren't alone when you made that witticism, you know. Besides, his act rather precipitated things. The little group of malcontents that he was part of and who have been so useful to me were quite upset with him."

"You mean people take him seriously?"

"People held together by a common sense of grievance frequently don't examine one another's character credibility too carefully. Besides, he can be quite convincing, and however illogical it may seem to you, the fact that his father is a Darcourt, instead of making him look like a nut with a grudge, lends him authority. And until recently, when he's gotten drunk a little too often, he's been quite impressive in his role of disinterested idealist, heart and soul for the people. After all, as he's often pointed out, by stirring up the islanders against Darcourt, he's endangering his own steady income, since Darcourt supports him. What he doesn't say, of course, is that he's after bigger game than a steady but small stipend. Like many such idealists, his passionate egalitarianism is based on envy."

"What a lot of bunk," I flared up, glad to have something I could reasonably get angry about. "I could tell you hundreds of—"

"Oh, spare me the rhetoric, Sally! I'm not interested in causes." He smiled. "Only in my own."

"But you use others."

"Of course. In this case, for Alix to inherit, her father has to die. Hence our tryst at the Devil's Cup."

"I see. And what was that yarn you were spinning Nicole . . . Mrs. Darcourt . . . about her having the pleasure of killing me and seeing Darcourt punished for it. I suppose you were using her in some way, too."

"Naturally. For one thing, she's rich in her own right, and she's been more than willing to give me the money for some of my . . . er . . . endeavors. To spite Darcourt, she was quite ready to see me marry Alix and have everything come back to the Charpentiers. But getting you . . . shall we say removed? . . . was the real carrot egging her on. She may be sick and demented, but she knows quite well Darcourt feels differently about you than he has about any other woman, and it's her possessiveness that's outraged."

"How are you going to explain Darcourt's death at the Cup to her—or anyone else for that matter?"

"A tragic but unavoidable accident. The story given out will be that Darcourt will have died—heroically, of course— trying to save his mentally disturbed wife from killing herself in the swamp. Nicole can be . . . persuaded . . . to back it up."

"And Alix? What will you tell her? Or is she so far gone in love she'll believe anything you say?"

André smiled. "I really think she is, you know. However, she believes her father plans to lock her up here on the island for the rest of her life."

"Another idea you've fostered?"

"Of course."

"And Nicole. I wonder how long she'll be around after you've married Alix."

"Not too long. Poor Nicole. Her many ailments will catch up with her."

I shivered, and, seeing me, he smiled again. "And you've made me a present of how to account for your death, Sally. That tragic navigational error. The dinghy which is now undoubtedly out at sea—or can very easily be put there—will be mute testimony to your lack of experience."

"Don't they require bodies?"

"In these conveniently shark-infested waters?"

He's quite mad, I thought, and then, no, not necessarily. Perhaps it was my orthodox upbringing, but I had never been able wholly to swallow the article of faith that held there are no evil people, only the sick and misunderstood. In André greed and envy, voluntarily nurtured, had become evil. It was incredible, I found myself thinking, looking up at him, how little light and depth his eyes showed.

Inevitably my mind went back to Darcourt and the fate that awaited him. Somehow, I couldn't make myself believe it.

"And I suppose," I said, "when you get Darcourt to the Devil's Cup, he'll just stand there and let you push him in. Fat chance! I'd back his guts any day against—"

His slap almost knocked me off the bed and made my head and ears ring. I managed—just—not to scream.

"I didn't ask for your opinion. I've brought pen and paper. Now write as I dictate."

Taking my right hand and turning it palm up, he put the pen and a sheet of paper on it, and tightened his grip on my wrist. "Knowing you, you'll try to throw them on the floor. But let me tell you what I will do if you don't agree to do what I say. I have some rope with me, just outside the door. I'll tie you to that table leg over there and let loose on you some choice bits of food—worms, crickets and roaches. The scorpions will be all over you. If you move or thrash around they'll become frightened and will sting you. One sting probably wouldn't kill you, although it might make you powerfully sick. It would be interesting—medically speaking—to see what several stings would do."

I stared at him with a sort of detachment that considering the horror I felt, surprised me.

"And," André went on, in the same almost casual voice,

"we'll tie up your dog with you. Oh, yes. We caught her."

"I don't believe you," I said after a minute, praying it was not true.

He smiled, and I knew that if I had had a gun at that point I would have killed him. Then he went back to the door and opened it.

"Nicole," he called out. "Pinch the little beast so her loving owner can hear."

"No!" I said, but my voice was drowned out by the yelping. André closed the door. "And now the letter—cousin."

I wrote it, the letter he dictated.

Tristram:

Please come. André will kill me if you don't. I need you."

And I signed it.

He read it. "That's better," he said. Then he went to the door. "I'll be back for you later." As he was about to close the door, he poked his head back in. "You'll be quite safe as long as you stay on the bed." Then he laughed again, closed the door and locked it.

Sister Teresa, the one who had started life as a Protestant, had always said, "When in a fix, first you pray. Then you think and act. Always remember that the will of God is more likely to be expressed in your bestirring yourself than in your sitting there, waiting for Him to rescue you." There was an ugly rumor afloat among those who did not admire Sister Teresa that she was still tainted with the remnants of the Protestant ethic.

Personally, I thought she was right. So I carried out the first part of her instructions. Then I applied myself to thinking.

As a result of this, some fifteen minutes later, I pushed myself over the end of the bed and regarded the number and strength of my roommates. Then I decided to examine the bed as thoroughly as I could. It was an unsavory task. Everything smelled of decay and mildew and crumbled in my hands. What I dreaded to see was more wildlife. Either it was too dark, or the wildlife had dispersed with all my thrashing around, or there wasn't any—a miracle almost too good to be true. I decided, realistically, to settle for it being too dark for me to see them, or for them to have dispersed, and ploughed my way on, pulling aside coverlet, sheets, and, when I got to it, chunks of mattress that came up, ticking and all, in my hands. Underneath the mattress, though, were slats, serving the purpose of springs in more modern beds. With no compunction at all, I pulled at one, breaking it off fairly easily near the frame. Then I broke it from the other end and pulled it out. It was light, and thanks to the pervading damp, not brittle. Two would be better, I decided, and broke off another one. Then I fished in my bag that had been brought up with me.

Yes. There was the scarf. Tearing it in strips, I tied the two slats together at intervals, making myself a handy swatter of about four and a half feet in length. It would be no use in helping me to defend my honor (whatever that old-fashioned phrase meant), but it would help with overcurious, overhungry or unusually aggressive scorpions. I was putting the remnants of the scarf back into my bag when my fingers encountered my pencil flashlight. Hardly an illuminating torch, I thought, but it might come in useful. And I put it in my pocket.

With the stave, then, I poked at the hangings above. Were they as rotten as the bed covers? Yes, I decided, as a cloud of dust descended on the bed, along with unpleasant-looking particles and bits of rotten cloth. Abandoning them, I picked up one of the bedside candles with my free hand and squirmed to the end of the bed. I really did not relish putting my feet on the floor, but, considering everything, including the fear that I had written a letter that might bring Tristram to his death, I had no choice. So I slid down.

Then swinging my stick in front of my feet in a wide arc—and sending a few what I had thought to be shadows scuttling to the corners—I walked over to one of the four high windows. Obviously this room was on a corner since the windows were two each on walls at right angles to each other. Like the windows at Darcourt Place, these were protected by blinds that had been pulled together and closed. The windows, opening in, were already opened flat against the inside walls, so, using the stick, I managed to raise the hook holding one set of blinds together, and, with a squeaking of hinges, got them pushed open. Then I put the candle on the nearest piece of furniture, blew it out so that it wouldn't prevent my eyes from becoming accustomed to the dark, and stared out.

I stood there for a while, until slowly the outside became lighter than the inside. And of all the things I did, just standing in the dark, not knowing what might run over my feet, was the hardest. But I had written that letter. Whether it was Susie's yelp alone or also the thought of being tied down as a giant smorgasbord for the scorpions that had sped my pen along the paper, I didn't know. And from Darcourt's point of view, what did it matter?

After a while, I could distinguish the shapes of trees against the lighter sky. A while longer and I could see some bushes lower down. But I still could not see what I wanted to: the ground. And until I could, I had no idea how high above it I was—or how far down I would have to drop. Further, I had more than a nagging belief that if the drop were at all feasible, André would not have left me alone in the room to make it—unless, of course, he thought the scorpions would keep me on the bed. Which was possible, but not likely. André impressed me as a man who would leave nothing to chance.

I still couldn't see the ground, which could mean it was anywhere from forty feet below me, to only ten or eleven; that is, just out of the range of my night vision.

I could, of course, risk a jump, but a broken leg—or a broken back—would not noticeably advance my cause.

I was about to pull my head back in when I thought I heard someone whisper my name. Since I assumed it obviously could not come from outside, I sprang around and looked into the room and towards the door. I had been staring out into the night, so the room was bright to my eyes, and it took a few seconds for me to be sure there was no one in the room.

I heard my name then, again, a whisper beyond the window. I turned back and stared down. Then I snatched the pencil flashlight from my pocket and shone it, a thin white stream of light, down.

"Put out that light," the voice said, with an incisive snap that I recognized instantly.

"Darcourt?" I said, disobeying him and extending the light as far down as it would go. At the point where the beam's strength gave out I saw his face turned up to me.

"I said put that damn thing out. Do you want everyone to know where I am?"

I put it out. "No, of course not," I said. Never would I have thought that I could be so glad to hear someone ordering me around.

"Stand back," the whisper came. "I'm going to throw something up. What do you have up there? Candles?"

"Yes," I whispered. "Four."

"Put them as near the window as you can. Then step back to one side."

"What—?"

"Just do as I say."

On the whole it seemed best to obey. Having placed the candles on the nearest pieces of furniture, I called down, "Okay." And stepped back. Two seconds later something came flying through the window and fell onto the floor. I looked at the four big hooks springing at right angles from one another and from a single base. Climbers of all types used them, I knew.

"Sally!"

I looked out. "Yes."

"Secure those hooks under or around the most solid piece of furniture you can find. Then let me know when they're steady, and I'll climb up."

Considering the condition of everything in the room, I wasn't sure I could secure the hooks. I went around the room, once nearly stepping on a large scorpion who didn't move fast enough. Somehow, with Darcourt out there, the wretched beasts didn't seem to bother me as much. And yet, and yet. . . . I reminded myself, pushing this piece, pulling that, if Darcourt's desperately ill wife were unhinged from being locked away, instead of being put into a hospital where she could be medically treated, whose fault was that? The fact remained, I needed his help. And hadn't it been Winston Churchill who had said in the darkest days of World War II that he would be glad for help from the devil himself. Well— so would I, I thought, tugging at the bed.

Of all the pieces of furniture, it was the only one that didn't move no matter how much I tugged at it. Darcourt, for all his leanness, was a big man. He could easily weigh, I calculated, about twice what I did. At that point it crossed my mind that I might, by helping Darcourt up here, be moving myself from the frying pan into the fire. I paused in my pulling. Well, I thought, better the devil I know!

I went back to the window. "How much rope do you have?" I whispered. "The only thing strong enough is the bed. It's at least twenty feet across the room and I can't move it."

"All you need. I brought plenty. Wrap the rope several times around the leg of the bed and then catch it in the hooks."

I did as he asked, went back to the window. "All right. It's done. I just hope it holds."

"Not more than I do. I'm standing on one of the few spots of firm ground around the fort," he whispered back. Then

244

I saw the rope straighten and grow taut. In a surprisingly short time Darcourt's head appeared, followed by the rest of him as he came walking up the wall, pulling himself hand over hand on the rope. For a man with a gimpy leg he seemed remarkably agile.

Unfortunately, my tendency to spit out, without thought, whatever sprang to my mind asserted itself. "That's pretty nippy for a—" Hastily I swallowed the last two words: lame person. But Darcourt, now sitting astride the window, finished for me, "A hunchback? Just call me Quasimodo. I was once a fairly respectable rock climber."

"I wasn't going to say that," I protested, as he brought both feet over and slid into the room.

"No, but you thought it, and with your face, as we discussed once before, that amounts to the same thing. And besides, I don't care. I'm not offended." He looked down at the floor. "You seem to have found your scorpion headquarters."

"Yes. Your delightful cousin André put me in here in the hope that they would drive me mad, especially if he tied me up and let loose a lot of their dinner over me. That's why— that's one of the reasons why I wrote that letter. Because"— I drew a deep breath—"I knew he meant to kill you when he got you here. I'm sorry."

Darcourt was watching me, his deep-set eyes hidden in the shadows. "First of all, I didn't get any letter. So don't lash yourself over that. I found out you were here and came on my own. Second, I know André wants to kill me—he's been plotting that for years. Third—"

"Well, if you've known that all the time, why didn't you do something about it, instead of letting him run free all over the place collecting scorpions with which to frighten your guests?"

"I'll answer all that in good time. You said that was one reason you wrote the letter. What was the other?"

"They have Susie," I said.

"I thought that might be it, which is why I asked. No. They do not have Susie. Your Susie is quite safe."

"You mean she crossed the marsh?"

"Hardly. I had ridden Sebastian here, leading the dogs, who had been instructed to find you, and they discovered her, sitting at the edge of the trees, waiting for you."

Relief surged over me. Then I said, "That . . . that *bastard* lied to me." I added, "My father would only allow the term to be used for the Ulster constabulary . . . and"—I hesitated

—"you. But I think André has earned it."

"Many times over."

"But I heard a dog yelping downstairs. They said it was Susie."

"That was probably Nicole's spaniel."

"Oh. André says he's going to marry Alix, you know."

"I do know. That was one of the reasons I hired you, and wanted you to ride with her."

"Well why didn't you *tell* me?"

He paused. "As you should know by now, I'm not given to explanations." He hesitated again. "I was always a natural loner, and everything that's happened in my life has simply . . . increased that tendency. It's probably wrong—but there it is. There are . . . I do have things to say, but I think you'd better tell me what's happened."

Never having heard doubt—or self-doubt—in Darcourt's voice, I found his hesitation oddly moving, and reached out and touched his shoulder. He put his hand over mine. And then his arms were around me and my mouth found his. It was just as well. Something ran over my foot and I gave a small shriek that came out a muffled gurgle.

"What's the matter?" Darcourt whispered.

"Something ran over my foot," I said.

His answer was brief and to the point. He picked me up and took me over to the bed. "How do you feel about bed bugs?" he said genially, about to deposit me.

"Amorously speaking, they do not inspire me."

He laughed and put me down on the bed. As he loomed over me I found I was shaking. And it was not with fear. I stared up at him. He was leaning over me, a hand on either side.

"Tristram—" I started.

"Yes?"

The electricity between us crackled almost audibly. Without thinking, I put my hands up to his shoulders against his rough riding jacket. We stayed there a minute. Then he leaned back and put his hands over mine.

"I'd give much," he said, sounding a little out of breath, "to continue this. But bed bugs apart, I don't think this is the moment. Not with André—who, by the way, is your cousin, not mine—planning our early demise."

But I dug my fingers into his shoulders. Even though what he said was unassailable, there was something I had to know. "Tristram, why didn't you send her . . . send your wife . . . to a hospital? She has leprosy, doesn't she?"

"Yes. I thought you'd made up your mind that I'd kept her here locked up out of sheer villainy."

"I don't want to believe that. As a matter of fact, I can't any more. Any more than I can believe you're selling out to the Arab oil interest."

"Oh—is that what you came to find out? You're going to lose your union card if you go on with that kind of thinking —exonerating me all over the place."

"Yes," I said sharply. "You're tailor-made to be a modern villain: too rich, too powerful, too arrogant."

"Then why the vote of trust?"

I stared up at him. "I don't know. Weakening of the moral fiber, I suppose. But I trust you."

He drew me to him very gently. "Do you, my darling. Do you?"

"Yes," I said, my face muffled against him. "I do."

He held me there for a while, then said, "It's a long story, and I'll tell you later. But Nicole is here because long ago, in a weak moment I promised her I would not send her to a hospital. Her mental balance was precarious, even then, and I was afraid she'd either kill herself or do what she finally did—lose her balance entirely. But I had given her my word, and I've never felt I could break it."

"But why fear of going to a hospital? Is she unbalanced because of her illness? Because of the leprosy?"

"Oh, no. Her horror and fear of the stigma—which unfortunately still exists—may have added to her mental instability. But they are quite separate. The Charpentiers have a streak of insanity running through the family. And, of course, the Charpentiers—and the LeVaux's, your mother's family—both came from the Cajun country, which is one of the few areas in the continental United States where leprosy is endemic."

"My mother's family," I repeated stupidly, suddenly afraid.

He looked down at me in the dim light. The candles flickered in a slight breeze from the window, their shadows dancing against the wall. From the floor came the faintly audible dry sounds I had come to dread. But at that moment I was unaware of anything outside the man in front of me.

"Of course." His voice was gentle. "Your aunt, your mother's sister, contracted the disease. She went to the hospital, the national leprosorium at Carville, in Louisiana, and lived the rest of her life and died there. That was the family skeleton in the closet."

(13)

AFTER a long moment, I said, "What—?"

"Look. I have to get you out of here now and try also to get André out, or he will not only kill you—or try to—but he will also kill Nicole. As long as she was useful, he used her, and exploited her persecution fantasies. But if he gets rid of you and me and marries Alix, he's not going to want her around as a witness, however demented, to his machinations."

"But—"

"I don't have time to answer all your questions." He kissed the top of my head. "So answer mine. I take it the door's locked?"

I nodded vaguely, still numb with shock.

Darcourt took my shoulders and shook me and said in a tone that reminded me of the feudal lord I resented so much, "Snap out of it, Sally. We have a lot of work to do."

That did it. "All right," I said, and pushed him away. "Yes. It's locked."

He stood there for a minute, thinking. Then he said, "I could, of course, just knock down the door—or try to, at least make such a noise that André would come running."

"He has a gun," I said.

"So do I." Darcourt pulled an ugly little black revolver from his jacket pocket.

"Then what are we dithering around for? I would like to get out *immediately*."

249

He grinned. "Is that what we were doing? Dithering?"

I felt my cheeks go warm and my traitorous heart start to beat faster. "Well, not entirely. But can't we—dither—elsewhere? I am not happy when I am locked in a mouldy fort entirely surrounded by scorpions."

"You have a point. But I have been waiting for some time for André to give himself away in a fashion that would not just amount to my word against his, and if you would be willing to play tethered goat while I appeared to cooperate with his note, we might just succeed. How was he going to send the note? By whom?"

"I don't know. The last thing I remember before waking up in this room was being knocked out with ether in the shack. I saw . . . Nicole." My voice wavered, as I remembered her and thought of my unknown aunt. "But besides her and André, I saw no one. Who could be here?" Curiously, I knew the answer before he spoke.

"Alix," he said. There was both sadness and resignation in his voice.

Darcourt stared at me for a moment, and then continued, "Because of my neglect—you were right about my failure there, by the way—André saw his chance and moved in on her affections. She liked you, I know, but André, I think, deliberately made her jealous of you by paying you marked attention, which would make it easier for her to follow his orders in using you. André, I'm pretty sure, was the inspiration behind the scorpions and the snake in your room."

"But—" I was remembering the envelope dropped at my door that first night.

"But what?"

I told Tristram. "And what really baffled me was that the envelope, which was hand-addressed to Mrs. Tristram Darcourt, like a letter from a personal friend, was postmarked only the week before. Of course, I didn't know she was here. And I thought everyone thought she was in France."

"They do. But begging letters from charity drives and invitations to classy fund-raising dinners are always hand-addressed. People with finishing-school handwriting are hired to do that kind of thing. And letters like that arrive all the time. All André or Alix would have to do would be to salvage one from the wastebasket where Mrs. Conyers throws them."

"Would it have been Alix that early?"

"Yes. I think so. After all, André didn't want anyone here, the fewer witnesses to his games the better. And if André didn't want you, you can be sure Alix followed him in that. It was probably just a shot in the dark, in the hope that if you were a nervous woman you might precipitate a fuss and leave immediately. But to get back to the moment, tell me in detail what happened to you this afternoon and how you got to this end of the island. I know about your taking the dinghy—the Coast Guard plane reported seeing you headed down the coast" (I remembered then the low-flying plane with the searchlight), "and later told me about seeing the boat empty and drifting out to sea. That was when I loosed the dogs and came here with them on Sebastian."

So I told him about the events of the afternoon and evening, including finding Petersen's body. "Did you know about that?" I asked.

"Yes. The Coast Guard told me that, too. Poor Petersen. He was a gloomy soul, but a loyal friend."

"Why do you suppose he was killed?"

"That was Boyd's doing, I'm afraid. I've been on the two-way radio with both the police and the Coast Guard, and, apparently, when the police found Petersen's body they also found enough incriminating evidence to arrest Boyd, who seemed to have run out of steam, anyway, and finally admitted that he had been caught by Petersen in the act of returning Susie. Boyd had been counting on Petersen's being busy taking me back to Darcourt Island. Only I took the big boat back myself, leaving Petersen to bring you. Anyway, when Boyd was putting Susie in the garage, Petersen, who had been testing the dinghy, heard him and came running back. When he saw Boyd and also recognized your dog, he wanted to know what the hell he was doing. Boyd, who has never been too bright, and probably wasn't too sober either, did the expected—panicked, and tried to run. Only Petersen was in his way. They fought. Then Boyd picked up the monkey wrench. He swears it was self-defense. Anyway, when he saw what he'd done, he panicked even more, picked Susie up and was making away with her again when he bumped into Norton and that lot. He didn't, of course, tell them about Petersen. He just said he'd had second thoughts about returning Susie. But they had had a chat with your friend the librarian and were not about to give you any excuse for writing up some bad publicity about them. When you told them Petersen was dead, of course, they knew they'd had it. I think if the police hadn't tracked down Boyd first, just as he was crossing to the mainland, they—Norton and company—would have killed him in sheer fury."

I searched his face. "I'm sorry about Boyd. I mean, were you fond of him?"

"No. Not at all. He was not only not too bright. He was thoroughly vicious. I suppose having a drunken mother and no father is not much of a start in life. But when you've said all that he still remained thoroughly obnoxious." The level brows came down. "Why are you looking at me like that?"

"Even granting his general obnoxiousness, that's a . . . cold-blooded way to describe your son."

"Son? Who told you that?"

"He isn't?"

"No. He was my brother Robert's son. The result of a summer's dalliance with Mother's maid just before he died."

"Oh." I made a not very successful effort not to sound pleased.

Darcourt touched my cheek. I put my hand up and took his, holding it against my face for a moment. Then I released it and said, "So you knew about Norton?"

"Oh, yes. He came up from New Orleans on André's recommendation, which should have made me suspicious in the first place. When André seemed unusually well informed about everything going on on the island, I did a little investigating and discovered that he was blackmailing Norton to act as some kind of island spy. It seems Norton had had trouble with bad checks. And André led him to believe that if he didn't do as he was told, he, André, would blow the whistle on Norton to me. And of course with my wealth and power, etcetera, I could have him put in jail for life. Norton, also, is not very bright, which is why André picked him as a tool as well as Boyd. What André had not counted on, though, was that while stupid tools can be easily threatened, they are the first, in a crisis, to lose their heads."

"André seems to have had an awful lot of conspiratorial irons in the fire."

"Yes. And considering all the disparate elements, he didn't do at all badly. I've often thought he was wasted in the twentieth century. What a Renaissance intriguer he would have made! And he was positively inspired in his way of using the materials at hand. He started rumors and kept flames going without—until just now—letting them get out of hand. So that, if, for example, I suddenly announced the opening of the new hospital section, I'd find a vocal opposition all set up. He knew I'd wait rather than ride over people, and that would give him more time to arrange credibly for my dispatch so he could marry Alix and get the island himself."

"I was astonished to learn in the library that St. Damien's still belonged to you."

"Oh, yes. But I have been negotiating to give it to the people there for some years."

"Negotiated? I should think they'd be delighted?"

"Yes, you would, wouldn't you? But the taxes on that island—all of which I pay—are considerable. When the islanders take it over, they'll have to pay the taxes themselves. So there's a group, especially among the older islanders on fixed incomes, to keep the island as my private property, for which they now pay not a penny tax."

"Oh," I said, digesting this.

"And it will come as no surprise to you to learn that André encouraged this group too. After all, if I sold the island, he wouldn't get it by marrying Alix."

"I begin to see what you mean about his being inspired in his use of the materials at hand."

"I thought you would. And besides all this, he loved intrigue for its own sake. I think it satisfied his frustrated desire for power. Anyway, he was keeping all these groups more or less where he wanted them when Boyd got mad at you, then got a little more tanked than he already was, and stole Susie, which resulted in his killing Petersen. At which point André knew he had to act, because with Petersen murdered I'd take steps to stop his games."

"Why didn't you stop them before?"

"I should have. And because I didn't, I feel partially responsible for Petersen's death. But the government was interested in André's Middle East friends and wanted to wait to let them—and all their domestic connections—show their hands."

"And you were willing to let André play with Alix's affections?"

He frowned. "I hadn't realized how far all that had gone. But you're right. I should have known."

"Speaking of Alix, if she gets back now to Darcourt place and finds you gone, won't she let André know?"

"How? The phone line has been cut—obviously André saw that that was done right after he heard from Norton about Boyd's hijinks and Petersen's death, whether or not he did the cutting himself or told Alix how to do it. But he forgot about my two-way radio, largely because I seldom have occasion to use it. That was the way I got in touch with the Coast Guard. Living on an island in the path of most of the hurricanes that come up the east coast, you have to be prepared for the possibility of all lines being blown down. But that hasn't happened since André started plotting to transfer my holdings to himself. Anyway, the Coast Guard relayed my messages to the police who were sending reinforcements over as I left. They will hold Alix. What was in the note?"

I told him, and, as I did so, felt again the pang of guilt. "I felt like I was summoning you to your death, Tristram," I said. "I'm sorry to be such a coward. But I couldn't let Susie . . . although now I realize he was putting me on over that, too. But you're so . . . so well able to take care of yourself."

"Am I?" he said drily. And I heard again that uncharacteristic note of self-doubt. I put my hands against his shoulders. "It's hard for me to think of you as anything but strong."

"And therefore perhaps beyond other human needs."

"Such as?"

"Such as love and tenderness and faith and warmth and belief—which should exist between two people who love one another."

"Perhaps no one ever knew how much you wanted it. Maybe you were too proud to let them."

After a moment he said, "I thought I let Giselle, your mother, know. That was why her letter came as such a shock."

"And it was because of her sister getting leprosy and having to go away?"

"Indirectly. The direct cause was that she was told by . . . someone . . . that if I knew about this I would want to break the engagement; and that if I didn't do so, it would be out of chivalry only!" He paused. "I told you, Sally, there was someone else moving around in this, pulling the levers, manipulating events, manipulating your mother's fear and the fear and horror she had like everyone else—of the disease."

"Who—" I started, when he interrupted me.

"What time do you have?"

I glanced at my watch. "Eleven fifteen. Just past."

"Yes. That's what I have. So it must be right. How long ago did André leave with that signed note?"

"Maybe an hour, maybe an hour and a half ago. Why?"

"If Alix rode, and I'm fairly sure she did, since both she

and her horse were missing when I got back from St. Damien's, then it would have taken her at least an hour to get to the house and another to get back, presumably bringing me."

"I forgot to tell you. You weren't to come here. You were to come to the Devil's Cup at six tomorrow morning."

"So it's to be the Devil's Cup," he said.

"Yes. Somebody—André—told me that your brother died in the Devil's Cup and that you were there. Is that true?"

"André leaves nothing out, does he? Yes. I was there."

He answered in the flat, indifferent voice that used to irritate me so much, but that I was beginning to see was as much camouflage for pain as my father's explosiveness. "What else did he tell you?"

"Nothing. Except that you were about seventeen." I touched him. "If you don't want to talk about it, don't. I understand."

He didn't say anything for a minute. Then he shrugged. "I suppose there's no hurry if André doesn't plan the rendezvous until six."

"Won't he expect Alix back sooner than that, as you said?"

"I doubt it. If that is the plan her role would be to persuade me to the meeting at the Cup. But he may come up to check on you, and I'd rather be nearby—within easy calling distance—but out of the room." He glanced around, his eye taking in the rope lying in coils near the window. My own eyes followed his. I said, "When you're out the window, I'll unhook the rope and throw it down. You can always throw it back in again."

"Suppose he decides to tie you up safe and comfy for the night among your six-legged friends."

I hadn't thought of that, and the prospect did not please me. But I replied bravely, "You'll think of something!"

"Your faith in me is inspiring, however much it may be a betrayal of your liberation principles. And it is well placed. I *have* thought of something."

Going over to the huge oak chest on the floor, he lifted the lid. "I could get into that quite easily. The question is, how long could I breathe if he decided to tie you up and then stick around?"

"Then don't get in. We'll have to think of something else."

"Look," Darcourt said. He went over to the rope, unfastened it from the foot of the bed, and put it in the chest. But before he shut the lid he pulled out the end and simply stuck it on top of one of the sides, the side away from the door. "If I lower the top—as you can see it's not a flat top but has a lip to it all the way around—I can put the end of the rope so that it stops it closing, but the lip covers the open join, so to speak. I'll get air, but André, unless he knows where to look, won't know."

Leaving the lid down, Darcourt went to the window and, leaning out, pulled the blinds shut. "We should have thought of doing this before. If André decided to take a stroll outside, he'd have seen the light from the candles, and known you had overcome your fear of scorpions and crossed the floor to open the window. And that might assure the fact that he would tie you up."

"Closing the blinds now is a little like locking the stable door after the mare has gone, isn't it?"

"Perhaps. Perhaps not." Hooking the blinds together he came back to the bed. "Now," he whispered, "let's keep our voices low. Not so much that he can hear us—if he's downstairs in the one habitable room, he can't—but so that we can hear him if he comes up here."

He stood for a moment listening.

"Why don't you sit down?" I asked. "Aren't you afraid of standing among the scorpions?"

"Not really. They're even less eager to bother me than I am to be bothered. And I have on boots. Standing, I can keep an eye on the door. About my brother's death—"

"You don't have to—"

"I know. But in a way, I do. It's time. Did André imply that I killed him? Or that I stood around doing nothing while he died?"

"Yes, the latter."

"Well, it's true. Only I wasn't seventeen, I was twenty-two, and had just been given a medical discharge from the navy. After graduating from Annapolis—all Darcourt younger sons went either into the army or navy—I went on my first long cruise. It was during that cruise that I got your mother's letter, by the way."

"Couldn't you have got leave to come home to see what it was about?"

"No. I don't think so. If we had been married, and it had been a question of the marriage, yes. But we weren't. And as a matter of fact, our engagement hadn't even been publicly announced. Back in those days things were more formal. And my pride was hurt."

I could believe that, and I couldn't even blame him. Under similar circumstances, I would have reacted the same. And my father? I found myself wondering. Wouldn't he have told the navy to go fly a kite and gone AWOL? Maybe. But then he didn't come from an old tradition of service.

"What are you thinking about?" Darcourt asked, his eyes on my face. I told him.

"Yes," he agreed. "I think your father would have told the navy where it could put itself and flown home. But—right or wrong—the Darcourts have always believed that feelings came after what they would probably describe as duty."

"I have no trouble believing that."

"And before you spit on the floor, suppose your father had been serving, not with the navy, the Establishment, but with, say the IRA. Would he have put down his molotov cocktail and hightailed it back to his girlfriend?"

I thought that one over. "You have an unpleasant way of putting things, don't you?"

"It's all in where your loyalties lie. Or, if you want to be really cynical—and I think you sometimes do—where your interests are invested. After all, the Darcourts' interests are with the current Establishment, so their tradition is to protect it. But don't the IRA and most other revolutionaries wish to become the Establishment, after, of course, they've unseated the present one?"

I had been half lying on the bed, but I sat up. "You know," I said indignantly, "until I met you things were nice and clear in my head. I didn't have to worry about other people's points of view, because I knew they were wrong."

"My apologies," he said drily.

I put up one hand and took his. "Go on. Why were you medically discharged from the navy?"

"Because I contracted an ailment that turned out to be tuberculosis of the bone. I was shipped back to the States and put in Walter Reed Hospital. After about a year of treatment and surgery I was sent home, with a hunch back and a slightly shorter left leg. There've been operations since, which have reduced the deformity. Anyway, my brother, Robert, and I were never the best of friends. When we were children he lorded it over me. Then, when I was in my late teens, I caught up with him in height and weight and even class work at prep school, and started beating him at his own games. I was highly competitive, and when I won, which

257

was more and more often, inclined to rub his nose in it, to make up for all the times he'd rubbed mine in his triumphs. Then I came home with crutches and a heavy brace."

Darcourt paused. "This is the part I'm not particularly proud of. Robert was genuinely sorry. He was a decent enough guy, and had grown into a nicer person than the adolescent he'd been, when he was feeling—I realized when it was too late—my hot, competitive breath coming up behind him. He came to the boat landing to meet me, and put his arms around me. He was always much more demonstrative and emotional than I. I took it as pity, and shoved him away with some biting comment or other. There were servants around and he was furious. But he forgave me. Because I was a cripple, he forgave me, and that was what I couldn't stand. Every time he came near I'd taunt him about this or that. Then, one day we were out riding. That was the one thing I could do. I'd had a special light brace made so I could sit a horse. We rode through the swamp. I've forgotten what started the quarrel that time. It could have been anything. I was full of self-pity and angry about your mother, about my illness, about having to leave the navy, about the fact that I would always be a cripple and that I would probably be able to do nothing but go into the family business as some kind of second-string step-and-fetchit for my older brother, who, in Darcourt tradition, would get all the real power.

"Anyway"—Darcourt took a deep breath—"he was boasting about what he would do when the holdings came to him. . . . Sally, it took years and more pain than I could have imagined for me to see that poor Robert's boastings were simply a defense against what we both knew: that he was neither as strong nor as self-confident as I'd always been. And knowing that, and feeling sorry for myself and angry at him, I taunted him. I told him that he had as much chance of improving and increasing the family empire as he did of jumping the Devil's Cup. You see, because he was lighter than I, the long jump was the one area where he continued to beat me, even after I was beating him in everything else. So my jibe hit both his strength and his weakness. Nevertheless, I did not—consciously—expect him to take me up on it. He did, however. So we got off our horses, who wouldn't go near the Cup, and walked over to it. By the time we got there I had regained enough sanity to try and talk him out of it. But not hard enough. He wouldn't listen. I then went after him physically. If I had been well, if I hadn't had that

258

brace, it would have been easy. But he was able to shake me off. I was yelling at him from where he had thrown me when he took a running jump. Even so, he might have made it. But he was wearing riding boots, and, just as he took off, his toe struck a stone, which cut back his thrust. There was nothing I could do. The Cup is more or less round—about twenty or so feet in diameter—and I couldn't reach him. The horses were too far away for me to use one of them to pull him out even if I had had a rope. He was gone in less than half a minute. But he had time to scream, 'You did this! You planned it!' And then he just screamed and screamed. . . ."

I was holding on to both his hands, and could think of nothing to say except, "Tristram, I'm sorry. I'm so sorry. It wasn't your fault."

He yanked his hands away. Then he leaned forward and grasped mine. "There I go again. Nobody must pity me or have sympathy for me." He squeezed them. "I've never been sure, you know, whether or not he was right: that I did, unconsciously, out of bitterness and frustration, plan it."

After a while I said, "Were your parents alive?"

"Oh, yes. I told them exactly what had happened. The shock killed my mother. Robert was always her favorite—he was very like her. She had a stroke immediately afterwards. And then, a few weeks later, another one that finished her off."

"And your father?"

"My father simply said, 'I don't think there is any need for me to say anything. The rest of your life will be more punishment than I could possibly mete out.' He was right."

After a while I said, "Tristram, your brother, Robert, he didn't have to jump."

"That's what Père de Sevigny—Father Mark's predecessor —said. I spilled it all to him once, and he put me in my place. He said, 'Take the responsibility that is yours—but not more than is yours. That's spiritual pride.' And, as I am sure, Sally, you would be the first to point out, pride is my besetting sin."

After a while I said, "Tell me about you and Nicole. When . . . when did it all happen?"

"If you mean the leprosy, probably when she was a child, probably from someone who nursed her or took care of her. But it has a long incubation period, and then when she started developing symptoms, which was a few years after we were married, it was diagnosed as half a dozen other skin diseases by doctors, perfectly competent men I suppose, except that they had never seen a case of leprosy in their lives and wouldn't ever even think to consider it as a possibility. It was a New Orleans doctor, finally, who diagnosed it correctly. And Nicole . . . well, you can imagine what her reaction would be. Rich, spoiled Nicole Charpentier, once debutante of the year, Queen of Carnival. If they'd handed her a white robe and a bell, as was done to people with leprosy in the Middle Ages, it couldn't have been a worse shock."

"I didn't know people even *had* leprosy anymore—certainly not in Europe or in the States."

Tristram moved around slowly. "In the world, there are about fifteen million. In the United States alone, two thousand, although that is probably a conservative figure. Because of the stigma and the fear there are people who simply won't turn up for treatment. They'll take other names, lose themselves. Anything. . . . It isn't as bad now. But did you know that until a decade or so ago, people who contracted leprosy had many of their civil rights taken away from them? Doctors have known now for a long time that of all communicable diseases it is the least communicable—and shortly after treatment is started, not at all. Yet, until a few years ago people who had leprosy could not travel with other people on public conveyances. They could not be treated at home. They could not be treated in ordinary hospitals, except temporarily, and they were forced by law to be isolated in the leprosorium at Carville. Even at Carville, patients were known by false names, so as not to injure their families or—should they be discharged as free of the disease—themselves. That's no longer true. But most Louisiana families—especially Cajun French families—know these old tales. And Nicole was born and brought up there. And—" He stopped.

"What?" I asked.

"It sounds crazy, but I've sometimes thought that Nicole must have known all along, on some level, what was the matter with her. She ran away from it so hard. She's wealthy in her own right, and she bought houses here and there—preferably as far away from Louisiana and the island here as possible. When she finally was diagnosed, she was devastated. But it was as though something that she had known was pursuing her had finally caught up with her."

We were silent for a while. Then Tristram said, "You know she was the one who renamed Damien Island St.

Damien's. Father Damien finally received his canonization, but from Nicole, not the Pope."

"But why? Why the island?"

"Because of the hospital already there. Doctor McIntyre's predecessor was a noted skin specialist who worked with doctors at Carville. It was his idea to add a section to the existing hospital for leprosy patients which I agreed to finance. With my permission, he renamed the island Damien, after the famous Belgian priest, Damien the Leper. Nicole added the 'Saint.' It was one of her last fully rational acts. Her irrationality had been showing up long before her physical illness was pinpointed. Then, as I said, fear of the stigma pushed her over the edge. Having—briefly—accepted the illness, she then did a right-about-face and since then has steadily refused to acknowledge it in any way, which means she has refused all medicine and all drugs. She thinks poor old McIntyre is about to poison her. And her disease has gone unchecked, which is a thousand pities, because it now can almost always be arrested. But, short of committing her to one hospital or another, there's nothing I've been able to do. She's half renovated the old plantation house. I offered to have the whole thing done, but she preferred to make over the upper story and part of the back, leaving the front a wreck to protect her privacy. As you obviously know, she even went into the old fort, building a bizarre maze out of stones and bits of plaster that have fallen in from the roof and the walls. As long as she didn't do herself, or anyone else, damage, I felt that leaving her alone was the kindest thing I could do."

"How long has she been like this? I mean, as ill, mentally and physically."

"Well, nothing stays still. She's grown worse. But she's been a recluse since Alix was a child."

"Does Alix know about her mother? I mean, she knows, or suspects her mother was back here. Or at least, so she's told me. Does she know why?"

"I don't think so. I'm not even sure that she's convinced her mother *is* here, even though she has said as much to me also. One can never be sure how much what she says is what she's been told to say."

"By André?"

"Yes. And what concerns me much more is whether André knows, or if he knows, has told her, that she herself has leprosy."

He said it so casually. But it was as though a lightning bolt had gone through me. "Then that's what—"

He smiled a little. "Yes. That's why everything." He sighed and sat down beside me. "I think I will sit down. Alix undoubtedly got it from her mother, who looked after her when she was a baby, although the first symptoms didn't appear till she was about thirteen. Fortunately she has a much milder form of leprosy. Because of our experience, I took her straight to Doctor McIntyre, who diagnosed it immediately, and she's been taking medicine regularly."

"Those vitamin pills!"

"Precisely. Which is why I—and the doctor—have been so adamant about making her take them. And why, in answer to the question you asked at the beginning, she has lived such an isolated life."

"But if it's not that communicable—"

"It isn't, but the stigma remains. Twice I have removed her from a school because someone there discovered what she was taking and what it was for. You know about the last time. It was pure bad luck that the nurse there had been a missionary nurse out in the Pacific islands and undoubtedly had seen the disease and recognized the medicine.

"One of the things I've learned is that once one person knows—however conscientious and well-meaning that person is—you might just as well assume that sooner or later others will know. Did you ever read the ancient story about the man who was given a terrible secret—I think it was that the king of the realm had ass's ears—and was told that if he ever passed it on to a single soul, dire calamity would follow? Well, he didn't tell anyone, but the burden of not talking about it was so great that one night he went out and knelt down and whispered it to the grass. Then, at peace, he went back to bed. But the wind blew over the grass and picked up the fearful secret, and gave it to the bells. And the next day everyone in the kingdom knew."

I shivered. Because I knew it was true. Hadn't I come down to publish whatever secret I had found? However, I couldn't resist saying to him, "You're a very odd businessman, with your spooky tales."

"How many businessmen have you known? I mean *known* as opposed to merely inciting other people to put their heads on pikes."

"Well, that's where the heads of most business czars ought to be. But not yours." I slipped my hand in his.

"I think your moral fibers are weakening again."

"I know they are."

He took his hand away and put it up behind me and rubbed my neck. "That's one of the many things I like about you. Your openmindedness."

"Tell me more about Alix."

"The first time someone at Alix's school—that was the first one—found out, I decided to wait and see. No one was unkind. Nothing seemed to happen. Until, suddenly, within one week, six sets of parents withdrew their children, and the headmistress called me and pleaded with me to take Alix out before the news leaked out generally. Apparently Alix, who thought her pills were vitamins, had shared them with some other kid, who proceeded to have some odd reactions, and the school nurse sent them off to a pharmacist friend for analysis. She then queried Alix pretty closely, but of course Alix honestly thought they were high-potency vitamins, so the nurse confided her findings to the headmistress— and she swore, no one else. Nevertheless, all those children started leaving. When the headmistress called me, she said if I took Alix out immediately she would lie to the parents and ascribe the pills and the medicine to some other more acceptable illness. I would like to have told her what she could do with her school, but the person who would suffer would be Alix. So I did as she asked. The next time it happened, I didn't wait to be asked. I just took her out."

"Wouldn't it have been better to have told her?"

"Perhaps. You may be right. But she is, or at least I thought she was, her mother's daughter, and that her reaction would be the same. I have been thinking now for some months I was wrong. To do him justice, McIntyre did, too, but I had forbidden him to mention it. She is responding very well to the medicine, and I was putting off the moment of telling her until it had been totally arrested."

Darcourt paused, got up, went over to the door and listened.

"Do you hear something?" I whispered.

After a moment he came back to the bed and stood and seemed to listen again. "I don't know. I thought I did." He stood silently and we both listened. But apart from little scraping noises from the edges of the room and the sighing of the wind through the treetops, I heard nothing.

"Tristram," I said, after another minute or two, "the St. Damien's islanders obviously have this same horror of leprosy you've talked about. And they've heard, or been told by somebody, that this new hospital, the new section of the existing hospital, for leprosy patients is going to be put there. I know you said this is what Doctor McIntyre's predecessor planned and you agreed then to pay for it. But is it still on?"

"Yes. McIntyre and some of the other doctors have long wanted to open up a new research center on that and other diseases generally associated with the tropics. It will involve some patients, but won't be a whole hospital such as at Carville. As a matter of fact, people who have leprosy are being treated more at home as outpatients. Only those who don't respond to the medicine, or who have neglected to get medical treatment and can't really care for themselves are put—entirely voluntarily—into hospitals."

"Then where do the people on St. Damien's get their scare from? The truth stretched and exaggerated by repetition?"

"Yes. Or, more likely, André. He would know how to play on ignorance and fear; how to set the fire and then fan it."

"But why? What good could a bunch of angry islanders do to him?"

"Soften them up for what I have reason to think he really has in mind: sell the island to some foreign—Middle-Eastern —syndicate that wants to make a massive resort out of it: another Miami or Palm Beach rolled into one. The islanders would be so relieved, with me out of the way and no hospital to be built, they wouldn't find out until it was too late that the resort wouldn't mean more jobs—which is what they'd be led to think—it would mean they'd be relocated on the mainland. Because if my investigations turn out to be true, they—the syndicate—want to raze the whole island and cut everything: village, woods, houses, so they can build their golf courses, swimming pools, air strip, beaches and other recreational joys. I also think that this island is part of the package, including the sanctuary, the swamp area, which they'd drain."

"You mean he wouldn't keep the island for himself?"

"I doubt it. Crazy as it sounds, I think he sees himself as some pre-Louisiana purchase French seigneur. I doubt if he'd live anywhere but Louisiana. And he's always hated the Darcourts."

"He said that you had inherited Charpentier holdings that he should have had, that they should have been left to his father."

"And they would have been, if Pierre, André's father,

could have been poured out of the bars on Bourbon Street long enough to see if he knew a shipyard from an oilfield. Nicole's father had no great love for me. He was a proud old French Louisianan who disliked the Anglo-Saxon and Protestant American almost as much as André did. That was the irony. But along with his French pride was a huge sense of responsibility. Do you know, Sally, how many people got their paychecks from him?"

I shook my head.

"More than fifty thousand, all told. A small city. If the Charpentier shipyards and shipping interests had gone bankrupt, that might have been the end of their jobs. That's why he made me his heir. I'm not even sure that that isn't the real reason he countenanced my marrying Nicole. He would have far preferred someone French and Catholic. But there were none in the woods around there of the right age who could have taken over his business affairs. And for all his religious and racial chauvinism, he was as shrewd as the French peasantry from which he sprang. Anyway, I promised him I wouldn't either sell his business or take it out of Louisiana or let it go down the drain. And I haven't."

Suddenly, and out of the blue, I remembered the file— "Javelin"—open on André's desk in the shack. "Tristram!"

He put his arm around me and smoothed my hair and then kissed me.

"Yes?"

"You're distracting me," I said breathlessly.

"Yes," he said, and kissed me again.

I emerged for air. "Successfully."

"All right. I'm sorry. Proceed."

I told him about the file and said, "What's 'Javelin'?"

"It's a code name the Intelligence people gave the operation of trying to find out what André was doing with his Middle Eastern friends. Given my vested interests, they were reluctant to use me—you can imagine the uproar it would cause. 'Multi-national head used as spy by government to protect own oil holdings.' Something like that. And you can also imagine how it would strike your chums in the press. On the other hand, I was certainly on the spot and could do more informed snooping than anyone else. And so they—the Intelligence people—gave me contacts here and on St. Damien's."

Darcourt was right about the headline, all right. I could see it on newspapers from New York to Washington out to

Los Angeles and on coast-to-coast network. There was the juicy bit that Brian would love to have. Not thinking, in reflex action, I asked:

"Oh? Who? What contacts?"

Darcourt, who had been walking around, came back and looked down at me. "Now, why should I tell you? You'd probably phone it through to some columnist or newshawk with your first dime as soon as you got out of here."

I reacted, of course, according to my guilt—indignantly. "After all . . . after everything . . . Tristram—you don't trust me."

"Should I?"

I didn't say anything.

"I have not been idle, my love. Didn't you get your initial start in journalism by an inflammatory piece called 'The Multinationals: How to Break Them; Who and Where to Attack.' I was looking it up earlier today in the St. Damien's library."

"You were there? When I was?"

"No. Somewhat before."

"I bet they would have allowed you to bring in Susie," I said bitterly.

"Yes. But for that reason I wouldn't have tried."

"Even so . . ."

"And besides, I gave them the library."

There was a silence.

"Well?" Tristram said. "Cat got your tongue? Where's your speech on feudal patronage?"

"If I'm going to marry you," I said typically, oh, so typically, not thinking. . . . And paused, horrified.

"You forget," Tristram said evenly. "I *am* married. Further, I gave Nicole's father my promise that I would not divorce her, no matter what. He was, as I said, French and Catholic, and he demanded it."

"In exchange for his shipyards," I said bitterly.

"That would confirm all your worst suspicions and beliefs, wouldn't it?"

I peered at him, towering over me as he stood at the bed's foot. "You said you were ambitious and competitive." I wanted, desperately, for him to deny it.

"Oh, yes. Very. I've been able to multiply all the property I inherited—or married."

A candle on the stone mantel flickered, guttered and went out. Tristram, kicking various creatures out of his way, went over and pinched the end to stop it smoking.

"And so, for all that, you tied yourself to——" My voice trailed off. Why didn't he deny it? Explain it? Justify it? Instead of just standing there and calmly agreeing with every accusation I flung at him.

"Shocking, isn't it? But then you knew it all along."

"Tristram——" I said.

"I'm not going to plead with you to believe in me."

I didn't say anything, mostly because I was concentrating on not crying.

"Pride, again," he said a little bitterly. "Well, to answer your question, old Pierre was indeed Catholic and French. But I doubt if even he would have asked that if Nicole's illness had not just been diagnosed. And because I felt guilty —I promised."

"Why did you feel guilty?"

"Because I was a lousy husband. Because if I had cared about her I would have sent her to a knowledgeable doctor instead of letting her bounce around with all the fashionable quacks she preferred. Because I married her for a lot of bad reasons—not including either love or money—but which did include both pride and vanity, which I took at the time to be love. Those were the years after World War Two. Nicole Charpentier was the leading debutante of French New Orleans. Queen of Carnival. Beautiful—far more beautiful than your mother, whom I *had* loved. She was what every man wanted. And I—hunchback, brace and all—got her. But Nicole married me for all the reasons you ascribe to me for marrying her. The Charpentiers were rich, but not as rich as the Darcourts, and nowhere near as well known in the outside world. The marriage started with vanity and pride on my side and greed and ambition on hers and went downhill from there. It didn't take long for one fact to emerge. She liked everything about being married to me, except me. So, it wasn't much of a union. She did her partying and playing elsewhere, and so did I. After a fashion. But that's all it was, as far as I was concerned, playing. A burnt dog stays away from the fire. So I kept my feelings, as they say today, uninvolved."

Unreasonably, I was hurt and angry—too much so to listen to what lay under his words. "That's reassuring to know," I commented. "I'm glad that with the coming and going of all your mistresses you didn't have time to be lonely."

"I didn't contract to be a monk." Which was exactly the way I had put it to myself.

And there we were, back to square one. Quarreling. Why, I thought dismally?

And it was at that moment that the door was unlocked and swung open.

André stood in the door, the key in his hand, blank surprise on his face. Then he plunged forward as though pushed. As indeed, it turned out, he was. Behind him, a gun in her hand, was Nicole.

"Get in," she said contemptuously, and then, sounding as rational as anyone, "Good evening, Tristram."

"Good evening, Nicole," he said calmly. "You've taken us by surprise. Not very clever of us, I'm afraid."

"Yes. I intended to."

(14)

SHE WAS a tall woman, and huge. A dark, shapeless garment dropped from her shoulders to the floor. From her head, falling to her shoulders, was a black veil, giving her figure that pyramid shape I had glimpsed in silhouette. The veil was now flung back, revealing the wrecked face. A tall cane was in her hand and as she came in a few steps, limping badly and dragging one foot, I heard again the step, drag, pause, step, drag, pause that I had heard in the forest, in front of Darcourt Place and, finally, behind me just before I walked into André's trap.

"Well, Miss Wainright," and I was, illogically, astonished again at the softness of her Southern voice. "Did you get what you came for?"

Since I was dealing with an unknown quantity, I hesitated before answering. Then I said, "I'm not sure what you mean."

"Come now, don't play coy games with me. You came here to get Tristram. You're not the first. You won't be the last, although I'll say this for you: you've succeeded, somehow, in getting more of his attention—and regard—than all the others who've come as so-called governesses. But that's all you'll get. Do you hear me!" She brought the cane down onto the floor with incredible force, and small shadows scattered away from her.

"Ach—!" She flayed about her on the floor with her stick.

Tristram took a step forward, but she was quick. With a

strange cry she abandoned her attack on the insect life around her and raised her stick with the obvious intention of cracking his skull in two.

"Tristram!" I cried, and at the same time heard André's voice.

"Cousin Nicole, not here!"

It was over in a minute. Tristram caught her arm. After a struggle that was ugly beyond words—the huge, tormented woman and the big man, his curved back distorted in shadow by the candle light—Tristram twisted the long black cane out of her hand.

"I'm sorry, Nicole. I'll give it back to you when we get back to your quarters."

"It was my father's," she said. "And my grandfather's from France." Absurdly, she sounded like a child lamenting her lost toy.

Tristram used her with a gentleness that was almost as shocking in him as the bizarre combination of child and fury was in her. "Yes, I know you value it. I'll return it when we get to your house."

There was a sudden movement, and André lunged for Tristram, obviously bent on taking advantage of the preoccupation with Nicole. But Tristram's perceptions were quick, and he was as agile as a cat. He met André's assault with one arm upraised and the other ready to return the blow. But he never delivered it.

The shot that rang out sounded, in that room, like a cannon. For what seemed like an extraordinarily long time we all stood there.

Then André, his eyes staring straight ahead to the doorway, said in a surprised voice, "*Mon Dieu, Mon Dieu, petite! Qu'est-ce que tu as fait?* What have you done?" The red stain sprang on his shirt front like a flower. He put his hand on it and the blood flowed over it.

"André!"

The cry came from the door. Alix flung the gun she was holding to the floor and sprang forward.

Tristram threw the long ebony cane on the bed and moved towards her. "Alix!"

André was bent over, one hand on the bed, a queer, dazed look on his face.

"Let me go to him," cried Alix, struggling in her father's arms. "Let me go!"

"Alix!" The whisper came from behind the veil which now

270

again covered Nicole's face. And then, still in a whisper, "Tristram, make her leave before . . . before . . ." In that nightmare scene it was pathetic to see the strange, possessed woman claw at the veil, pulling it down, fumbling with it to make sure it was in place. "Tristram . . . she doesn't know . . . she mustn't!"

Tristram stared at his wife for a moment and then released Alix. "It's all right," he said very quietly. "She won't know."

Alix flung herself towards André. "André, André darling. Don't die. Please don't die. I didn't mean to hit you. I fired into the air to scare Father so he'd let you go. Truly. I don't understand . . ." Her voice ended in a sob.

I saw Tristram look up and followed his glance. There, on the stained ceiling, was a new gash. "Riccochet," he said quietly.

"*Quel dommage, petite*," André whispered. "What a pity." In that light it was impossible to be sure. But it seemed to me his color was ghastly.

Tristram stepped forward. "Just a minute, Alix."

She swung around to him. "It's your fault. I hate you. I *hate* you." Her voice, borne up by hysteria, was rising. It ended abruptly when Tristram took hold of her shoulders and shook her. "Be quiet!" he ordered.

Alix caught her breath and held it for a minute. Then broke into a desolate weeping. Her mother, who had backed into the shadowy doorway, stood silent. I had no way of knowing, but I felt that she, too, was crying. One hand crept up under the veil. I then heard a soft sob.

"Sally," Tristram said. "Come and give me a hand."

We pushed André onto the bed and bent over him. Tristram tore away the bloody shirt. Gunshot wounds were outside my experience, but even I knew that there was not much that could be done.

André opened his eyes and looked at Tristram. "You won," he said tiredly. "And it was Alix . . . Alix! who did it for you. What a joke! What a terrible joke!" He coughed, and bloody foam came to his lips.

"Be quiet, André," Tristram said. "You'll lose what chance you've got."

André's eyes looked black as he stared up at his enemy. "I don't have any chance at all, Tristram. And you know it. Get me a priest."

"Hang on till morning, André. And I'll get you one then."

André closed his eyes and then opened them again. "What's

271

the matter with telephoning now?" Then, "I remember now. I cut the line." He coughed again. His breath grew shallow and wheezy. Then he said, "I had it all worked out. And then Alix's bullet. . . . And I can't even die shriven, because I cut the line. God must be laughing."

"André darling—" Alix pushed me out of the way. "André —I didn't mean . . . it was an accident . . . I'll get you a priest."

"Alix!"

The voice this time came from behind the veil. One hand gripped, once more, the ebony cane, which she must have retrieved from the bed. The other hand, with fingers shortened and deformed, was held out in an age-old gesture of supplication. "Alix!"

Alix drew back. "Who are you?"

I stared back at the young girl. "Alix," I said. "You were the one who told me your mother lived here."

She looked at me impatiently. "I told you that because André told me to. My mother's in France." Her voice caught on a sob. "It was part of everything we planned. André told me who this woman is. She's just some poor dotty servant that's allowed to live here because she once worked for us and otherwise would be in a booby-hatch."

"But—" I said.

Tristram suddenly spoke. "Just be quiet, Sally."

But I couldn't. Greedy and ambitious she might have been. Only half rational she had certainly become. And her present state was as much the result of her own choice—after all, she had deliberately and constantly refused all medical attention—as of malignant fate or others' indifference. Yet my pity for her, and for this final rejection by her daughter, won over judgment.

"Alix, this is your mother. She is very ill. But she is your mother."

Alix turned towards me. "You're lying. Of course you're lying. You've seen my mother's portrait. She was beautiful. Like me." Her hand strayed towards her face and touched the round macule on her cheek.

The tall woman in the shadows gave a cry that pierced the heart.

"Sally," Tristram said again.

But something—expiation?—was driving me on. I, too, in so many ways had rejected my mother, resenting the adoration my father had for her. "Alix," I started again.

The girl looked at me. Then, in a quick gesture, stepped forward and pulled the veil off her mother's face. I wondered if Alix would find in the ruined features anything of the mother she had not seen since she was a child.

Then, as Alix stared, I knew there could be no mistaking. Behind the distorted features, still visible, was the beautiful woman whose portrait hung in the Darcourt library.

This time the cry came from Alix. "No, no, no, no."

The sound came back as Alix fled the room and down the stone hall outside, the sound of her feet fading.

"Alix!" Nicole cried. "Alix!"

Then she whirled around towards Tristram. "You have to follow her. She will go into the swamp!" Her voice shaking, she turned to me and cried, "This is your doing. You came here to take my husband and my child. I told André not to use you. You would put the evil on me as your mother did."

"My mother——?" I repeated.

Her voice now rose in rhythmic waves. Almost, I found myself thinking, as though it were some ancient chant or incantation.

"Your mother's sister had this curse on her and I found out about it when she visited us. Tristram came to the house to meet me, but he met your mother and then he never looked at me, even though I was much more beautiful——" The chant ceased abruptly. She whirled on Tristram and said in an ordinary voice, "Wasn't I?"

"Yes," he said wearily. "You were. But it was Giselle I wanted."

"Well, you may have wanted her, Tristram. But I decided that Giselle shouldn't have you." It was astounding, I thought, how her voice revealed what her face couldn't. Now she sounded both crafty and smug, like a child, successfully plotting to get her way. "So when you went off on that navy cruise, I told that Irish builder who was always around, while the new wing was being put up at home, and who looked like a sick cow every time Giselle appeared, that if you knew about her sister you wouldn't want to marry her. After all, you were a Darcourt, and the Darcourts had to be careful who they married. Oh, was I clever. I knew Giselle's pride. After all, she was a poor relation and all poor relations are proud. So I told that oafish, stupid Celt that you, Tristram, you of all people, would be too chivalrous, too gentlemanly, to tell her that yourself. And of course he told her, just as I planned, because he wanted her for himself."

Her laugh rang out and rose, reminding me again of the waves of Alix's hysteria. But there was something eerie and horrible about Nicole—far more dreadful than the disease that had ravaged her. After all, I had seen worse when I had worked as a hospital aide one summer vacation. I had been in cancer wards and helped take care of burn victims and accident casualties. The real horror of Nicole lay within her, in the furious will that bent everyone to her purpose and desire.

"So that," Tristram said slowly, "was the unknown agent, the person I knew was there." It was a statement, I noted vaguely, not a question.

"Of course. And he did exactly what I knew he'd do. He got Giselle up to New York and married her."

"Of course he did," I said. "He . . . he *was* chivalrous."

She laughed again. "Do you think so? So you know what he said when I told him that Tristram would want to jilt Giselle? He said, in that dreadful brogue, 'You're a lying, scheming vixen. No man would be that daft. You've got some plan of your own. But it suits my purpose, so I'll tell her so. She'd never be happy with him anyway.' I only half twisted your mother's life, Miss Wainright. He twisted her the rest of it. For himself."

I wanted to say, that's a lie. But I knew it wasn't. So many things were now clear.

She turned, her mood switched. "We have to go. Why are you waiting?"

Tristram glanced at André.

"Leave him," Nicole said. "He's dying. He's no use anymore."

Tristram looked at her. Then he went over and picked up the limp hand. With the other hand he lifted André's eyelid. "Yes. He's dead," he said matter-of-factly.

Because I was in a daze, the journey through the crumbling remains of that old fort, along a colonnade and into the back of the old plantation house, seemed like an unconnected collection of passing impressions.

Tristram started out first, holding the flashlight that André had brought in attached to his belt. I sarted to follow Tristram. Behind me, with her cane and the pistol she had retrieved from some pocket held rigidly alert, was Nicole. Then, just as I was leaving the room, I saw the revolver that Alix had flung down and bent to pick it up. Nicole knocked my arm with her stick and snapped, "Put that down!"

Tristram turned back and saw Nicole's revolver. "Surely that isn't necessary, Nicole."

The shortened fingers tightened on the weapon. "But I like to have it. I like to have it when you and this woman"—she suddenly pointed it at me—"don't."

We stood there. I thought about the pistol in Tristram's pocket and wondered if he would use it. I wondered also whether Nicole would use hers, or was it merely a power toy to be brandished.

"Go on," Nicole said to me, and rammed the pistol against me. "Go on," she repeated, and I was shocked by the hatred in her voice.

"If you use that pistol, Nicole," Tristram said calmly, "I will kill you."

The mouth of the pistol did not move from me, but her gaze shifted to Tristram. "Good!" she said. "Why should I want to live anyway? First we will kill your lady friend here, your mistress. That's why I made André come up. He was trying to put me off with some silly excuse. He thought he was using me." She gave a short laugh. "I was using him. But now, after we kill her, your mistress"—she gestured towards me with the gun—"we will die together. Suitably. As man and wife." She smiled.

"Sally is not my mistress," Tristram said.

"Don't lie to me!"

"And if we have a suicide pact," he went on calmly, "what will become of Alix?"

"She will marry—" And she glanced back toward the room where André lay, and looked suddenly confused.

"No," Tristram said. "She will not marry André. And she needs care and protection. She, too, has leprosy."

There was a silence, then Nicole screamed, a terrible noise filled with rage and pain. Whether consciously or not, her hand loosened and the pistol dropped.

"Sally, come beside me quickly," Tristram said, and I found myself yanked back by my arm. "No, Nicole, don't pick that up. I don't want to hurt you. I've never wanted to hurt you. But if I must, I will."

In Tristram's other hand was his own pistol. Then he stepped in front of me. "Come, now, Nicole. Let me take you back to your rooms."

Against common sense, undoing the protection that Tristram's body afforded me, I shifted so I could see her. But it was as though I had no choice.

"Tell me," her voice from behind the veil said, "please tell me you're lying, Tristram. That you just said it to get the pistol, to save Miss Wainright. Alix doesn't have leprosy. That's one of the reasons why I left, you know that. So she wouldn't get it. You're lying," she repeated, and the half-chanting note came back in her voice. "You're lying, you're lying, you're lying, tell me."

"No, I'm not lying. Alix has a mild form of leprosy, which was diagnosed immediately. She's been taking medicine, and her disease is being brought under control. She will have to take medicine all her life, but if she does, and with care and luck, there is no reason she shouldn't live a perfectly normal life. If you had been willing . . . but even now, if you let Doctor McIntyre—"

"Do you think I'm a fool? Have you seen my face lately?" The gloved hand tore back the veil. "Have you seen my hands?" She held out one, ungloved, the ends of the fingers reabsorbed back into the bone. "The lesions on my leg? You are saying that these will go away, that I can be as I once was?"

"No. Not now. But if you would just submit to medical care, it could be arrested, and if it were, then there is surgery—"

"That's what you told me before. And I know it's a lie. All those doctors lied. And you are now lying. Everyone lies, to get the better of me. That's why you're telling me this lie about Alix. Isn't it? Isn't it?"

"Be quiet!"

He stood, grasping her arms above the wrists. "Do you want us to go after Alix or not? If you keep this up, she can ride straight into one of those swamps."

For what seemed a long time there was silence. Then the woman shuddered. "Let us go, quickly."

Tristram said quietly, "Sally, pick up her pistol and walk behind us. Gently now . . ."

He didn't need to caution me. Moving as evenly as I could, I got Nicole's pistol and walked around her.

"Now, Nicole," Tristram said, in the same gentle voice, "let me escort you back into your home. Give me your arm."

For a moment she didn't move. Then she said with weary bitterness, "Aren't you afraid?"

"Of what?"

"Of me. Of what I carry in my body."

"No. There's nothing to be afraid of."

276

"If I had believed you——"

"It's still not too late."

"Yes. It is. Everything's too late. But we must not be, for Alix."

Tristram took her arm. For a moment, I thought she would reject it. But she moved forward and, as though he were leading Nicole Charpentier into the cotillion at the Rex Ball, where she was to be crowned Queen of Carnival, he led her through the old fort's crumbling rabbit warren of corridors, doorways and passages.

Tristram, of course, had the flashlight and I stumbled after them, using my own pencil light. Crawling things scuttled out of the way. Wings suddenly whirred above our heads. Once Tristram turned the flashlight up and shone it on row upon row of bats, all hanging upside down. The stink of mildew and damp and rotting substances and animal and bird waste was overpowering.

And then, almost abruptly, we emerged from a rubble-covered passageway onto a high walk, made of wood, covered above but open to the sides above a low railing. At the other end of that was a wooden door. Around us were the branches of leaves of trees, and long streamers of moss. I took a deep breath of cool fresh air and smelled a heady mixture of sweet and sour: the flowering sweet olive and cape jasmine, mingled with salt from the sea and the rank acrid odor of the marsh. But rank or sweet, after the fetid, stagnant atmosphere of the fort, it was like champagne, and I almost made myself dizzy with the deep draughts I sucked into my lungs.

Then Tristram opened the wooden door, and a few minutes later I was in another world. The door had been built into what was obviously a back porch. Here and there was a wicker easy chair, a table, rocking chairs, and a lamp or two. Screens covered the entire porch which was further protected by the surrounding evergreens and thus probably invisible from below. But Tristram and Nicole were moving straight ahead towards a door opposite the wooden one. Opening that, they went through, and I followed, and entered into a gracious ante-bellum mansion, looking, with the exception of softly globed electric lights, very much as it must have in 1850. There was no decay here, but polished wood and warmth and the smell of wax and potpourri. This was a short, wide hall, almost a landing. At right angles to it was another much wider hall branching left and right. And as we turned left into it, I could see the walls were lined above with portraits and framed prints and below with chests and tables, bearing polished silver, crystal and china ornaments. Who keeps this up? I wondered, and just in time kept myself from posing the question. An unwelcome question could jar the precarious calm Tristram had gone to so much trouble to establish.

Glimpses into rooms on our left showed me the same care and taste as the hall, but it dawned on me that all the rooms to the right of this long wing were closed. I was puzzling over this as we walked down the hall, Tristram holding his pace to Nicole's step, drag, pause, and I bringing up the rear, when the obvious reason struck me: the rooms to the right opened on the front. And suddenly in my mind I saw again the eyeless windows, their panes broken, their shutters hanging, the whole front of the house a desolate ruin. What better camouflage could there be? Who would guess that behind the wrecked façade lay a home in active use?

At that point in my cogitations, the right wall gave way to a staircase. Glancing down as we passed, I saw where I had stood with André. There, across the lower part of the stairs, was the beam, slanting up as though fallen from above, an effective barrier, dust-covered and splintered.

Once, I suspected, there had been a wide, graceful stairwell and landing, but now all except a narrow opening at the actual head of the stairs had been plastered up, so that anyone looking from below would see nothing except an expanse of stained wall. I paused and peered down. The place where André and I had stood when he offered to show me upstairs—banking on my recoil from the wreck and decay with its threat, always present in the tropics and subtropics, of a myriad of living creatures—would be, though invisible, highly audible to any listener in the hall above. Had Nicole listened up there and laughed as André maneuvered me into my refusal to explore further?

I saw Tristram glance behind and frown, and knew that by loitering I was risking the peace he had bought. Making as little sound as I could, I caught up.

"Nicole," Tristram said, slowing, "I want you to wait here while we go out and look for Alix. We will find her much more quickly if we move fast."

I thought for a moment she was going to refuse. Then she drew down her veil again and nodded. "Very well."

"Is André's car outside?"

"Yes."

"Did you take the key?"

Pause. A long silence. Then, "Yes." She fumbled under the voluminous folds of her long dress. "Here it is."

Tristram took it and looked across at me and moved his head, indicating that I was to go to the door at the end of the hall directly behind him.

I moved as casually as I could, bent on not triggering Nicole's alarm or anger. The door was very like the one leading from the colonnade to the porch. I opened it and stepped out onto a narrow iron balcony, forming the top of iron stairs leading to the ground. I paused, wondering whether Tristram meant to go down, and then knowing that of course he did. Still, I lingered. Along with my pity for Nicole was a conviction that her acquiescent calm was not to be trusted, and if she turned on Tristram, much as I was convinced he could take care of himself, I wanted to be there. But the door swung open again and Tristram appeared.

"Go on down, for God's sake!" he said.

"Are you coming?"

"Of course. Hurry! But be as quiet as you can. Something —a noise, anything—can set her off." Fortunately, my crepe-soled loafers enabled me to comply with this, and I noticed that Tristram, in well-worn riding boots, did the same.

The small foreign car appeared as we got below the screen of leaves and foliage and reached the ground. "Get in," Tristram said tersely, and went around to the driver's side.

"Now we see whether this really is the key," he said, getting in.

"Did you really think it mightn't be?"

"Oh, yes. Nicole loves to play tricks. But I think that her concern for Alix might inhibit her this time." Pushing the key into the ignition, he turned it. The motor caught.

"Now," Tristram said, "let's get the hell out of here."

"Are you really worried about Alix?" I asked. "Or was that just a ploy?"

"No. I'm worried. I know she rides in the swamp all the time, but not at night. She can see like a cat and she knows the path as well as anyone, but she's not on Brutus. He cast a shoe this—yesterday—morning, and Duncan, who had the day off, hadn't yet given him a new one. So Alix took out Bolero, who's nervous and high strung. If that mare put a foot on unfirm ground, she wouldn't simply back off, but would buck and do her best to throw Alix off. Alix's been forbidden to ride Bolero—not, of course, that that would do anything but induce her to do so at the first opportunity, but I hadn't counted on Brutus losing a shoe."

Tristram switched on the headlights and handed me the flashlight he had been carrying. "You may have to use this in addition, if I ask you to shine it on the road to either side." He put up his head like an animal and sniffed a little. "It should be light before long."

He eased the car along a small, winding path, thickly lined on either side with shrubbery. I had lost all sense of direction, and the shrubs never thinned out long enough for me to see anything else in the car's headlights.

"You should get a surprise in a moment," Tristram said.

"What—" I started, but at that moment, he said, "Look," and taking the flashlight from me, switched it on and beamed it slightly to one side. There were five huge dogs, lying asleep. In the middle of them, not asleep, sitting bolt upright on her haunches, was Susie.

"Susie," I said, not altogether surprised to find myself near tears.

Tristram slowed the car and I opened the door preparatory to getting out.

"Stay where you are," he said.

"I'm just—"

"I'll give her to you. I want you in there."

"Why?"

"Because this is treacherous ground, because I don't know where Nicole is, because I told you to stay in there." With that, he got out, picked her up and handed her to me. "Satisfied?"

"You're a good, *brave* dog," I said to Susie, ignoring him.

He gave a wry smile. Then leaning forward, he opened the glove compartment and rummaged in it.

"What are you looking for?" I asked.

"Anything I can find that might belong to Alix."

After a minute or two he pulled out a book and flipped open the cover. "Yes, this is hers. Poetry . . ." He opened it at random. "Ah, yes. She's just the right age for this, 'I have been faithful to thee, Cynara, in my fashion.'" He snapped the book shut. "I hope that bastard didn't hurt her too much." He took the book and handed it around under the noses of the dogs, all of whom were now up and plunging around. "All right. Go and look for her."

He got back into the car and put the book away.

The dogs, barking now, were speeding up the road ahead, running.

It was an eerie ride. Ahead raced the dogs, sometimes beyond the reach of the powerful headlights. There were trees and bushes and a road that twisted and turned. On either side of the road, and lower, was the swamp, pockets of mud covered by grass that in daylight, I remembered from my drive with André, were bright green.

"In what direction are we heading?" I asked.

"North. Towards the swamp."

"I thought you said the ground here was unfirm."

"The whole southern end of the island has swampy patches, but the swamp proper doesn't start till we get to the line of trees. You can't miss them. There . . . there they are."

And there they were, ghostly and threatening in the powerful lights from the car. And as we got nearer to them, there came on the air, much stronger than before, the sour, marshy smell.

We entered the trees, turning and twisting through them, and as we drove, I caught Tristram looking once or twice in the rear-view mirror. "Who would follow us here?" I asked.

"Nicole."

"You mean she has a car?"

"She has something that was specially made for her—it's a cross between a golf cart and a dune buggy. It enables her to get around the island, which she does mostly either when it's night, or when she thinks no one is around."

"Then that accounts for my hearing her in the forest that day, and in front of the house late at night."

"Oh, yes. She gets around."

"Do the servants know about her?"

"They think, as Alix did, that she was an old family retainer. I never told them that. But André did, and I let it go."

"You think she'll come after us?"

He didn't answer for a moment. Then he said, "I'm sure of it. Either that or she'll take one of the other two or three paths into the swamp. Wasn't it Polonius who said of Hamlet 'There's a method in his madness'? Well, there's a method in Nicole's. And if it is what I think it is, then she will certainly follow."

"What do you think it is?"

"Sally, I could be wrong. If I am, I would rather not have put it into words."

"All right."

Suddenly he reached with one hand and took mine. "I haven't said this before, and I don't know, under the circumstances, what good it will do either of us, but I must say it. I love you very much."

My heart felt as though it gave a shout.

"Tristram, I—"

Suddenly, faintly, came a sound.

"What was that?"

Tristram abruptly stopped the car and turned off the engine. We sat there in an unbelievable stillness. Turning my head, I saw light coming up from the horizon on one side of the sky. And it was as though a conductor had risen his baton. Everything living seemed to break loose into sound. It was the kind of celebration of the day that I had read about but never witnessed, and it was beautiful and satisfying beyond description. Then, among the songs and twitterings, came another sound that was unmistakably human, a cry.

"There she is," Tristram whispered. It came again. "Over there."

The eastern sky was pearl gray and, at the rim of the horizon, fiery red. But over the swamp itself lay a thick white mist, covering the ground completely and surrounding the car.

"We could drive off the path into the swamp in this," Tristram said. "Which would not help Alix. Sally, I'm getting out and walking ahead in the general direction of that voice. I want you to follow me. Keep that decoration on the center of the hood exactly on me—not to one side or another, or you may find your front wheels sinking."

"All right, what was that?"

"The sound I've been afraid of. Nicole's cart. Its engine was constructed deliberately to be as near noiseless as possible but I've been listening. We have to hurry."

Taking the flashlight, he got out of the car and moved ahead. I put Susie on the seat beside me.

Afterwards, I decided the slow drive, with Tristram walking in front, probably took only a few minutes. At the time it felt like an hour. Above was the sky, clear and sparkling, going through its technicolor metamorphosis. But for several feet off the ground was the swirling, moving mist, not yet burned dry by the sun. As I drove sounds came from either side—cheerful sounds, like bird song, unpleasant sounds, like plops and vague noises that made me think of soft mud and suction. Tristram, directly in front of the car, would occasionally become, not invisible, but cloudy, and I would be torn between the two fears of running him down and losing him.

Then suddenly, much louder, a cry, unmistakably from Alix. "No. Stop it. Don't . . ." And a scream.

Tristram speeded up. Which turned out to be dangerous, because his foot slid and one foot went down into mud that seemed to come up and grasp it like greedy lips. But he pulled himself out and stumbled on. And then, rearing up in front of him, was a horse, or mare, her reins dangling, her head up, ears forward. As Tristram came up she whinnied and frisked away.

Remembering what Tristram had said about her not putting a foot on unfirm ground, I decided she would not, unlike less intelligent humans, stumble into the swamp.

Then, suddenly, there were Nicole and Alix, struggling, and Tristram struggling with them. Wondering what I could do, I jumped out of the car and felt my feet slide. Clinging to the car door, I got back in, and wriggled over to the passenger side, where I put my feet out again. The ground felt firm, and, still holding on to the car, I got around it. But before I could reach the three figures, Alix was suddenly thrown clear. Half sitting half lying, she stared at me. "She tried to push me into the Cup."

"The Devil's Cup?"

"Yes. There. Behind them."

I turned. The mist had partially dispersed. There was the wide marsh, like a huge saucer, with its brilliant green reeds and black mud.

"My God!" I said, and turned to the two figures, still struggling, as they had struggled back in the fort.

"She must die," Nicole cried suddenly. "Tristram, you don't understand. She's cursed like me. She must die. That's the only way to save her. She must die!"

"No, Nicole. She will be all right. You must let her go. Now go back to your house. I will talk to you." His words had that same calming note I had heard before, and I understood what he was trying to do. "I'll drive you back, Nicole," he said. "We will talk about it there."

All of a sudden she seemed to relax. "All right, Tristram. I will do as you say."

I saw him straighten his curved back, as though it pained

him. Her veil was thrown back. I saw her eyes before she moved.

"Tristram—" I cried out.

But I was too late. They had twisted so that he was standing on the edge of the Cup and she pushed him with all her might. Then she turned and ran, stumbling, to her cart.

But I paid no attention, because I had jumped to where Tristram, frantically clawing the grasses and roots at the edge of the Cup, was slowly sinking.

"Hold me," I said. "*Hold..me.*"

I will never forget his eyes, curiously calm. "If I do," he panted, "I'll drag you with me. Take care of Alix."

I heard Alix's voice. She said with a terrible slowness, "There's a rope in the back of André's car."

"Get it, Alix," I called quickly. "Get it!"

But she didn't move.

Whether my hold was helping to sustain Tristram I couldn't be sure. But nor could I let him go to get the rope.

"Alix," I cried. "Alix—he's just saved your life."

And with that, as though she had stepped from one world to another, she took a breath. "All right." And I heard her run to the car.

"Tell her to tie it to the car," Tristram said. "Oh, my God." One of the pieces of firm earth he was holding broke away. I was clinging to his jacket, where I could get better purchase than I could on him. But he was going down, albeit more slowly.

"Tie it to the car, to the steering wheel, and bring it here," I cried.

It seemed a long time. "Hurry, hurry," I called.

Then she was there with the end of the rope.

"Get it under my shoulders," Tristram said.

Somehow we did.

"Is it tied to the car?"

"Yes."

"Then get in the car and start backing it. Carefully."

Alix ran back. I heard the motor, saw the line grow taut. "Let me go, darling," Tristram said.

"I love you. I love you."

Incredibly, he smiled. "Yes. I know. Now move."

The swamp did not give him up easily. The car backed and he pulled on the rope, and eventually, with a dreadful sound, his legs and boots emerged from the mud, and he lay, panting, on the hard surface of the path.

It was then we heard the cry from somewhere far beyond us. Terrible and eerie, it rose and rose, and then died away.

A little later, when the mist had cleared, we found her long ebony cane on the path beside a black saucer of swamp and a piece of black veiling torn and speared by spiky reeds a foot or two inside the edge.

"Do you think she slipped, or did she mean to do it?" I asked Tristram.

"I don't know. But I suspect she wanted it that way. Maybe she thought that by killing herself she was killing what she always thought of as the curse on her and freeing Alix."

Then, as he said that, we both turned and looked at Alix, wondering if she understood.

Alix picked up the cane. "She told me that this thing I have"—with her other hand she touched her cheek—"is leprosy. Is that true?"

Tristram walked over to her, the filthy black mud still clinging to the lower part of his legs and boots. "Yes. It's true. But you've been taking medicine and it's going to be arrested. The doctor is certain of that as he can be."

Alix didn't say anything for a while. Then she said, "Those vitamin pills?"

He nodded.

I stood there, apart, wondering what she would do, how, in view of her frequent hysterical behavior, she'd take it. She looked up at both of us. "Why didn't you tell me?"

Tristram said, "To do Sally justice, she felt you should be told. It was my fault that you weren't. I'm sorry. I guess I thought . . ."

His daughter looked at him, "That I'd behave like a child?"

He nodded.

"It wouldn't do me much good, would it?" She took a breath. "Maybe, if you stopped treating me like a child, I'd start growing up."

Her voice faltered a little. Her father put his arms around her and kissed her head.

Alix went on, "Mother . . . Mother said André was using me. He didn't really love me. He just wanted the Darcourt money and the islands."

Darcourt looked down at her. "I'm afraid he was using all of us. But if you hadn't been so alone, you wouldn't have been so . . . vulnerable. I've been a rotten father, Alix. I'm sorry. I'll try to do better."

I went back to Susie, who was asleep on the seat of the car. Around the car were the five other dogs.

Back of the car, quite visible in the clearing mist, was Bolero, nibbling bits of grass here and there. I eyed her, noting the hanging reins, remembering various aspects of equine lore that had been imparted to me, such as, *never let the reins dangle. The horse can trip and break a leg, which is much more serious than if you break yours.*

That phrase reminded me of the old, dictatorial, feudal-tyrant Tristram which, not entirely to my surprise, cheered me up enormously. I decided to tie the rein to Bolero's saddle, and with that worthy notion approached the mare, who happened at that moment to turn her back to me.

I was within a few feet of her when the voice of the feudal-tyrant exploded behind me. "Of all the bumble-headed— Stop, Sally. Haven't I told you again and again, *never* approach a horse from behind unless you want to have your head kicked off?"

He came up beside me. "Now, in the future—"

"Future?" I heard myself ask.

"Yes." He looked down at me. His face was tired and strained but his eyes smiled. "Future. A long, long one. Together. After all, it will take you at least eternity to try and reform my reprehensible views and ways."

"Don't think I won't!" I said. But my heart was singing.

Victoria Holt

Over 20,000,000 copies of Victoria Holt's novels are in print. If you have missed any of her spellbinding bestsellers, here is an opportunity to order any or all direct by mail.

- ☐ BRIDE OF PENDORRIC   22870-3   1.75
- ☐ THE CURSE OF THE KINGS   Q2215   1.50
- ☐ THE HOUSE OF A THOUSAND LANTERNS   X2472   1.75
- ☐ THE KING OF THE CASTLE   X2823   1.75
- ☐ KIRKLAND REVELS   X2917   1.75
- ☐ LEGEND OF THE SEVEN VIRGIN   X2833   1.75
- ☐ LORD OF THE FAR ISLAND   22874-6   1.95
- ☐ MENFREYA IN THE MORNING   23076-7   1.75
- ☐ MISTRESS OF MELLYN   23124-0   1.75
- ☐ ON THE NIGHT OF THE SEVENTH MOON   X2613   1.75
- ☐ THE QUEEN'S CONFESSION   X2700   1.75
- ☐ THE SECRET WOMAN   X2665   1.75
- ☐ SHADOW OF THE LYNX   X2727   1.75
- ☐ THE SHIVERING SANDS   22970-X   1.75

Buy them at your local bookstores or use this handy coupon for ordering:

FAWCETT PUBLICATIONS, P.O. Box 1014, Greenwich Conn. 06830

Please send me the books I have checked above. Orders for less than 5 books must include 60c for the first book and 25c for each additional book to cover mailing and handling. Orders of 5 or more books postage is Free. I enclose $_____ in check or money order.

Mr/Mrs/Miss_____

Address_____

City_____ State/Zip_____

Please allow 4 to 5 weeks for delivery. This offer expires 6/78.   A-3

Dorothy Eden

Ms. Eden's novels have enthralled millions of readers for many years. Here is your chance to order any or all of her bestselling titles direct by mail.

☐ AN AFTERNOON WALK	23072-4	1.75
☐ DARKWATER	23153-4	1.75
☐ THE HOUSE ON HAY HILL	X2839	1.75
☐ LADY OF MALLOW	Q2796	1.50
☐ THE MARRIAGE CHEST	23032-5	1.50
☐ MELBURY SQUARE	22973-4	1.75
☐ THE MILLIONAIRE'S DAUGHTER	23186-0	1.95
☐ NEVER CALL IT LOVING	23143-7	1.95
☐ RAVENSCROFT	22998-X	1.50
☐ THE SHADOW WIFE	22802-9	1.50
☐ SIEGE IN THE SUN	Q2736	1.50
☐ SLEEP IN THE WOODS	23075-9	1.75
☐ SPEAK TO ME OF LOVE	X2735	1.75
☐ THE TIME OF THE DRAGON	23059-7	1.95
☐ THE VINES OF YARRABEE	23184-4	1.95
☐ WAITING FOR WILLA	23187-9	1.50
☐ WINTERWOOD	23185-2	1.75

Buy them at your local bookstores or use this handy coupon for ordering: